A
Hopeful
Heart

Books by

Kim Vogel Sawyer

FROM BETHANY HOUSE PUBLISHERS

Waiting for Summer's Return

Where Willows Grow

My Heart Remembers

Where the Heart Leads

A Promise for Spring

Fields of Grace

A Hopeful Heart

In Every Heartbeat

A
Hopeful
Heart

Kim Vogel

A Novel by
Sawyer

BETHANY HOUSE PUBLISHERS

Minneapolis, Minnesota

Published by Bethany House Publishers
11400 Hampshire Avenue South
Bloomington, Minnesota 55438

Bethany House Publishers is a division of
Baker Publishing Group, Grand Rapids, Michigan.

Printed in the United States of America

Library of Congress Cataloging-in-Publication Data

Sawyer, Kim Vogel.
    A hopeful heart / Kim Vogel Sawyer.
        p.   cm.
    ISBN 978-0-7642-0509-5 (pbk.)
    1. Ranch life—Kansas—Fiction.   2. Kansas—History—19th century—Fiction.
I. Title.
    PS3619.A97H67   2010
    813'.6—dc22

                                                                    2010004146

With a big hug to *Aunt Lois*,
who always made me believe I was someone special.

"For I know the thoughts I think toward you, saith the Lord, thoughts of peace, and not of evil, to give you an expected end."

JEREMIAH 29:11

1

Curling her fingers around the leather handle of the battered carpet-bag that held her carefully selected belongings, Tressa Neill fell in line behind the tittering row of young women disembarking the train. She didn't mind being last. In the homespun dress and outdated straw hat acquired by Aunt Gretchen, she felt dowdy and conspicuous. No matter that her attire closely matched that of her traveling companions—with the exception of Evelyn. She still harbored an intense desire to hide.

She peered out one of the train car's dusty windows. A solitary thick-waisted woman wearing a calico bonnet and matching apron over a pale blue dress stood at the edge of the white-painted depot's wooden walkway. The woman cupped her hand above the bonnet's brim and stared at the train, obviously seeking someone. In the telegram that had outlined Tressa's travel itinerary, her benefactor indicated she would meet her pupils at the train station, so Tressa surmised this woman must be the school's founder, Mrs. Hattie Wyatt. The woman's round face held a warm smile, reminding Tressa of her favorite childhood nursemaid. At once, she felt drawn to her.

Then Tressa's gaze drifted to a small crowd gathered in the slash of shade offered by the depot's overhanging porch roof. All men. All gawking with obvious interest. A bead of sweat trickled down her back. In the acceptance letter Tressa had received from the Wyatt Herdsman School, Mrs. Wyatt had vowed the men of Barnett desired wives, but Tressa hadn't anticipated a welcoming band of prospective suitors. The sight of those sunburnt, cowboy-hat-topped men sent Tressa's stomach into spasms of nervousness.

A giggle pierced the air. After days of traveling with the other girls, Tressa recognized its source: Luella. The girl had talked incessantly, interjecting her chatter with high-pitched squeals of laughter. Luella turned from her position at the head of the line and grinned down the row of girls. "Look outside. Do you see? The men have lined up to meet us!" She touched a hand to her dimpled cheek, her lips curving into a smile. "Oh, won't they be pleased that we've arrived?" Another giggle erupted.

"Then kindly give them the pleasure of seeing us depart the train." Evelyn's sardonic command brought an abrupt end to Luella's annoying laughter, but the girl still remained rooted in the middle of the aisle.

"Shouldn't we wait for the conductor?" Repeatedly during the journey, Luella had batted her eyelashes and made frivolous requests of the portly conductor.

"For what purpose?" Evelyn pointed to the opening at the end of the car with the tip of her satin parasol. "The train has stopped. We've reached our destination. We can leave the car without the conductor's approval. Now go!"

Luella bolted forward, and the others followed. Tressa's dry tongue stuck to the roof of her mouth, and she kept her eyes on the curled-by-nature ringlets cascading from beneath the rolled brim of Evelyn's satin hat. Evelyn's fashionable cinnamon-colored gown provided a perfect backdrop for her shining golden locks. The obvious quality and stylish cut of the dress reminded Tressa of the world she'd left behind. A world in which she was no longer welcome.

"Tressa, no man of breeding will wed a dowryless woman. Your unfortunate situation with Tremaine Woodward certainly proves my point." Aunt Gretchen's emotionless voice echoed in Tressa's memory. *"This herdsman school in Kansas offers you an opportunity to gain a husband and enjoy a life of family, if not of leisure."* Her aunt had shrugged, fanning herself with the printed advertisement that sealed Tressa's fate. *"Second best, perhaps, but a second-best chance is better than no chance at all."*

Homesickness swelled, but not for Aunt Gretchen and Uncle Leo's grand estate. Tressa longed to return to Evan's Glen, her childhood home, with Papa and Mama and—

Giving herself a shake, she dispelled the desire. One could not live in the past. She must march into the future, no matter how bleak it appeared. So she squared her shoulders and followed Evelyn onto the passenger car's small iron landing. A fierce blast of wind stole her breath and lifted the straw skimmer from her head. She dropped her bag and reached for the hat, but the lightweight piece of millinery sailed over the heads of the girls standing at the base of the platform. A thick strand of hair whipped loose from her simple bun, effectively shielding her eyes. Dizziness assailed her. She groped for the handrail, but her fingers closed over air.

Plunging forward, she landed hard against Evelyn's back. Squeals erupted as Evelyn tumbled into the group and, like a row of dominoes, the girls fell into a heap on the dusty street, with Tressa on top. The men on the porch roared, pointing and slapping their thighs in amusement.

"Tressa!" Evelyn's demanding voice carried over the other girls' complaints. She jabbed Tressa with her elbow. "Get off of me, you bumbling idiot!"

Tressa tried to right herself, but the wind tangled her skirts around her legs, trapping her in place. Suddenly, fingers grasped her waist and lifted her. The woman Tressa had identified as Mrs. Wyatt set Tressa to the side and then reached into the fray. "Stop that caterwauling," she chided as she grabbed Evelyn's upper arm and pulled her from the pile. Tressa marveled at the woman's strength.

"Ah, Aunt Hattie, are these the hardy farm wives you promised us? Look more like wilting daisies to me," one man called. The others clapped him on the back, their laughter boisterous. Tressa staggered over to retrieve her abandoned bag, her face burning with humiliation as the men continued to hurl insults.

Mrs. Wyatt assisted Luella to her feet and spun to face the raucous men. "What're these girls s'posed to think about our town with you carryin' on like banshees?" She plunked her fists on her hips and sent a glare across the small crowd. "Gage Hammond? You the leader o' this sorry bunch?"

A young man with a cocky grin stepped forward. He yanked his hat from his head, revealing thick black curls. "Yes'm, Aunt Hattie. When I saw you waitin' at the depot, I figured your girls was comin', so I fetched the men."

"Well, your fun is over. You brought 'em, so now you take 'em an' git." Mrs. Wyatt waved her hand at the crowd and then offered the girls an encouraging smile. "Never mind them ill-mannered fellas. Don't get much excitement in this little town, so they're feelin' their oats. You all just dust yourself off an' hold your heads high, like the ladies you are."

One by one, the men drifted away, their laughter continuing to roll. But one man—tall and lean, with a deeply tanned face and a low-tugged cowboy hat nearly hiding his eyes—ambled toward Tressa.

He held her skimmer. Its faded pink ribbons trailed over his knobby knuckles, the picture somehow unsettling.

"I believe this is yours, miss."

Tressa snatched the hat from his rawboned hand and crushed it to her chest. Too embarrassed to meet his gaze, she focused on the tan wedge of skin revealed by his open shirt collar and mumbled, "Thank you, sir."

His hand rose to briefly touch his hat brim, and then he moved away with long strides, dust rising with every fall of his boot against the ground. Tressa plopped the hat over her tangled hair, pulling it clear down to her ears before turning back to the group. Her stomach clenched at the steely glares of her traveling mates. She didn't dare look at Mrs. Wyatt. After her clumsy display, the woman would certainly send her straight back to New York. And then what would she do?

❧

Abel Samms headed for the Feed and Seed, where his wagon waited. It took great self-control to avoid sneaking a glance over his shoulder. Aunt Hattie's voice carried on the wind. "Now, gather 'round here, ladies, an' load your bags in the wagon. No fellers'll do it for ya. You're here to learn to fend for yourselves, an' this is the first lesson— totin' your own bags." He swallowed a chuckle as a single protesting wail rose, followed by Aunt Hattie's stern "There'll be none o' that sniveling. Hoist it, girl, hoist it!"

Seemed as though the men were missing a good show.

When Gage Hammond had clattered down the boardwalk, announcing that Aunt Hattie was waiting at the station so her pupils must be coming, Abel's curiosity had stirred. So he'd turned on his heel and, instead of entering Hank's Feed and Seed, followed the cluster of men to the newly constructed depot. Under ordinary circumstances he wouldn't pay any mind to Gage Hammond. The spoiled son of Barnett's richest rancher was usually up to mischief. Only a fool believed everything the kid said. But the herdsman school had been the talk of the town for the past four months, ever since Aunt Hattie'd stood up in Sunday service and questioned the ranchers on what qualities they'd like in a wife.

Abel had kept his mouth closed that day—he had no interest in taking a wife—but he'd listened in as the others shouted out their preferences. Aunt Hattie had written down everything on a pad of paper, her face serious. Then she'd stated her intention to open a school on her ranch. Everybody knew the West was long on men and short on women. Aunt Hattie's plan to bring women from the East and teach them all they'd need to know about ranching and then match those women with bachelor men from the community had brought a rousing cheer of approval from the unmarried men in the congregation. With the exception of Abel.

So he hadn't headed to the depot to lay claim to a potential wife; he'd just wanted to see how Aunt Hattie's plan had worked out. He held a fondness for the older widow, as did most everybody in town. And sure enough—just as Aunt Hattie had promised, a passel of young ladies arrived on the iron horse. At first glance, it seemed she'd been able to meet some of the men's requests. The ladies all looked to be in their early twenties—old enough to have some maturity but young enough to birth babies. None had appeared sickly or ill-tempered. His friends had elbowed each other, grinning and whispering in approval, right until the last one stepped onto the platform. Then the appreciative whispers changed to ridicule.

Looking more like a lost waif than a woman, that last one hadn't fit Aunt Hattie's description of a "hardy farm wife." Small and spindly, he couldn't imagine her hoisting her own bag, let alone wrestling an ornery calf to the ground. But his pity had been stirred when her hat went flying . . . then she went flying.

His jaw muscles tightened as he recalled the unkind comments the men had hollered. In Abel's family, they abided by the Golden Rule.

How many times had Ma advised, "Son, treat others the way you'd want them to treat you; then you'll always be fair"? He sure hadn't appreciated the townsfolk poking fun at his misfortune two years ago. So nobody would find him hurling insults, not even in sport.

Abel planted his toe on the hub of the wagon wheel and hoisted himself into the high, springed seat. The sight of those eastern ladies stepping off the train had stirred too many memories—things better left buried. Snatching up the reins, he gave the leather traces a flick. "Get up there, Ed."

The roan gelding shook his head, as if irritated to be wakened from his nap, but he obediently strained against the rigging and pulled the wagon into the street. Abel rolled past Aunt Hattie's high-sided buckboard, where the town's new arrivals now sat in a wilted row on top of their piled luggage. But he kept his face aimed straight ahead and pretended not to see when Aunt Hattie raised her hand in a friendly wave.

Guilt pinched the edges of his conscience. His ma had taught him better manners than ignoring a neighbor's greeting, but she'd also taught him to be truthful. And Abel didn't want to give any of those young ladies so much as an inkling that he might be interested in taking a bride.

2

"Whoa." Abel pulled back on the reins, drawing the horse to a halt. He leaped from the wagon seat and walked around to release Ed from his rigging. The smell of burnt hide and scorched metal carried on the wind. Branding must be well underway. In the past, Abel had waited until the calving season was complete before rounding up all the calves and branding in one fell swoop. But this year he couldn't afford to wait.

"Hey, boss! Been watchin' for ya." Cole Jacobs, the youngest of the three hired hands who lived on Abel's small ranch, trotted across the grounds. Catching the tailgate of the wagon, he peered into the empty bed and then shot Abel a startled look. "Ol' Hank out of that new-fangled barbed wire already?"

Abel jolted. With the arrival of the train—and Aunt Hattie's girls—he'd plumb forgot to ask the Feed and Seed owner about a roll of barbed wire. He tugged on the bridle, guiding Ed toward the barn. "I'll have to check when I go in next."

Cole trailed along beside Abel, swishing his hands against his dusty pant legs. "Might be just as well. I heard Mr. Hammond's had to replace a string of fence three times already. Somebody keeps cuttin' it. Gotta be costly, puttin' it back up time and again."

Abel led the big roan into a stall and reached for the curry brush. Feelings ran strong for and against barbed wire fencing. Local ranchers liked the idea of keeping their own beef penned in, but those who drove their herds to the new railroad to send the beef to market found the fences a nuisance. More than one fight had broken out when drovers cut a fence to shorten their distance to the railroad's loading pens.

"Yep, suppose it is an aggravation." Abel nodded toward Cole. "But how many head've we lost in the last couple of years 'cause they . . . wander?" Even though he couldn't prove it, nothing would convince Abel those cattle didn't have help leaving his land. He had no cash to spare, but he hoped a barbed wire fence might discourage more "wandering."

"You're prob'ly right. Fence'd decrease the losses. Well . . ." Cole backed toward the barn door. "I'll tell the others you're back and we won't be puttin' up wire fence tomorrow. Just about got the calves branded. Want us to put 'em back on the range with their mamas when we're done or keep 'em in the corral overnight?"

"Keep 'em in."

Cole grimaced. "You sure? They're a-bawlin' somethin' fierce. Might keep us up tonight."

Abel slipped the leather traces over Ed's head. "Well, then pull the mamas in with 'em, but I want 'em kept in."

"Yessir." Cole shot out the door, his thudding footsteps receding quickly.

Abel stroked the brush across Ed's withers, and the horse nickered, nudging Abel's shoulder with his nose. Normally Abel would laugh at the horse's antics, but Cole's comment about fence-cutting brought up a new worry. As if he needed a new worry. Between the increased ranching in Dakota, Montana, Wyoming, and Colorado lowering the price per head and the frustration of losing a significant portion of his herd in each of the past three years, he was barely keeping himself afloat.

As much as he hated to consider it, he might have to let one of his hired hands go. But being short-handed meant less supervision of the cattle, which could lead to greater losses. Besides, who would he cut loose? Releasing the newest hire, Cole, seemed the fairest, but the man knew the business; Abel didn't want to fire a knowledgeable, willing worker. Made more sense to let Vince go. The weathered cowboy was fast approaching his fiftieth birthday and was slowing down considerably.

Abel's hand paused in the brushing as his thoughts tumbled onward. If he cut Vince, his son Ethan would go, too, leaving only Abel and Cole to work the ranch. Two men couldn't possibly see to everything that needed done. Besides that, Pa would turn over in his grave if Abel sent Vince from the ranch. The two men had worked side-by-side for nearly two decades. Pa considered Vince as close as a brother, and Ethan had grown up alongside Abel. The men were like family.

"Pa, sure wish you were here to give me some advice." Seemed the older he got, the more he missed his father. Without conscious thought, he turned his head toward the northwest, where Pa and Ma, along with Abel's newborn twin brothers, rested in the gravesite on the far corner of the property. If Abel had his way, he'd be buried right next to them when his time came to leave this earth. Of course, it would be nice to pass this ranch on to his son, just as his Pa had done for him, but that didn't seem too likely seeing as how he wasn't interested in taking a wife.

Immediately a face flashed in his memory—delicate cheekbones, upturned lips, sparkling eyes fringed by thick lashes . . . He shook his head hard, dismissing the image. Last thing this day needed was thoughts of Amanda!

He thumped the curry brush on the shelf and then stood facing the wall, worry making his throat dry. Ever since Pa's death, the losses had outweighed the gains on the ranch. First that hard winter, then the mysterious disappearance of a good portion of his herd. Abel wasn't sure how to turn it all around. If he didn't get a good return on his beef this year, he might be forced to sell his spread to Mr. Hammond. The man was interested, and he'd give Abel a good price.

Abel swished his hand through the air, shooing away the thought. Selling out wasn't an option. Pa and Ma had poured their sweat into this land. On his deathbed, Pa made Abel promise he'd hang on to the land, and Abel would honor that promise. He needed to stop this worrying. Ma always said worry never added a single hour to anybody's life.

He gave a little jerk, setting his feet in motion. "Get to work, Abel. Standin' around here stewin' isn't helping a thing." He gave Ed a pat on the neck and headed toward the branding pen.

&

"Well, ladies, here we are."

Tressa roused at Mrs. Wyatt's announcement. The gently bouncing wagon ride across the rolling prairie had lulled her to sleep, but she sat up and yawned discreetly behind her hand. Squinting against the sun, she peered over the wood side of the wagon. A tall, square house sat on a smooth, grassy rise. Although plain with whitewashed clapboard siding, its neatly paired windows glinted in the sunlight and seemed to send a welcoming wink. Tressa struggled to her knees to get a better look.

"Now, now, gawkin' can come later." Mrs. Wyatt bustled to the back of the wagon and lowered the tailgate. "Grab your effects outta there an' then follow me. It's pret' near suppertime, an' my men'll be comin' in soon expectin' to get their bellies filled."

"Men?" Luella's brows shot high as she shoved her bag to the end of the wagon bed.

"Yes, missy, my ranch hands." The older woman went on conversationally. "But your path an' theirs won't be crossin' for a good long while, not even at mealtime. Dinin' room'll only hold eight at a time, so we'll be eatin' in shifts. 'Sides that, the men're here to work, an' you're here to learn, an' that'll keep all o' you plenty occupied."

Luella seemed to wilt momentarily, but then she lifted her chin and sent a saucy grin around the group. "But if we're living on the same grounds, surely there will be time for—"

"There'll be time for workin' an' learnin'." Mrs. Wyatt cocked her head to the side and gave Luella a puzzled look. "You thinkin' you'll be pitchin' woo right from the start?"

Luella held her hands outward. "Isn't that why we're here?"

"Well, sure. Eventually." Placing a hand on her hip, Mrs. Wyatt bounced a serious look from girl to girl. "But I don't plan on lettin' the men spend time with you till you've learnt all you need to be a good helpmeet to one o' the fellers around here."

"But why do we have to wait until *then*?" Luella's tone turned petulant. A couple of others murmured their agreement.

A slight frown creased the older woman's brow, but she replied patiently. " 'Cause you come here to learn to be a herdsman—somebody who knows ranchin' inside an' out. There's lots to learn, from cookin' for a crowd to stampin' a brand on the hindquarters of a wrigglin' calf an' drivin' a wagon across roadless pasture. No sense in gettin' a fella's hopes up an' then have you decide ranchin' life ain't for you an' you skedaddle back to New York, leavin' him empty-handed an' sore-hearted."

She nodded, as if agreeing with herself. "Yep, it's best you gals learn the skills first, *then* get to know the fellers." Mrs. Wyatt shrugged, an impish grin rounding her full cheeks. "If you're in a hurry to get hitched, you can either head on back to New York an' seek out a likely prospect there, or you best set your mind to learnin'."

Luella's full lips formed a pout, but much to Tressa's relief, she climbed out of the wagon without another word. Tressa found the girl's ceaseless chatter and flirtatious ways disquieting. Had no one taught Luella the meaning of decorum?

Mrs. Wyatt stood to the side, her arms folded over her ample chest, and allowed the girls to heft everything out of the wagon bed. Once the trunks and bags stood in a disorganized tumble on the ground, she waved her hand. "We'll carry things in after we've figured out your rooms. Come with me."

Once again, Tressa fell into the last position as the six girls trailed Mrs. Wyatt over a walkway formed of flat stones. She released a little breath of relief as she stepped onto the wide, railed porch, where the roof provided protection from the harsh sun. Back at her aunt's home in New York, tall trees and flowered trellises offered refreshing shade, but trees and manicured gardens were sorely lacking here on the prairie. Another twinge of homesickness attacked, but Tressa resolutely pushed the feeling away. New York held nothing of value for her anymore.

Inside, Mrs. Wyatt charged directly up a spindled staircase. The girls clattered up behind her. A long, wallpapered landing divided the upper floor down the middle, with two pairs of doors facing each other from across a narrow expanse of wood-planked floor.

Mrs. Wyatt pointed to the first door on the right. "This here is my room. The others're up for grabs. You girls break into twos and choose a room."

"We must *share?*" Evelyn stared at Mrs. Wyatt in dismay.

Mrs. Wyatt took in a deep breath, as if gathering patience. "Yes, you must share. That's part o' the learnin'." She sent a firm glance around the circle of girls. "An' please, no room-changin' once you've settled in—too much fuss an' feathers. So choose careful."

Luella immediately looped arms with Evelyn. Although Evelyn appeared dubious about the pairing, Luella seemed disinclined to release her hold. With a sigh, Evelyn nodded her assent. Mabelle and Paralee exchanged a quick nod, sealing their agreement. That left Tressa and Sallie.

Sallie angled a hopeful look in Tressa's direction. "Do ye mind sharin' a room with me, Tressa?" Her lilting Irish brogue carried a note of timidity.

Even in her aunt and uncle's home, a shelter provided dutifully albeit reluctantly, Tressa had enjoyed the pleasure of a room to herself. On the long journey by train, she had traveled in a private berth—her uncle's parting gift to her. The idea of having no privacy held little appeal, yet Tressa wouldn't complain. Mrs. Wyatt had apparently been unaffected by Tressa's clumsiness at the depot; she dared not give the woman a reason to reject her now.

Tressa nodded. "Certainly we can share."

Sallie's freckled face split into a grin.

"Well then, that's that." Mrs. Wyatt clapped her thick palms together. "The rooms're nothin' fancy, but you won't be in 'em over-much." She turned and clumped down the stairs, still talking. "Just claim one an' get your things moved in an' put away while I fix my hired hands their supper. I'll call you when they've cleared out an' I'm ready to feed you." She disappeared around the bend at the base of the stairs.

With murmured comments, the girls plodded down the stairs and outside to retrieve their items. Tressa shielded her eyes with her hand as she walked across the yard and bent to grasp her carpetbag. Having brought, at her aunt's insistence, only one small bag, she anticipated no difficulty carrying it up the stairs. But Evelyn grunted with the effort of lugging her heavy trunk across the sparse grass toward the porch.

Sallie dropped her satchel and trotted to Evelyn's side. "Could ye be usin' some help?"

Evelyn's brows rose in a superior manner, but she nodded. With Sallie hoisting one end and Evelyn the other, the pair managed to cart the sizable trunk across the yard and into the house. Once inside, they faced the steeply angled stairway.

Sallie flashed a grin over her shoulder at Tressa. "I'm thinkin' it will be best for ye to stand well back till we get this all the way up. If it drops, it'll squash ye flat!"

Tressa stood to the side of the stairs while Evelyn and Sallie wrestled the trunk upward. Behind her, Luella held her breath, her lips sucked in and eyes wide. Mabelle and Paralee peered between carved posts, whispering to one another. Luella's breath whooshed past Tressa's ear when Evelyn dropped her end of the trunk on the upstairs landing with a resounding thud.

Sallie leaned over the railing, her smile bright. "Safe it is now, girls! Bring your own things." She scuttled down the stairs and out the front door to reclaim her discarded bag.

Talking and jostling, the girls zipped around Tressa and scrambled up the stairs. The sound of their pounding footsteps created a slight ache at the base of her skull. Her own footsteps slowed. Sallie moved in unison with Tressa up the stair risers. She poked Tressa's ribs lightly with her skinny elbow.

" 'Tis relieved I am that Evelyn an' me made it all the way up with that heavy box. I'm thinkin' she must be cartin' bricks of gold along with her fine dresses—maybe believin' she'll be able t' buy herself a groom." Sallie snickered and then lowered her voice to a conspiratorial whisper. "Why do ye suppose a well-to-do girl's come to this school? Surely her da could've found her a husband, don't ye think?"

Tressa chose not to answer. Her mother had frowned at gossiping. Furthermore, Sallie's disparaging tone when uttering the words "well-to-do" seemed to affirm Aunt Gretchen's warning. While packing

Tressa's bag with articles of clothing scavenged from a local church's charity barrels, Aunt Gretchen had stated firmly, *"If you're to find acceptance in that untamed western town, you must be one of them. The classes do not mix, Tressa. If they suspect you have breeding, they'll disdain you as a suitable mate. So bury your affluent background and pretend it never existed."*

The question that had burned on her tongue but went unasked now fluttered through Tressa's mind: Was it possible to forget one's personal history? Wasn't her past woven into her very being? If her past ceased to exist, then *she* did not exist.

Flopping the bag onto the quilt-covered mattress of the creaky iron bed, she glanced around at the simple, mismatched furnishings and faded floral wallpaper. Had she ever inhabited such a sad, tired-looking space? Despair overcame her, and she sank down next to her bag. For the first time since she'd set out on this adventure to become the wife of a Kansas rancher, she allowed tears of sorrow to pool in her eyes.

Her only hope lay in convincing Mrs. Wyatt that she was an adept worker and a desirable mate for a man she had yet to meet. Given her background of luxury, hope was fleeting at best.

"Amen." Hattie Wyatt closed the prayer of gratitude for the meal, opened her eyes, and snatched up the bowl of steaming turnips. She scooped a sizable portion, clunking the wooden spoon against her tin plate to release every bit of the mashed buttery turnips, then plopped the bowl into the hands of the tall girl sitting on her right.

"Take some, then pass it on." She bobbed her head toward the plat-ters of food filling the center of the planked wood table. "If somethin' is close to you, get it started goin' 'round." She chuckled. "The food won't jump from those bowls an' onto your plates on its own."

A titter went around the table, and Hattie grinned. Maybe there was some life in these girls after all. When she'd called them down for supper, they'd stumbled into the dining room as if they'd been rounding up strays all day instead of sitting on a train. But then, maybe travel wore a body out. Hattie wouldn't know—she hadn't ventured more than fifteen miles from her ranch since she and Jed had settled this land.

"So did you get your bags emptied an' everything put to right in your rooms?" Hattie asked around a bite of green beans. The beans, well seasoned with onion and bacon, pleased her tongue, and she eagerly forked another hearty bite.

The girl on her right—the one with yellow curly hair and the air of a princess—glanced down the length of the table before answering. "I would like to request the use of a wardrobe. I had to leave several items in my trunk. The bureau won't accommodate all of my garments."

"Um . . ." Hattie pressed her brain for the girl's name. "Evelyn?"

The girl nodded.

"Well, Evelyn, if the things in your trunk are as high-falutin' as the dress you're wearin' right now—" Hattie let her gaze sweep over the lacy bodice of the shiny red-brown dress—"you might be better off leavin' it all in the trunk. Won't be much need of fancy wear like that out here. You did bring work clothes, didn't you? Something simple—calico or muslin?"

The girl's eyebrows arched high. "I should say not."

Hattie sighed. "That means a trip to Barnett's general store, then, to order you a workin' dress from the catalog. With me teachin' you pupils, I won't have time to stitch you up one. But you'll need somethin'. You'll ruin that fancy material in no time." She pinched a bit of the glossy cloth between her fingers, releasing it when Evelyn threw her shoulders back and sucked in a sharp breath.

"In the meantime," Hattie mused, "maybe one o' the others could borrow you a dress to make do." But if she remembered correctly from seeing the girls all lined up in a row, Evelyn stood a good two inches taller than any of the others. She released a low chuckle. "Or you can wear one o' mine. We're eye-to-eye from top to bottom, but it'll be a loose fit side-to-side." She gave her midsection a pat. "I got a bit more girth than you do."

The girl sitting next to Evelyn—Luella—let out a giggle that ran the scales. Evelyn sent Luella a stern glare, and the giggle ended abruptly. With her face glowing, Luella leaned over her plate and spooned up a bite of stewed beef.

Hattie shook her head. That Evelyn would need to come down a peg or two or she'd be of no use to anyone. "What about the rest o' you? All settled in your rooms?"

A chorus of assurances sounded, and Hattie smiled. "Good. 'Cause come tomorrow mornin', bright an' early, we'll be startin' your classes."

Classes. Hattie savored the word. Back in her early years, she'd fancied becoming a teacher. But Jed had won her heart, and she'd given up the idea of teaching to become his wife. Never regretted it, either. How could she lament even one minute of nearly forty years with a godly man like Jed? But getting the chance to teach these young ladies was like recapturing the long-ago dream. God was good to give her this gift so late in her life.

"W-what exactly will we be doin' tomorrow?" The timorous question came from the one named Mabelle. Although buxom and with well-formed arms, the girl's hunched shoulders and low-held head made her seem mousy.

"Well . . ." Hattie leaned back in her chair and tapped the edge of her plate with her fork. "Tomorrow mornin', as the sun's risin', you'll get your first taste of cow-milkin'. Any o' you milked a cow before?"

The red-haired gal with the foreign brogue sat straight up. "Oh! I've milked me share o' cows, Mrs. Wyatt."

"Call me Aunt Hattie—everybody does." Hattie nodded her approval at the girl. "Glad you got some experience. You lived on a farm, did you?"

"Indentured I was to a dairyman for three years." For a moment, something akin to fear flashed in the girl's eyes, but then a bright smile chased away the look. " 'Tis able I am to milk, an' churn, an' even make cheese if it'd be pleasin'."

"Cheese?" Hattie gave the tabletop a light smack. "That'd be a real good thing for all of us to learn. We'll let you teach us . . ." She scrambled for the girl's name. "Sallie."

Sallie beamed as if she'd been handed a jeweled crown. "Yes'm!"

"Ya see—" Hattie pointed her finger at each girl by turn—" 'round here, we make our livin' from the livestock. Everybody's got at least a milker or two. Everybody's raisin' a herd o' beef, be it a big herd or only a dozen head. No matter where you wind up throwin' out your bedroll, you'll be dealin' with cattle. So it's important that you learn to handle yourself around those ornery critters."

Her lips twitched as she recalled the conversation that had prompted her to open up the Wyatt Herdsman School. Bob Clemence had let loose a stream of tobacco on the street right next to her feet. She'd scolded him, admonishing that if he had a wife, he'd give up such ugly habits. He'd replied with tongue in cheek, *Aunt Hattie, if you show me a woman who can milk a cow, cook somethin' more'n beans with fatback, and knows which end of a horse to attach to a plow, I'll snatch 'er up.*

Looking at the circle of faces around the table, Hattie speculated that sprightly little Sallie might make a good match for Bob—he'd need someone with a touch of sass. She'd do some praying on that. But the matching would come later.

She propped her elbows on the table. "Out in my barn, I got an even half dozen milkin' cows. That means each o' you'll claim one an' see to its milkin' an' care every day."

She examined her pupils. No one fainted dead away, although Evelyn looked like she might have swallowed something bitter, and the girl with her brown hair pulled into a scraggly bun—what was her name?—clutched a quivering hand to her throat.

Keeping a brisk, confident tone, Hattie went on. "Just like I said in the letters I sent each of ya, there'll be lots to learn—milkin', gardenin', cannin', cookin' an' cleanin', ropin' an' ridin' . . . even some plowin' and plantin'. But we'll take it one step at a time. A person crawls before she walks, an' walks before she runs. So don't be frettin' any." She sent the brown-haired gal, who looked white around her mouth, a reassuring smile. "You'll all be good strong runners by the time I'm finished with you.

"But now . . ." Pressing her palms to the table, she rose. "Supper's done, the sun's losin' it's battle with dark, an' there's dishes to wash. So everybody grab your own plates an' such an' take 'em to the kitchen— right this way." She led them through the dining room doorway into the large kitchen. "Leave 'em on the dry sink there. We'll be takin' turns with cleanup, but it bein' your first night, I'll take care of it this time. You all go on up to bed an' get a good night's rest. You'll need your energy come mornin'."

Hattie shooed the cluster of girls to the base of the stairs and then watched as they climbed to the upper story. When the red-haired gal named Sallie reached the top, she turned back and waved. "G'night to ye, Aunt Hattie." One by one, each girl added her good-night wish to Sallie's.

Heat built from the center of Hattie's chest. She fanned herself with her apron skirt. "Night, Sallie. Night Evelyn an' Luella. Sleep well, Mabelle, Paralee, an' . . . an' . . ." The name of the remaining girl still escaped Hattie.

"Tressa," the girl supplied in a near whisper.

Hattie met the girl's eyes with a steady gaze. "Sleep well, Tressa. An' sweet dreams to you."

"Thank you, Mrs. Wyatt. You have a pleasant night, as well."

Hattie chuckled softly to herself as she returned to the kitchen, replaying each girl's good-night wish. A soft meow greeted her. She bent over and scooped up Isabella, the long-haired cat who spent most of her day snoozing beneath the stove. "You been hidin' from all the strangers in the house? Better get used to it—they're here to stay. Leastwise, for as long as it takes to learn to be good ranchers' wives—an' that might be quite a while for some of 'em."

Nuzzling the cat's warm fur, she said with wonder, "Didja hear 'em, ol' Izzy-B? First time this house has had young ones lined up on the stairs, callin' down good-nights to me." Although she and Jed had built a big house to accommodate a sizable brood, God hadn't seen fit to bless them with children. Hattie sighed. "Felt good to hear that chorus o' voices wishin' me a good night."

Isabella purred in response, working her paws against Hattie's shoulder. Hattie rubbed the cat's chin with her knuckles, chuckling when the purr deepened. After a few moments she released a little huff. "Well now, I can't be expected to pet you all night. I got work to do."

She pulled a ladder-backed chair from the small worktable in the corner of the kitchen and placed the cat on the smooth seat. "You sit here out from under my feet an' keep me company while I get these dishes washed." The cat assumed a regal posture, folding her paws beneath her full white bib and staring at her mistress with round, yellow eyes.

Hattie ladled hot water from the stove's reservoir into the wash pan and stirred in soap flakes to make suds. "Yes'm, Isabella, I think this school idea is goin' to work just fine. Men in town sure showed interest! An' already I feel myself growin' attached to those girls—like they're a little bit mine." She furrowed her brow. "But there's somethin' odd about . . ." A detail tickled the back of her mind, hiding in shadow instead of making itself clear. Shaking her head, she set to work. Not until she finished scrubbing the last plate did she catch the illusive thought. Spinning toward the cat, she announced, "That's it!"

Isabella leaped from the chair and dashed under the stove, her fur on end. Hattie crouched down and crooned to the startled animal, coaxing her out once again. Cradling the cat in her lap, she whispered, "Ain't it odd that the one named Tressa wears clothes like a workin'-class girl, but her speech is all refined, like an educated lady?"

Hattie looked toward the ceiling, imagining the girls snug in their beds. The image of Tressa lingered. She gave the cat a final scratch behind her ears before releasing her. "Yes'm, Izzy-B, I'm thinkin' we got ourselves a puzzle sleepin' upstairs."

❧

Tressa stood at the window, peering across the moonlit ranch grounds. The girls hadn't been allowed to explore when they arrived at Mrs. Wyatt's ranch. Curiosity, combined with the unfamiliar silence that permeated the area, held sleep at bay. Sallie snored softly in the featherbed, her tangled red hair scattered across the white pillowcase. Tressa envied the girl's ability to drift off to sleep, unencumbered by worries.

Before slipping between the sheets, Sallie had stretched her arms over her head and released a happy giggle. "What a grand place t' be, with so much space an' only Aunt Hattie givin' orders. She's a mite crusty, but I'm willin' to wager she has a tender heart. So different from—" Her smile had dimmed momentarily, but then she'd spun herself in a little circle and clapped her hands, her grin wide. " 'Tis happy I am to be here, an' eager to be startin' me new life. An' ye, Tressa?"

Tressa had forced a smile and mumbled something about being happy, too. But her conscience pricked now as she examined the purplish shadowed landscape scattered with gray outbuildings. She wasn't happy to be here. Not really.

Slipping to her knees, she propped her arm on the windowsill and rested her chin on the back of her wrist. Stars glittered overhead, beautiful against the velvety backdrop of black sky. How often had she sat in the window of her childhood home and made wishes on the stars?

Just as she had when she was six, Tressa scrunched her eyes tight. Her most frequent little-girl wish replayed in her heart. *I wish I could marry a man like Papa.* She opened her eyes, blinking out at the soft night scene. Though she was now a grown up twenty-two, the desire lingered.

Surely happiness would be hers if she could find someone like Papa—someone tall and strong, with a ready smile and gentle hands.

Someone loving, with a boisterous laugh. A man who would adore her the way Papa adored Mama. Papa had adored Mama so much that when she died giving birth to Tressa's baby brother, he lost much of his will to live.

He hadn't even seemed to care when his cotton mill burned to the ground, leaving him without a means of income. His apathy when forced to sell Evan's Glen, the home where Tressa had been born, had filled her with anguish, yet even as an eleven-year-old she understood the root of Papa's lack of caring. Why would he fight to keep a home where his beloved wife no longer resided? Tressa was certain the pneumonia would not have claimed her dear papa if he hadn't been so heartsick from mourning.

Tears stung her eyes. Although Mama and Papa had been gone for years, she missed them as much as if they'd only left her yesterday. Memories from her early years—carefree, joyful, surrounded by love and laughter—were the only happy possessions she carried into adulthood. Fortunately, her long, somber years with Aunt Gretchen and Uncle Leo hadn't succeeded in washing away the precious memories.

The stars wavered, distorted by her tears, but she stared hard at the flickering bits of light. Papa and Mama lived somewhere behind those stars. Papa believed the Bible when it said the Father's house had many mansions. After Mama's death, he had held Tressa on his lap and explained that the Father's house was Heaven, and that Mama now lived in a beautiful mansion built by God. Tressa easily envisioned the mansion—built of tan stone, with turrets and beautifully colored windows, a replica of Evan's Glen. And she knew Papa and Mama were there, along with the little baby boy who'd lived only a few hours. They resided happily together.

While she was all alone.

Sallie's snore increased in volume. Tressa turned from the window and gasped when a small, fuzzy animal darted across the floor and jumped into her lap. The animal—a cat with long black-and-white fur—kneaded its front feet against Tressa's leg and set up a mighty purr that competed with Sallie's snore.

Too startled to react, Tressa simply planted her palms against the wood floor and stared at the cat. A creaking noise from the hall shifted her attention from the cat to the doorway. Mrs. Wyatt poked her head into the room.

"Oh! Tressa, my apologies, dearie. I was tryin' to put that old scalawag in the pantry, where she spends the night, but she got away from me." The woman tiptoed into the room, casting a furtive glance toward the bed where Sallie slept on, unaware. "I forgot to tell you the latch on the door to this room doesn't always hook. Izzy-B here can bat it right open. I'll have one o' my men take a look at it tomorrow an' get it fixed so she won't be sneakin' in here an' botherin' you."

The cat examined Tressa with round, curious eyes before turning itself and coiling into a ball on her lap. Despite the start she'd been given, Tressa felt a small bubble of laughter form in her throat. "Oh, she's not a bother, ma'am. She's actually quite . . . nice."

Mrs. Wyatt's smile warmed. "It's good of you to say so. She's a special girl to me, havin' been a gift from my husband—God rest his soul—when she was just a scrawny kitten. She spent lots o' years in the barn, chasin' away the mice, but she's earned her spot 'neath the stove in her later years."

Tressa stroked her hand down the length of the animal's back. The cat responded by twisting around and bobbing her head against Tressa's palm. The giggle trickled past Tressa's lips.

"I'll take her now so I can put her to bed."

Somewhat disappointed, Tressa lifted the cat and handed it to its owner. Mrs. Wyatt cradled the cat beneath her chin. Suddenly she frowned. "What're you doin' over here on the floor instead of bein' in bed at this hour?"

Tressa struggled to her feet, careful to shield her bare limbs with the generous folds of her white cotton nightgown. She kept her gaze averted as she replied. "I was looking at the countryside. It's so big . . . and open. Not like—" She started to say "home," but had her aunt and uncle's three-story townhouse ever truly been home?

"I remember it seemin' mighty big when Jed an' me first settled here. An' quiet, compared to the city." Mrs. Wyatt paused, and then her quiet voice came again. "You missin' the city?"

Truthfully, Tressa didn't miss the city, but she missed her former life. Her life with Mama and Papa. But she'd been missing that life since she was twelve years old. She shook her head, still clutching the cotton fabric of the worn nightgown.

"I know it's different here, Tressa, but it's a fine place to put down roots. Good folks—salt o' the earth, no matter what you might've thought about the men's orneriness today. As a whole, they're hard-workin' an' God-lovin', even if some are a bit rough around the edges." Mrs. Wyatt chuckled softly. "But nothin' softens up a man like the care of a good woman."

Tressa lifted her head. The woman's face, even shadowed by the scant moonlight shining through the window, appeared kind. For a moment she considered sharing her thoughts. Mrs. Wyatt had lost her husband; she would understand the deep hurt Tressa still carried at having to say good-bye to her parents far too soon. But her aunt's warning about keeping her past a secret held her tongue. So she blurted, "I . . . I should go to bed now."

She scurried to the bed and climbed in, careful not to bounce the mattress and disturb Sallie. Mrs. Wyatt padded silently to the door and stepped into the hallway. Her whispered voice, crooning to the cat, slowly faded as she headed down the stairs. Tressa lay, wide-eyed, staring out the window. Although she wanted to sleep, a question kept her awake: If her childhood wish to marry a man like Papa came true, would this lonely ache finally depart for good?

4

"Hey, boss?"

Abel paused in lifting the pitchfork of hay to look at Cole. The hired hand straddled a low stool beside the milk cow, squirting an even stream of creamy milk into the tin bucket between his knees. A lopsided grin stretched across his face.

"Reckon Aunt Hattie managed to get them girls out of bed with the rooster's crow?"

Abel tossed the forkful of hay into the horse's stall. Cole was a good worker and more than earned his pay as a hand on Abel's ranch, but once he latched on to an idea, he was like a fox with an egg in its mouth—all the hollering in the world wouldn't make him drop it. Last night at supper Abel made it clear he didn't want to discuss the herdsman school or its pupils. Cole had hushed his speculations when Abel got cranky, but here he was, starting in again first thing this morning.

Drawing in a lungful of air, Abel prepared to tell Cole in plain language to get his mind off those girls at Aunt Hattie's ranch, but before he could speak, Cole continued.

"Seems to me it wouldn't be so bad to have one of 'em on your ranch, seein' to the cookin' and milkin' an' such." Cole rested his cheek against the cow's flank, his expression thoughtful. "Free us men up to focus on other things."

"Like I said last night . . ." Abel forced the words through clenched teeth, jabbing the pitchfork into the mound of hay with enough force to bend the tines. "I wish Aunt Hattie well with her school, but I'm not interested in those girls." He pointed at Cole, squinting one eye. "An' I'll thank you to keep your nose out of my business."

"Well . . ." Cole lifted the bucket from beneath the cow's slack udder and rested it on his knee. The man's sparsely whiskered cheeks blotched red. "I wasn't necessarily thinkin' of you so much as . . ."

Abel waited, his body tense.

"Me. Maybe takin' a look-see at 'em an' seein' if . . . well . . ."

Abel's jaw went slack. "You thinkin' of marryin' up with one of those girls?"

Cole shrugged one shoulder while keeping a grip on the bucket. "Dunno why not. Most men think of gettin' hitched at some point. An' I'm gettin' up there, ya know. Be twenty-two on my next birthday. . . ."

Abel swallowed a laugh.

"Why, even you must think it's a good idea for a man to have a wife. 'Member two years back when you—"

Abel snatched up the pitchfork and stabbed it into the mound of hay. "Two years back I didn't have the sense I have today." He tossed the load over the stall's door and then moved to the next stall. "Besides, we weren't talkin' about me—we were talkin' about you." Abel faced Cole, hooking his elbow on the rounded end of the pitchfork's handle. "Seems to me that before you start courtin', you ought to think where you'd keep a wife. You forget you live in a bunkhouse with two other men? No woman I know would cotton to a setup like that."

"I reckon not." Cole rose, catching the bucket by its rope handle and letting it dangle from his hand. His shoulders slumped, his chin low. "Just thinkin' . . . Them girls, they're bound to be pretty."

Abel double-fisted the pitchfork's handle. "Eastern women." He didn't try to hide the disgust in his voice. "Pretty packages with not much inside."

Cole heaved a sigh as he ambled toward the barn's wide opening. "Yep . . . Reckon you'd know." He exited, leaving Abel alone.

"Reckon you'd know . . ." The words buzzed like a persistent horse-fly. Abel reached to scoop another load of hay, but then his hands stilled, an old hurt rising to pinch his chest. When would the humiliation of Amanda's rejection ease?

More than two years had passed since he'd offered his heart through letters and then paid for her transport west. But even now, if he closed his eyes, he could picture how she'd looked as she stepped out of that stagecoach, wearing a gown the color of the Kansas sky, her big eyes as green as fresh clover. His heart had fired into his throat when he'd realized how lovely his bride-to-be was. Wouldn't every man in town be jealous? But instead of becoming the envy of the town, he became Barnett's laughingstock—the man duped into believing a highbred eastern woman would want to carve out a life on the Kansas plains.

He banged the pitchfork on the stall door, shaking the hay loose. If only it were as simple to shake loose the unpleasant memories. As much as he hated to admit it, Cole was right—a man naturally thought of matrimony. But thoughts of marriage led Abel straight to thoughts of Amanda. Why would he want to relive a hurt such as that?

He hooked the pitchfork on a wooden peg in the tack room and then headed for the house. By now Cole should have breakfast laid out so the men could eat and get the day started. Abel grimaced, considering Cole's sorry excuse for cooking. But there was no cure for it—each of the men took their turn, and this week was Cole's.

"Wouldn't be so bad to have one of 'em on your ranch, seein' to the cookin'..."

Cole's words returned to haunt Abel. He came to a dead halt in the middle of the yard and gave his forehead a firm whack with the butt of his hand to send the idea far from his mind. The last thing he needed was another eastern woman leaving him high and dry!

He set his feet in motion again, but his heels dragged, his thoughts refusing to go where he demanded. Amanda had been a woman of wealth. She'd claimed she found the high society life unbearably dull and without challenge. So she'd agreed to join him on his ranch. After a few weeks, however, she admitted her pampered life hadn't prepared her for the ruggedness of the Kansas plains, and she broke her agreement with Abel to return to the East.

But was it fair to compare these women Aunt Hattie had brought in to Amanda? They weren't wealthy and spoiled like Amanda. Aunt Hattie had invited working girls, girls accustomed to labor. And time under Hattie's tutelage would surely provide them with all the skills needed to meet the demands of being a rancher's wife.

"Abel?" Ethan Rylin called from the open doorway of the house, yanking Abel from his reverie. "Cole's got breakfast cooked." Ethan made a face as Abel trotted up to the porch. "Burnt pancakes and raw bacon. But I figure we've eaten worse on his week. . . ."

Abel followed Ethan into the house, wrinkling his nose at the acrid smell of burnt food permeating the dwelling. He sank into the chair at the head of the table and stared at the pitiful mess substituting as breakfast on his plate. "Vince, would you give the blessing?"

Vince offered thanks for the food while Abel's thoughts rolled onward. Cole was right—it would be beneficial to have a woman on the place, seeing to the cooking and cleaning. Should he check into hiring a housekeeper? But how would he pay her? He couldn't afford a housekeeper, but a man didn't have to pay a wife a wage. . . .

He jabbed his fork into the pancake on his plate. *No wife.* Not for him. Having his heart stomped once was plenty for any man.

≈

"Why, Sallie, you do know your way around a cow."

Tressa peeked over her shoulder. Sallie stood next to Mrs. Wyatt, a triumphant grin on her face and a full bucket in her hand. With a frustrated sigh, Tressa turned her attention back to the cow she'd chosen as her own. The brown and white beast, with its large eyes and incredibly long eyelashes, had seemed a cooperative sort. Unlike the one Mabelle chose, Tressa's cow stood complacently rather than shifting her feet. But the gentle animal refused to release more than a weak dribble of milk into Tressa's pail.

Despite the measly return, she dutifully continued her squeeze-and-pull on the cow's teats, just as Mrs. Wyatt had instructed. She also kept her lips tightly clamped against complaint. Evelyn openly and loudly proclaimed her opinions on rising at such an early hour, sitting in such an unladylike position, and being forced to endure the odors of the barn. Her comments couldn't quite drown out the whiz of milk streams connecting with the tin sides of the buckets. Obviously the others were experiencing success in emptying their cows' full udders. If Tressa couldn't compete with skill, she could at least be noted for her long-suffering behavior. Hopefully it would be enough to retain her position in the school.

Her shoulders pinched from leaning forward. Her hips ached at being held in the straddle-legged position for so long. Her fingers, cramping and stiff, resisted squeezing just one more time. She bit down on her lower lip and willed herself to continue. A hand descended on Tressa's shoulder. She peered up into Sallie's freckled face.

"The others've all taken their milk to the house for churnin' an' such. Aunt Hattie asked me to stay with ye."

Tressa spun on the stool, searching the barn. With the exception of Sallie, a row of cows contentedly munching from hay boxes, and a bird peeking over the edge of a nest snug against the rafters, the barn was empty. How could she not have heard everyone leave?

Sallie crouched beside Tressa and angled her head to peek into the bucket. She reared back in surprise. "Why, it's not even half full! Is she wigglin' too much for ye to hit the bucket?"

Tressa wrinkled her nose. "She's been a patient beast and very well behaved, but . . ." She sighed, flexing her tired fingers. "I can't seem to coax the milk from her."

"Scoot aside. Let me be givin' it a try."

Tressa's feeling of incompetence increased as a full, sure stream of milk fired into the bucket with Sallie's first pull. "Oh, Sallie . . ." Tressa sank down in the soft hay, resting her chin in her hands. "I'm an utter failure at milking."

Sallie gawked at her. "*Udder* failure?" The girl laughed, startling the cow into nervous shifting. With a wide grin, she gave Tressa's shoulder a light push. "Not at all, Tressa. It just takes time an' patience . . . and a wee trick. Ye must roll your fingers down the teat, like so . . ." Sallie demonstrated, squeezing one finger at a time and giving a gentle pull with the final finger. "See?"

"I see, but . . ." Tressa bit off the last words. Hadn't she decided not to complain? "I'll try again." Sallie shifted off the stool, and Tressa resumed her position, working her fingers just as Sallie had shown her. A drizzly stream released—much improved over the drip, drip, drip of moments ago. Heartened, Tressa squeezed again and was rewarded by another meager stream.

"There now, you're gettin' it!" Sallie beamed, giving Tressa's shoulder a pat. "But why don'tcha let me finish for ye?"

"Oh, no, I—"

"Aren't your hands achin'?"

Tressa sat back on the stool. In all honesty, her fingers hurt so badly she feared they'd be useless the rest of the day.

Sallie held up her hands. Calluses dotted her palms and the pads of her fingers. "My hands're used to milkin'." She caught Tressa's arm and urged her from the stool. Tressa stood to the side, rubbing her aching knuckles while Sallie quickly seated herself and emptied the cow's udder. Finished, she pulled the bucket free and grinned.

"Now, let's get this girl into a stall with some breakfast, an' we can head to the house to see what we'll be doin' next."

Tressa took the bucket with both hands. Its weight settled against her knees, and she waddled as she followed Sallie between stall rails, where the girl piled clean hay in the waiting feed box. The girl's confident actions stirred a question in Tressa's mind. "Sallie, you possess so many skills. . . . Surely you could have found employment in the city. Why did you choose to attend Mrs. Wyatt's school?"

Sallie led the cow to the feed box, her face puckered with sadness. "Right ye are that I be havin' many skills. I've been workin' from the time I was a wee lass, an' there's not much I can't do. No, t'wasn't the promise of new skills that brought me to Kansas. . . ." She scratched the cow's forehead while the animal munched. "I'm wantin' a kind man an' the chance to build a family of me own. Been many years since I been part of a family, Tressa." She tipped her head, sending Tressa a thoughtful look. "And ye? Why did ye come to this place?"

Heat built in Tressa's face. How could she explain that coming hadn't been her idea? Sallie would certainly scuttle away in shock if she learned that Tressa's aunt had deemed the school a means of ridding her of the obligation of providing a dowry for a niece. Tressa felt a developing affinity with Sallie despite the vast differences in their backgrounds. But if she were to mention those differences, Sallie might withdraw her offer of friendship.

She chose her words carefully, unwilling to deceive Sallie but also unable to divulge the full truth. "Like you, I'm here to gain a husband . . . and a family."

Sallie grinned, stepping away from the cow and reaching for the bucket. "Well, I'd say with your pretty face an' sweet way of talkin', the men around here would be foolish to pass ye by. I be thinkin', once you've learnt what ye need to cook an' clean an' be a help with the animals, you'll have no trouble snaggin' a man."

Tressa couldn't decide if she found Sallie's validation encouraging or frightening.

"An' besides, if ye don't find any of the men here pleasin', I'm thinkin' you'd make a fine schoolmarm. I can tell by your way of speakin' you've had more learnin' than most. You must've lived with a fancy family at some time an' picked up their habits. . . ."

Tressa's pulse raced. Why hadn't Aunt Gretchen warned her of the need to temper her speech? Working clothes weren't enough—Tressa must somehow present the complete picture of a lower-class girl. She made a silent vow to choose her words carefully lest she give her secret away and lose her opportunity to find a new life in this barren land.

She followed Sallie out of the cool, shadowy barn into full daylight. The brightness took Tressa by surprise. The sun had been a golden promise resting on the horizon line when they each chose a cow and began milking. But now the gray sky had turned robin's egg blue, the sun a huge yellow ball climbing toward the heavens. How much time had she wasted trying to draw milk from that cow?

Sallie also gave a start, squinting at the sun. "Aunt Hattie's surely got breakfast waitin'. We best be hurryin', Tressa."

They scuttled through the back door, which led directly into the kitchen. Sallie plunked Tressa's milk bucket beside the dry sink, where a row of upended buckets dripped from a recent washing. The room held a pleasant aroma, giving evidence that breakfast had been prepared. But no one was around. Then the sound of voices carried from the dining room. Sallie grabbed Tressa's hand and pulled her in that direction.

Mrs. Wyatt gestured toward the two open chairs when the girls entered the room. "Sit. Eat. The eggs're probably cold by now, but that's the price paid by stragglers." Her smile softened the reprimand. She waited until Tressa and Sallie sat before speaking again. "We were discussin' the cookin' schedule. Each of you will take your turn pre-parin' meals. First just for us, an' then for my whole crew."

"So we'll meet the men after we've learned to cook?" Luella tittered, hunching her shoulders and winking in Evelyn's direction. "Oooh, I'll be first."

Mrs. Wyatt continued as if Luella hadn't spoken. "Most o' the ranches around here have a full work crew livin' on the property, an' the wives're responsible for feedin' not only their own families but the fellas who work the place. So cookin' for a crowd is somethin' you all need to learn."

Tressa slid an egg onto her plate, noting the slight tremble in her hand. Not once had she prepared a meal. At Evan's Glen, she'd often visited the kitchen, receiving treats from the cheerful cook. But at Uncle Leo's, she wasn't allowed to enter the kitchen. Consorting with staff had been strictly prohibited. But then her aunt and uncle had callously thrown her into a situation for which she was ill-prepared. Indignation filled her at the unfair circumstances. If only Mama and Papa were still alive, how different her life would be. . . .

"Tressa, are ye all right?" Sallie's compassionate voice broke through Tressa's inner reflection.

Tressa shifted to look at Sallie, surprised to discover the girl's image seemed blurred. She swiped her hand across her eyes, removing the shimmer of tears, and held her volume to a whisper to match Sallie's. "Yes. Yes, of course, I'm quite—" Then, remembering Sallie's comment about her speech, she scrambled to reply in a simple manner. "I'm fine.

Just . . . tired." Her voice sounded stilted and unnatural. But Sallie smiled and relaxed into her seat, apparently reassured.

At the head of the table, Mrs. Wyatt turned to Luella. "Well, missy, since you're all fired up to take on the cookin' chores, you can have kitchen duties this week." She rose, swinging a grin around the table. "C'mon, girls, let's leave Luella to the cleanup an' get started on turnin' some o' that cream into butter."

Ignoring her stiff hips and aching shoulders, Tressa pushed to her feet and followed Mrs. Wyatt. She hoped it was easier to extract butter from cream than it had been to draw milk from that cow!

5

Abel rose with the congregation for the closing hymn. Beside him, Cole turned to gawk backward. Again. Abel focused on the words of the song, determined not to join his hired hand and sneak a peek over his own shoulder. Cole, Ethan, and even Vince, who was old enough to know better, had sent glances toward the back pew of the church more than once during the lengthy sermon. Constant shuffles from the pews behind Abel had indicated several others were more interested in getting a gander at the newcomers than focusing on Brother Connor's sermon.

Abel refrained from looking, but he was keenly aware of the women's presence somewhere behind him. The chorus of higher-pitched voices added a whole new quality to "Cast Thy Burden on the Lord." And with the service now ending, he'd have to turn around and make his way out of the church. In all of his years of attending the Barnett Community Church, he had never gone a Sunday without shaking hands with every other member and offering a greeting. But how could he greet Aunt Hattie today without acknowledging those women she'd brought to town?

His stomach churned, and it had nothing to do with the lumpy oatmeal he'd eaten for breakfast. Aunt Hattie meant well. She really thought she was doing the men of the town a favor with her herdsman school. Abel suspected if the widow had any idea how much it affected him to have those eastern women sitting in church, she would've driven over to Pierceville and attended service there instead this morning.

Telling her might make things easier for him, but he'd never let on to Hattie. There wasn't a purer soul in all of Ford County. She'd been the first one to come calling after Pa fell ill. She'd invited Abel to Sunday dinner more times than he could count. But if she invited him today, he'd say no for the first time.

The hymn ended on a long note, the harmony echoing from the rafters. Then with a wave of his hand, Brother Connor brought the singing to an end. Abel drew a deep breath and stepped into the aisle between the two rows of pews. On an ordinary May Sunday, the women clustered to share the latest gossip, and the men—married or single—smacked one another on the back, talked about the weather, or bragged about the number of calves born on their spread.

Today, however, wives captured their husbands' arms and escorted them straight out of the church building without giving them a chance to say a word. The single men stood for long seconds, their gazes bouncing between Aunt Hattie's girls and one another. Then, as if someone had fired a warning shot, they all leaped into action, crowding into the aisle and gathering around the pew at the back of the church, where Aunt Hattie stood like a mother bear shielding her cubs. Ethan and Cole crowded past Abel and clattered down the aisle to join the others.

The men all talked at once, creating a bigger hullabaloo than the summer day a hound dog pup sneaked into church and crawled under old Widow Parker's skirt. Rumor had it the shock of having the long-legged hound tangled up in her petticoats—followed by the uproarious laughter of her very own congregation—led directly to her decision to close up her café and move to Junction City and live with her oldest daughter. Abel hadn't thought any event could best that one, but the excited chatter from the back half of the church proved him wrong.

Vince stepped beside Abel and shook his head. "Fool men. They act like they've never seen females before." He shrugged. " 'Course, with ladies bein' scarce as hens' teeth around here, I reckon we can't fault the fellas for struttin' a bit." He nudged Abel with his elbow and added, "If I was a mite younger—say maybe twenty-six . . . or twenty-seven . . . I'd be over there lettin' those gals know I was available, too."

Abel grunted. Vince knew Abel's age, and Abel suspected it was no accident the old cowhand chose to name the number of candles that would decorate his next birthday cake, assuming Aunt Hattie made one for him again like she'd done in the years since his ma's passing. But he also figured Vince was smart enough to know why he didn't hurry over and make his presence known to those women.

Crushing his hat against his thigh, he strode toward the double doors that led out into the sunshiny churchyard. Vince followed. As they edged past the group, Aunt Hattie's voice carried over the fray.

"Mr. Samms! You hold up there a minute."

Stifling a groan, Abel came to a halt.

Aunt Hattie's stern frown sent the men scuttling out of her way. She stepped to the end of the pew, creating a formidable block between the men and the girls. "Cole an' Ethan was just sayin' you got a couple o' cows due to birth in the next day or so."

Keeping his gaze angled toward the wide opening only a few feet ahead, Abel gave a brusque nod. "That's right."

"I was wonderin' . . ." She caught his sleeve and gave it a tug, forcing him to look at her. "My pupils need to see a birthin', maybe bottle-feed a baby or two. Think we might be able to work somethin' out where they come to your place an'—"

"Brewster Hammond's probably got more cows than me still needin' to birth." Abel shifted slightly, removing his sleeve from her light grasp. "Might have better luck at his place."

"That's right, Aunt Hattie." Hammond's son, Gage, stuck his nose into the conversation, his smirk wide. "Nobody's got more cows than my pa. You're sure to see a birth or two at our place on any day of the week during the calvin' season." He winked at the cluster of girls, but Abel noticed only one responded to his brazen gesture.

"Brewster Hammond might have more births on a given day," Hattie countered in an even tone, shifting her frame to block Gage from the girls' view, "but his spread's farther out. Makes it harder for me to get the pupils there an' back without wastin' most of a day."

Abel licked his lower lip, his mind racing. "Don't you have cows birthin' on your place?"

" 'Course I do, but you know I don't bring 'em in close like you do. They have their babies out in the pasture an' my men tend to 'em out there."

A thought flicked through Abel's mind: *Why haven't the other ranchers near my place lost part of their herds the way I have? Why is the rustler targeting me?* He pushed the silent question aside to focus on Aunt Hattie, who continued in a persuasive tone.

"It'd be easier on the girls—them bein' new around here an' all—to see their first births in a barn rather than out in the open."

Seemed to Abel a birth was a birth whether out on the open range or in a barn, but he wouldn't argue with the lady. Not when she'd done so many kind deeds for him in the past. "I reckon it'd be all right if you brought 'em over."

A smile lit her face. "Thank you. Just send one o' your hands by"—Cole and Ethan jabbed each other with their elbows, grinning like they didn't have good sense—"when you think a cow's fixin' to deliver. I'll bring the pupils quick as a lick."

Abel made a mental note to instruct Vince to oversee the delivery and supervise Aunt Hattie's pupils. "That'd be fine, Aunt Hattie. Have a good day now." He slammed his hat onto his head and charged out the door.

~

Tressa tucked a strand of hair behind her ear, her gaze following the tall cowboy as he strode from the church. She recognized him as the man who had retrieved her hat the day she arrived in Barnett. That day, she hadn't looked directly into his face, too embarrassed by her clumsiness to raise her head. Today, however, with him caught up in conversation with Mrs. Wyatt, she'd had an opportunity to peruse his features without his knowledge. And she liked what she'd seen.

His thick, wavy hair, combed straight back and shiny with oil, reminded her of Papa's hair. Where Papa's was black with streaks of gray, however, the rancher's was dark brown with streaks of lighter brown, probably from time in the sun. His eyes were just as warm and brown as Papa's, though, and something in his reserved expression conjured pictures of Papa's reticence after Mama died. Looking into his eyes had ignited something akin to compassion in her breast.

She followed Mrs. Wyatt and the other girls out of the church, holding her arms stiffly to her sides in an attempt to shrink herself. The men crowding close made her uncomfortable. For reasons she couldn't explain, one in particular—the one Mrs. Wyatt had called Gage—left her feeling as though bugs crawled under her skin. When he sidled into her pathway, she sidestepped past him and scurried to Mrs. Wyatt's wagon. His laughter followed her, creating a rush of anger. She would keep a watch on that man. She didn't trust him.

Luella, however, took her time sashaying to the wagon. She cast her dimpled grin over her shoulder, batting her eyelashes. When she reached the wagon, she spun to face the men and waved good-bye with a little waggle of her fingertips.

Mrs. Wyatt made a *tsk-tsk* sound and shook her head. "Luella, save up your flirtin' till it's time to use it."

With a pout, Luella climbed into the back and flumped down beside Evelyn. Mabelle and Paralee scrambled in, followed by Sallie. Tressa took hold of the back and started to heave herself in when a hand curled around her elbow. She gasped in surprise and peered into the face of a tall, weathered man with striking dark eyes and thick pewter hair.

"Let me help you, miss."

His low, polite voice did little to calm her racing pulse. She tensed as he lifted, assisting her into the back of the wagon. Seating herself, she smoothed her skirt over her ankles. "Th-thank you, sir."

He closed the hatch and then touched the brim of his hat, reminding her of the man who'd retrieved her hat. A bit of her nervousness drifted away. Without another glance in her direction, the man strode around the side of the wagon and rested his elbow on the edge of the wagon's side.

"Harriet."

Mrs. Wyatt held the reins in her hands. "How-do, Brewster."

Tressa couldn't determine from Mrs. Wyatt's tone whether she was pleased or perturbed to be delayed by this tall, courtly man.

"My son tells me you're wantin' your pupils to witness the birth of a calf or two."

"Gage spoke rightly." Mrs. Wyatt jiggled the reins, signaling her impatience. "But I've solved the problem. Abel Samms said he'd let the girls come on to his place when the time comes."

Abel . . . Close in sound to Athol, Papa's name. Tressa's heart gave a little flutter, and she filed the name away for safekeeping.

The older man frowned, the leathery skin between his eyebrows folding into a tight crease. "Now, you know my herd's five times the size of Samms', Harriet. You'd have a better chance of seein' a birth any day of the week if you just came out to—"

"Appreciate your willingness to help us, Brewster." Mrs. Wyatt bobbed her chin toward the man. "But things're set, an' I'm content to let 'em be. You have a good Lord's day. Bye now." She clicked her tongue on her teeth and flicked the reins. The horses trotted forward, leaving the gray-haired rancher standing in the churchyard, staring after the wagon.

"Now *he's* a handsome man." Luella's low-toned comment brought Tressa's attention from the rancher. Luella flicked a knowing look around the circle of girls in the back of the wagon. "Just like his son." She heaved a dramatic sigh. "Oooh, Gage is my pick of the men in town."

"Gage . . ." Evelyn sniffed, snapping her parasol open over her head. "Why, he's just a boy. He probably hasn't been shaving for a full year yet."

"Even so," Luella said in an insistent voice, "he's the most eligible man in town. The son of the most successful rancher. I can't believe all of you aren't itching to be matched with him."

Evelyn rolled her eyes and double-fisted the parasol's bamboo handle, gazing out across the passing landscape with her lips pursed tight.

Sallie's eyes sparkled. "Seems to me the father's the most eligible, since he's the one who owns the biggest ranch. An' perhaps he's taken a fancy to our Tressa here."

Luella snickered, and Tressa gawked at Sallie in horror. "To me?"

"Why, ye didn't see him scurryin' forward to help any of *us* into the wagon, did ye?" Sallie grinned. "An' wouldn't it be a fine thing, Tressa, to be chosen by him?"

"Oh, he's far too old for Tressa," Paralee contributed.

Mabelle hunched her shoulders as she leaned forward. Her cheeks blotched red, matching her sunburned nose. "In lots of Beadle's dime novels, the woman's lover is double her age. She never seems to mind."

"Mabelle!" Paralee squealed.

Luella clamped her hand over Paralee's mouth. She tipped her head in the direction of Mrs. Wyatt. When the older woman didn't even glance over her shoulder, Luella lowered her hand, but she hissed, "Hush now! We don't want Aunt Hattie tellin' us to quit thinkin' of the men." She giggled. "As if I could do it."

Tressa wriggled backward, distancing herself from the group. The conversation left her feeling as though her breathing was constricted. The purpose in coming to Kansas was to secure a husband—she knew that—but shouldn't marriage be a dignified topic? Somehow Luella's smirks and the others' teasing comments made a mockery of the beautiful union her parents had shared. Sallie, Luella, Paralee, and Mabelle sat with their heads close together, whispering and giggling. Tressa shifted even further into the corner of the wagon.

Evelyn scooted sideways and tapped Tressa on the shoulder. "Ignore them. What do you expect from factory workers and household maids? They lack even the pretense of civility."

Evelyn's haughty tone was no easier to bear than the others' flippancy, but Tressa simply nodded.

"To be perfectly frank, Tressa, if you must complete this school and be matched with a man from the community, the older rancher would be the best choice." Evelyn glanced at the others, rolled her eyes in obvious distaste, and turned back to Tressa. "You *do* understand what I'm saying?"

Tressa licked her lips. Although the girls had worked side-by-side for the past several days at Mrs. Wyatt's ranch, she and Evelyn had never exchanged more than a few words in passing. Confusion clouded her mind at having the girl offer advice. "No. I confess, I don't understand."

Evelyn released a long-suffering sigh. "Think about it, Tressa. You marry a man twice your age. He dies while you're still young, leaving you his money. Then you're free to take that money and leave this godforsaken territory and have a decent life somewhere else."

Tressa reared back. How could Evelyn be so coldhearted? As if Tressa would marry someone merely to assume control of his possessions! Then something else occurred to her. "But if he's the best prospect in town, why don't you pursue him yourself?"

Evelyn's gaze drifted to the prairie once more. "I have no intention of marrying any of these bumpkins, no matter how well established." She pursed her lips. "I'm only here because my father is trying to teach me a lesson. I refused to wed the man he chose for me. He sent me away to give me an opportunity to regret my rebellion." A wry smile curled her lips. "His plan was successful. Now that I've seen the alternative to accepting Father's choice, I'm ready to concede defeat. Besides . . ." Her smile turned cunning. "The doddering old fool Father has selected can't last more than a few more years. When he's gone, I'll be his heir. My father was right all along."

Tressa turned away from Evelyn's smug face. To her relief, Mrs. Wyatt's house loomed in the distance. Pressing her palms to the floor of the rattling wagon, she battled the urge to leap over the side and run the remainder of the distance so she could be free of the present company. Luella's flirtatious ways, Evelyn's heartless conniving, and the others' frivolous behavior made her wish to be anywhere but there.

But where would she go? The thought brought her up short. When she left Mrs. Wyatt's for good, it would be to another ranch in the area. To be a rancher's wife. Heat flooded her cheeks as the faces of the men from church paraded through her memory. She shuddered, remembering young Gage's leering wink, and her skin prickled in memory of the elder Hammond's hand on her arm. But when the image of the rancher named Abel crossed her mind, she relaxed.

Abel . . . the man with eyes like Papa. The man whose serious expression seemed to indicate he needed cheering as much as Tressa did. The man who had rescued her hat.

Lifting her eyes to the crystal blue sky overhead, Tressa wondered who Papa might choose as her beau if he were still alive.

6

"See there, Isabella?" Tressa tipped the pail slightly so the cat could peek over the brim. "A full bucket. And look." She held her hands outward, flexing her fingers. The nails were chipped and calluses decorated her palms—such a change in appearance in a week and a half of labor— but the movement proved effortless. "They hardly hurt at all. That means I'm getting better at milking, wouldn't you agree?"

The cat twitched the white tip of her tail and stared at Tressa with unblinking yellow eyes.

Tressa grimaced. "You're right, I *am* the last one in the barn . . . again. But I didn't need anyone else's help, and the bucket *is* full. So I still assert I'm showing improvement."

Isabella yawned and then lifted one paw to give it a thorough wash with her rough pink tongue.

Tressa laughed. "You aren't very encouraging, puss, but I'm glad you're here anyway." She scratched the cat's chin, raising an immediate rumbling purr. Over the past days, she and Isabella had become fast friends. Although puzzled by the cat's fondness for her, she still found it flattering that Isabella preferred her company over that of the other girls on the ranch. She also welcomed the cat's presence.

With Evelyn's departure for New York two days ago, Luella had appropriated Sallie's attention. Paralee and Mabelle remained very close, which left Tressa without a partner. During the years she lived in her uncle's home, she had often felt alone, as her four younger girl cousins had never fully accepted her into their circle. She should be accustomed to being the odd person out, yet loneliness still created an empty ache in her chest.

"I'm glad you like me, Isabella. The others certainly don't." Isabella placed one front paw on Tressa's knee and batted at her chin with her other paw. Tressa scooped the animal into her lap. "I can't honestly fault them. I'm completely inept at most of the required tasks, so I make a mess of nearly everything I touch."

She ran her hands through Isabella's soft fur, enjoying the answering purr of appreciation. At least she could do something right. "I hear them whispering about me." Her throat tightened, recalling the embarrassment of those moments when the others sent supercilious looks of disapproval her way. "I do the best I can, but . . ."

Her gaze fell to the bucket of milk waiting to be delivered to the house. She was already well behind the others. Sitting here petting the cat wouldn't get the butter churned. "I need to get inside, kitty."

With a sigh, Tressa put Isabella on the ground and pushed off of the stool. "Would you like to help me put old Rosie in her stall?" Isabella wove between her feet while Tressa saw to the cow's needs. Then, with bucket in hand, she headed for the house. The cat trotted ahead, tail sticking up as straight as a poker. She glanced back now and then as if to ascertain Tressa was still following. Despite her momentary melancholy in the barn, Tressa released a laugh at the cat's antics.

Just as she reached the back door, the sound of horses' hooves caught her attention. Isabella's tail puffed to twice its normal size, and she dashed under the short bench that sat below the kitchen window. Tressa turned to see a cowboy rein in next to the house. He grinned broadly when he spotted her, snatching off his hat to reveal a thick thatch of straw-colored hair.

"Howdy, miss. My name's Ethan Rylin—I work for Abel Samms. Is Aunt Hattie in the house?"

Tressa nodded.

"Tell 'er Abel sent me to say we got a calf on the way."

Tressa crinkled her brow. "A calf?"

"Yep. If you're wantin' to see a birthin', head on over to the Lazy S."

"Oh!" Tressa remembered Mrs. Wyatt's desire for the girls to witness a birth. With so many activities packed into a day, she had forgotten the conversation at church. "I'll tell her. Thank you."

Ethan smacked his hat back on his head, tugged the reins, and galloped off without another word. Tressa hurried into the house, stumbling a bit to avoid stepping on Isabella, who darted between her feet. "Mrs. Wyatt! Mrs. Wyatt?"

The older woman bustled from the pantry, wiping her hands on her apron. A white streak of flour decorated her left cheek. "You got that milk ready to go? An' call me Aunt Hattie. Land sakes, girl, I don't rightly know how to answer to Mrs. Wyatt."

"I . . . I'm sorry." Tressa placed the bucket on the dry sink beside the door.

"Apology accepted. Now, soon as you get that milk separated an' the cream churned to butter, you can mix up some biscuits for lunch. Reckon you've watched me enough times to do that on your own by now." She jabbed her thumb toward the pantry. "I been siftin' the flour to remove the weevils for ya—I know the sight o' them bugs doesn't set well with your stomach." She shook her head. "But, Tressa-darlin', you're gonna hafta to set aside that weak tummy o' yours or you'll never make it around here. A person can find worse'n weevils hidin' in a barrel."

Tressa's stomach rolled as she considered what else might lurk in a flour barrel. "Yes, ma'am. I'll do my best." But she must tell Mrs. Wyatt about the cowboy. "Ma'am, a man just rode up. He said to tell you if we hurry to the Lazy S, we'll have the opportunity to see a birthing today."

Mrs. Wyatt clapped her palms together. "Oh, that's good news." She grimaced. "I hate leavin' your bucket o' milk sit out, though. Heaven only knows when we'll be back." She tapped her chin with one finger. "I tell you what, throw a piece of damp cheesecloth over the top o' that bucket an' take it down to the root cellar real quick. It'll stay cool as the underside of a rock down there. I'll gather up the others. Meet us in the barn an' we'll drive on over to Abel's ranch." She started toward the doorway, but then she turned back. A smile broke across her face. "You're in for a real treat today. Ain't nothin' more special than a birthin'."

Tressa pondered Mrs. Wyatt's comment as she carried the bucket outside and headed toward the root cellar. Her only experience with birthing was the night her baby brother was born. She remembered little more than being sent to the kitchen with the old cook who sang songs and rocked her to distract her from the piercing cries coming from her mother's bedroom. She'd fallen asleep, and the next morning her father had sorrowfully explained that Mama and the baby were in Heaven with Jesus.

By the time she returned from the cellar, the others were all waiting in the wagon. She climbed in, and even before she could sit, Mrs. Wyatt smacked the reins onto the horses' backs. "Yah!" The wagon jolted forward, throwing Tressa flat onto her bottom with her feet in the air. Luella nudged Paralee's arm, and the two snickered. She turned her head, clamping her lips tight to hide the quiver in her chin.

The ride to the Lazy S took them in the opposite direction of town, but the view still seemed familiar. The prairie rolled endlessly in all directions, knee-high grass gently waving in the wind. The sun shone bright overhead, glinting off the blades of grass and warming Tressa's uncovered head. She hadn't taken time to put on a bonnet before leaving the house, and the wind tore her hair loose from the unpretentious tail she had tied with a piece of ribbon. She held the side of the wagon with one hand and used the other to hold her hair and prevent it from blowing.

The wagon rolled onto the dirt yard of a simple one-story ranch house. Tressa wrinkled her nose at the sight of the unpainted, unappealing dwelling. This structure made Mrs. Wyatt's modest house seem like a mansion. Mrs. Wyatt brought the team to a stop, then she grinned into the back of the wagon. "Barn's straight ahead. If I know Abel Samms, he'll have the stall all mucked out an' ready for us, so head on over."

Before the girls could climb from the back, a weathered cowboy emerged from the barn and trotted toward them. He waved his hand.

"Hold up there, Hattie, an' let me help you down." He offered Mrs. Wyatt his hand, and she allowed him to assist her from the seat.

"Thank you, Vince. I don't believe you met my pupils in church last Sunday." She led the man to the back of the wagon and released the hatch. "This here is Miss Mabelle, Miss Paralee, Miss Sallie, Miss Luella, an' Miss Tressa." She pointed to each girl in turn.

Vince nodded, offering a broad smile. "Welcome to the Lazy S, ladies. It's been my home for nearly twenty years, an' I'm right fond of the place." He held out his hand to Tressa. "Let's get you gals into the barn. I figure there won't be a long wait—this mama's just about ready to deliver."

He caught Tressa around the waist and lifted her from the back of the wagon. She scurried to Mrs. Wyatt's side as he helped the others. When he reached for Luella, she batted her eyelashes and tittered. The too-familiar sound set Tressa's teeth on edge. Vince placed Luella on the ground, and her hands lingered on his shoulders. Vince grinned and offered Luella his elbow. With another high-pitched giggle, she slipped her hand into the curve of his arm and sashayed along beside him as they led the way to the barn.

Tressa shifted her gaze from Luella and the angular cowboy to the waiting barn. She found its massive size astounding. Constructed of rough-cut tan stones and towering two stories high, it dwarfed the barn on Mrs. Wyatt's property. Doors yawned wide in the arched opening at the front as if offering an invitation to enter. Tressa released a little shiver as she stepped from the sun into the cool, shadowed interior of the huge structure. Although this barn was at least triple the size of the Mrs. Wyatt's barn, the smells were the same—musty hay, musky animals, and moist soil. Tressa put her finger under her nose to stave off a sneeze.

Staying close to Mrs. Wyatt, she followed the others to a stall about halfway down on the east side. Vince removed Luella's hand from his arm with a dapper bow and entered the stall. Mrs. Wyatt put her hand on Tressa's back and propelled her to the edge of the stall. Tressa rested her fingertips on the highest rail and peered over the top at a tawny brown cow. It lay on its side with its neck arched and legs stretched straight out. Pieces of hay clung to its head and nose, tempting Tressa to climb over the rails and brush the bits away.

Vince hunkered beside the beast and placed his hand on the cow's bulging stomach. He grinned up at the row of girls. "See how big her belly looks? That's not all baby. She's holdin' her breath, which means she's in the middle of a birthin' pain."

Tressa's stomach muscles tightened in compassionate response to the cow's discomfort.

Vince went on. "Her water bag ruptured right before you got here. Won't be long now, an' we'll see some little feet come through the canal."

"Feet?" Mabelle squeaked the word and then clapped her hand over her mouth.

Vince chuckled. "Yep, feet. We wanna see feet an' then a nose. Sometimes calves're born rump first, but that's awful hard on the mama. So we need to be hopin' for a nose instead."

The cow huffed, lifting her head slightly. She released a low moo and pawed the air with her front hooves. Tressa took an involuntary step backward while the others pressed forward.

Vince propped one hand against the ground, tipping his head toward the cow's rear quarters. "Uh-huh, here we go!"

Two tiny hooves appeared. Luella climbed onto the lowest rail and leaned into the stall, her eyes wide and mouth forming an O of wonder. Sallie sent a grin over her shoulder. "I seen my share of birthin's when I worked for the dairyman, but it's an amazin' thing to watch. Are ye wantin' to come up, Tressa?"

Tressa shook her head wildly, and Sallie shrugged. "Suit yourself." She clambered up beside Luella. Paralee gasped, reaching for Mabelle's hand. Mabelle caught hold, and the two clung. Tressa swallowed. She wished she could hold someone's hand. Mrs. Wyatt stood near. Without turning her gaze from the laboring cow, Tressa reached blindly. Her fingers encountered a hand, and she grabbed hold.

At first the fingers lay loose within her grasp, but when the cow mooed again—louder and more panicked—Tressa squeezed, and the fingers curved securely around her hand. The touch offered a measure of comfort, and she clung hard while she watched the birth. A white nose followed the hooves. The cow moaned again, and the calf's head emerged.

Tressa held her breath, her fingers squeezing hard on Mrs. Wyatt's hand while the cow bawled in complaint. Suddenly the calf's wet, slick body wriggled through the opening in a rush and sprawled in the hay. It thrashed its spindly legs, nosing the ground. The mother staggered to her feet and circled the baby. She began licking it, and the calf folded its legs underneath itself. It hiked its rump in the air first and then raised its wobbly head to stand on four shaky legs.

Vince laughed out loud. "We got ourselves a little bull." He patted the cow's side. "Good job, mama."

Tressa's breath whooshed from her lungs, her knees sagging with relief that the mother and baby were fine. She turned to thank Mrs. Wyatt for the comforting support of her hand, but to her shock, instead of Mrs. Wyatt, the brown-eyed rancher named Abel Samms stood beside her. And she held tight to his hand.

7

Abel watched the young woman's face blaze red. She yanked her hand free of his so fast she nearly threw him off balance. Scuttling sideways, she ran smack into Aunt Hattie, and then took two backward steps that bounced her against the stall rails. There she stood, staring at him in silence with wide, pale blue eyes before she whirled around and presented her back.

He resisted releasing a snort of amusement. Considering *she* had latched on to *him*, she didn't need to act all put upon. He'd entered the barn intending to tap Aunt Hattie's shoulder and draw her out to the yard for a private conversation. But before he could follow through on his plan, that girl had grabbed hold of his hand and wouldn't let loose. So he'd stayed.

Now he swiped his palm down his trouser leg to remove their joined moisture and faced Hattie, who offered a knowing smirk. Did she think that hand-holding had been *his* idea? He cleared his throat.

"Aunt Hattie, couldja step out here with me for a minute?" He didn't wait for a response but turned and clumped outside, trusting her to follow. The excited chatter of Aunt Hattie's pupils and Vince's drawling responses to their questions carried through the barn door's opening, so he stepped well out into the yard.

He squinted into Aunt Hattie's grinning face. "What're you smilin' at?"

"You."

"Why?"

She touched his arm. "That was a kind thing you did, Abel, holding Miss Tressa's hand."

He started to explain that he hadn't meant to hold her hand, but the girl's name echoed through his mind, stilling his tongue. Tressa. An unusual name—as unusual as her eyes. He'd never seen such pale eyes—the color of wild sweet William, his ma's favorite blossom. He'd picked dozens of sweet William bouquets as a little boy. But it'd been a while since he'd picked one for her grave. He needed to do that before the early spring wildflowers all died away.

Aunt Hattie continued. "New experiences can be frightenin', so I know you gave her a real gift by holdin' on tight."

That girl'd taken his hand—he hadn't given it—and he shouldn't take credit. But there was something more important to discuss. "Aunt Hattie, I gotta ask you a question, an' I'm trustin' you to keep it quiet."

Her heavy eyebrows knitted together. "You can trust me."

Abel flicked a glance toward the barn. The murmur of voices told him the pupils and Vince were still occupied. He crossed his arms over his chest. "You heard about any ranchers around here losin' lots of cattle the last couple of years?"

Hattie smoothed her hand down her bonnet strings. "Well now, Abel, every rancher loses a few head ever' winter, an' I reckon I've lost a calf or two to coyotes."

"No, not that kind of loss."

"Then what?"

"Rustlers."

Aunt Hattie's jaw dropped. "Rustlers? In Barnett?"

"Shh!" Abel caught her elbow and propelled her to her wagon. He propped his arm on the side and dipped his face close to hers. "Started after Pa died. I lost a good ten percent of my herd last year an' even more'n that the year before. I know we had a hard winter in '85. That took its toll on lots of ranchers, but in the past two years I haven't found carcasses to account for comin' up so short. There'd be somethin'. Even a pack of coyotes can't drag off every bone from a steer."

"Oh, my . . ." Aunt Hattie's tone reflected dismay. She shook her head. "I never heard o' such a thing 'cept in Texas. Don't like to even think of it." Her frown deepened. "You talk to the sheriff?"

Abel blew out a snide breath. "Naw. Lazy ol' coot. He'd want proof of somethin' before he'd sling himself on a horse an' look into things. An' I don't got proof. All I got is my instincts."

"Well, instincts is sometimes wrong, Abel."

She sounded hopeful, and Abel couldn't blame her. He didn't like to think someone was deliberately stealing his animals. Especially considering it seemed his ranch was the only one bothered. Why would somebody target his ranch? He didn't know of anyone with a grudge against him.

He sighed. "Aunt Hattie, I don't think I'm wrong."

"So what're you gonna do?"

"Put up some of that barbed wire fence. Keep my herd closer in. Make it harder for the thief." He let out a humorless chuckle. " 'Course, makes it harder on me an' my hands, too, 'cause we'll be hauling in hay rather'n lettin' the cows graze. But what else can I do?"

Aunt Hattie clasped his wrist. "You can pray that the thief'll get an attack o' conscience, repent, an' stop his wicked ways."

Abel bit down on his tongue to hold back words of protest. Oh, he went to church regular just like his ma had taught him, and he prayed over his meals—especially when Cole did the cooking. But the last times he'd prayed—*really* prayed—God hadn't paid him any mind. Pa still died of that infection. Amanda still returned to the East. Abel didn't see much sense in giving God another opportunity to let him down.

Aunt Hattie nibbled her lower lip. "Could you use an extra hand to keep an eye out? I could spare one o' my men since the pupils're doin' a lot o' the chores around my ranch."

Abel considered her suggestion, but in the end he shook his head. "Naw. I appreciate the offer, but the fewer people who know about this, the better. I don't want the thief gettin' wind that I'm on to him. I'm hopin' he'll get lazy . . . be easier for me to catch him."

"I hope you're right."

A flurry of movement in the barn's opening caught his attention. The girls spilled into the yard with Vince in the middle of their throng. They headed toward the wagon, still jabbering and laughing. Except for the one called Tressa. She trailed behind, her unsmiling lips pressed shut.

Abel caught Aunt Hattie's arm. "Remember—it's our secret."

" 'Course it is. Ours an' God's."

As Abel ambled away, he muttered, "Let's just keep it between you an' me."

❧

Facing a corner of the bedroom, Tressa slipped her nightgown over her head, buttoned it, then turned away from the corner. Sallie stood in front of the bureau in her chemise, pawing through the bottom drawer. Tressa spun to face the corner again, her cheeks hot. The drawer banged shut and still she waited, giving Sallie adequate time to slip into her nightclothes. Finally she directed a cautious glance over her shoulder to find her roommate, attired in her simple cotton gown, grinning at her.

"You're a strange one, Tressa. Never met anybody so shy about herself." Sallie laughed lightly, shaking her head. Her spiraling red curls bounced on her shoulders. "Luella asked me to move into her room now that she's all alone, but I told her no. Now I'm thinkin' maybe you'd be happier without someone else in your room?"

Tressa's heart gave a little leap. If Sallie had refused to move in with Luella, perhaps she was still interested in pursuing her fledgling friendship with Tressa. Clasping her gown closed at the neck, she sat gingerly on the edge of the bed. "You told Luella no?"

Sallie flumped into her bed, making the springs squeak. "You heard Aunt Hattie the day we moved in. No room changin'." She offered a pensive look. "But if you'd be happier without me underfoot, I'll ask about makin' the change."

Tressa hung her head. "No. No, that's fine, Sallie." She swallowed. "Unless . . . Would you rather room with Luella?"

Sallie shrugged and pulled the covers to her chin. "Oh now, Luella's a laughy sort. A mite daft sometimes, too, but even that makes me laugh. But . . ." She yawned, wriggling farther down into the mattress. "I'll be stayin' here instead. Movin' is too much fuss an' feathers."

Tressa blew out the lamp that sat on the little table beside the bed, plunging them into darkness, and then slid between the sheets. Lying perfectly still, she listened to Sallie's steady breathing give way to soft snoring. She willed herself to succumb to sleep, too. But her mind resisted. Tossing the covers aside, she rose and crossed to the window. Perhaps some stargazing would cheer her and help her sleep.

But a hazy band stretched across the sky, hiding the stars. Frowning, Tressa dropped the curtain into place. Did the clouds cover the entire sky, or only this view? Determined to get a glimpse of the flickering lights that gave her heart a lift, she snatched her tattered robe from the corner of the bed and tiptoed out the door.

She crept down the stairs, cringing as her foot hit the creaky fourth riser. Pausing, she listened intently. Had anyone been disturbed? No sounds carried from any of the bedrooms, convincing her the others slept on. She hurried down the remaining stairs and crossed to the front door. To her surprise, the door stood open, allowing in the night air. Did Mrs. Wyatt leave the house completely open during the night? Her heart pattered at the thought. Then she assured herself she was no longer in the city—locked doors probably weren't necessary here in the country.

The heavily scented night breeze stirred the tails of her robe as she stepped out onto the porch. She padded to the railing, the pine boards cool and smooth against the soles of her bare feet, and rested her fingertips on the top rail. Leaning her hips against the sturdy railing, she turned her gaze to the sky, her eyes eager to feast upon a host of sparkling stars. But disappointment sagged her shoulders. Clouds shrouded this view, as well.

Sighing, she turned to go back into the house, but a flicker of light from the far end of the porch caught her attention. The flicker became an undulating glow accompanied by a thin ribbon of aromatic smoke. She froze, a chill attacking her frame. And then a chuckle rumbled.

"Well, Tressa, don't stand there with your mouth hangin' open. Come on over here an' join me an' Izzy-B since you're up."

She wilted with relief when Mrs. Wyatt's familiar voice reached her ears. Her eyes adjusted enough to make her way to the edge of the porch, where Mrs. Wyatt sat in one of two rickety straight-back chairs. Tressa sank into the second chair, smiling when Isabella stretched out her paw and meowed in greeting.

She wrinkled her nose, however, at the object Mrs. Wyatt held in her hand. A pipe, out of which a thin band of smoke continued to rise, flavoring the air.

Mrs. Wyatt's low-toned chuckle came again. "You don't hide much with those big eyes o' yours, girlie." She bounced the pipe in Tressa's direction. "You find this thing objectionable?"

Honestly, the cherry-scented smoke wasn't unpleasant. Tressa shook her head. "No, ma'am. I'm just . . ." Never had Tressa imagined a woman smoking a pipe. She found the practice unseemly at best. Fearful of insulting her hostess, she fell silent.

But Mrs. Wyatt completed the thought. "Shocked that a lady would smoke?"

Heat flooded her face, but Tressa offered a quick nod.

"It's a nasty habit, I'm sure." Mrs. Wyatt took a draw on the pipe, creating a soft glow in the bowl, and blew the smoke toward the ceiling. She examined the pipe and a soft smile curved her lips. "My husband, Jed, smoked of an evening. Sometimes when I get to missin' him too much, I come out here an' light up his pipe. The smell of his favorite tobacco takes a bit of my loneliness away."

Compassion filled Tressa's chest. "I understand."

"An' you, Tressa? You sneakin' out here to find a salve for your loneliness?"

The woman's astuteness took Tressa by surprise. "I . . . I . . ."

Another chuckled sounded. "Aw, Tressa-darlin', I can tell you ain't exactly comfortable here on the ranch. Oh, you try hard. Got more stick-to-it-iveness than you let yourself admit, I wager. But I know you aren't here 'cause it was your choice." A short pause gave Tressa the opportunity to rise and escape to her bedroom, but she remained rooted to the chair. Mrs. Wyatt continued softly. "Are you like Evelyn, sent here by a daddy who means to teach you a lesson?"

Tressa curled her hands around the seat of the chair and jerked to face the older woman. "No! My papa would never have sent me away! He loved me!"

"Ah." Mrs. Wyatt nodded wisely, tucking the slim stem into the corner of her mouth. "*Loved.* Not *loves.* That means he's gone?" Gentle puffs of smoke rose from the pipe's bowl.

Tressa aimed her gaze across the dark landscape, blinking rapidly to control the attack of tears. "Yes, ma'am."

"An' you got no other people?"

Tressa couldn't find an honest answer to that question. Yes, she had people, but they didn't want her. She sat in silence.

"Well, Tressa, that puts you in a fix, don't it? 'Specially since you don't exactly feel wanted here, either."

Turning her head slightly, Tressa met Mrs. Wyatt's sympathetic gaze.

"Don't take the others' tauntin' to heart, Tressa. Y'see, people sometimes behave like a flock o' chickens, peckin' on the one they see as the weakest."

Tressa nodded. She had witnessed the hens' ill-treatment of one poor bird in the coop. Her heart stirred with pity each time she glimpsed that bedraggled, skinny hen huddling in the corner of the coop by itself while the others scratched in the dirt together.

"Don't let 'em make you feel bad. It's clear you haven't had the same experiences as the others, an' that puts you at a disadvantage. You'll learn eventually if you keep tryin' hard as you have been. But, Tressa-darlin', you gotta get some gumption. Stand up for yourself!"

Mrs. Wyatt punched the air with her fist. Isabella released a meow of protest and leaped from the woman's lap into Tressa's. Tressa ran her fingers through the animal's soft fur, finding comfort in the warm, purring body.

"Somethin' you gotta learn, girl, is people will push you only as far as you let 'em. They'll keep makin' you the pecked hen unless you ruffle your feathers and show 'em you aren't gonna stand for their peck-peck-peck." She pulled the pipe from her lips and jabbed the air with the pipe's stem to punctuate her words. "Look 'em in the eye 'stead o' hangin' your head. Speak up 'stead o' standin' quiet. Jump into the middle 'stead o' holdin' off by yourself. *Make* those girls see the fine, hardworkin', capable person I know you to be. You'll feel a whole lot better about yourself."

Tressa licked her lips. "You . . . you think I'm capable of learning all there is to know?"

Mrs. Wyatt leaned toward Tressa, her expression serious. "I *know* you are. But what's more important, Tressa, is for *you* to know you are."

Swallowing, Tressa offered one slow nod. Mrs. Wyatt had given her much to consider. She started to scoop Isabella from her lap so she could return to her room, but Mrs. Wyatt clamped her hand over her wrist, holding her in place.

"Tressa, can I ask you a question?"

"I . . . I suppose."

"Where you lived before, did anybody teach you to believe in God?"

Memories rolled through Tressa's mind. When Mama and Papa were alive, they had attended a lovely stone chapel together as a family. The messages delivered from the pulpit about a loving God had given the child Tressa a sense of security and peace. But after her aunt and uncle took her in, church attendance had been limited to special holidays, and Tressa had nearly forgotten the lessons of her childhood.

Her years with Aunt Gretchen and Uncle Leo cast a shadow over her years with Papa and Mama. Tressa formed an answer. "No, ma'am."

A deep sigh heaved from Mrs. Wyatt. "Well, then, darlin', here's lesson number one." She pointed skyward. "There's a Father in Heaven who cares about you. Loves you. Loves you dearly. An' He's got willin' ears to listen when His children speak to Him. So anytime you're feelin' sad or lonely or upset, you can tell it to Him an' He'll give you the help you need."

Shreds of memories from long ago, when Papa held her on his knee and read to her from a big black book, whispered through her mind. But reality chased the wispy memories away. Her father resided in Heaven, and he was too far away to offer any help to her now.

"Yes, missy, you can always depend on God."

Tressa tipped her head. Had Mrs. Wyatt meant to intimate that God was her father?

Slapping her thighs, Mrs. Wyatt rose. "Lots more I could say, but it's late an' we both need our rest." She walked to the edge of the porch, turned the pipe upside-down, and tapped it on the railing. Coals scattered across the ground. They flickered briefly and then died, reminding Tressa of stars disappearing from view as sunshine captured the sky.

Mrs. Wyatt slipped the pipe into her apron pocket and plucked Isabella from Tressa's lap. "Bed now." She smiled, reaching out to briefly cup Tressa's cheek with her warm palm. "Things'll look brighter in the mornin'. Wait an' see."

8

"Boss! Boss!"

Abel jerked upright. The pan of corn bread he was removing from the oven fell from his hand. The pan bounced from the open oven door to the wide-planked floor, sending chunks of steaming yellow bread in every direction. Clamping his lips against a mild oath, he turned toward the kitchen door, where Cole stood, wide-eyed and panting.

"What is it?" Abel didn't bother to hide his aggravation as he bent to pick up the mess. The hot corn bread burned his fingers, and he tossed the pieces back into the pan as quickly as possible.

"Don't know how it happened, but four of our calves . . ." Cole took a deep breath, shaking his head. "They're gone. Just disappeared from the pen overnight."

Abel jolted to his feet. "Gone? From the pen?" The large holding pen where Abel had decided to corral the newest calves until the scars from branding were completely healed stood between the barn and the bunkhouse. A thief would have had to come well onto the property, in plain sight of the bunkhouse as well as the main house, in order to remove any calves. "Didn't you hear nothin' last night?"

"Not a thing," Cole claimed. "Think it could be coyotes?"

"A pack of coyotes might take down a calf an' scare off the others, but there'd be plenty of noise an' a mess left behind. You see any blood or clumps of hide out there?"

"No, sir. Just a jumble of prints headin' right out the gate."

"Then it's gotta be men." Abel kicked at a clump of corn bread with the toe of his boot. The chunk crumbled into bits. The broken corn bread painted an ugly picture of his ranch—everything was falling apart, and he was helpless against it.

Cole crushed his hat in his hands. "Want I should ride in for the sheriff? Make a report?"

Abel hesitated. If he notified the sheriff, it wouldn't be long before word spread through all of Barnett and the surrounding ranches. Everyone would be on alert, aware of strangers in the area. While that might be a good thing, Abel knew it could also lead to mayhem. When he was a boy, his pa had told him about a group of angry, suspicious ranchers lynching two men suspected of horse-thieving only to discover later that the real horse thieves were already in the Dodge City jail. Abel had taken the lesson to heart—don't be brash.

"Not just yet." Abel snatched his hat from the peg beside the back door. "Tell Vince an' Ethan to eat." He grimaced at the ruined corn bread. At least the bacon waiting hot and crisp in the frying pan would be edible. "But you take turns eating. I want somebody watchin' the pen at all times."

"You think somebody'd try to steal in the light of day?"

Abel wished he could laugh at Cole's astounded expression. Unfortunately, he could believe anything after having calves snatched from beneath their very noses. "Just rather be safe than sorry. I'm headin' to town." If it took every penny left in his bank account, he'd buy enough barbed wire to discourage anybody from putting a foot on his property, night or day.

❧

The clouds that had shielded the stars from view during the night still hung like a gossamer canopy when Tressa headed to the henhouse in the morning. She swung a basket on her arm, her gaze sweeping from horizon to horizon, seeking a peep of blue. But wispy gray greeted her eyes no matter where she looked. Despondence tried to seize her—the sun always made a day seem cheery—but she resisted letting the feeling take hold. Today was her emancipation day! She wouldn't allow clouds to dampen her spirits or her resolve.

Last night, after returning to her bed, she had lain awake, considering Mrs. Wyatt's advice. Was it possible that the others berated her because she allowed them to do so? Might she be able to bring an end to their condescension by exhibiting more confidence? She wanted to explore the notion, and she had made a decision. No more suffering in silence. If someone spoke ill of her or to her, she would calmly but firmly defend herself. She gave a little skip, discovering a sense of freedom in the contemplation of fending off the pecks of the others.

She entered the henhouse and made her way down the row of nesting boxes, reaching beneath each sleeping hen to remove the egg from the nest. The hens wriggled at the intrusion, one or two releasing a soft cluck of irritation. One tried to peck her hand, but she had learned to be quick. The poor mistreated hen with missing feathers and small scabs showing in the bare spots sat in the last box. Her nest contained only straw, no egg.

Tressa took a moment to run her hand over the hen's back, smoothing the stiff feathers into place. Suddenly the fat hen in the closest box stretched out and gave a vicious peck on the injured hen's neck, narrowly missing Tressa's hand.

"You stop that!" Tressa smacked the errant hen, toppling it onto its side. It righted itself with a wild flapping of its wings and began squawking in earnest. Within seconds, every other hen in the coop took up the cry. Ignoring the hubbub, Tressa shook her finger in the offending hen's face. "You will behave yourself or suffer the consequences!"

Ducking past the flying feathers, Tressa left the henhouse to return to the kitchen. The squawks followed, ringing in her ears. When she was halfway across the yard, the kitchen door flew open. Mabelle stood in the opening with her hands on her hips.

"What on earth did you do to those chickens? I could hear them fussing from here even with the door closed!"

Tressa glanced over her shoulder. The raucous clucking continued; a few feathers flitted from the slatted window openings. With a shrug, she looked directly into Mabelle's face. "One of the hens tried to peck me, so I clopped her good. She'll settle down in time." She stepped past Mabelle and set the basket of eggs on the dry sink. With a smug smile, she added under her breath, "Let my lesson to the hen to be a lesson to you, too. No more pecking, or else!"

❧

"There you be, Abel." Hank Townsend rolled the last bale of barbed wire into Abel's wagon and then swished his beefy hands together. His belly bounced with a chortle. "You got enough wire there to hem in the entire county."

"Might not be a bad idea," Abel muttered. "Keep out the riff-raff." He slammed the gate and dropped the locking pins into place. "Thanks, Hank. What do I owe you?" He cringed when Hank stated the price, but he counted out the needed amount from the funds he'd withdrawn from his bank account and placed the bills on Hank's waiting palm.

The man grinned. "Wear good sturdy gloves when you're stringin' that wire or you'll be as pricked as a woman's pincushion."

"Will do."

Just as Abel turned to pull himself into the high seat, Hank smacked himself on the forehead and said, "Oh! Abel, hold up a minute." He bustled to Abel's side. "You hafta ride right past Hattie Wyatt's ranch when you go home, don'tcha?"

Abel nodded.

"She ordered a dozen pairs of gardenin' gloves for her pupils. Ever'thing I had in stock was too big for their hands. The order come in yesterday an' I hadn't got around to lettin' her know. Reckon she'd like to have 'em. They're all paid for. Would'ja take 'em out to her—save her the trip in?"

Although Abel preferred to hurry home and get started stringing his new wire fence, he couldn't refuse doing a favor for Aunt Hattie. "Sure, Hank. Toss 'em in the back an' I'll drop 'em by."

Moments later, Abel turned the wagon toward home. He battled a strong urge to speed the horses along the road. But even if the horses suddenly sprouted wings and flew him to the ranch, it wouldn't bring back the missing calves.

He passed the church building and the little house where Brother Connor lived with his wife and two youngsters. His fingers tightened on the reins as the desire to stop, to enter the little clapboard chapel and spend some time in prayer, nearly overwhelmed him. His ma had taught him there wasn't any problem too big for God. Whenever he'd felt burdened, she'd said, "Give it to your heavenly Father, son. He's big enough to carry it for you." Even one of the newer hymns they sang in church—the one about having a friend in Jesus—advised the singers to take their problems to the Lord in prayer.

As a boy, there'd been sweet release in handing his problems to God. But his boy-sized problems were insignificant compared to the challenges facing him as an adult. Pa had entrusted him with the ranch. Somehow, he had to keep it operating. He needed the sale of cattle—lots of cattle—to pay the ranch hands and the taxes and to purchase supplies. This latest theft had his gut twisted into knots. Would he have enough calves to sell to make ends meet?

Whoever was stealing his cattle had easy access to his ranch. He envisioned the faces of his neighbors—Aunt Hattie to the west, Brewster Hammond to the north, Jerome Garner to the east, and Glendon Shultz to the south—but he couldn't imagine any of them stealing from him. Not even Jerome, who kept to himself and was one of the few Barnett residents to often skip church on Sundays.

Suddenly a thought struck. Brewster's son, Gage, was an ornery sort, prone to jokes and mischief. The whole town tsk-tsked about Gage's lack of discipline—Brewster had pretty much spoiled Gage rotten since his wife died when the boy was still knee-high to a pack mule. Might Gage be sneaking off with Abel's cattle as a means of playing a prank? It would be easy to hide a dozen or so cattle in the midst of hundreds.

Abel decided that after he'd delivered the gloves to Aunt Hattie, he'd head to Brewster's place and ask some questions.

He guided the team onto the lane leading to Hattie's ranch. A woman worked in the garden patch beside the house, tapping the soil with a hoe. A poke bonnet hid her face from view, but Abel knew from her slender form it was one of Aunt Hattie's pupils rather than the teacher herself. He drew the team to a halt and called, "You there! Good mornin'!"

The woman straightened and turned, giving him a view of her face. The back of Abel's neck grew hot when he recognized her as the one who'd grabbed his hand in the barn during the calf birthing. He internally kicked himself for not just plopping the box on the porch and leaving.

"G-good morning, Mr. Samms." Her hesitant voice carried across the yard, increasing the heat in his neck. She must be remembering their hand-holding, too, because she stood grasping the hoe two-handed like a weapon. "Did you need something?"

He pointed to the small crate that held the gloves. "Hank at the Feed an' Seed asked me to make a delivery to Aunt Hattie."

She set aside the hoe and picked her way out of the garden patch, holding her skirt just above the tops of her lace-up shoes. Abel averted his gaze until she left the garden and dropped her skirt back into place. She scurried across the ground to the wagon and peeked over the side. The wagon's tall sides made the reach difficult for her—she didn't have much in height—and Abel considered hopping down and offering his help. But fear of accidentally touching her hand kept him planted on the seat. She rose up on tiptoes, angled her elbows high, and reached in to take hold of the crate. But as she started to lift it out, a rip sounded. She released a yelp and dropped the box.

Abel leaped off the seat and dashed to her side. "Are you all right?"

"Something caught me." She examined her elbow, where a tear in the blue calico fabric exposed a bleeding wound.

Abel gave himself another mental kick. He should've helped her. Of course all that barbed wire would get in the way. With one hand he plucked the box from the back and with the other grasped her uninjured arm. He guided her toward the back of house. "Where's Aunt Hattie?"

"She took some of the others to the northeast pasture. They're practicing using the plow."

"An' you got left behind?"

They reached the back door, and Abel opened it. She answered as she stepped into the house. "I'm on household duty this week, so I'm cooking, cleaning, and gardening. I'll probably learn to use the plow next week."

Abel wished Aunt Hattie were there to see to the girl's wound so he could get on home. Then he berated himself for the selfish thought.

His inconsiderate actions had caused her injury; the least he could do was wash and bandage it.

"Where does Aunt Hattie keep her doctorin' supplies?" Every rancher worth his salt kept a box of medical necessities handy. A person never knew when an emergency might strike.

She pointed. "In the pantry."

He started toward the door.

"But I can take care of it. It's just a little scratch."

Abel paused, chewing his lower lip. While Miss Tressa's scratch wasn't as serious as a snake bite or a broken bone, Abel knew scratches could get infected. Memories of his pa's lingering death hovered in the back of his mind, and sweat beaded across his forehead. Her being new on the plains, she surely didn't understand the importance of cleaning that scratch good before slapping a bandage on it. He'd see that things were done right.

"You just sit down at the table there an' I'll get the supplies." He stepped into the pantry and searched the neatly organized shelves. "I'm sure Aunt Hattie's got everything from tincture of iodine to snake oil." He spotted a small, hinged wooden box on a top shelf and lifted it down. A glance inside confirmed it contained medical supplies.

Stepping back into the kitchen, he found Tressa sitting on a kitchen chair, holding her elbow aloft. Her bonnet hung down her back by its strings. Tangled brown hair stuck out in every direction around her dirty face and Aunt Hattie's house cat sat on her lap. The young woman looked as bedraggled as anything he'd ever seen. Despite himself, he laughed. The cat startled and jumped down, slinking under the stove.

"I'm sorry. Didn't mean to scare your friend."

Tressa looked after the animal and sighed. "It's all right. She would have needed to get down anyway." She nodded toward the box. "Please put the box on the table over here and I'll see to my scratch."

"Naw, I'll do it." He thumped the box on the table and pawed through it, removing a brown bottle of iodine, a puff of cotton batting, and a roll of bandages.

"Really, I can take care of it myself, Mr. Samms." Her cheeks blotched bright pink. "You don't need to bother."

Abel propped his hands on his hips. "Now, see here, Miss Tressa. Around these parts, we don't take injuries lightly. Scratch like that might not seem like much, but if infection sets in, you could get mighty sick in a hurry." With thoughts of Pa strong in his mind, his tone turned stern. "You just stick that elbow up here an' let me get it cleaned without any more fuss."

She sighed. "Should I roll my sleeve out of the way?"

If she were one of his hired hands, he'd just rip the sleeve clean off, but he figured rolling it up was a better solution this time. He nodded and waited for her to work the sleeve upward. She grimaced as she coaxed the wadded fabric past the wound, but she managed to push the sleeve well above her elbow. Her arm was slender and pale, the wrist delicate. He swallowed and focused on unscrewing the cap on the iodine bottle.

Her wide, uniquely colored eyes followed his hands as he sprinkled a goodly amount of the brackish liquid onto the cotton puff. He bent down on one knee beside her and pulled his lips into a sympathetic grin. "This might sting a little."

She hissed through her teeth when he applied the iodine to the scratch, but she didn't try to pull away. He gave the entire area a thorough scrub, staining a sizable portion of her arm in the process. When he'd determined the wound had been adequately cleaned, he reached for the roll of bandages. "All right, hold your arm out."

Without a moment's hesitation, she stuck her arm straight out. Gingerly, he wound the bandage around her elbow, taking care not to bind it too tight. He bit the fabric and ripped it loose from the roll, then tucked the severed end under the band. Slapping his knee, he rose. "Well then, that's that."

"Thank you, Mr. Samms. You were very kind."

Her timid, appreciative smile sent warmth through his belly—an unaccustomed feeling. He cleared his throat. "You're welcome, Miss Tressa."

She started to roll her sleeve back down, but the fabric was wadded up tight and wouldn't budge.

"Here, let me help you." Abel gently unrolled the bunched sleeve, easing it past the bulky bandage and down to her wrist. A tiny button closure at the cuff proved tricky, and he lifted her hand to get a better view of the buttonhole. They were nearly nose-to-nose, both focused on the button, when a third voice intruded.

"Well, well, well, what have we here?"

9

Tressa gasped. Mr. Samms spun toward the door. Luella stood in the opening with a knowing smirk on her face. Sallie crowded behind her, her mouth forming a perfect O of astonishment. Tressa frantically scrambled to fasten the button at her wrist, but her clumsy fingers refused to complete the task.

"Hmm . . ." Luella tapped her full lips, sending a smug glance over her shoulder to Sallie. "Aunt Hattie's harped at me about saving my flirting until we've learned all we're supposed to. Looks to me like Tressa here needs the same talk."

Sallie tipped at the waist, shaking her finger at both Tressa and Mr. Samms. "Shamed ye ought to be, dallyin' here in the house together all alone." She clicked her tongue on her teeth.

Mr. Samms balled his hands into fists. "Now you hold on there! We—"

"Don't deny it." Luella's lilting voice matched her high-raised eyebrows. She held out her arms to indicate the kitchen. "No one around . . . Tressa's button undone . . ." She nodded toward Sallie. "We aren't fools. We know what you've been doing."

Mr. Samms pointed at Luella. "You'd best listen to me, miss. I—"

"Tressa-darlin', you gotta get some gumption. Stand up for yourself!" Mrs. Wyatt's admonition rang through Tressa's mind. With her heart pounding, Tressa dove in front of the man. "Mr. Samms and I have done nothing of which to be ashamed. I cut my arm on some wire while removing a box from the back of his wagon." She thrust out her elbow, displaying the white bandage peeping through the torn sleeve. "He was kind enough to see to my wound, and that is *all* that has transpired. I shall not allow you to malign our characters with lewd and fallacious accusations."

Both Luella and Sallie stared at Tressa, open-mouthed. Tressa couldn't remember a time when she'd been more pleased by someone's reaction. She flashed Mr. Samms a triumphant grin. But to her surprise, he also stood with his jaw hanging slack. As their gazes met, he snapped his mouth shut and took a step away from her.

"Since you're all right, Miss Tressa, I'll head on. Keep that scratch clean now, you hear?" Without waiting for a reply, he charged past the two girls. The door banged shut behind him.

Tressa's elation flickered and died. Fending off the others' pecks had felt wonderful; silencing the ever-blabbering Luella had given her tremendous pleasure. But apparently her bold behavior hadn't met with Mr. Samms' approval. Confused and embarrassed, she felt tears prick behind her eyes.

Suddenly Luella sprang to life, twisting her lips into a horrible scowl. Her eyes became slits of malevolence as she advanced on Tressa. "You little snip! How dare you talk to me like that? Acting so high an' mighty . . . You won't be so full of yourself when I tell Aunt Hattie you were here in the house alone with a man!"

"But I told you, we did nothing wrong!"

"So you say. But we know what we saw, right, Sallie? It wouldn't surprise me if Aunt Hattie sent you packing straightaway!"

Tressa cast a helpless look in Sallie's direction. "You believe me, don't you, Sallie? You know Mr. Samms and I weren't doing anything improper."

Luella caught Sallie's arm. "Sallie, you must report what you saw."

Sallie's face glowed so red her freckles vanished. "I want to be stayin' out of this. I'm not one for makin' trouble."

Luella huffed, tossing her head. "Well then, I'll speak to Aunt Hattie alone. I can be very convincing when I want to be. I don't need Sallie's help to make her believe that we caught you and Mr. Samms spooning."

Tressa stomped her foot. "We were not spooning!"

Luella angled her chin high. "Try telling that to Aunt Hattie when I'm done." She flounced out the back door.

"Sallie." Tressa rushed forward, wringing her hands. "You must tell Mrs. Wyatt the truth, that Mr. Samms and I were only—"

Sallie backed toward the door. " 'Tis sorry I am, Tressa, but I can't be sayin' what ye want me to. I saw him holdin' your hand . . . so that's all I can claim to know." Fear glittered in her eyes. "I'd like to be helpin', but I learned long ago gettin' mixed up in others' problems is a foolish way to spend my time." She darted out the door.

Tressa sank down into a chair. Isabella crept from beneath the stove and crawled into Tressa's lap. Tressa wrapped her arms around the cat, burying her face in the animal's furry ruff. "Oh, Izzy-B, I only did what Mrs. Wyatt encouraged. I refused to accept their pecking. What will I do if she believes Luella? I have nowhere to go. . . ."

❧

"Git up there, Ed." Abel gave the reins a stern flick. The big roan obediently pulled the wagon out of Hattie's lane and onto the road. Abel left the Flying W behind, his heart continuing to pound in confusion.

While kneeling before Miss Tressa, tending to her wound, an odd feeling of kinship had wound its way through his middle. Her complete trust in him, even though his ministrations must have caused her discomfort, gave him an accountability toward her that he couldn't explain, yet he knew it existed. And to his surprise, he'd found the experience pleasurable.

Then the others had come in, thrown accusations, and Miss Tressa had spouted off with words no common girl would know. She'd sounded like Amanda with her high-class talk, and all the warm feelings of moments before had burst apart as surely as that corn bread had shattered when it hit the floor. He groaned aloud, rotating his head to relieve the tension in his neck. He shouldn't have let himself get close to that girl. In the future, he'd exercise better judgment.

When he neared his own ranch, he considered pulling in and relieving the wagon of its load of barbed wire. The sooner he and his men set posts and ran wire, the sooner his herd would have a protective barrier. But in the end he decided against it. If it turned out that Gage Hammond was the one sneaking off with his cattle, Brewster would have to put an end to it. And if Brewster ended it, then Abel could return all that barbed wire and get his money back. He turned north on the rutted dirt road on the far side of his ranch and aimed the wagon toward the Double H.

The lane to the Hammonds' ranch waited ahead. Brewster Hammond had constructed a sign of bent iron shaped into letters that announced the name of the ranch. The sign arched above the lane's wide opening. Abel glanced at it as his wagon rolled beneath it, and the knotted muscles in his neck cramped again. A man who could afford something like that overhead announcement had no reason to steal cattle from his neighbors. But that didn't mean his son wouldn't do it anyway just for fun. Abel'd sure seen the boy pull other stunts nobody else found funny. He wondered why Brewster hadn't taken a strap to that son of his years ago.

He stopped his wagon at the hitching post that ran the length of the long gingerbread-trimmed porch of the rambling rock house. Even before his feet hit the ground, the front door opened and Brewster stepped out onto the porch. A napkin hung from his open collar, and the man yanked it loose and swiped it across his mouth.

"Abel." Brewster gave a nod of greeting. "Saw the wagon turn in at the gate. Want to come in an' have a bite? Got plenty of pan-fried steak and potatoes on the table. Cookie sure knows how to prepare a piece of beef."

Abel knew of no other rancher besides Brewster Hammond who kept a cook on his payroll. Having skipped breakfast, he found the invitation tempting. But he'd already spent the entire morning away from his ranch—he had no more time to spare.

"Thanks, Brewster, but I better not. I . . . ." Suddenly he wasn't sure how to approach the subject of the missing calves.

Brewster moved to the edge of the porch. He propped his forearm against the nearest turned post, still wadding the napkin in his hand. "What's on your mind?"

Abel shifted from one foot to the other at the base of the porch stairs and formed his thoughts into a query that wouldn't be read as an attack. Wouldn't do him any good to make an enemy out of the most powerful rancher in Ford County. "I wondered . . . your men notice any spare calves show up on your spread?"

Brewster puckered his lips for a moment. "You missin' some?"

" 'Fraid so. Four of 'em managed to escape a pen last night." Although all told he'd lost more than four calves, it seemed best to focus on the most current loss. "They're just barely weaned, so they might be bawlin' for their mamas. Make 'em easier to spot, if you'd ask your men to keep an eye out for 'em."

"I can do that, Abel." Brewster stepped off the porch, forcing Abel backward a step. He flicked the napkin against his trouser leg. "But you know, with my land all fenced in, it'd be a mite difficult for calves to accidentally wander onto my property. Somebody'd either have to cut my fence to let 'em in or bring 'em through a gate."

Abel licked his dry lips. "Reckon that's true . . ."

"You let your other neighbors know about these missin' calves?"

Although Brewster's face remained friendly, Abel sensed a shift in his tone. "No, sir."

"Just me, huh?" The older man rubbed his lips together for a moment, his dark eyes boring into Abel's. "Four ranches surround yours. Could've gone to any of 'em, but you came here first. Must be a reason." The napkin flicked faster. "Speak plain, boy."

Abel drew in a breath that expanded his chest and raised his shoulders. He plucked his hat from his head. "Well, to be honest, Brewster, I wondered if Gage might be—"

"Stealin'?" There was no denying the defensive current in Brewster's voice. "My boy's got a mischievous streak, I'll grant you that, but I've taught him right from wrong. An' he's got no reason to steal, considerin' his allowance is sufficient to purchase pret' near everything he wants. Not sure I take kindly to the insinuation."

"I wasn't insinuatin' Gage is a *thief*, Brewster, I was just—"

"I know what you was doin'. Lookin' for whoever might've stole away with your calves. An' you come here. But you won't find 'em here, Samms, so you can just take your searchin' elsewhere."

Abel should've known Brewster would defend Gage. He always had. He scratched his cheek and sighed. "Well, if somethin' should change, I'd—"

"Tell you what." Brewster curled his hand over Abel's shoulder, turning him toward the wagon. "I'll let my men know some of your calves have turned up missin' an' to watch for a Lazy S brand. If those calves're spotted, we'll shoo 'em straight back to your land." He applied gentle pressure, urging Abel to climb into the wagon seat. His focus flicked to the rolls of barbed wire in the bed. "You fixin' to run some wire, are you?"

Abel nodded.

"Good idea." He perused the bed's contents, his lips moving as he silently counted the rolls. "Appears you got plenty . . ." Meeting Abel's gaze, he said, "I suggest runnin' four lines per post instead of three. Makes it harder for somebody to cut through, an' it reduces the possibility of critters creepin' between the lines."

"That's sound advice, Brewster. Thank you."

Brewster's expression hardened. "And here's one more piece of advice: Head on down the road an' alert your other neighbors about these calves so they can be lookin', too. I think that's best."

Only an idiot would have missed the subtle warning. Abel slid onto the seat and took up the reins. "I'll do that, Brewster. Thanks for your time." He smacked the reins onto Ed's back.

As he rode toward home, he outlined the afternoon's tasks: Put Vince in sole charge of seeing to the calving; set Ethan and Cole to chopping down saplings that grew along the creek for fence posts; and as for him, he'd nose around the grounds and look for evidence that might help him catch last night's thief. He figured he also better put some lunch on the table for his men—this was his week to cook.

When he turned in at his gate, he noticed a wagon parked in front of the house. Aunt Hattie's mare stood within the traces, her head low, apparently dozing. Abel drew his wagon alongside hers, and Ed nosed the visiting mare. She stirred and nickered in reply. Leaving the horses to get acquainted, Abel hopped down and trotted onto the porch.

Wonderful aromas greeted his nose as he stepped into the house. His mouth watering, he hurried directly to the table, where Aunt Hattie had served up steaming bowls of stew to his men. A platter of flaky biscuits sat in the middle of the table. Even while Abel's stomach turned over in anticipation of the enticing meal, confusion clouded his mind.

"Look here, Abel." Ethan tipped his chair back on two feet, allowing Aunt Hattie to ladle a hearty portion of stew into his bowl. "Aunt Hattie brung us lunch." He licked his lips. "Looks mighty good, don't it?"

Aunt Hattie pointed to the empty chair at the table. "Sit down, Abel, afore this stew gets cold an' the biscuits dry out. Few things worse'n cold stew an' dry biscuits."

Abel moved to his chair on stiff legs and seated himself. She ladled stew into his bowl, the steam rising and filling his nostrils. His belly twisted with desire. "Aunt Hattie, it's not that I don't appreciate you bringin' us lunch, but . . . what's the occasion?"

She looked at him with one brow arched high. "Well now, Abel, let's just say I learnt a thing or two durin' my years o' marriage to Jed, an' one o' the most important is that men can take bad news easier on a full stomach."

10

Hattie's heart panged as Abel's expression turned uneasy, but she wouldn't mislead him. She hadn't come for a social call, and it was best he knew the truth straightaway.

He pushed away from the table. "Maybe we should go outside an' talk."

"Don'tcha wanna eat first?" She hoped he would. He might not be hungry after she'd spoke her piece.

But he shook his head. "Nah. Rather find out what you need." He turned on the worn heel of his boot and headed for the front of the house.

Hattie flashed a smile at the three hired hands seated around the table. "Don't you fret now, just enjoy that stew an' those biscuits. Lots of fresh-churned butter in them biscuits, so you won't even need jam to flavor 'em." She waited long enough to see the three men reach for biscuits before trotting after Abel.

He was pacing on the front porch, his hands in his pockets. When she closed the door behind her, he whirled on her. "All right, Aunt Hattie, what's wrong?"

Hattie folded her arms over her chest and raised her chin. "What's wrong is I got two upset pupils at my house, one sayin' one thing an' one sayin' another. I come to get your side o' the story so's maybe I can set things to right."

Releasing a groan, Abel sank down on the rough-hewn bench that stretched across one end of the narrow porch. "It's not what it looked like, Aunt Hattie. Miss Tressa an' me weren't doin' anything indecent."

Hattie sat beside Abel and smoothed her rumpled apron over her knees. "Why don't you tell me what happened?" She resolved to ask questions only if she needed something clarified. Both Luella's and Tressa's claims hung heavy in her mind. Abel would confirm one story as truth if she just let him talk.

"Miss Tressa cut her arm on some barbed wire from the back of my wagon when she was taking out the box of gloves Hank sent from the Feed an' Seed." He grimaced. "I should've took the box out myself, but I was in a hurry, so I let her do it. An' she got cut. I felt real bad about it, so I doctored her arm." Abel shifted in the seat and faced Hattie. "Her sleeve got stuck above the bandage, so I helped her roll it down. I was just tryin' to hook that little button on the cuff of her sleeve when the other girls come in an' saw us. That's all that happened."

Hattie nodded, heaving a sigh of relief. Abel's story matched Tressa's, which was what she'd expected. Still, it lifted her spirits to hear it from his lips. "I believe you, Abel. I know you was raised to be an honest man. I just needed to hear it from you so I could sort things out."

"Well then, I'm glad that's settled." He started to rise.

Hattie caught his sleeve. "Hold up there, Abel. Somethin' else I need to say."

He plunked his hindquarters hard on the bench, wariness in his eyes. "What?"

"Miss Luella . . . she's a strong-willed girl. An' she's taken a dislike to Miss Tressa. No sound reason for it that I can see—seems some people just need somebody to bully or they're not happy, an' Luella's chosen to torment Tressa."

"I don't see that I can help with—"

Hattie waved her hand. "Not lookin' for your help, Abel, just need you to understand somethin'. When I go back to the ranch an' tell Luella that you upheld Tressa's story 'stead o' hers, she's not gonna be happy. She's one who likes to talk—she's been a-yammerin' about this, that, an' the other thing ever since she arrived. An' if she yammers about this an' folks in town get wind, it could cause trouble. For Tressa, for me, an' for you."

"Me?" Abel jabbed his chest with his thumb. "How'd I get tangled up in this?"

"You got tangled up by bein' a man an' payin' attention to someone besides Luella." Hattie formed a knowing expression. "That girl's got one purpose for bein' here: snaggin' a man. Never saw a woman so bent on snaggin' a man. I've put off teachin' her to lasso for fear she'll aim the loop at a two-legged critter instead of a four-legged one." Shaking her head, she mused aloud, "Makes me wonder what kind o' upbringin' she had."

Hattie had clearly indicated in her advertisement that only women of good moral reputation should apply to attend her herdsman school. According to a letter of recommendation from a former employer, Luella fit the requirement, but Hattie found the girl's behavior troubling. She suspected that Luella thought so little of herself she needed attention to feel important and wanted. Hattie vowed to keep praying for her.

Abel's jaw thrust out. "Still don't see how that brings trouble on me. *I* didn't do nothin' wrong."

Giving his knee a pat, Hattie chuckled. "Now, Abel, you didn't get this far in life without knowin' how a rumor can cause problems even if it holds no truth." She frowned, fighting back a wave of worry. She wanted her school to be a success—wanted to build something that would last. She'd been so certain bringing girls from the East to match up with western men would be of benefit to the community— and give her some much-needed companionship. But a trumped-up story could cast aspersions on the entire operation and bring things to a halt before she even had a chance to get started.

Abel's eyes narrowed. "You sayin' this girl'll spread lies about me an' Miss Tressa?"

"I'm sayin' she *might*. An' if she does, it'll take some doin' to set the record straight. Barnett's peopled with good folks, but somehow even good folks lose their reasonin' abilities when they're chewin' on a meaty piece o' gossip."

Abel shot from the bench and clumped to the edge of the porch. A frustrated huff of breath exploded from his lips. "As if I'd be interested in someone like Miss Tressa."

Hattie's hackles rose at his derogatory tone. Wasn't it enough that the other girls in the school made Tressa feel like a misfit? What did Abel hold against the girl? She stomped to his side and gave his shirt sleeve a good yank. "An' just what's that s'posed to mean?"

"Aw, c'mon, Aunt Hattie, you have to know that girl's not all she appears to be."

Balling her hands on her hips, Hattie fixed Abel with a fierce glare. "Son, you're treadin' on dangerous ground right now. You'd best explain yourself, an' make it quick. Why're you speakin' ill of Miss Tressa?"

He folded his arms across his chest. "Here she is attendin' your school, dressed in homespun, makin' out like she's a workin' girl lookin' to better herself. But she's no workin' girl. She's high society—I'd bet my bottom dollar on it."

"And you'd lose it. 'Cause I know what you mean when you say 'high society,' an' you're not meanin' to be complimentary."

"Yep. Won't argue."

"But you're wrong about Miss Tressa."

He raised his eyebrows in a look of skepticism.

Hattie pointed her finger at Abel's nose. "You need to do some soul searchin', Abel Samms. You're lettin' what happened with Amanda make you bitter an' distrustful."

Red streaked his suntanned neck. "This has nothin' to do with Amanda. It's those girls out at your ranch who're causin' problems for me."

She chose to counter his belligerent tone with gentleness. "Like it or not, Abel, Amanda's still got a hold on you. An' you makin' Miss Tressa accountable for Amanda's choice is just as wrong as Luella makin' Tressa the scapegoat for her troubles." She placed her hand on Abel's forearm. His muscles felt like knotted rope beneath her palm. She gave his arm a slight squeeze. "Maybe nothin'll come of it—I'm prayin' Luella'll let things drop. But I'd rather know up front what I might be facin' so I can be prepared. Figured you'd prefer that, too."

Abel relaxed, sliding his thumbs into the front pockets of his trousers. "Thanks, Aunt Hattie. I do appreciate your warnin'. An' . . ." He hung his head, drawing in a deep breath and then letting it out between puckered lips. "I'm sorry I got cranky with you. I just got a lot on my mind."

She glanced at the rolls of barbed wire in the back of Abel's wagon. "An' a big job waitin'. I know you said you intended to put up some fence, but . . . you plannin' to string all o' that?"

"Don't see as how I have much choice." Abel's tone turned hard. "Lost four calves last night. Somebody took 'em right out of the holdin' pen next to the barn."

Hattie's knees nearly gave way. "Oh, Abel . . ."

"So I got bigger problems than rumors."

She shook her head. "Well, I'll keep prayin' this thievin' ends. Just ain't right . . ."

The front door burst open and Abel's hired hands thumped onto the porch. Cole slapped his hat onto his head and shot Hattie a wide grin. "Thanks for bringin' that lunch to us, Aunt Hattie."

"Good as always, Hattie." Vince nodded his graying head in a gentlemanly fashion.

"Yes'm. Thank you." Ethan supplied his thanks when his father bumped him with his elbow.

Hattie flapped both hands at the men. "Oh, now, don't give me the credit." She flicked a quick glance at Abel. "Miss Tressa's on cookin' duty this week, so she's the one who made that stew an' the buttery biscuits, too—she asked me to bring 'em over here as a way o' sayin' thanks." She sent Abel a meaningful look. By his splotchy cheeks, she knew he understood.

❧

Tressa set the last plate in the cupboard and closed the door. Turning from the cupboard, she lifted the wash pan from the dry sink. The evening breeze wafting through the open back door caressed her face, and she moved eagerly into the opening for a deeper draw of the scented air before heaving the wash pan's cloudy contents onto the ground. A swish with a length of toweling removed the remaining drops of water and tiny bubbles of soapy foam from the speckled pan. That task complete, she placed the pan upside-down on the dry sink and headed to the pantry to retrieve a pair of tin pails.

She swung the empty pails as she crossed the uneven ground beneath a dusky pink sky. After placing the pails on the ground beside the well's rock wall, she turned the crank, grunting a bit as she brought the bucket from the depths of the well. In New York, water came right into the house thanks to piping and a brass spigot. Her tasks would be simpler if Mrs. Wyatt possessed indoor plumbing, but she chose not to complain.

The sides of the wooden bucket were slick and cool from laying in the water. She gripped the bucket tightly between her hands and filled both of her pails, then she tossed the bucket back into the well. After wiping her wet hands on her apron, she lifted the full pails and turned toward the house.

A sense of pride washed over her as she carried both pails. When she had first been assigned to kitchen duty three weeks ago, she could only carry one bucket at a time. But now she could carry two. Her strength was increasing by the day, giving her confidence that, regardless of Luella's disparaging remarks, she could become a herdsman and successfully live on the plains.

In spite of the sun's low-hung position and the light breeze, sweat beaded across her upper lip. When she entered the kitchen, she scooped a dipperful of cool water and took a drink before emptying the pails into the stove's reservoir. Then she returned the empty pails to their spot on the pantry shelf. As she exited the pantry, Isabella trotted from the dining room in her typical high-tailed fashion.

Tressa swept the cat into her arms and nuzzled her neck. "There you are! You didn't keep me company while I washed dishes tonight. It was lonely without you." She carried Isabella to the work table and sat, holding the cat in her lap while she examined every inch of the kitchen.

Not so much as a crumb dotted the floor or an errant drop of water stained the sink, but the toweling she'd used to dry the dishes lay rumpled on the edge of the dry sink. "Oops! Excuse me, kitty." She transferred Isabella to the chair and skipped across the wood floor, snatched up the towel, and hung it neatly over a bar attached to the wall beside the window. Satisfied with the appearance of the kitchen, she untied her apron and dropped it into the washbasket that rested near the back door. Isabella dashed across the floor and batted at the apron tie that dangled over the edge of the basket.

Giggling, Tressa knelt and stroked the cat while Isabella continued to attack the strip of flowered cloth. "Izzy-B, I have my chores finished, so it's time for me to turn in." She raised her face to the ceiling. Through the floor joists, she could hear the creak of footsteps and the soft mutter of voices. Mrs. Wyatt had turned in early, complaining of a headache, so Tressa surmised the other girls were moving around upstairs. Her chest constricted. The others were no doubt gathered in Luella's room, sharing a few minutes of conversation and relaxation before heading to bed. They'd assembled on numerous occasions, but Tressa had never been invited.

Even though she'd proven herself capable of performing the necessary duties in the house and garden, the other girls continued to view her with disdain, following Luella's lead. And especially since Mrs. Wyatt had believed Tressa over Luella, the other girl had been particularly spiteful. Luella never engaged in mistreatment in the presence of their teacher, but she was sly. One night, Tressa had slipped into bed only to discover that her pillow was littered with cockleburs. As a result, she'd had to snip away a few curls of her hair. Another time she'd found several dead crickets in her underclothes drawer. Neither of the pranks were harmful—clothes could be washed and hair would grow back—but they were clear messages that Luella was angry and would have her retribution.

Tressa knew, despite Luella's sneakiness, that Mrs. Wyatt suspected the other girl of being unkind. She had assigned Tressa to kitchen duty three weeks in a row and sent Luella to the fields to walk behind the plow and then plant the alfalfa that would help feed the animals during the winter. The girls' pathways only crossed at mealtimes and bedtime, giving Luella few opportunities to deliver verbal attacks. But although the attacks were few, they left Tressa feeling as pecked and scarred as that poor little chicken in the coop. As soon as she had time, she intended to build a separate enclosure for the mistreated bird. If only she could separate herself from Luella's tormenting. . . .

With a sigh, Tressa carried the cat to the pantry and set her inside. After giving Isabella one final stroke, she closed the pantry door. Her face against the crack between the door and the doorjamb, she whispered, "Good night, kitty. Sleep well."

She trudged toward the stairs, tired and ready to bring the day to a close. Just as she placed her foot on the lowest stair riser, she sensed a movement. Had Isabella escaped the pantry? Tipping sideways, she glimpsed a full skirt slipping through the shadows and past the kitchen doorway. Moments later, the back door to the house squeaked open and clicked closed.

Tressa frowned. All of the bedrooms were upstairs, so someone had to have been hiding in the dining room, waiting for Tressa to leave the kitchen, or she would have met the person on the stairs. A chill went down her spine as she thought of someone standing around the corner, listening to her hum as she went about her work, watching her play with the cat. She hugged herself, contemplating whether or not to alert Mrs. Wyatt that one of the girls had sneaked outside. But then she shook her head. Perhaps one of the girls needed to use the outhouse. If so, she'd return shortly. Tressa sat on the lower step, chin in hand, to wait.

Minutes ticked by, measured by the pendulum clock that hung on the wall of the seldom-used parlor. Tressa yawned and leaned against the wall. Her eyelids grew heavy, and still she waited. Suddenly she jerked. Her head bounced against the wall, and she realized she'd fallen asleep. She staggered to her feet, her muscles stiff, and squinted at the pendulum clock. Eleven fifteen! She'd slept for over an hour! Why hadn't she awakened when the wanderer returned to the house?

Holding to the handrail, she climbed the stairs and crept past her own room, where Sallie's snore signaled deep sleep. No sound came from any of the other rooms. Feeling like a burglar, she turned the doorknob on Mabelle and Paralee's room. Two lumps in the bed gave witness to their presence.

Tressa eased the door closed and tiptoed across the hall, her heart pounding. If Luella caught her peeking into her room, there would be no end to the screech of protest. Holding her breath, she opened the door a crack. Tressa sagged against the doorjamb. Moonlight streamed through the window and painted a path to the empty bed. Luella was gone.

11

Tressa placed a steaming pile of flapjacks in the center of the table and then sat in her chair next to Sallie. Mrs. Wyatt offered her customary blessing for the meal, and the girls passed around the platters of flapjacks, crispy bacon, and fried eggs. Covertly, Tressa watched Luella, noticing that the girl's short night of sleep showed in the purple smudges beneath her eyes, but she held her head high and engaged in conversation as if it were a normal morning.

Questions crowded Tressa's mind. Where had Luella gone last night? Had she met someone? Had she ever sneaked off before? And—most pressing of all—should Tressa tell Mrs. Wyatt about Luella's nocturnal wandering? Tattling would certainly bring another tide of retaliation from the vindictive girl, yet it seemed dishonest and irresponsible to keep the information to herself. Mrs. Wyatt had lectured the girls on the perils of the open plains. She always had them work in pairs when she sent them away from the ranch house. Luella could stumble upon all kinds of dangers, wandering alone in the darkness.

"After church today," Mrs. Wyatt announced, interrupting Tressa's thoughts, "we've all been invited to the Double H Ranch for lunch."

"The Double H? The Hammond ranch?" Luella sent Mrs. Wyatt a wide-eyed look. Did a note of panic underscore Luella's tone, or was it mere excitement?

"That's right. Every summer, Brewster Hammond hosts a get-together and invites the whole church out for pit-roasted beef an' all the fixings."

"Ooooh!" Sallie clapped her hands, her eyes glittering. "What fun!"

"Yep, it's always a treat to gather with friends an' neighbors for a time of fellowship an' good food." Mrs. Wyatt rested her elbows on the table and clasped her hands as if in prayer. "Mr. Hammond's planned his pit roast a mite early this year. I was hopin' to put off fraternizin' until closer to the end o' the summer. By then, you'll all be pret' near ready to leave the school an' be matched up with fellers in the community."

Tressa's heart began to pound. She put down her fork and clamped her hands together in her lap. Her aunt's words haunted her memory: *"A second-best chance is better than no chance at all."* Mrs. Wyatt had never indicated how the girls would be paired up with the men of the community. Might they be lined up and ogled like horses on an auction block, selected for one's good teeth or muscular structure?

"But we're not ready for the matchin' yet, so I want you girls to mind your p's an' q's at the get-together. I'm wantin' you to get acquainted with the townsfolk—if you choose to stick around an' be matched after your schoolin' is done, these'll be your friends an' neighbors. But it's not yet time for hobnobbin' with single fellers." Mrs. Wyatt fixed her gaze on Luella, who yawned and broke a piece of bacon into small pieces.

Paralee leaned forward. "When will we be matched, Aunt Hattie?" She and Mabelle exchanged quick, worried looks.

"At the end o' the summer, we'll have our own party here at the ranch. Whole town'll come out, an' interested men'll have the chance to get to know each of you an' start courtin' under my supervision."

Sallie blew out a little breath. "Then you'll not be throwin' us to the wolves? You'll be keepin' a watch?"

Mrs. Wyatt's eyebrows rose. " 'Course I'll be keepin' a watch! Since you gals don't have parents here to keep an eye over you, I promise I'll oversee the courtin'." She leaned forward, her expression fervent. "You pupils're my responsibility, an' I want only the best for you. I been prayin' since before you came that each o' you would find a godly mate. Don't want any of you endin' up in situations not of your choosin'."

Luella giggled. "Rich and handsome, that's all I need."

Sallie sighed. "I'd like my man to be even-tempered an' kind."

Paralee and Mabelle each offered their opinion of the perfect husband, and then Sallie looked at Tressa. "An' ye, Tressa? What kind of man would ye be wantin'?"

She wanted a man like her papa—strong but gentle, ambitious but honest, with a quick smile and a ready laugh. But she wouldn't open herself to more ridicule by sharing her thoughts. She shook her head, and Luella snorted.

Mrs. Wyatt glanced around the table at each girl in turn, ending with Luella. Her expression turned wary. "If it wouldn't be considered rude, I wouldn't go to Brewster's ranch today—not sure all of us are ready for socializin'. But folks'd think it odd if we didn't come. So . . ." She pressed her palms to the table and rose. "You girls do as I said. Be friendly with the women—you'll need to be formin' relationships with them—but no time alone with any o' the men." Her gaze lit on Luella and lingered. "I'll be watchin'. . . ."

"Why do I hafta stay behind?"

Cole sounded like a petulant child rather than a grown man. Abel couldn't honestly say he faulted Cole for being disappointed—everyone in Barnett looked forward to the Hammonds' yearly pit roast. But given the rash of thefts on his property, Abel wasn't going to leave his land unattended even for a church service and party.

"Like it or not, Cole, you're last hired, so that means fewer privileges." Abel squinted against the midmorning sunlight, squelching the impatience that churned in his gut. For two bits he'd stay home himself instead of going to the Double H, but as the owner of the Lazy S, he'd be expected. Might damage his relations with his neighbors if he didn't go. He glanced skyward, hoping a rain cloud might magically appear. It'd be a heap easier if the pit roast was canceled. But not so much as a white wisp decorated the robin's-egg-blue sky.

Cole smacked his leg with his hat. "But I put on my new shirt an' bay rum an' everything."

Abel didn't need Cole's words to confirm his use of bay rum. The man was stout enough to fend off a dust devil. "Look, I'm sorry, but—"

"I'll stay." Vince hopped down from the wagon seat and strode to Abel's side. He tugged loose the black string tie from beneath his chin. "Been to many of the Hammonds' pit roasts—won't bother me none to miss one. 'Sides . . ." A grin twitched the cowboy's weathered cheeks. "You young'uns will want to take a gander at the girls Hattie'll be bringin' with her. Ol' coot like me ain't got no need for a wife. So you go on ahead an' I'll keep a watch on things here."

"Are you sure, Vince?" Abel didn't think it fair to make Vince stay behind. The older man had served the Lazy S faithfully for nearly all of Abel's twenty-seven years of life. He'd earned his time of relaxation.

"I'm sure. You go on in with Cole an' Ethan." Vince's grin widened. "But save me a piece of Hattie's apple pie. She's sure to bring one to the party."

"Will do." Abel clapped Vince's bony shoulder. "Thanks, Vince."

He climbed into the wagon and slapped down the reins. As he passed the Flying W, Aunt Hattie's wagon rolled from her gate and fell in behind his. She raised her hand in a cheery wave. "Mornin', Abel . . . Cole . . . Ethan. You goin' to the big doin's at Brewster's place after church?"

"Sure are, Aunt Hattie!" Cole turned in the seat to smile back at the wagonful of young ladies. "I'm hopin' there'll be music—maybe get to do a little dancin', too."

"Had dancin' at the last ones," Hattie replied, "but don't be askin' none o' my girls to join you in a do-si-do. They haven't learned the steps."

Cole spun back around and shot a sour look at Ethan. Disappointment sagged both of the men's faces. But Abel nearly heaved a sigh of relief. Every year Brewster Hammond's cook broke out his fiddle and played tunes so the attendees could dance. Knowing Aunt Hattie's girls wouldn't be joining any of the circles meant he didn't have to worry about encountering Miss Tressa. He needed to keep his distance. He wouldn't give the town any fuel to stoke the flame of Miss Luella's claims, assuming rumors had reached Barnett's citizens.

❧

Brother Connor cut the service short—probably because he knew he wouldn't be able to hold the attention of his congregants, who were all eager to get out to the Hammond place and fill their plates with succulent roasted beef, vegetables fresh from area gardens, and desserts carried in by the ladies of the community. People headed straight to their wagons instead of standing around to chat—they could visit at the Double H. The line of wagons stretched half a mile long as everyone fell in behind Brewster's fancy rig.

Abel's wagon ended up in front of Aunt Hattie's. Cole and Ethan climbed into the back and hollered back and forth to Aunt Hattie while Abel drove. By the time he rolled onto Brewster's yard, he was as tightly wound as a new watch. Courtesy dictated he help Hattie and her pupils from their wagon, so he hopped down and squared his shoulders. But before he could take two steps, Cole and Ethan beat a path to the back hatch of her wagon and assisted Aunt Hattie's pupils to the ground.

Aunt Hattie clambered down without help and trotted to the rear of the wagon. "Thank you, gentlemen. But we'll be fine now—you go on an' get yourselves a plate."

Cole stuck out his elbow in invitation. "You sure we can't—"

"Go on," Hattie said in a kind yet no-nonsense tone.

With slumped shoulders, the pair ambled toward the house, where townspeople were milling in noisy groups on the grassy yard. Abel fiddled with his horse's rigging for a few minutes, giving Aunt Hattie and her pupils time to be absorbed by the gathered crowd before he joined the others.

The smell of roasting beef drifted on the breeze, and Abel's stomach rolled over in anticipation. He and his men didn't get a decent meal often, and as much as he might have preferred to avoid today's festivities, he had to admit a plateful of beef sounded mighty good. He'd be sure and take back a good portion for Vince, too. Brewster wouldn't mind—there was always plenty of food to go around.

While Abel mingled, plate and fork in hand, he couldn't help but wonder if one of the people laughing and chatting under the noonday sun might be sneaking off with his cattle after dark. Guilt pricked as he considered the idea that a neighbor could be his thief, but reason dictated the rustling had to be done by someone living close by. A stranger might hit a ranch once and move on, but the repeated thefts indicated the perpetrator had regular access to his land and his cattle.

"All right, folks!" Brewster Hammond stood on the edge of the porch with his arms in the air. "Listen up!" His booming voice carried over the combined conversations, and folks fell silent. "Food's still a-plenty, so feel free to keep fillin' your plates as well as your bellies"— an appreciative laugh broke from the gathered guests—"but right now Cookie is tightenin' his fiddle strings, an' in a few minutes we'll have a square or two goin'. So grab yourself a partner!"

A cheer rose. Wives immediately commandeered their husbands' elbows, tugging them to the center of the yard. Abel backed out of the way of the eager throng. He inched toward the food tables, and out of the corner of his eye he spotted Cole and Ethan dashing toward Aunt Hattie.

The older woman had kept her pupils close to her side since they'd arrived, stepping into the pathway of any single man who tried to steal a few words with one of the girls. Cole and Ethan addressed Hattie, and even though the distance prevented Abel from hearing what they said, he suspected they were asking permission to dance with the pupils. Several other single men, including Gage Hammond, were angling in behind Cole and Ethan.

Abel chuckled when Aunt Hattie shook her head and waved the men away. Apparently when she'd said the girls didn't know how to dance, she'd also meant she wouldn't allow anyone else to teach them. Abel had to commend Aunt Hattie—she had starch, shooing the fellows off that way. But he wondered how long she'd be able to hold them at bay. A handful of pretty young girls created a mighty temptation to a passel of women-hungry men.

Picking up a clean tin plate, Abel made his way down the food table, choosing beef, pickled beets, and boiled butter beans to take back to Vince. The twang of the fiddle filled his ears and the ground reverberated with the pounding of feet as the dancing commenced. Single men partnered with one another in the absence of female companions, just as they'd done dozens of times before. When the first circle ended, the dancers applauded the fiddler. He gave a sprightly bow and raised the fiddle to begin a second set, but a voice intruded.

"Afore we start again, let's get Aunt Hattie's girls out here! Don't seem right to have men dancin' with men when there's women available."

A mutter of agreement rolled across the single male population. Everyone, male and female alike, turned to face Aunt Hattie. Abel paused in carrying a slice of apple pie to the plate. A tingle crept across his scalp—men could get fractious when denied something they wanted, and he didn't want to see Aunt Hattie get caught up in an ugly exchange.

She balled her fists on her hips and shook her head, her eyes seeking the crowd. "Len Meyer, was that you?"

The lanky cowboy separated himself from the murmuring throng. "Yes'm, it was me. An' I'm tired of dancin' with Glendon. He keeps steppin' on my toes." He paused while the crowd roared. "If I gotta get tromped, I'd rather it was by somebody with dainty feet. So let your pupils dance, Aunt Hattie. What would it hurt?"

An answering chorus rose, all men's voices begging Hattie for a chance to partner with one of her girls.

"Now, fellas, don't think I'm not sympathizin' with you." Hattie kept a friendly smile on her face, letting her focus bob across the eager cowboys. "If I was you, I'd rather dance with any o' my girls than Glendon Shultz. He's got a big heavy foot, an' there's no denyin' it."

Once more, laughter rang, and Glendon's face turned bright red.

Chuckling, Hattie continued. "But y'see, these girls're new around here. They need a chance to feel at ease before we throw 'em out in the middle. 'Sides, this won't be the summer's only party. End o' August, when these young ladies've had a chance to really settle in, I'll be hostin' a big party, invitin' everybody in the county. These ladies'll know how to dance by then, as I'll be teachin' 'em myself." She gave a little jig that brought another round of laughter. "An' I promise you'll get the chance to fill their dance cards with your marks. But . . ." She shrugged, pursing her lips. "For now, they're just watchin'."

Mumbles started again, but Hattie turned her back on the crowd and herded her pupils to the other side of the food tables, well away from the dancing circle. Abel noted a couple of the girls looked longingly toward the dance floor, and the one who'd accused him and Miss Tressa of dallying lagged behind, but Aunt Hattie looped elbows with the girl and hurried her along.

The fiddler started a new tune, and the dancers set their feet into motion once more. Abel finished filling Vince's plate, glancing back and forth from Hattie's pupils to the single men. Although Hattie had managed to squelch an open rebellion, tension was still hanging in the air.

He tossed a napkin over Vince's plate and carried it to his wagon. After sliding the plate under the seat, he turned and looked across the grounds. Aunt Hattie's girls were standing in a tight circle peering over Hattie's shoulders at the dancers. Even from this distance, he could read frustration on several faces. He whistled through his teeth. The end of August was a ways off. Aunt Hattie might be hard-pressed to keep the men—and some of those girls—reined in that much longer.

12

Tressa heaved a sigh of relief when Mrs. Wyatt suggested they head for home. As the afternoon lengthened, the sun had seemed to burn a hole through the top of her straw skimmer, searing her scalp. She was ready to return to the ranch she now thought of as home.

Mrs. Wyatt pointed to the wagon. "You gals go ahead and climb on in—I'll say our thank-you an' good-bye to Brewster an' be with you in a jiffy."

"Can't we say our own good-byes to everyone?" Luella folded her arms over her chest. "You've hardly let us say two words all day . . . except to the women." Luella made "women" sound like a dirty word.

Aunt Hattie shook her head. "Now, you knew up front we'd be makin' friends with the ladies but not the men today, Luella. No sense in cryin' in your buttermilk over it now. Mr. Hammond'll accept a group thank-you from all of us, so get on with you. Evenin' chores're waitin'." She spun and charged in the direction of the porch, where Mr. Hammond stood with a few other townspeople.

Tressa eagerly turned toward the wagon, but she walked slowly. Her full stomach didn't encourage rushing. How she had enjoyed the food! The simple but tasty fare had rivaled that served at any of her aunt's lavish dinner parties in New York. After weeks of cooking for the others residing at Mrs. Wyatt's ranch, she'd found great pleasure in eating someone else's cooking.

She passed the roasting pit, giggling a bit at her initial reaction to the skinned calf turning on a spit over the fire-filled pit. Her stomach had trembled at the sight, but with the first taste of the meat from that calf, the image fled. She'd never eaten such succulent beef.

Sallie, Paralee, and Mabelle darted ahead of her, their heads together, tongues wagging. Luella sidled up to Tressa, her face angled over her shoulder. She swayed her hips in a way that made her skirts twirl around her dusty hightop shoes. Raising one hand, Luella waggled her fingers at someone behind them. Tressa glanced over her shoulder and spotted Gage Hammond leaning on a fence post, toe planted in the dirt, grinning after them. He tipped his hat and winked. Tressa spun forward, her face hot.

Luella snickered. "No need to get all pink-cheeked. He wasn't winking at you."

Tressa shot the girl a questioning look. "How do you know?"

"Never you mind." Luella tossed her head, her dark locks flying over her shoulders. "I just know." She gave a little skip, scurrying forward to climb into the wagon.

Tressa's footsteps slowed even more. Might Luella have sneaked out of the house to meet Gage Hammond? She risked another quick glimpse over her shoulder. Gage remained at the post. His tugged-low hat shielded his eyes, but it couldn't hide his smirk. A chill wiggled down Tressa's spine. Why did she find that young man so disquieting?

"Come now, Tressa." Mrs. Wyatt hustled to Tressa's side and captured her elbow. "We got critters at home waitin' to be fed, so we need to hurry."

"Yes, ma'am." Tressa trotted the remaining distance to the wagon and climbed in. As she settled into one corner, she looked at Luella. The other girl wore a secretive grin that matched Gage's. Despite the summer afternoon sun, another chill attacked. Tressa needed to talk to Mrs. Wyatt about Gage and Luella. But first she needed proof.

❧

Tressa deliberately dragged out the kitchen cleanup after supper, delaying the final tasks until the sun touched the horizon and painted the sky in a soft peach glow. Mrs. Wyatt shuffled into the kitchen dressed in her unpretentious cotton gown and tattered housecoat. Her light brown hair, streaked heavily with gray, lay in thick waves across her shoulders.

Hands on hips, she shook her head. "Land sakes, girl, you're slower'n molasses in February tonight. What ails you?"

Tressa ran a soapy cloth over the worktable, lifting one shoulder in a slight shrug. "Nothing, ma'am. Just feeling . . . pensive, I suppose."

"Pensive?" The woman tucked her chin down and raised one brow high. "What'n dried beans is pensive?"

With a soft laugh, Tressa said, "Pensive . . . thoughtful . . . dreamy."

Mrs. Wyatt chuckled. "Well, I reckon every young woman is entitled to a dreamy evenin' now an' then." She folded her arms across her chest. "Would that dreaminess be connected to someone? Maybe a particular fella who caught your eye this afternoon?"

Two pictures immediately vied for prominence in Tressa's mind— one of Gage Hammond leaning on the fence post with a smirk marring his face and one of Abel Samms standing on the outside of the circle of dancers with a look of loneliness creasing his brow. Gage's image brought a shiver of distaste; Abel's a wash of sympathy coupled with a splash of confusion. He'd gently tended to her wound but then escaped as quickly as a mouse fleeing Isabella's pounce. She found his behavior puzzling and her own concern toward him even more bewildering.

But her reason for delaying bedtime had nothing to do with either man. Uncertain how to respond, she headed for the pantry to retrieve the water pails. "I need to fill the stove reservoir."

Mrs. Wyatt chuckled again, her eyes twinkling. "Pretty sure you've got more on your mind than fillin' the stove's water tank, but I won't force nothin' out o' you."

For a moment, guilt teased the edges of Tressa's conscience, and she considered divulging the reason she wanted to be downstairs when night fell. But until she knew for sure what Luella was scheming, she'd only be telling tales. She hadn't cared for Luella jumping to conclusions about her with Mr. Samms; she'd discover the truth before opening her mouth to Mrs. Wyatt.

"Thinkin' I might sit out on the front porch an' breathe in a little pipe smoke. Watchin' all that dancin' today . . ." Mrs. Wyatt sighed. "Got me lonesome for Jed. Why, nobody could hold a candle to Jed an' me when it came to dancin' a square."

Tressa tried to imagine Mrs. Wyatt swinging around the circle with her husband, but the image eluded her. Then she jolted, her thoughts unfolding one on top of the other. If Mrs. Wyatt were out on the porch, she'd surely see someone creeping around in the yard. If Luella tried to sneak out again tonight, she'd find it difficult to evade Mrs. Wyatt's notice. And if Mrs. Wyatt caught Luella, there would be no reason for Tressa to play Pinkerton detective.

She wrung the cloth into the washbasin and hung it over the edge of the dry sink. "It *is* a pleasant evening to sit outdoors. . . ."

Mrs. Wyatt yawned widely, not bothering to cover her mouth with her hand. "Then again I might go straight to bed. The others've all gone up—already hear snorin' comin' from Sallie. Even though it was a day o' rest, bein' out in the sun can wear a body out."

Tressa held her breath, waiting for Mrs. Wyatt to make up her mind.

The older woman crinkled her brow in thought. Then she blew out a long breath. "Oh my, I think I'm too tired to even light a pipe. I'm goin' on up to bed. Tressa-darlin', be sure to blow out all the lamps when you're finished down here, will you?"

"Certainly, ma'am."

The woman shook her head as she moved toward the doorway, mumbling, " 'Ma'am,' she says. . . . Land sakes, girl, just call me Aunt Hattie. Everybody does. No need to be so formal. . . ." Her voice faded away as her shuffling footsteps led her around the corner.

Tressa quickly filled the stove reservoir, put the buckets on the pantry shelf, and then fetched Isabella from her spot beneath the stove. She hated disturbing the sleeping cat, but Mrs. Wyatt preferred the animal spend the night in the pantry. With Isabella safely tucked away, she blew out the remaining lamps. Darkness engulfed the kitchen.

Feeling her way, she moved along the wall to the staircase and thumped to the top, deliberately setting her feet down firmly enough to be heard. When she reached the top, she paused for a moment and then turned and tiptoed back down. The actions felt deceitful, but if she was going to catch Luella, it would take a small measure of stealth.

She darted around the corner into the dining room. The heavily draped windows prevented even a hint of moonlight from entering the room. Cloaked completely in dark, Tressa leaned against the wall, her heart pounding. She aimed her ear toward the doorway and listened intently. Several minutes ticked by before a creak on the stairs warned of someone's approach. The thud in her chest carried to her ears, nearly covering the sound of footfalls, and she tried to slow her pulse with a slowly indrawn breath.

Just as she released the breath, a shadowy figure in a full skirt crept around the corner. Tressa flattened herself against the wall, but despite the effort to make herself disappear, the woman walked straight into her. Both released a squeak of surprise, and then a hand clamped around Tressa's arm.

"Who is it?"

"It's me—Tressa."

"What're you doing down here?"

Although deep shadows hid the woman's features, Tressa recognized the voice. She whispered back, "What are *you* doing, Luella?"

Maintaining a painful grip on Tressa's arm, Luella dragged Tressa through the dining room and into the kitchen. Soft moonlight sifted through the uncovered window above the sink, giving Tressa a glimpse of Luella's fury.

"You little sneak! You were watching for me, weren't you?"

"Yes, I was!" Tressa wrenched her arm free. Luella stood several inches taller, but Tressa squared her shoulders and looked directly into the other girl's face. "I saw you leave the house last night, and I thought you might do it again. Mrs. Wyatt made it quite clear that it isn't safe for us to wander away from the ranch alone, and especially not at night."

"I can take care of myself." Luella hissed the words through clenched teeth. Then a sly smile curved her lips. "Besides, I won't be alone for long."

Gage's face flashed in Tressa's memory. "Are you sneaking off to meet Gage Hammond?"

Luella's eyes narrowed. "That's none of your affair. And if you dare say a word to Aunt Hattie, I'll make your life miserable!"

Tressa couldn't imagine how the girl could create any more misery than she'd already accomplished. She tossed aside the threat. "It would be irresponsible for me to keep silent." Despite Luella's past unkind treatment, worry rose in Tressa's breast. "Luella, I don't think it's wise to spend time with Gage Hammond. That man—"

"That man has the means to give me everything I want." Luella's tone turned hard. "I won't risk being passed over by refusing to give him what he wants."

The insinuation struck Tressa so forcefully her knees began to tremble. "Luella, you aren't . . ." She couldn't bring herself to speak the words.

Luella emitted a short, scornful snicker. "Stop being such a baby, Tressa. You think some man is going to choose you because of your cooking and cow-roping skills? No matter what Aunt Hattie says, a man wants more from a woman than three meals a day, a tidy house, and help with his critters. I know what pleases a man, and I intend to let Gage Hammond know what he can expect if he chooses me. Now get out of my way."

She pushed past Tressa, nearly knocking her against the dry sink. But then she whirled back and grasped Tressa's arm again. Her fingers clamped down on the bandaged cut, and Tressa cried out. Luella squeezed harder. "Keep quiet about this, Tressa."

Tressa tried unsuccessfully to pry Luella's finger from her arm. Her wound throbbed painfully. "Luella, let go!"

"Do you promise not to tell?"

"I *have* to tell! It's against Mrs. Wyatt's rules to—"

"Forget the confounded rules!" She shook Tressa by her arm and then abruptly released her.

Tressa caught her balance and clutched her aching elbow.

"Think about this, Tressa." Suddenly Luella's tone turned wheedling, almost friendly. "You like Aunt Hattie, don't you?"

Gooseflesh broke out on Tressa's arms. She nodded slowly.

"Well, think how her reputation could be tarnished if one of her pupils managed to sneak off in the middle of the night with a local rancher's son. The fine townspeople of Barnett wouldn't take too kindly to that, now, would they?"

Tressa stared in shock. "How could Mrs. Wyatt be held accountable for what you chose to do?"

"She's supposed to be in charge, isn't she? So she'd be blamed." Luella advanced on Tressa, a malicious smile playing at the corners of her lips. "If you want to protect your dear Mrs. Wyatt, you'll keep your mouth shut." She patted Tressa's cheek with her open palm, then spun and slipped out the back door.

Tressa started after Luella, but then turned and took two stumbling steps toward the stairway. But she stopped again, her entire body quivering in worry and indecision. "I don't know what to do . . ." she whispered to the empty room. Suddenly Mrs. Wyatt's advice from weeks ago flitted through her mind: *Missy, you can always depend on God.*

Crossing to the window, Tressa pressed her fingertips to the glass and raised her gaze to the star-laden sky. The beauty of the night sky created a tug on her heart, but at the same time an emptiness engulfed her. Tears stung her eyes, blurring the twinkling stars. Mrs. Wyatt had told her she could depend on God to help her, but Tressa had no idea how to ask for His help.

৯

A fierce pounding wakened Abel from a restless sleep. He sat up, blinking into the murky bedroom and trying to make sense of the unexpected noise. The pounding came again, accompanied by a frantic voice. "Abel! Abel, wake up!"

Abel stumbled out of bed, tripping over the boots he'd abandoned in front of his night table. Muttering, he kicked the boots out of his way and clumped to the bedroom window. He pulled the yellow-checked curtain aside and squinted out at the peaceful night scene. No barn on fire, no bawling cattle, no reason he could see for someone to scare him out of a year's growth.

Grumbling under his breath, he charged to the front door and swung it wide. "Ethan, why're you bangin' on my door in the middle of the night?" He rubbed his eyes and yawned.

"Pa's bed is empty—he's gone."

Abel resisted snorting. "Did you check the outhouse?"

Ethan nodded hard enough to dislodge his head from his neck. "Checked everywhere, includin' the barn. His horse is gone, too. I figger he must've heard somethin'. Maybe the thieves came back an' he went after 'em."

Abel came full awake. "Vince went out alone?" His heart thumped in fear. The older man would be no match for desperate men. He hurried to his bedroom and scrambled into his trousers and boots and then tugged a jacket over his longjohns. "Any idea when he might've headed out?"

Ethan trotted alongside Abel as he thumped toward the barn. Worry created a deep crease in his brow. "I visited the outhouse around ten. Pa was in his bed then. What time is it now?"

Abel came to a halt and dug in his pocket for the watch he always carried. A flick of the catch opened the round cover. He angled the face toward the meager moonlight. "Eleven forty-five." So Vince could have been gone for an hour or more. He groaned. In the dark, they'd never be able to figure out which direction he went. Vince could be in grave danger, and Abel was powerless to help him.

"Are we gonna saddle horses an' go out?" Ethan stood poised, ready for action.

Abel flung his arms wide. "Which way, Ethan? Where do we go?"

"I . . . I don't know. . . ."

"Neither do I." Abel ran his hand through his hair, frustration sharpening his tone.

"But we gotta do somethin'! Pa . . . he shouldn't be chasin' rustlers on his own!"

Abel well understood Ethan's fretfulness, but what could they do? He needed guidance. Ethan tapped his boot on the ground, his breath coming in little huffs of impatience, but Abel stood stone still, uncertainty nailing him in place.

Suddenly the sound of hoof beats intruded. Both men spun toward the sound. As they watched, a rider reined his horse to a stop on the far side of the house and swung from the saddle. He led the horse toward the barn, his head low and his heels dragging. When he was within twenty feet of the barn, Ethan released a cry of relief.

"Pa!"

The man's head shot up, revealing a sparse gray beard and wide eyes. "Ethan—an' Abel . . . What're you two doin' out here?"

"We were goin' after you, Pa." Ethan raced to his father's side. "When I saw you were gone, I got worried. I told Abel you'd probably gone after the rustlers. Did you catch them?"

Vince's gaze flicked to Abel. Regret flashed in his eyes, and then he lowered his head. "No. No, didn't catch nobody."

Abel strode forward. "I appreciate you tryin' to protect the cattle, but it wasn't wise, Vince, goin' out on your own like that. Thieves are bound to be dangerous—likely to shoot anybody who gets in their way."

Vince rubbed his finger under his nose. "You're right, Abel. I'm sorry."

Ethan swung on Abel. "We gotta get the sheriff in on this, Abel. Just the four of us—we can't keep these rustlers away."

"No." Abel barked the word. But then uncertainty smote him. "Or should I, Vince? Is it time to get the sheriff in on our problem?"

Vince angled his face toward the barn, his brow puckering. "You're the boss, Abel, an' if you think we oughtta contact Sheriff Tate, I'll go along with ya. But I'm thinkin' the fewer people involved the better. Whole county'll get in an uproar if you make an official complaint. Men'll be firin' weapons in the dark, an' who knows what kind of harm might come."

"But—" Ethan started.

Abel inserted, "I agree with your pa, Ethan. Sheriff Tate's likely to do little more'n talk about it, an' rumors can build to misconceptions quicker'n a fox can raid a henhouse. No, we gotta handle this ourselves. But, Vince . . ." Abel gave the man's shoulder a squeeze. "Next time you hear somethin' at night, come get me. I should be the one takin' the risks. After all, the cattle're mine."

Vince sucked in a breath, as if preparing an argument, but then he gave a brusque nod. "Whatever you say, Abel."

Tiredness underscored the man's tone. Abel needed to let him get back to bed, but first he needed a question answered. "Do you know . . . are we missin' any head?"

"Won't know till mornin' how many, but I'm pret' sure we lost some tonight. Rode clear out to the north side of the far pasture. Wire's been cut." The muscles in Vince's jaw clenched.

Abel clamped his lips tight to hold back a curse. "Can't do nothin' tonight. We'll do a count in the mornin'. You two get some sleep."

"I'll see to your horse, Pa. Go on to bed." Ethan caught the reins and guided the horse toward the barn. Head slung low, Vince scuffed his way to the bunkhouse.

Abel's arms pumped and his feet pounded as he crossed the ground to the house. Vince'd said the north fence of the far pasture had been cut. That created an opening directly onto Hammond land. Tomorrow he'd pay another visit to Brewster Hammond.

13

Hattie pushed aside her empty breakfast plate and drew in a deep breath. "Ladies, today might be a bit hard on your tender sensibilities, but . . ."

Five wary faces turned in her direction, giving her pause. She'd put off calf branding because she suspected some of the girls would be squeamish about the task. But it couldn't be delayed any longer or those calves would be too big to wrestle to the ground. Besides, she'd helped Jed every year. Chances were these girls' mates would depend on their help one day. So, squeamish or not, they'd need to learn.

"Laid out on the sofa in the parlor are a half dozen shirts an' just as many pairs of trousers. I don't expect you'll find a perfect fit with any of 'em, but if you tuck the shirts in and then tie a length o' good strong twine around your middle, you'll be able to keep the pants up. So scoot upstairs an' change out o' your skirts, then meet me in the front yard. We'll be stampin' the Flying W brand on my new calves this mornin'."

A flutter went around the table. Mabelle's mouth fell open. "You . . . you want us to wear pants? But . . . but . . ." She shook her head, coils of frizzy brown hair springing loose from her ponytail. "Ladies don't wear pants!"

"City ladies sure don't," Hattie agreed, "but in case you hadn't noticed, this ain't the city. You think you can tussle a calf to the ground while you're wearin' a skirt? 'Sides that, skirts flare out in the wind. Last thing we want is for a skirt to drag through the firepit where we heat the brandin' iron."

Mabelle clapped her hand over her mouth, her eyes widening in an expression of horror.

Hattie nodded. "Nope, skirts have no place in the brandin' corral. So go on now—get yourselves into britches an' meet me outside." Without waiting for compliance, she rose and headed for the back door.

"Mrs. Wyatt?"

Hattie turned back at Tressa's hesitant voice. She had to bite the insides of her cheeks to keep from grinning at the girl's apprehensive expression.

"Shouldn't I clear the breakfast table before coming out?"

Emitting a low chuckle, Hattie shook her head. "Oh no, missy, you aren't gonna miss out on the fun. Just stack them dishes in the wash pan an' come out with the others. When the brandin' is done, we'll worry about the dishes."

Tressa's shoulders sagged, but she obediently followed the others out of the dining room. Still chuckling, Hattie made her way through the kitchen and into the yard. The wind tugged at the fabric of her full skirts, reminding her she'd need to instruct the girls from outside the pen so her wind-tossed calico wouldn't frighten the calves or—worse—catch flame. She smiled, recalling how Jed always told her she was cuter'n a baby bunny in spring clover in a pair of britches. Giving her padded hips a pat, she grinned to herself at how he'd fibbed, but she'd still liked hearing it.

Her gaze drifted to the corral, where the new calves jostled one another and bawled in protest at being penned up. All that bawling was music to a rancher's ears—the more calves, the more money to be made. Her ranch hands were there, too, stoking the fire and spinning lassos in readiness. Their faces lifted toward the house, and they poked one another with their elbows, grinning like fools. She pursed her lips into a frown. Appeared they were a little too eager to have the girls join them.

She'd already warned them to keep these lessons professional, but she suspected it would be hard considering it was the first time she'd allowed her hands and her pupils to be in close proximity. But staying focused was crucial considering the task. Many a man had come away from branding with a broken bone—a finger, wrist, or ankle—or a burn from the fire. Carelessness caused accidents, and she didn't want any injuries today. They'd best all keep their minds on their work. Scowling, she decided to give the men one more stern warning before the girls came out.

As she headed across the yard, two horses with riders loped through the gate at the end of the lane—Brewster Hammond and Abel Samms. Neither looked happy. Trepidation created a lump in her belly, but she hitched up her skirts and trotted to meet them.

"Harriet." Brewster touched his hat's brim and nodded.

Abel removed his hat. "Mornin', Aunt Hattie." The greeting carried no cheer.

Hattie plopped one fist on her hip. "I can already tell it's bad news. Just go ahead and tell me."

The two men exchanged looks. Abel scratched his head. "Fence between my place an' Brewster's got cut last night, an' we found tracks headin' right for your land."

Hattie gawked in amazement. "You think somebody deposited your beef on my land?"

"Wouldn't be hard to cut through your place, Aunt Hattie, seein' as how you don't have fence around your grazin' land." He glanced at the noisy calves. "Mind if I take a peek in your corral over there at the calves? Want to make sure none of 'em are carryin' my brand."

"Not likely, Abel, since my men rounded 'em up yesterday afternoon and penned 'em overnight. But you're welcome to take a look, if it'll ease your mind."

Abel hesitated, pulling his lower lip between his teeth. Finally he gave a nod. "You're prob'ly right, but I'll go look just in case." He replaced his hat and gave the reins a tug. The horse turned sharply toward the corral.

As Abel clopped away, Brewster swung down from his horse. "Abel come to my place first thing this mornin', all a-dither. At first I thought he was imaginin' things, so I agreed to go out an' do some snoopin' just to prove him wrong. Couldn't believe it when I saw those tracks cuttin' along my property line. Makes me madder'n hops that someone would stoop so low as to run off his cattle. No secret that I wouldn't mind addin' his land to my holdings since it's right next door an' has a good source of water, but I sure can't abide rustlin'."

Hattie wondered why Brewster felt the need to defend himself to her, but she didn't ask. Men were funny creatures. Sometimes they talked without thinking, but they were mostly prone to think without talking. At least she assumed there was thinking going on behind their closed mouths. Her Jed had been the exception, engaging in long conversations in the evenings while they sat together on the porch.

Brewster tipped his head toward the branding pen, his gray eyebrows high. "You're brandin' a little late, aren't you? Those calves look well beyond weaned. Be tougher to hold 'em down, given their size. . . ."

A hint of defensiveness tickled Hattie's chest. "It is later than usual, but I had my reasons." She didn't offer to share the reasons, however.

Brewster's face puckered for a moment, and he opened his mouth as if to say something else. But at that moment, the girls spilled out of the house dressed in shirts with the sleeves rolled above their wrists and pant legs dragging on the ground.

Brewster gaped. "What in blue blazes?" He pointed at the girls as they straggled to the branding pen and lined up along the fence. "Harriet, are those your pupils gussied up like a pack of miners?"

She laughed at his disbelieving face. "Yep, Brewster, them's my pupils. They're gonna be brandin' the calves today, an' they needed to be dressed for it."

"You're lettin' 'em brand?" Brewster pushed his hat to the back of his head. "Harriet Wyatt, have you taken leave of your senses? A woman's got no business in a brandin' pen!"

Hattie drew back. "Now, see here, Brewster, I'm a woman, an' I branded more'n my fair share o' calves when Jed an' me were gettin' started. Hasn't hurt me a bit to know every aspect o' ranchin'. A wife is a *helpmeet*, an' these girls're gonna learn to be helpmeets in every sense o' the word."

"But, Harriet—"

"Brewster, if you'll excuse me, my pupils're ready to start their lessons. If you've a mind to, you can stick around an' watch. Might surprise you what a *woman* can do." She swept past him, her nose in the air. But after only a few steps, guilt attacked. Brewster's late wife, Amy, God rest her soul, had been a fragile woman who had no business setting foot in a branding pen. Brewster had cause to express concern. But her girls were strong and able. They'd do just fine with the right instruction.

As she neared the pen, Abel stepped into her pathway. He held the horse's reins in one hand and his hat in the other. "Thanks for lettin' me look, Aunt Hattie. You were right—I didn't see any calves carryin' the Lazy S brand."

She touched his arm. "Don't lose heart, Abel. Just keep prayin' for that thief to let go o' his wicked ways."

He clapped the hat onto his head. "I've lost a total of ten calves, three cows, an' a bull this season." He heaved a deep sigh. "Much as I hate to, I reckon it's time I get the sheriff in on the situation."

"Well now, I've always had better luck with God than with the sheriff."

The corner of Abel's mouth twitched. "Not sure either one of 'em have done me much good."

Hattie gave him a fierce scowl. "Shame on you, Abel Samms. Your mama would wash your mouth out with soap if she heard you! I couldn't name two more godly people than your ma an' pa. Why would you make such a claim?"

A frown pinched his face. "Got my reasons."

She jabbed her finger at his nose. "Man's reasonin' is foolishness in the sight o' God. You remember that, Abel." Leaning in close, she added, "Just 'cause things don't go the way we want 'em to doesn't mean God's quit carin'. He cares deep, but His ways aren't ours. His ways are always better."

Abel turned his face away, his jaw thrust out.

Stubborn coot . . . Hattie shook her head. "Well, if you won't pray, I will. An' when that thief is caught, you'll owe me a big thank-you for handlin' your problem for you. Now, unless you want to help with brandin' today, you best get on to town an' let the sheriff know what's been happenin'."

He swung onto his horse and clopped toward the gate without a word. She stood looking after him for a moment, her heart heavy. She'd be praying for the thief, but she'd also be praying for Abel to put his trust in God again.

The smell of smoke reached her nose. The fire would burn out before they got started if she didn't put somebody to work. She charged over to the row of girls and grinned down the line. "All right, ladies, Clyde is gonna show you how to lasso a calf, drag it to the fire, and sear the brand into his rear flank. Who wants to go first?"

Both Luella and Paralee stuck a hand in the air. Although Paralee's gesture was less confident than Luella's, Hattie chose Paralee. "Good girl." She peered into Paralee's pale face. "You sure you're ready?"

Paralee gulped twice, ran her hand down the length of her gold-tinged braid, and squared her skinny shoulders. "I reckon so."

Hattie rewarded her with a wide smile. "Spoken like a true rancher's wife! Crawl between those rails now an' show us what you can do."

❧

Tressa dropped the filthy pair of pants on top of Sallie's discarded clothing. A puff of dust rose from the pile. She hoped Mrs. Wyatt would put someone else on laundry duty for the week. She had no desire to scrub the stains from those clothes. Turning toward the corner, she began unbuttoning her shirt. A groan from the opposite side of the room caught her attention. She peeked over her shoulder and caught Sallie examining her bare limbs in the oval mirror that hung above the bureau.

"Sallie!" Forgetting her own state of dishevelment, she dashed to Sallie's side and gingerly touched a large purple splotch on the girl's shoulder blade. "Oh my!"

Sallie grimaced, pointing to a series of smaller walnut-sized bruises running down the front of her shin. "It's terrible marked up I am." Holding out her arm, she ran her fingers over a bluish blotch on the inside of her elbow. She sighed. "I haven't been so black an' blue since—" She clamped her mouth closed and scrambled in the drawer for her nightgown. She whisked it over her head and snatched up her hairbrush, viciously attacking her tangled hair.

Tressa stood in the dusty half-buttoned shirt, staring at Sallie's pale reflection in the mirror. Suddenly the reason for the fear she'd witnessed in Sallie's green eyes on previous occasions became far too clear. She gently cupped her hand over Sallie's shoulder. "Sallie? Has someone . . . mistreated you?"

Sallie's eyes darted to the side and then returned, meeting Tressa's in the mirror. Her lips formed a grim line. "*He* did. But no more. I tricked him by gettin' far away. He can't ever be hurtin' me again." Her expression hardened. "No man will."

Although Tressa had received little affection from her aunt and uncle, at least they had never raised a hand to her. How could someone be cruel enough to strike Sallie hard enough to leave marks behind? She squeezed Sallie's shoulder. "I'm so sorry."

Sallie shrugged, dislodging Tressa's hand. "Don't be wastin' your sorry on me. As I said, it won't be happenin' again." She smacked the brush onto the bureau and spun around, a smile dimpling her cheeks. "An' ye might want to check yourself where ye sit down. I saw ye fall when the calf worked its head free of the lasso."

Despite the remembered embarrassment of that moment, Tressa released a giggle. She rubbed her sore hip and nodded. "The fall was a surprise. But I managed to brand him after all." Pride filled her. Never would she have believed she would have the courage to press a red-hot iron against the flank of a thrashing calf. But she'd done it!

"Oh, ye branded him, for sure." Sallie's eyes twinkled. "But I wish you could've seen yourself—eyes squinched shut an' arms out as straight as the iron itself, keepin' as much distance as ye could from the poor dumb creature." Sallie acted out her words as she spoke. " 'Tis a wonder ye didn't brand one of the hired hands instead of the little cow!"

Laughter spilled from Sallie's lips, and a grin grew on Tressa's face with no effort. Not since their first days on the ranch had the girls shared such a moment of mirth, and Tressa discovered she didn't want the feeling of companionship to end. Clasping her hands together, she said, "Would you like me to fetch the liniment bottle from the pantry and rub some on your bruises? It might take some of the ache away."

"Oooh, I'd be thankin' ye for it, Tressa."

Tressa scurried toward the door.

"But, Tressa?"

She turned back.

"Ye might want to be changin' into somethin' more presentable before going down to the kitchen."

Tressa glanced at her bare legs sticking out from beneath the tail of the shirt. She clapped her hands to her cheeks and stared at Sallie in horror. Sallie broke into gales of laughter. And despite her tiredness and her continued worry about Luella and Gage, for that moment Tressa cast off her concerns and let her own laughter ring.

14

Tressa placed the liniment bottle back in the box of medicinal cures and slid the box onto the pantry shelf. A smile still hovered on her heart. The time of ministering to Sallie, of shared laughter, had taken a load from her shoulders. She whispered good-night to Isabella, who curled on her rug in the corner of the pantry, then closed the door and headed toward the stairs. But the creak of footsteps from the dining room brought her to a stumbling halt. Was Luella planning to meet Gage Hammond again?

She held her breath, watching the doorway, and her breath whooshed out with relief when Mrs. Wyatt bustled into the kitchen. "Mrs. Wyatt . . . it's you."

"Who were you expectin', a burglar?" The older woman balled her fists on her hips. "An' when're you goin' to give up callin' me 'Mrs. Wyatt'? Does the name 'Aunt Hattie' stick in your craw?"

The teasing grin that accompanied the rebuke made Tressa laugh. "No, ma'am." How could she explain to this woman that the title "aunt" carried an unpleasant connotation? It seemed unfair to apply that title to someone so vastly different from Aunt Gretchen.

"Well, it'd do my heart good to hear 'Aunt Hattie' out o' you instead o' that formal 'Mrs. Wyatt.'" She puckered her lips into a sour expression. "Makes me feel like some doddering old woman." Shaking her finger at Tressa, she added, "An' don't let this gray hair fool you! I might look old on the outside, but my insides are still plenty spry!"

Tressa nodded in agreement. She'd never met a more lively woman—young or old—than Mrs. Wyatt.

Suddenly the woman heaved a sigh. "Where does the time go?" Her introspective tone left Tressa feeling like an eavesdropper. "Seems just yesterday Jed an' me were buildin' this ranch, dreamin' of the future, and now . . . Jed's gone, I'm comin' up on my sixty-second year, an' . . ." She stopped abruptly, giving herself a little shake. "An' here I am, keepin' you from goin' up to bed."

Tressa took a forward step, lifting her hand toward Mrs. Wyatt. "Oh no, ma'am! You aren't keeping me. I . . . I enjoy talking with you."

"An' I enjoy you, too, Tressa-darlin'." Mrs. Wyatt's eyes crinkled with her smile. "The good Lord planted a tender heart in your chest, an' it's a pleasure to see you openin' up, like a rosebud bloomin'." Her grin turned teasing. "You did good today on the brandin', hittin' your target even with your eyes closed."

Tressa grimaced. How foolish she must have appeared!

Mrs. Wyatt laughed, shaking her head. "Do you know how proud it made me to see you climb into that pen an' fling that lasso? Why, when you first come, you seemed scared o' your own shadow. But now you jump in an' do what's needed, even when it scares you. Yep, Tressa, you are blossomin' for sure."

The compliment washed Tressa with delight, the reaction almost dizzying. She gulped, seeking words of gratitude, but before any formed, Mrs. Wyatt went on.

"I'm grateful God brought you to Barnett—I just know He's got somethin' special planned for you here."

Tressa's pulse sped, and an argument spilled from her lips. "*God* didn't bring me to Barnett. My aunt and uncle sent me because—" She clamped a hand over her mouth, aghast at her defiant tone.

For long moments she and Mrs. Wyatt stared at each other across the quiet kitchen. Tressa's heart pounded so hard she feared it might explode. But Mrs. Wyatt stood calmly, her eyes sad. Suddenly, without warning, Mrs. Wyatt stepped forward and wrapped Tressa in her arms. She guided Tressa's head to her shoulder and gently rocked back and forth.

Tears pricked behind Tressa's eyes. The comforting embrace, so unexpected, swept away the hurt anger of moments before. How many years had passed since she had received a hug? Papa had been affectionate, but not since his death had anyone offered her the comfort of an embrace. Closing her eyes, she relished the moment, fondness for this dear woman filling her with gratitude.

Mrs. Wyatt gave Tressa a pat on the back and then released her. Twin tears winked in the woman's faded gray eyes. "Tressa-darlin', you listen to me an' you memorize these words. There's a verse in the Bible—found in Psalm 139—that says our days were planned by God even before we were born. Your aunt an' uncle might've sent you here, but they were actin' as God's hands."

Gently curling her fingers around Tressa's upper arms, Mrs. Wyatt lowered her voice to a whisper. "He brought you here for His reasons, so you quit feelin' like you've been cast aside an' consider that you've been *chosen*. Will you remember that, Tressa?"

She swallowed hard. The concept of God taking such an active interest in her—Tressa Neill, the orphaned, unwanted niece of Leo and Gretchen Neill—was too large to accept in one portion. She would need to digest it slowly. But she nodded, silently vowing to give Mrs. Wyatt's astounding statement some serious reflection.

"Good girl." Mrs. Wyatt released Tressa and scuffed toward the back door. She turned the skeleton key that always rested in the lock, then pulled it free and hung it on a nail pounded into the doorjamb.

"Why are you locking the door?" Not once since she'd arrived on the ranch had Tressa witnessed Mrs. Wyatt locking up the house. She hugged herself as an unnamed worry seized her.

Mrs. Wyatt laughed, but to Tressa's ears the sound seemed forced. "Oh now, it's just a precaution. I've not had any trouble here, but one o' my neighbors has had a theft or two at his place."

The worry grew into fear. "Thefts? At night?" Her heart began to pound. "*Last* night?"

Mrs. Wyatt's brows knitted together. "That's right. How did you know?"

Tressa's mind raced. Luella had sneaked off to meet Gage last night. She had suspected the pair was behaving in a wanton manner, but might they also be involved in something unscrupulous?

Mrs. Wyatt took Tressa's hand. "Why, girl, you're pale as a ghost. Somethin's ailin' you. Tell me."

Her mouth went dry, and Tressa licked her lips. "Mrs. Wyatt, I—"

The creak of a floorboard intruded. Both women jumped when Luella crept into the room. When she spotted Tressa and Mrs. Wyatt, she stopped so suddenly her feet slid on the polished wood floor. After only a second or two, her startled look transformed into a too-bright smile.

"Oh, Aunt Hattie, I thought you'd gone to bed. I . . . I came down for a glass of milk. Would you like one, too? I'll pour one for you." She flounced to the icebox and removed the tin pitcher of milk.

Mrs. Wyatt caught Luella's arm, preventing her from taking glasses from the cupboard. "You always get dressed to fetch a glass of milk?"

Luella glanced down her length, appearing surprised by her own attire. She laughed, raising her shoulders in a self-conscious shrug. "This dress was at the foot of my bed. I guess I put it on without thinking about it being bedtime. After my milk, I'll change into my nightgown."

Mrs. Wyatt gave the girl a steady, unsmiling look. "You sure you only came down for milk?"

Luella shot a short, venomous glare in Tressa's direction before bestowing an ingenuous look on Mrs. Wyatt. "Of course."

Drawing in a deep breath, Mrs. Wyatt stepped back. "Well then, drink your milk an' head on up. You'll be doin' laundry tomorrow, an' after today's activities, it'll take some effort to get those clothes clean again."

Luella downed a glass of milk. Humming to herself, she returned the pitcher to the icebox, placed the glass in the wash basin, and then pranced around the corner without a backward glance.

Tressa expected Mrs. Wyatt to question her again, but instead the woman marched to the door. With a grim expression, she deposited the key in her robe pocket. "Bed now, Tressa." Her tone didn't invite further conversation.

❧

Abel pinched his lips around three nails and held his hammer against his thigh, standing still and tense as he watched Aunt Hattie approach. Her expression was grim, and he wondered what more could have gone wrong. She reined in next to the partially completed fence and remained astride her horse. Her husband's prized Stetson pulled low on her head shielded the upper half of her face from the midmorning sun. Without so much as a greeting, she wrapped the reins around the saddle horn and spoke in a terse tone. "I don't like to think of it, Abel, but I'm wonderin' if one o' my pupils might be tangled up in your rustlin' problem."

Her announcement was so ludicrous, a snort of laughter grated in his throat. Bouncing the hammer handle against his leg, he squinted against the sun and spoke around the nails. "You gotta be misunder-standin' somethin', Aunt Hattie. Your pupils only just arrived a month or so ago. The thefts have been goin' on for more'n two years."

Returning to his task, he held the string of barbed wire in place with his gloved thumb and pulled a nail free from his mouth. With several deft whacks, he pounded the nail into the wood below the string of wire. When the nail was half buried in the post, he tapped the extended half into a loop over the wire to hold it in place.

He took a step back and looked down the row of empty fence posts. Still a far piece to go. He removed another nail from his mouth and gestured with it. "Besides, why would your pupils want to steal cattle? They're all here to cozy up to some rancher an' make a home in this area, right? Stealin' sure wouldn't endear them to anyone around here. Nope . . . it don't make sense."

"Don't make much sense to me, either—yet." She doubled her hands over the saddle horn and tipped closer, lowering her voice even though they were alone on the far side of the north pasture. "But I never saw a person try so hard to look innocent. That girl's hidin' somethin'. An' earlier in the evenin' another o' my pupils said somethin' that made me think . . ."

She looked back and forth, like she expected someone to jump out from the tangle of tumbleweeds. "I'm uneasy, Abel. Somethin' ain't right."

He swallowed a grunt and pounded in another nail. Things hadn't been right for a good long while. Pa's death, Amanda's rejection, the loss of a significant portion of his herd, wondering if he'd be able to hang on to his land . . .

"I'm just sayin' that it might be best for you to demand our lazy sheriff hire a few men to keep watch around your place."

He released one huff of laughter. "Aunt Hattie, you know Sheriff Tate only wears that badge for show. He's never done one thing to act like a sheriff." The man had scratched his head and mumbled something about looking into things when Abel reported the thefts, but Abel held no real confidence that anything would be done.

"Well, it's high time he earned his keep!" Aunt Hattie aimed a stern look down at Abel. "You just remind him our taxes go for protection."

Abel gave the post a smack with his open palm. "Me tellin' him won't guarantee he'll do anything, but if it'll make you feel better . . ." He grabbed the end of the wire and headed for the next post.

Aunt Hattie tapped her horse with her moccasin-covered heels and followed. "Abel, I got another idea, too."

Urgency to protect his remaining herd nudged him to keep hammering—this wire wouldn't string itself—and impatience at the delay made him twitch in place. "What?"

"You run a short-handed ranch, with just three men on your payroll, an' it gets even shorter when you keep one of 'em on kitchen duty. I was thinkin'—my pupils've done a fine job of learnin' their way around a kitchen, an' now it's time for 'em to try some . . ." She scratched her chin. "Well, I guess you'd call it apprenticin'."

He stared up at Aunt Hattie. Was she suggesting . . . ? He shook his finger at her. "Oh no, Aunt Hattie, you aren't sendin' one of those girls to my place. I'd never get any work out of Cole or Ethan if they knew one of your pupils was at the house all day."

"Now, give it some thought, Abel." Her wheedling tone set his teeth on edge. He wasn't a little boy to be cajoled into eating his turnip greens. "You need your men on the range, watchin' the cattle. Besides that, you'd be doin' me a favor by givin' one o' my girls the experience of runnin' a kitchen all on her own."

"Aunt Hattie, I—"

She held up her palm. "I know, I know, you carry a grudge against eastern women. But it's time you let loose o' that, an' gettin' to know one o' my girls might just convince you that not all eastern women are bad." Angling her head to the side, she sent him a saucy grin. "I promise not to send you the one I suspect o' bein' a party to the rustlin'."

Despite himself, Abel laughed. He chewed the inside of his lip, contemplating her suggestion. Having all of his men free to ride the range, make sure the fence stayed up, and do a count of cattle every day would give him some assurance. And eating decent cooking on a daily basis appealed to him. His mouth watered, remembering the stew and biscuits Aunt Hattie had brought by. But there was one concern she hadn't addressed.

"Most times apprentices get a little somethin' for their efforts. What kind of payment are you expectin' me to give?" His bank account wouldn't hold up to much more strain.

"No payment. This is part o' their trainin'."

His eyebrows shot up. "You sure? That's a heap of work for no return."

Aunt Hattie chuckled. "Oh, there'll be a return—experience an' knowledge. A person can't put a price on somethin' as valuable as experience an' knowledge."

Abel rubbed the underside of his nose with his finger. Although he still wasn't keen on having a woman in his house—especially one from the East—he could see the benefit for him and his ranch. Besides, he'd only encounter her at mealtimes. "Well, I guess it's all right as long as you'll bring her over each day. I haven't got time to cart somebody back an' forth."

"No need for either of us to do any cartin'. She'll bring herself." Aunt Hattie's grin broadened. "This week I'm teachin' the pupils to ride an' assignin' 'em the care of a horse. Ought to be ready to start sendin' 'em out for trainin' next Monday. That suit you?"

Monday. That gave him almost a week to prepare himself and his men. He scowled. He'd need to set some firm ground rules for Cole and Ethan or having this woman around might prove more trouble than she was worth.

He jerked his head to look into Aunt Hattie's face. "If things don't work out, you'll change the arrangement without pesterin' me?"

She sighed. "Abel, you are the most contrary man I ever met. . . ." She shook her head. "Let's compromise, hmm? You promise to give one o' my pupils a week o' trainin'. One week. Then I'll move 'er somewhere else. That sound fair?"

Abel popped off his glove and stuck out his hand. "Fair enough." They shook.

"Good." Giving the reins a yank, she turned her horse from the fence line. "You won't be sorry, Abel!"

He waved and then faced the waiting fence post. Aunt Hattie's parting comment hung in the air. He gave the post a bump with his boot and mumbled, "That waits to be seen. . . ."

15

"Of all the things we've learned since coming to Kansas, I think I like horse-riding the best." Tressa flashed a smile at Sallie as they trotted side-by-side down the road toward the Lazy S ranch.

Sallie grinned. "An' ye surprised me, for sure, with the way ye've taken to a horse's back. I would've thought of ye bein' too prim an' proper to straddle a horse."

Heat built in Tressa's cheeks. Surely her aunt would be appalled to witness her sitting astride the tall speckled beast with her skirts hitched up above her ankles and draped across the horse's rump. Tressa admitted to some momentary misgivings when Mrs. Wyatt had scoffed at her query about a sidesaddle. "You aren't gonna be trottin' through some namby-pamby park; you'll be ridin' over pasture land and rain-washed roads. If you don't have your feet firm in a stirrup, you're liable to be unseated, an' it's a far piece to the ground. No, ma'am, you'll be ridin' astride."

Tressa bounced her heels lightly against her horse's ribs, and the horse tossed his head, making his black mane ripple. He broke into a gentle trot. Tressa laughed with pleasure. What freedom she experienced, riding beneath a pale sky with the sun peeping over the edge of the horizon and the dew-scented breeze tossing the ties of her bonnet over her shoulders.

She longed to coax the horse into a run, but Mrs. Wyatt's warning about the dangers that could befall an animal should it step into a gopher hole or stumble in a rut in the road kept her from giving in to her desire. Besides, a run would shorten the ride. The longer the time on the back of the horse, the less time in Abel Samms' kitchen.

"I'm glad we'll be working at the Lazy S together, Sallie." Tressa didn't know why Mrs. Wyatt had decided to allow the girls to work in pairs rather than individually, but she felt much more secure knowing Sallie would be with her.

" 'Tis pleased I am, too." Sallie giggled. "But did ye see the look on Luella's face when Aunt Hattie said she'd be stayin' to do duties at the Flyin' W?" She clicked her tongue against her teeth. "Poor Luella . . . as if Aunt Hattie would've sent her to the Double H. The Hammonds already have a cook on staff. They've no need for one of us settin' foot in their kitchen."

Tressa sent Sallie a sidelong glance, a question burning her tongue. Did Sallie know about Luella's secret meetings with Gage Hammond? Obviously Sallie recognized Luella's infatuation with the man, but if she was unaware of Luella's nighttime dalliances, broaching the subject would make Tressa a talebearer, so she held her tongue.

"Do ye remember how many men we'll be feedin' at the Lazy S?" Sallie urged her horse to trot up alongside Tressa's mount.

"Four." Tressa licked her lips, her mouth suddenly dry. Mrs. Wyatt had sent Paralee and Mabelle to the Shultz ranch. Tressa had considered asking to trade with one of them so she could avoid further contact with Abel Samms. Never had she experienced such odd feelings toward a man—drawn to him while simultaneously apprehensive of him.

Of course, her only relationship with a man of her age had been her short-lived courtship with Tremaine Woodward.

Her heart twisted in remembrance. She had genuinely liked Tremaine. He was handsome, funny, smart, and very polite. After several weeks of carefully supervised get-togethers, she had begun to long for moments alone with him and had even imagined what it would be like to become Mrs. Tremaine Woodward. But then he asked permission to become betrothed to her and her uncle informed him that, as an orphan, Tressa would be a dowryless bride. Tremaine had wished her well and begun courting Emma Lowery. Even now, almost a year later, the memory stung. Was she, as a person, worth so little?

"Only four, after feedin' six hired hands an' as many women at Aunt Hattie's will be like playtime." Sallie grinned again. "We'll be havin' a holiday, Tressa."

Tressa wasn't sure being in close proximity to Abel Samms would be a holiday for her, but she didn't argue. They would work the Lazy S for one week. Surely she could set aside her strange feelings concerning the man for one week.

"There it is!" Sallie pointed to the gate leading to the Lazy S. She glanced at the rising sun. "An' they're prob'ly eager for breakfast so they can be startin' their day. We best get inside quickly an' set food on the table."

They left the horses, still saddled, inside the barn, intending to return and remove their saddles as soon as breakfast had been served. Sallie tapped lightly on the front door. It swung open so quickly Tressa felt certain someone had been watching their approach from a window. The thought gave her a little chill.

Abel Samms stood in the doorway. His thick brown hair lay across his forehead in damp waves, his clean-shaven cheeks shiny from a recent wash. Attired in a simple cotton shirt, tan trousers, and scuffed square-toed boots, he had a rugged appearance that made Tressa's stomach flutter in an unfamiliar yet not unpleasant way.

He gave them a hesitant nod in greeting and gestured for them to step over the threshold. Then, wordlessly, he led the way through a fairly large sitting room that contained a velvet-upholstered parlor set, as well as a dining table and matching chairs. The furnishings seemed out of place in the otherwise rustic dwelling.

On Abel's heels, Tressa and Sallie entered a lean-to that apparently served as the kitchen. Compared to Mrs. Wyatt's spacious kitchen, this space felt like a closet. Tressa hoped her dismay didn't show on her face. A dry sink and punched-tin cupboard stood along one wall, and the stove crouched on the opposite wall with a scant three feet of distance between them. A small square table—the only available workspace—filled a corner. Unpainted warped wood shelves lined the walls at shoulder height and held pots, pans, dishes, and woven baskets with various kitchen implements poking out of them. Taking in the cramped space, Tressa wondered how she and Sallie would manage to avoid stepping on each other.

"Chicken coop's out back." Mr. Samms crossed to a windowless door in the corner next to the jelly cupboard and propped it open with a smooth gray rock. The morning breeze washed through the opening, instantly cheering the dismal little room. "Cellar's just around the corner. You'll find meat, cheese, an' vegetables down there. Cole milked the cow this mornin', so there's fresh milk an' cream, too. Make use of whatever you want from the cellar an' the cupboard." He pulled a folded piece of yellow paper and a pencil stub from his shirt pocket and placed them on the edge of the dry sink. "But write down what you use so I can be sure an' replace everything when I go to town Saturday."

Tressa huddled in the doorway, trying to make herself as small as possible, but Sallie crossed to the cupboard and swung both doors open. She flashed a smile over her shoulder. "I see the makin's for flapjacks. Would it be pleasin' ye to have a stack of flapjacks an' fried eggs for breakfast this mornin', Mr. Samms?"

"Whatever you decide is fine." The man inched his way toward the open door. "When breakfast is ready, ring the bell." He pointed to a tarnished brass bell hanging just outside the door. "We won't bother you until you call for us."

"Yes, sir, Mr. Samms."

At Sallie's agreement, he turned on his boot heel and disappeared around the corner.

Sallie put her hands on her hips and shook her head after him. "Never saw such an' unsmilin' man." She whirled, winking at Tressa. "But nothin' brings a smile like a good meal. So let's get to cookin', shall we, Tressa?"

When the first batch of flapjacks was ready, Tressa rang the little bell and then allowed Sallie to serve the men while she remained at the stove, flipping additional flapjacks and dropping eggs into the sizzling grease. Sweat beaded across her upper lip and tickled between her shoulder blades. Even with the door open, the tiny room became unbearable with the fire roaring in the belly of the stove. Relief flooded her when Sallie finally carried in the dirty dishes and the slam of the front door signaled the men's departure from the house.

Sallie dumped the dishes onto the dry sink. "Since you did the cookin', I'll do the cleanin' up. Why don't you go out an' see to our horses? The poor beasts'll be ready to be free of their saddles, for sure."

Tressa eagerly shot out the back door. She stood for a moment, blinking as bright sunlight attacked her eyes. The breeze, although warm, felt heavenly after being cooped up in the stifling little room. Somewhat refreshed, she headed for the barn. As she neared the wide opening of the rock barn, a horse and rider emerged. She recognized the rider as the man who had come to Mrs. Wyatt's ranch to let them know a cow was ready to birth. When he spotted her, he brought his horse to a stop and grinned down at her.

"You goin' to take care of your horses?"

She nodded.

"I did it for ya. Put the saddles over the stall wall an' gave the horses some hay an' water, too. After they eat, you can put 'em in the corral over there." He pointed with his hat and then settled it over his straw-colored hair. "When you an' Miss Sallie're ready to head on back to Aunt Hattie's, you just let me an' Cole know. We'll saddle 'em for ya. A lady shouldn't hafta fling a saddle over a horse's back."

His friendly grin was impossible to resist. She offered a hesitant smile in return. "Thank you." She wished she could remember his name.

"Welcome, Miss Tressa. Have a good mornin' now." He clicked his tongue, and the horse galloped off around the barn.

Grateful at being relieved of the cumbersome chore of caring for the horses, Tressa returned to the kitchen. She and Sallie spent a pleasant hour together, churning butter, mixing bread dough, and peeling and chopping vegetables for a hearty stew. "We should take stock of Mr. Samms' cupboards an' make a plan for the week's meals," Sallie suggested while kneading the huge lump of dough on the tiny work table. Flour streaked her cheek, hiding some of her freckles. "Aunt Hattie'll surely have some suggestions, too, if she knows what stores're available to us."

Tressa nodded, stirring the bubbling pot on the stove. Although she'd become quite adept at cooking, her list of memorized recipes was scant at best. The men would quickly tire of stew, biscuits, and chicken and dumplings. She glanced at the paper and pencil Mr. Samms had left behind. "We'll need to bring paper with us tomorrow, then. There isn't enough room on that single piece to record everything."

Sallie lifted her shoulder and pushed her hair from her face. "Don't ye think Mr. Samms must be havin' more paper around here somewhere?"

"Of course. You can ask him at dinnertime."

Sallie divided the ball of dough into three equal portions with deft twists of her wrists. She patted one portion into a smooth oblong ball, her grin saucy. "An' why won't ye be askin' him?"

Tressa reached for the little bag of salt and tossed several pinches into the pot. "You suggested recording the available items, so I suppose you can make arrangements for it." Her voice took on an unintentionally tart tone.

Sallie laughed. "Uh-huh, an' that's just what I was suspectin'. You're sweet on Abel Samms."

Tressa whirled to face Sallie. "Don't say such things!"

"But why? There's no harm in bein' sweet on a man. That's why we're here, ain't it? To find a man an' build a family with 'im?"

"Well, yes, but—"

"Then why're ye gettin' so flustered? He's a single man, an' he's got this fine house to offer ye. I can see no reason why you'd want to turn him away."

"But . . . but . . . " Tressa gathered her racing thoughts. "He hasn't offered anything more than the opportunity to practice our skills in his kitchen. The man isn't interested in me. He . . . he avoids me as if I had some sort of foul odor." Strange how it pained her to utter those words aloud. Did she really care what Abel Samms thought? His warm brown eyes appeared in her memory—eyes as dark and tender as Papa's—and she swallowed a lump of sadness that formed in her throat.

"To my way of thinkin'," Sallie said, plopping the last ball of dough into its waiting pan, "when a man works so hard to avoid a woman, what he's doing is avoidin' his own feelin's." She placed the pans in a row on top of the stove's warming hobs. "I'd wager he's sweet on ye an' tryin' hard to keep it a secret."

Tressa bit down on the end of her tongue, stilling any further protest. Arguing would only add fuel to Sallie's fire, and anything she said might be repeated to the other girls. She stirred the stew with a vengeance and refused to even look in Sallie's direction.

149

They worked in silence for a few minutes, and then a finger tapped Tressa's shoulder. "Are ye goin' to stay mad at me all day? 'Cause it'll make for a dreary time."

With a sigh, Tressa turned from the stove and met Sallie's contrite gaze. "I'm not angry, Sallie, I'm just . . ." But once again, she fell silent. She couldn't begin to explain how she felt about Abel Samms. Plus, she couldn't truthfully deny Sallie's assumption. A tiny piece of her was, as Sallie had put it, sweet on the man.

Sallie's face brightened with a quick smile. "If you're not angry, then I'll do a little searchin' for some paper an' get started writin' down what supplies are available to us."

Tressa grabbed Sallie's arm as the girl headed for the door that led to the main room of the house. "Searching? You mean snooping!"

Her eyes sparkling with mischief, Sallie nodded. "For sure, snoopin'! But it's hardly out of line. We'll be cleanin' his house, too, so we must be knowin' what's here." She tugged loose from Tressa's grip and charged around the corner.

Tressa scuttled after her, wringing her hands. "Sallie, I think we should wait and receive Mr. Samms' instructions on what he wants us to do. He might not appreciate—"

"Oh, bosh." Sallie waved Tressa's concerns away. "Any man who lives alone'll appreciate havin' his house cleaned. Now . . ." She tapped her lips, looking back and forth between two doors that stood at the far end of the main room. "Which of those rooms do ye suppose will have paper?"

Without waiting for Tressa's reply, she skipped to the one on the right and swung it wide. Tressa got a peek of two single-sized beds draped with bright quilts and a tall four-drawer chest before Sallie snapped the door closed again.

"No desk in there," Sallie chirped and turned toward the second door.

Tressa bolted forward and closed her hand over the doorknob.

"Sallie, we shouldn't go into these rooms until Mr. Samms has given us permission to do so. Would we want someone barging into our room at Mrs. Wyatt's house and rummaging through our things?"

Sallie bit down on her lower lip, her brow furrowed with indecision. Finally, she sighed. "All right, Tressa, I suppose you're right. I'd not be pleased to have someone diggin' in my bureau drawers without me knowin'."

Tressa's breath whooshed out in relief.

"So we'll wait for the men to come in for lunch, an' we'll find out then what duties Mr. Samms would have us be performin'."

"Good." Tressa gave Sallie a gentle push in the direction of the kitchen. "Go stir that stew. I'm going to put the horses in the corral. When I get back, I'll set the table for lunch."

Tressa led the horses, one at a time, to the corral and released them to spend the day lazing in the sun. Then she hurried back to the house. When she entered, she found Sallie standing in the middle of the main room with a secretive smile on her face.

"Tressa, you'll never guess what I found."

Trepidation formed a stone in Tressa's stomach when she saw the second door standing wide open. "Sallie, did you—"

"Yes, I did. An' look!" She thrust out her hand and unfolded her fingers to reveal a delicate gold frame.

The tiny, filigreed frame drew Tressa like a magnet. She leaned close. A beautiful woman peered up at Tressa from an amazingly detailed portrait.

"Ain't she a pretty one?" Sallie rubbed her thumb along the edge of the frame. "Makes me wonder who she is, an' if she's the reason Mr. Samms is so standoffish."

Jolting upright, Tressa glared at Sallie. "Shame on you! You shouldn't have gone rummaging through his things. This might very well be a portrait of his mother. Put it back, Sallie, at once!"

Sallie closed her fist over the picture and put her nose in the air.

"Well, ye needn't turn so high-an'-mighty. Ye enjoyed lookin' at it, too." She flounced through the doorway. Tressa remained rooted in the middle of the floor, deliberately avoiding so much as a glance into the bedroom. A moment later Sallie emerged and closed the door behind her. "There now, it's safely back in the top drawer of his highboy."

Tressa gawked at Sallie in dismay. "You opened his highboy?" Tressa remembered her father keeping his most intimate items in the highest drawer of his own highboy.

"I wanted paper." Sallie placed her fingertips against her bodice in a gesture of innocence. Then an impish grin creased her face, and she grabbed Tressa's wrist. "Aren't ye curious now who she is?"

"Let's get lunch ready." Tressa stomped toward the kitchen. Although she refused to respond to Sallie, her traitorous heart mulled the question all afternoon, and her inability to set the image aside provided the answer. The curiosity nearly turned her inside out. Who was the lovely woman in the little frame?

16

The aroma of cinnamon and apples greeted Abel's nose when he stepped into the house Friday evening. In response, his stomach turned a flip of desire. A glance around the living area showed throw rugs neatly placed, all wood surfaces gleaming with a fresh polish, and the pillows on the parlor set fluffed and ready for a man to sit down and relax. A feeling of satisfaction wrapped itself around him. What a difference a woman made in a house—she turned a dwelling into a *home*.

He then gave himself a mental kick, dislodging the thought. He and the men had gotten along well enough before the women came; they'd manage just fine without them again, too.

Ethan stopped beside Cole, lifted his chin, and sniffed. A smile broke across his square face. "Mmm, betcha the gals made apple pie for dessert. Smells just like Ma's used to." Suddenly his cheerful countenance crumbled. "But this's the last day Miss Tressa an' Miss Sallie'll be comin', ain't it?"

An unexpected knot of regret formed in Abel's throat. He swallowed hard and offered a brusque nod. " 'Fraid so. Our arrangement was for one week."

Ethan shook his head, sending a sorrowful look over his shoulder at Cole and Vince. "Sure will miss 'em. Been real good havin' a hot meal waitin' every mornin', noon, an' evenin'."

"An' laundry done up an' folded at the foot of my bed," Cole added.

Vince gave Ethan's shoulder a slap. "Now, son, you knew this was a temporary setup meant to give them gals a little practice at housekeepin'. They never intended to *stay*."

"But, Pa, don't you wish they could?" Ethan's youthful voice belied his age. He turned a pleading look at Abel. "Don't you, Abel?"

Abel chewed the inside of his lip. Truthfully, the past week had been the most peaceful in months. Not one head of cattle had disappeared. Having all four of the men working the grounds had apparently kept the thieves at bay. He also had come to appreciate the ready meals, the fresh laundry, and the spit-shined house. Not so much as a speck of dust lurked in the corners of the rooms, and the kitchen hadn't been so clean since Ma was alive. No one could deny that Aunt Hattie had trained the girls well. Even the fancy one masquerading in commoner's clothing had pulled her weight. But he wouldn't admit all that to his men.

"As Vince said, they only planned to be here for a week. No point in wishin' for what can't be." He maintained a terse tone that went against his inner feelings.

"Wouldn't hafta be only one week if one of us was to—"

Abel talked over the end of Ethan's comment. "So let's just enjoy this last meal tonight, an' next week we'll get back to our old routine."

Ethan and Cole exchanged disgruntled looks but sauntered to the neatly set table with no further protests. Just as Abel and Vince pulled out their chairs, Miss Sallie bustled around the corner with a bowl of steaming mashed squash in her hands. She swept a quick glance across the men.

"Did ye get your hands good an' clean at the wash bucket?"

Cole groaned. "Aw, Miss Sallie, we been workin' hard an' we're hungry. We'll wash after we eat."

Miss Sallie shook her head, dislodging several corkscrews of red hair from her bun. "No, sir, ye wash an' *then* ye eat. Won't be havin' dirty hands at me table."

Abel raised one eyebrow. Since when had his ma's dining room table become Sallie's?

"Miss Tressa's got the full bucket, soap, an' clean towels waitin' on the back stoop. Just march yourselves out there an' clean up good. Then we'll be puttin' your supper on the table."

Grumbling, Cole and Ethan clumped through the kitchen doorway. Vince held up his palms to Sallie. "Already did my washin' in the barn 'fore I come in."

Sallie placed the bowl on the table and flashed a quick grin at the old cowboy. "Ye're a good man, Mr. Rylin." Sallie turned to Abel. "An' did ye wash in the barn, too, Mr. Samms?"

Abel stared at her in surprise. "Why, no—no, I didn't."

"Then take yourself out an' wash," she chided. Grabbing her skirts, she whirled toward the kitchen doorway. "By the time ye're finished, Tressa an' me'll have the food on the table." She shot a grin over her shoulder. "Tressa made apple dumplin's for dessert—ye won't be wantin' to miss out on them, now." She disappeared around the corner.

Vince chuckled. "That Miss Sallie—she's a spirited one. Life'd never be dull with *her* around."

Abel nodded slowly in reply, but his thoughts skipped past Vince's comment to his strange reaction to Sallie's mention of Tressa's name. A bolt of lightning had fired from his scalp to his toes.

Over the past week, he'd done his best to keep his distance from the women working in his house. He'd succeeded, too, except for two encounters. Once he'd come in to retrieve a fresh pair of pants after being bumped into a mud puddle by his ornery horse, and he'd caught Tressa stripping the sheets from his bed. She'd gone scuttling out the door with her face all pink, but seeing her in the room where he slept was enough to send her drifting through his dreams for the next two nights.

Then yesterday he'd come around the barn to find her nose-to-nose with the Appaloosa she rode. He feared the image—her hands cupping the beast's jaws, her cheek resting against the horse's muzzle—would be burned into his memory forever. He couldn't help but compare Tressa's obvious ease with the big animal to a recollection of Amanda squealing and ducking from his horse's friendly snuffle on her neck.

As much as he wanted to continue thinking of Tressa as an upper-class girl—too sophisticated and spoiled to survive on the plains—the encounter by the barn had forced him to look at her in a different light.

"So, you think you might consider askin' that Miss Sallie to . . . stay around?"

Abel gave a start at Vince's voice. "No." The denial came out too loudly. Vince smirked. But before Abel could say anything else, Ethan and Cole charged into the room, followed by Sallie, who carried a platter of fried steaks. She scowled across the table at him.

"Haven't ye gone to wash your hands yet, Mr. Samms? Ye best be hurryin'—Tressa's dishin' up the stewed tomatoes, an' then it'll be time to eat."

Although the water bucket waited outside the back door, Abel decided to leave through the front door. That way he wouldn't have to pass through the kitchen and risk seeing Tressa at his ma's stove, looking as though she belonged. He didn't need any more pictures to carry in his head.

❧

"Tressa, might I be makin' a confession?"

Tressa shifted her gaze from a hawk circling high overhead to Sallie. Since leaving the Lazy S, they'd ridden in silence, the whispering wind, distant lowing of cattle, and call of birds providing the only intrusions. At Sallie's serious question, Tressa crinkled her brow. "What is it, Sallie?"

"I'm feelin' rather sad." Sallie puckered her lips, her eyes downcast. "I wasn't ready to be done at the Lazy S."

Tressa offered a sympathetic nod. Although she wouldn't admit it to Sallie, her heart felt heavy, too. The week of seeing to the needs of Abel Samms and his ranch hands hadn't been unpleasant. Despite her earlier misgivings, she'd found the men appreciative of all the women provided, and she'd discovered an element of contentment in seeing to their needs.

Thinking back to her years living with Aunt Gretchen and Uncle Leo, she couldn't recall the household servants behaving as though they enjoyed serving. In fact, she'd frequently heard them grumble about their endless responsibilities. Yet essentially she and Sallie had acted as servants in Abel Samms' home. So why had the experience been rewarding rather than a burden?

"Know what I'm goin' to miss the most?" Sallie's pensive voice cut into Tressa's thoughts again. "Seein' Cole dig into his plate while smilin' so big his whole face lit up." She chuckled, the sound affectionate. "He's a man who enjoys eatin' for sure."

Tressa smiled. Yes, Cole wasn't bashful about his enjoyment of their cooking. None of the men had voiced a single complaint about anything placed on the table and were especially fond of the pastries Mrs. Wyatt had taught Tressa to bake.

"An' ye know, I'm thinkin' he might be missin' me, too." Sallie flitted a sidelong glance at Tressa before looking forward. Her cheeks streaked with pink, masking the spattering of copper-colored freckles. "Him an' me . . . we had a couple of moments alone, an' . . ."

Tressa spun on the saddle, nearly upsetting her seat. She clutched the saddle horn as the horse shifted nervously beneath her. Mrs. Wyatt had cautioned them about spending time alone with any of the men. The day Abel had walked in while she was removing the sheets from his bed, she'd nearly tripped over herself trying to escape, lest she give Sallie the mistaken idea she'd intended to steal a moment of time with him.

"Sallie, you spent time *alone* with Cole?"

Sallie nodded, her blush increasing to a fiery red that matched her flame-colored hair. "Yes. An' once in the barn, when I was puttin' away the horses, Cole . . . he kissed me." She whispered the last words. "An' I didn't go runnin' in fear." Her eyes widened in wonder as she faced Tressa. "I never thought I'd be able to—" She clamped her mouth closed and looked down at her thumbs, which twitched on the horse's reins. "It was a precious moment to me, Tressa, for many reasons."

Tressa carefully processed Sallie's words. Her heart pounded as she realized the hidden meaning behind the whispered admission. Perhaps living with Aunt Gretchen and Uncle Leo wasn't the worst plight that could befall a person.

Giving the horse's reins a gentle tug to slow his pace, Tressa looked at Sallie. "So if Cole were to ask Mrs. Wyatt for permission to court you, would you be agreeable?"

Sallie offered a shy smile. "I would be agreeable." Then she sighed, shaking her head. "But he won't be askin'. Not that he doesn't like me—he already told me he does—but he's not a rancher, just a ranch hand. He has no place of his own. He shares a bunkhouse with Mr. Rylin an' his son. Where would he keep a wife?" Another heavy sigh told of Sallie's disappointment. "It's best we aren't at the Samms' place anymore. Bein' around Cole, knowin' we can't ever be together, would be too hard. For him . . . an' for me."

Tressa pondered the unfairness of the situation as she and Sallie continued plodding toward the Flying W. If a person genuinely cared for another, then something so simple as a dwelling place shouldn't stand in the way. Tressa dared to offer a promise. "Tonight, when the others have gone on to bed, I'll talk with Mrs. Wyatt. Surely she can find a way for things to work out between you and Cole." After all the difficulties Sallie had faced prior to coming to Kansas, she deserved the chance to capture happiness with Cole, if she so desired.

"Aw, I'd thank ye, Tressa, if you'd be doin' that for me." A grin twitched her cheek. "An' what of ye, Tressa? Will ye be missin' Mr. Samms or the young Mr. Rylin?"

Tressa turned a frown on Sallie. "And why, pray tell, should I miss them?"

Sallie clicked her tongue against her teeth. "Oh, you're not foolin' me with that monstrous scowl. Do ye think I've not got eyes in me head?" She tapped her forehead. "I saw the way the men watched ye, an' I saw how careful ye were to avoid lookin' at 'em."

Tressa jerked her face forward, refusing to meet Sallie's teasing expression. Sallie's assessment wasn't incorrect—she had kept her focus on working rather than fraternizing. It had proved amazingly simple with Mr. Samms, as he seemed as determined as she to avoid contact. But Ethan Rylin had openly sought snatches of time with her, moseying by the garden when she was picking vegetables or appearing in the barn when she was preparing to saddle her horse. She had recognized his ploys and managed to remain kind but cool in the face of his attentiveness, accepting his assistance without encouraging him to pamper her.

Raising her chin, she offered a tart rejoinder. "I merely attempted to remain committed to the tasks at hand rather than allowing one of the men to distract me from my duties."

To Tressa's aggravation, Sallie burst out laughing. "Ah, Tressa, ye're such a funny one, drawin' on that fancy talk when ye're rattled. It's a sure giveaway that I've struck a sore spot."

Tressa drew in a sharp breath. Would she ever learn to speak like a working-class girl? The last time she'd spouted in such a manner, she had sent Abel Samms ducking for cover as if she'd hurled rotten apples at him. Her heart ached, remembering how his tender attention had changed to apprehensive avoidance. If she wasn't careful, she would lose her friendship with Sallie.

Tressa offered Sallie a weak smile. "I'm sorry, Sallie. I didn't mean to be haughty. Will you forgive me?"

Sallie waved her hand in dismissal. "Oh now, don't be apologizin'. I provoked ye, for sure, an' deserved the sharp side of your tongue. I was just hopin' that maybe ye *would* be missin' one of them."

"Why?"

Sallie's grin turned mischievous. "Well, if ye were to take up with Ethan Rylin an' I took up with Cole Jacobs, then we could keep workin' together at the ranch. It's a mite easier to share the cookin' an' cleanin' chores rather than handlin' it all alone, y'know."

Tressa agreed that Sallie's plan to share the chores sounded pleasing. She had enjoyed her week working with Sallie. "But you said you couldn't take up with Cole because—"

"I know what I said, an' it hasn't changed. It isn't to be. But . . ." Sallie sighed, her expression becoming wistful. "A girl can hope, can't she? Sometimes all a person has to hold on to is hope."

A snippet from Brother Connor's sermon two Sundays ago drifted through Tressa's mind. She frowned, trying to recall the exact wording, but it escaped her. Something about placing one's hope in the Lord to discover renewed strength. She would ask Mrs. Wyatt about the reference when she visited with her about Sallie. "There's nothing wrong with hoping things will work out between you and Cole." And was there anything wrong with her hoping Abel Samms might set aside his aversion to her company? She pushed that fleeting thought aside.

"Then I'll keep hopin'. An' I'll be hopin' for ye to find favor with Ethan Rylin, for I'm certain he'd be willin' to court ye if he thought you'd be interested. Maybe we could live in the bunkhouse with the two of them an' old Mr. Rylin could move into the ranch house with Mr. Samms. There's the two sleepin' rooms, an' Mr. Samms has the house all to himself."

Tressa laughed at Sallie's plan. "You have it all worked out, don't you?"

"Oh, I'm a fine one for dreamin', Tressa." Sallie aimed her wistful gaze at the sky. "Hopin' an' dreamin' . . . I been doin' it for years. But only since I came here did I dare believe some of the dreams might come true."

They topped the final rise that led to Mrs. Wyatt's ranch, and the horses bobbed their heads, snorting in impatience when the ranch came into view. Tressa gave her horse its head and it lunged forward, breaking into a canter that forced her to clamp her knees against the saddle's soft leather fenders and hold tight to the horn to avoid being bounced from the seat. The pounding of hooves behind her let her know Sallie's horse was just as eager to reach the barn.

She and Sallie reined in outside the barn's opening, and one of Mrs. Wyatt's hired hands emerged from the structure. He tipped his hat back on his head. "Climb on down an' head to the house. I'll take care of the horses for you."

Tressa swung down, but she held tight to the reins. "Thank you, sir, but it's our job to see to the horses' needs."

Sallie kept her fist wrapped around her horse's reins, too.

The man laughed, slapping his leg with his open hand. "An' that's just what Miz Wyatt told me you'd say. But she said for you to come on up to the house. Somethin' she needs to discuss with you right quick. So go on now an' let me care for the horses."

Tressa sent Sallie a puzzled look, which Sallie returned. Reluctantly, they handed the reins to the waiting cowboy and turned toward the house. Sallie's face seemed pale in the fading light. "Do ye suppose we've done somethin' wrong?"

Tressa shrugged. "If we have, we'll know soon enough."

Sallie caught Tressa's hand. "Let's hurry. If it's good news waitin', I'll want to be hearin' it quick. An' if it's bad news waitin', I'll want to be gettin' it over quick."

Tressa couldn't argue with Sallie's logic. Catching her skirt with her free hand, she broke into a trot.

17

"I been thinkin' . . ." Hattie let her gaze drift around the parlor and touch each girl in turn. "Even though I didn't intend to host our courtin' party until late August, you gals've made quicker progress than I expected. You all can be real proud o' yourselves." A lump formed in Hattie's throat, making her voice come out gruff. She'd miss these girls when they went on to their new homes. "Truth is, I think you're ready to start bein' sparked by fellas."

A variety of expressions danced on the girls' faces—everything from elation to out-and-out fear. Hattie pressed on. "If we move the party up closer, then you'll have more time to get acquainted with the single men o' the community. My next group o' students won't be arrivin' until after Christmas, which'll give you a good five months to make your matches an' plan your weddin's." Slapping her palms on her thighs, Hattie leaned back in the chair. "So, what do you gals have to say?"

Luella shrugged one shoulder. "It makes no difference to me." She flashed a smirk. "My choice is already made, so I won't even need to attend the courtin' party."

"We'll *all* be attendin' the party." Hattie gave Luella a stern look. "There'll be no matchin' done without my consent. The agreement you signed before comin' here clearly outlined how the matches are made, an' I haven't agreed to any just yet."

Luella's jaw dropped. "But *I've* made an agreement with—"

Hattie raised her brows, and Luella fell silent. That Luella was as headstrong as a mule and twice as ornery. She needed to have a firm chat with the girl, but she wouldn't do any arguing in front of the others. "We can talk about it later. Right now we're discussin' the party." Rubbing her palms together, she offered a smile. "I was thinkin' maybe the Saturday after the fourth o' July."

Sallie's green eyes flew wide. "Why, that's less than two weeks away!"

"Think it's too quick?" Hattie paused, giving the girls time to voice their thoughts. But they sat as quiet as scarecrows in a garden, so she filled the silence. "Folks'll still be in a celebratin' mood, an' the watermelons'll be ripe for pickin'. Seems like a fine time to host a party, if you gals are up to the work it'll take to get all the food ready."

Sallie, crowded between Tressa and Luella on the sofa, sat up straight. Her freckles fairly glowed. "I'm game." She nudged Tressa with her elbow. "An' what about ye, Tressa? Are ye ready to be courted?"

The teasing grin on Sallie's face coupled with Tressa's embarrassed flush made Hattie wonder what had transpired at the Lazy S over the past week. Could it be Abel had finally let down his guard and allowed his heart to open?

Tressa sent a nervous glance at Hattie and nibbled her lip before dropping her gaze. Clearly the idea of courting scared the bashful girl more than a mite. Hattie's resolve wavered. She didn't want these girls to think she was throwing them out of the nest before their feathers were developed enough to let them fly. "We can wait until August if you'd rather. Just means the courtin' time'll be shortened up. Still doable. It's up to you girls." A long silence followed.

Impatience stirred in Hattie's breast. She gave the little marble-topped table next to her chair a smack. "Come on now, speak up! If you're gonna be ranchers' wives, you're gonna have to be strong. Them men'll run roughshod over ya if you don't open your mouths an' speak." She pointed at Mabelle. "Now or later, missy?"

Mabelle gulped twice, glanced at Paralee, who sat with her eyes wide and her lips pinched up tighter than the strings on a miser's purse, and then barked out one word: "Now." She clamped both hands over her mouth and giggled hysterically behind her palms.

Hattie resisted rolling her eyes. "Paralee?"

Paralee's cheeks twitched as if a bumblebee fought for release from her mouth. "I . . . I reckon now is . . . fine." The last word came out on a strangled yelp.

"All right, now we're gettin' somewhere." Hattie heaved a sigh. "Sallie, Mabelle, an' Paralee are for doin' the courtin' party ahead o' the original plan." She glanced at Luella and decided not to ask her opinion. That gal would leap out of a window into a man's arms if Hattie let her. She turned her attention to Tressa. "Tressa, what're you thinkin'?"

Tressa's face faded from rosy pink to white. "I shall bow to whatever decision you make, Mrs. Wyatt."

Hattie frowned. That highbrow talk only came out when the girl was upset. "Now, Tressa, didn't I just say ya gotta learn to speak your own mind? Just 'cause the others've agreed don't mean you need to get swept along like a twig in a creek. If you have strong feelin's in another direction, now's the time to say so. This's gonna be an all-or-nothin' proposition. I don't want nobody bein' pushed into courtin' until she's ready."

Every other girl seemed to suck in air and hold it. Hattie leaned her elbows on her knees and looked steadily into Tressa's pale blue eyes. "You be honest with me now, missy. You ready to start courtin' or would'ja rather wait? Nobody'll hold it against you if you need more time." She flashed a warning look around the room before settling her gaze on Tressa again. "No matter what, there'll be courtin', so nobody'll lose out by waitin'. I want to do what's best for *all* of you."

Tressa glaced at Sallie. She pulled in her bottom lip for a moment. "If I'm to be completely truthful with you, Mrs. Wyatt, this past week proved quite enlightening. I do feel adequately prepared to take on the responsibilities of housekeeping. I am not as certain I'm ready to be a wife, in every s-sense of the word."

The slight stutter combined with her high-falutin' talk communicated the source of the girl's misgivings. Hattie offered an assuring smile. "Now, missy, that part'll come natural when you've found a fella that makes your heart go a-patterin' in your chest. You'll know when you're bein' courted by the right man."

Tressa's trembling smile offered a silent thank-you.

Hattie sighed, closing her eyes for a moment. Memories of her years with Jed—and these lonely ones without him—crowded her mind, bringing a rush of mingled joy and sadness. She opened her eyes, surprised to find the girls' images wavering through a veil of tears. "Even before you gals came, I was prayin' for each o' you an' the man who'd be claimin' you. I've been askin' God to pave the way for you to find good mates. Marriage is the most beautiful union in the world when it has God's blessin'."

She blinked, whisking away the moisture that clouded her vision. "Now that you all have the skills you need to see to a house an' garden an' livestock, all that's left is findin' a man—one who'll cherish you, an' who you can cherish in return."

Mabelle's chest heaved with a mighty sigh. "That's bound to be harder than ropin' a calf."

Hattie snorted with laughter. "Oh, now, missy, nothin's too hard for the good Lord in heaven. An' He's got the perfect husband all picked out for each o' you. You just gotta listen to your heart an' follow His lead. God always plans the best for His children."

☙

Tressa looked hard into Mrs. Wyatt's sincere, honest face, and a longing the likes of which she'd never before experienced caught in her breastbone and held with an intensity that prevented her from drawing a breath. Her pulse raced, just as Mrs. Wyatt had indicated would happen when she met the right man to be her husband, yet no man was nearby. So what was the source of the strange ache in the center of her heart?

Mrs. Wyatt clapped her thick palms together and rose. "Well, girls, now that our decision's been made, we got work to do. Cakes an' pies to bake, an' meat to smoke—I'm thinkin' a brisket'll make good party food. An' maybe—"

"Aunt Hattie." Luella bounced to her feet, her smile conniving. "Could we do something fun at the party? Each of us—" she gestured to the girls, her eyebrows rising superciliously when she looked across at Tressa—"make a dinner basket, and the men can bid for the pleasure of eating with us."

"You mean a box social?" Mrs. Wyatt's brows beetled together.

"That's right." Luella toyed with a curling strand of hair at her temple. "Don't you think the men would enjoy a little competition?"

"But then they'd have to pay for their dinner." Mabelle cast a worried look at Paralee. "I don't know that any man would pay to eat with me."

"Now, that's a silly thing to say, Mabelle." Mrs. Wyatt shook her index finger at Mabelle, then swung to face Luella. "An' this isn't supposed to be a money-makin' party. It's a get-acquainted social."

"But what would be the harm?" Luella held her hands outward. "I think it would be great fun for each of us to stand in front of the crowd with a gaily decorated basket heaping with food and let the men battle for who gets the privilege of lunch with that girl." Luella's eyes gleamed.

"The harm would be bringin' in money when this isn't supposed to cost the men anything more than their time." Mrs. Wyatt frowned. Although the woman was one of the most uncomplaining people Tressa had ever met, it appeared Mrs. Wyatt's patience was nearly spent with Luella.

"Oh!" Mabelle jumped up, her hands clasped beneath her chin. "Aunt Hattie, remember in church two Sundays ago when Brother Connor said the congregation needed money to fix the roof on the church building? He asked for a special offering."

"Yes, I recall the request." Mrs. Wyatt tapped her chin with her finger. "Are you thinkin' we could turn the men's biddin' money over to the church for a new roof?"

"That's perfect, Mabelle!" Luella flung her arm around Mabelle's shoulders, and the shorter girl grinned with delight. "Don't you think so, too, Aunt Hattie?"

Tressa's head spun. Stand in front of the crowd with a basket in her arms and allow men to call out bids? Why, prairie or not, she could never be so brazen as to offer herself in such an unsophisticated manner. She opened her mouth to voice her protest, but Mrs. Wyatt cut in.

"I think it's a fine idea to want to raise money for the church roof, but that standin' up an' auctionin' off yourselves . . ." She shook her head. "I'm not keen on that."

"Oh, but, Aunt Hattie—"

Mrs. Wyatt gave Luella a scowl that stilled her protest. "Now, if you want to decorate box lunches an' have the men bid on the lunch without knowin' who made it, that's a different thing altogether. Then it's kind of a luck-o'-the-draw sort of thing, an' the men might find it amusin'."

"But what if a man who holds no interest in us wins our basket?" Paralee wrung her hands, her brow wrinkled in concern.

"There'll be opportunities to mingle with all the men. After all, the party'll include dancin'—I'm sure Mr. Hammond's cook will be willin' to bring his fiddle an' play some tunes—an' we'll plan some games an' whatnot, too."

Mrs. Wyatt's response seemed to satisfy Paralee because the girl relaxed in her chair and shot a relieved look at Mabelle.

"Now, it's late," Mrs. Wyatt said sternly, "an' as I've already said, we got lots o' work to do—our regular chores plus preparin' for this party. So all of you on up to bed. Scoot." She shooed the girls toward the staircase.

Tressa, out of habit, fell to the rear of the group. As she stepped onto the first riser, she remembered her plan to discuss Sallie's situation with Mrs. Wyatt. She spun around. "Mrs. Wyatt, may I ask you a question?"

"Go ahead, but make it quick. I'm about ready to topple, I'm so tired." The older woman yawned noisily, then grinned. "This week's plumb wore me out. I got so used to you girls doin' all the work, I almost forgot how to take care o' my own kitchen an' garden!"

Tressa couldn't imagine the busy, knowledgeable woman ever slowing down. "I wondered . . . which men from the community will be welcome at the party? Only ranch owners, or any single man interested in taking a wife?"

The woman's eyes narrowed speculatively. "You got a certain young man weighin' heavy on your thoughts?"

"Yes, ma'am. You see—"

"Well, missy, I plan on invitin' everybody in Barnett an' the surroundin' area—families an' single men from eighteen to eighty. They're all welcome to come an' spend time gettin' to know you gals better, since it's always good to know one's neighbors, but only the men who're able to provide for a wife will be allowed to do any courtin'."

Tressa envisioned Sallie as she'd appeared earlier in the evening, her face bright with hope. Cole, although willing, surely didn't meet Mrs. Wyatt's stipulation of being able to provide for a wife. Tressa hung her head. "I see. . . ."

Mrs. Wyatt cupped Tressa's chin, lifting her head. "My responsibility is to make sure you girls are well cared for. I brought you all the way out here. Can't put you in a situation where you'll be lackin', or you're no better off than you were in New York. You understand, don't you, Tressa?"

Tressa swallowed hard. How her heart ached for Sallie and Cole. If only Cole had his own ranch. . . . "Yes, ma'am, I understand."

The older woman smiled. "Good. But don't you be worryin'. There're plenty of good men with successful ranches who are more'n able to take care of a wife. So none o' you will be left wantin'."

Tressa nodded, but she couldn't force her lips into a smile.

Mrs. Wyatt gave Tressa's cheek a pat. "An' remember, I've been prayin'. I'm trustin' God to open the right man's heart to each o' you."

The odd desire that had pressed at Tressa's chest earlier returned, making her gasp. Mrs. Wyatt's brow immediately creased. "Tressa? What is it, darlin'?"

Tressa caught Mrs. Wyatt's hands. "Ma'am, how can you be so certain that God wants what is best for us?" Long-buried memories of her father reading from a big black book tried to surface, but so much time had passed, the remembrance was like a wisp of smoke— impossible to grasp.

Mrs. Wyatt chuckled. "Why, I know because I've witnessed His goodness again an' again. He an' me . . . we've been on a first-name basis, you might say, ever since I was a young girl. I trust Him."

Tressa considered her parents' deaths, the lonely years with her aunt and uncle, the rejection of the other girls at the ranch. "But not everything that happens is good."

Mrs. Wyatt pursed her lips for a moment, and when she spoke, her low, husky voice wavered with emotion. "We can't really define good, can we, Tressa? Good for one person might be ruination for another. The problem with our human eyes is that we can only see the right now. But God? He sees around the corner, over the hill, and clean to the horizon. He knows what's comin', an' He knows what we need to be prepared for what's comin'. So sometimes those things we face that we don't understand—the things we think of as bad—are really for our good down the line. Does that make sense to you, Tressa?"

She shook her head, releasing a rueful laugh. "No, ma'am, it really doesn't."

Mrs. Wyatt squeezed Tressa's hands and released them. "Someday it will. You just gotta trust. Even when you don't understand, you still gotta trust. That's called faith, an' it'll always carry you through."

After wishing Mrs. Wyatt a good-night, Tressa climbed the stairs and crept into her room. Sallie was already asleep, her red curls tumbling across her pillow and her face bearing a slight smile. Was she dreaming of the kiss she had shared with Cole in Abel Samms' barn? Tressa's heart ached anew at the realization that Cole wouldn't be allowed to court Sallie.

"There is no hope for you, Sallie. Not with Cole." Tressa whispered the words into the quiet room. Then she shifted to gaze out toward the pale, star-dotted sky. Mrs. Wyatt had indicated God knew what was best. What might God deem best for Sallie?

She tiptoed to the window and rested her fingertips against the smooth glass. "God, do You have something good waiting for me, too?"

18

Tressa awakened to a dark room, lit only by pale moonlight. Through the lace-covered window, she could see stars twinkling like diamonds in a black velvet sky. Although the dark sky should have lured her back to sleep, thoughts of the upcoming courting party—and all the work Mrs. Wyatt had said must be done in preparation for it—prevented her from relaxing. The older woman had looked so tired last night. Perhaps Tressa could prepare breakfast and allow her benefactor a few extra minutes of rest.

She slipped from her bed and dressed in the murky gray, cringing against the groan of the bureau drawer and the creak of the floorboards. With her hairbrush in hand, she tiptoed downstairs, where she lit a lantern and brushed her long tresses into a neat tail.

A plaintive meow sounded from the pantry. With a smile, Tressa opened the door, and Isabella dashed out, tail straight up and whiskers splayed in every direction. With a little cry of delight, Tressa scooped the cat into her arms. Isabella alternately purred and meowed a funny little *mrrp* that sounded more like the chirp of a bird, bumping her head against Tressa's chin. Tressa laughed softly in response.

"Yes, I missed you, too. I didn't see you at all last week! How are you, kitty?"

The purring increased in volume, and Isabella worked her paws against Tressa's shoulder. Being so enthusiastically greeted filled Tressa with warmth. Pressing her face into the cat's soft ruff, she released a sigh. "Oh, Izzy-B, it will be very hard to leave the ranch when Mrs. Wyatt finds my match. I don't wish to leave you behind. . . ."

Carrying the cat, she crossed to the table and sat. Isabella perched on Tressa's lap, her golden eyes peering into Tressa's face as if inviting her to share her thoughts. Tressa wound her fingers through the cat's warm fur as she replayed Mrs. Wyatt's assurance that God had good plans for His children. A fear stabbed fiercely in the center of her chest, and her hands stilled on Isabella's neck.

"What if . . . what if God has no plans for me because I . . . I'm not one of His children?"

Tressa hugged the cat close, her heart pounding. "How can one know for sure that she belongs to Him?"

A rustle at the kitchen door startled Tressa, and Isabella wriggled from her grasp to dart beneath the table. Mrs. Wyatt shuffled around the corner in her nightgown, her scraggly gray hair sticking out around her face. Isabella scampered out and wove around the woman's feet. Mrs. Wyatt leaned down and gave the cat a stroke before facing Tressa.

"Land o' mercy, girl, you gave me a fright. Heard somebody talkin' down here an' couldn't figure who'd be wanderin' the house at this hour." Her brow crinkled. "You all right? Feelin' poorly? I can get the tonic from the medicine box if you need it."

Tressa did feel sick, but she knew the kind of illness that plagued her—a heart sickness—wouldn't be cured by a tonic from a bottle. Rising, she held out her hands to Mrs. Wyatt. "I didn't mean to wake you, but since you're up, would you . . . would you please tell me how one can be certain she is a child of God?"

Mrs. Wyatt gaped at Tressa with such a look of astonishment that Tressa shrank back in embarrassment. Clasping her hands against her ribs, Tressa ducked her head. "I'm sorry, ma'am. I shouldn't be so bold."

Mrs. Wyatt bustled forward and took Tressa's hands. She squeezed hard, tears glittering in her faded eyes. "Oh, Tressa-darlin', I need to apologize to you. No, you shouldn't *need* to be so bold. I should've explained this to you long ago. I knew your people hadn't . . ." Her voice caught, and she gave Tressa a little push toward the table. "You sit down. I'm gonna fetch my Bible, an' you an' me'll have us a serious talk."

For the next half hour, Mrs. Wyatt shared passages of Scripture with Tressa, beginning in Isaiah where God promised to send a Messiah to save the people from their sins and ending in Luke with the death and resurrection of Jesus. Her fervent tone, the tears that continued to wink in her eyes, communicated the sincerity and depth of her beliefs. Tressa battled tears as the knowledge that God loved her enough to allow His own son to die as a sacrifice for her wrongdoings took root in her heart.

"So you see, Tressa, to become a child of God, you just need to accept what Jesus did. Ask Him to be *your* Savior. An' from that day forward, you'll be one o' His—a true child of God." Mrs. Wyatt closed the Bible and rested her palms on the worn black cover. Her gaze bored into Tressa's, her expression serious. "Is that what you're wantin' to do, child?"

A lump in her throat prevented Tressa from speaking, but she nodded eagerly. Everything within her strained toward the peace and assurance of belonging to God.

"Then talk to God, Tressa. Tell Him you're wantin' His Son to be your Savior."

Tressa linked her fingers together and pressed her knuckles to the underside of her chin. Eyes tightly closed, she whispered, "God, I . . . I want You to be my Father. I thank You for sending Jesus, and I ask that He wash away my sins, just like Mrs. Wyatt read in Your book." A tingling warmth built from the center of Tressa's chest outward, filling her with a joy beyond anything she'd ever known before. She identified the source of the joy: love—a deep, pure love that felt like it would be a part of her until her last days.

Tears escaped from behind her closed lids, and a smile broke across her face. "Thank You, God, for this wonderful gift. Thank You for making me Your child. Thank You for loving me. . . . Thank You. . . ." Her praises continued while warm tears ran down her cheeks and across the backs of her hands. When she finally opened her eyes, tiny fingers of sunlight were slipping through the lace curtains, casting a soft glow on Mrs. Wyatt's beaming, tear-stained face. Tressa released a giggle. "You look like an angel!"

Mrs. Wyatt blasted a guffaw and smoothed down her rumpled hair. "Lands, girl, what a thing to say."

Swallowing a bubble of laughter, Tressa reached out and embraced the older woman. She pressed her wet cheek to Mrs. Wyatt's. "Thank you for telling me about God. I feel loved again now, thanks to you."

Rough hands patted Tressa's back. "You've always had love, darlin'. You're just recognizin' it now. An' you don't owe me any thanks. That love's open to anyone who asks. So thank God, not me."

Tressa knew she would thank God every day for the rest of her life for the precious gift He'd given her. Her circumstances hadn't changed. She was still the unwanted niece of Leo and Gretchen Neill; she still faced an uncertain future in an unfamiliar land. But somehow the fears and heartache had melted away. In their stead, a glimmer of hope resided. Only God could create such a change.

Tressa offered a shy smile. "But if you hadn't told me how to know Him, I wouldn't be His child. So thank you, too, Aunt Hattie."

The woman beamed. "Ah, Tressa-girl." They shared another hug.

Footsteps sounded overhead, indicating that the other girls were awake. Tressa leaped from the table. "Oh! I came down early to start breakfast, but—"

Aunt Hattie scuttled toward the door, holding her robe closed at the throat. "I'll go get dressed an' then come help you. Just make flapjacks—don't take much time an' they'll fill everybody nicely."

Tressa stayed busy frying flapjacks for nearly an hour. But finally the girls' and ranch hands' bellies were filled, and Aunt Hattie handed out the assignments for the usual Saturday chores and the additional responsibilities of preparing for the courting party. The list went on and on, and Saturday faded in a blur of activity. By the evening, Tressa was almost too tired to climb the stairs, and she fell into bed with a sigh of relief that nighttime had arrived.

Sallie tugged her nightgown over her head and grinned at Tressa. "You look as worn out as an old man's slippers."

Tressa managed a weak laugh at Sallie's analogy, and the other girl blew out the lamp and climbed into the bed. The mattress bounced as Sallie settled herself against the pillow. Tressa closed her eyes, sleep wrapping itself around the fringes of her mind. But then Sallie's voice pulled her from the cocoon of slumber.

"You've been lookin' all day like a cat with a bellyful of cream. Did ye have a talk with Aunt Hattie?"

A smile lifted Tressa's lips as she remembered her quiet moments with Aunt Hattie and the wonderful change that had come into her life. "We had a talk."

"Dare I hope your contented smile means she found a way for me an' Cole to be matched?"

Regret washed away the peace of only seconds ago. Tressa rolled sideways. "Oh, Sallie, I'm so sorry. I should have told you last night, but you were already asleep . . ." She swallowed, seeking words that would offer the least amount of pain. "The only men who will be allowed to court us are those who have established ranches. It . . . it's just as you feared. I'm so sorry."

Seconds ticked by silently. Sallie lay on her back, staring at the ceiling. Although the darkness of the room hid the girl's features from view, Tressa sensed sadness emanating from Sallie, and her heart ached along with her friend's.

After a long while, Sallie emitted a short, humorless chuckle. "Ah, well, I should've known it weren't to be. A girl like me . . . the good breaks don't come."

"Oh, but, Sallie—"

"G'night, Tressa." Sallie rolled over and tugged the sheets high, hiding her face. But the slight vibrations of the mattress spoke of silent tears flowing.

Tressa lay back and closed her eyes. The peace that had held her captive during the day wavered in light of Sallie's deep heartache, but rather than giving in to despair, she closed her eyes and asked her Father to bring comfort to Sallie. She fell asleep, certain God's good plan for Sallie would be revealed.

❧

Abel watched Aunt Hattie charge up the church aisle with her usual arm-swinging pace. She spun to face the waiting congregation with a huge smile. "Well, fellers, the time has come for that courtin' party I promised you. Celebration'll be at my place the ninth o' July."

An excited murmur rolled through the church. Abel sensed Cole and Ethan exchanging grins, but he didn't turn his head to look. Instead, he focused on Aunt Hattie's round, flushed face. She looked tickled as could be. Seeing her stand in front of the church and make her announcement reminded him of the day she'd queried the men on what kind of women they'd choose for marrying. Now, just like then, his stomach rolled in nervousness. Maybe he wouldn't even go to the party. But from the gleeful whispers bouncing from pew to pew behind him, he figured none of the other single men would miss it.

Aunt Hattie continued. "Reckon our springs'll still be twangin' from the big Fourth of July doin's in town, but that'll be all right—make the party more fun. The gals an' me've cooked up somethin' special, too." The excited whispers rose in volume as Aunt Hattie explained auctioning off basket lunches to raise money for the church roof. Her grin wide, she pointed to the men. "You fellas bring your dancin' feet an' full pockets so we can get a good start on that roof fund."

Her smiling face swung to include everyone in the pews. " 'Course you know everyone's invited—party's for the whole county, an' I'm hopin' it'll be a rip-roarer. Ladies, if you want to bring a pie or cake or special dish to add to the table, I won't complain. So plan on bein' at my place on the ninth." She clapped her hands together and gave Brother Connor a nod. "That's it. Thanks for lettin' me have a minute of your time."

The service ended with a rousing rendition of "Praise God From Whom All Blessings Flow." Abel felt certain by the booming bass voices echoing off the rafters the men were already thinking how blessed they'd be if they managed to capture the heart of one of Hattie's girls.

After engaging in their customary greetings, he and his men headed for the wagon. His stomach was growling, but Abel didn't look forward to the cold lunch waiting. He glanced across the churchyard and spotted Aunt Hattie and her girls climbing into her wagon. His mouth watered, remembering the fine meals Miss Tressa and Miss Sallie had placed on his table during their week in his kitchen.

"I'm goin' to that party, an' I'm buyin' Miss Sallie's basket."

Cole's bold declaration matched Abel's thoughts so closely Abel wondered if he'd spoken aloud.

Ethan punched Cole's shoulder. "You buy Miss Sallie's an' I'll buy Miss Tressa's."

Abel prickled at Ethan's comment. He placed his Bible on the wagon seat and then plunked himself beside it. "You fellas have grand ambitions, considering how many men'll be biddin' on those baskets." His voice came out harsher than he'd intended, but he made no effort to gentle it. "Best figure on spendin' a good month's pay to win the privilege of time with either of those girls. The ranch owners'll be biddin' high."

Ethan's brow crunched. "You plan on biddin', Abel?"

Vince folded himself onto the opposite half of the wagon seat and released a snort. "Abel's too smart to squander his money that way. He'll put his dollar in the offering basket in church to contribute 'stead of actin' like a plumb fool an' hollerin' out amounts at a party."

Abel flicked the reins, battling a grin. The grumpiness in Vince's tone made Abel think the old cowboy was wishing he was a few years younger so he could court one of those girls. Abel answered Ethan's question. "I've got no plans to bid, Ethan. I figure the competition'll be stiff—men outnumber gals at least five to one. 'Sides that, Aunt Hattie'll be doin' a mess of cookin', so nobody'll go hungry, whether he bids or not."

"But to get to sit an' eat with one of them gals—'specially Miss Tressa . . ." Ethan whistled through his teeth. "I'd give two month's pay for that honor."

Abel bit down on the end of his tongue. No sense in stomping Ethan's hope, but the man had as much chance as a wax cat in a burning barn to win the bid for Miss Tressa's—or any of the gals'— baskets. The area ranchers would snatch them up before cowhands put one finger in the air. Besides that, Aunt Hattie had made it clear only ranchers would be allowed to court the girls. A cowboy's wage wouldn't support a wife, and Aunt Hattie was set on those girls being well provided for.

They drove the remainder of the distance in silence, Vince dozing on the seat. When they reached the ranch, Vince snuffled and climbed out of the wagon as if his joints had stove up during the ride. Abel had intended to ask Vince to take the wagon to the barn and release the horses, but given the man's stiff gait, he gave the responsibility to Ethan instead.

"Cole, you head on in an' set lunch on the table," Abel directed, swiping a trickle of sweat from his forehead. "Cold beef an' cheese're in the cellar, an' bread's in the breadbox. Open a tin of beans, an' that oughtta be good enough. Lay it all out, an' we'll be in shortly to eat."

Cole slapped his leg with his hat. "Boss, am I gonna have kitchen duty this week?"

Abel propped his fist on his hip. "One of us has to take it, Cole. Food don't find its own way to the table."

"Why can't we have Aunt Hattie send the gals back again this week? Sure was nice, not havin' to cook our dinners."

Ethan trotted to Cole's side, providing a united front. "Sure was. An' it let us all work the cattle, like we're paid to do. I say bring 'em back."

Abel opened his mouth to voice his opinion, but Vince stepped forward, his jaw jutting and his eyes sparking with anger.

"You two're like little kids throwin' a tantrum." He yanked his hat from his head, leaving his sparse, wiry hair standing on end. "Since when do you question Abel when he gives an order? Ethan, I'm ashamed of ya. An' Cole, we been sharin' cookin' duties for more years than you've been on this ranch—ever since Abel's ma took ill an' died. We've all managed just fine without a lady in the house. So stop actin' like a mollycoddled baby an' put lunch on the table, like Abel told ya to do. I'm hungry." When the pair didn't move, he waved his hat at the young cowboys. "I said *git!*"

Cole spun and took off for the house at a trot. At the same time, Ethan swung into the wagon's seat and gave the horses' backs a quick flick with the traces. Vince glared at the wagon as it rolled by, then turned a satisfied grin in Abel's direction.

"There now. That's how you get things done." He plopped his hat back on his head. "Have Ethan bring a sandwich to the bunkhouse for me. I'm gettin' out o' these church duds an' layin' down for a while. Sunday's a day of rest." He ambled toward the bunkhouse without waiting for a reply from Abel.

Abel watched him go, scratching his head. The man's age was bringing out a cranky side. But at least Cole and Ethan had followed his orders. He reckoned he could handle Vince's crustiness as long as it had good results. He started toward the house, but changed course and walked to the branding pen instead.

Resting his elbows on the highest rail, he stared into the empty pen and considered Ethan's comment. The men had been hired as cowboys, not housekeepers. It didn't make much sense to pay them a cowpoke's wage to cook and clean. But there was no other way to make sure the household chores were completed . . . unless they had someone living on the ranch and seeing to those duties.

Another bead of sweat broke loose and rolled down Abel's temple. He turned his face toward the wind to dry the moisture. His gaze swept the pasture beyond the pen, the sight of his grazing cattle reminding him that he hadn't lost one head during the week the girls had taken over the house. Working all the men on the range was his best means of preventing more rustling.

Much as he hated to admit it, it made sense to have someone besides his ranch hands in the kitchen. But he didn't have the funds to pay a housekeeper. Which meant *somebody* needed to take a wife. None of his hired men were eligible, given Aunt Hattie's rules. That only left him.

"Sure wish Pa was here for me to talk to. . . ."

"Wal, I ain't your pa, but—"

Abel spun around.

Vince stood a few feet away. He shuffled forward, glancing left and right, as if embarrassed to intrude. "Saw ya standin' out here, lookin' lost. Figured on checkin' on you."

Although Vince wasn't his father, he was an older man Abel knew and trusted. Surely the older cowboy could offer sound advice. "Maybe you can help me sort somethin' out. . . ."

Vince slung his arms over the top rail and fixed Abel with a steady look. "I'm listenin'."

"Well, I'm wonderin' if Cole an' Ethan are right—" Abel rubbed his nose, suddenly feeling shy—"an' somebody should take a wife."

Vince's brows shot upward. "Only person eligible, accordin' to Hattie, is you." His lips twitched. "You interested?"

Abel swallowed. "Might be."

Vince chuckled. "Well now, Abel, takin' a wife . . . that's a big responsibility. An' a new wife'll be wantin' lots of time. You got it to give?"

Abel stood silently, pondering Vince's question.

The older man gazed across the ground, his voice pensive. "Seems to me you got plenty to handle around here, 'specially with them rustlers targetin' your spread. You really want my advice?"

Abel nodded.

"I'm thinkin' it'd be better to get the rustlin' situation under control before you say 'I do.' " He clapped Abel's shoulder. "Hattie's plannin' on bringin' in another class of pupils after this one's moved on. There'll be other girls—other chances. You don't need to be latchin' on to one right now."

"Reckon you're right, but . . ." Abel dug his toe into the dirt. "Next class won't have Miss Tressa in it."

"Ah." Vince nodded wisely. "She is a purty one. She's turned Ethan's head, too." He sighed. "Sure would hate for a female to come between the two of you. You boys've been almost like brothers since you was young'uns."

The clang of the dinner bell intruded. Abel pushed off from the fence. "You're right, Vince. Foolish of me to be takin' a wife when things are so uncertain."

Vince flung his arm around Abel's shoulders and aimed him toward the house. "You're young yet, Abel. Don't be rushin' into somethin' you might later regret." He yawned and scratched his chin. "I'll be waitin' for that sandwich—tell Ethan to hurry, would'ja?" He turned and ambled to the bunkhouse.

Abel's feet slowed as he pondered Vince's final piece of advice. Which would he regret more—taking Miss Tressa as his wife or letting her go?

19

"They're comin', Aunt Hattie, they're comin'!"

At Mabelle's shrill shout, Tressa looked up from placing her basket on the makeshift table created by laying boards across two sawhorses. A roiling cloud of dust offered proof that wagons and buggies were on their way to the Flying W. And many would carry eligible men eager to take a wife. Tressa's stomach fluttered. Which man might God have chosen for her?

Each night of the past week, before drifting off to sleep, she had spent time reading in the Bible Aunt Hattie had given her. The older woman had made a list of Scriptures for Tressa to study, and she absorbed the promises she encountered on the pages. She'd also developed the habit of slipping to her knees in prayer, talking to God and seeking His plans. She relished the peace that enveloped her during times of prayer, and she'd begun winging brief prayers skyward during the day—requests for strength or patience, appreciation for the beauty of nature, or simply praise for His presence. Those prayers, from simple to in-depth, drew her closer to her Father. Tressa clung to Him with both hands.

Sallie stepped off the porch and crossed to Tressa's side as she adjusted the ribbon on her basket. Each basket bore a colored ribbon, signifying its preparer. Tressa had chosen yellow, the color of sunshine. Sallie's basket sported a bold red ribbon. Sallie fingered the wide band of bright satin and released a sigh.

Tressa put her arm around Sallie's shoulders. "Don't be sad, Sallie. If you're meant to be with Cole, God will make it possible for you."

Sallie cast a quick, hopeful glance at Tressa before lowering her gaze to the baskets again. "Don't know why God would be troublin' Himself over the likes of me. But if ye have a mind to appeal to Him on my behalf, I'd be grateful. My heart does pine for Cole. He's a *kind* man, Tressa. . . ."

Tressa gave Sallie's shoulder a squeeze, sending up a silent prayer of blessing for her friend. Aunt Hattie burst out of the house, waving her hands to the girls. "C'mon over here an' be ready to greet our guests!"

Tressa gave Sallie's arm a little tug, and they joined the others at the base of the porch steps. Tressa smiled as Aunt Hattie fussed with the rows of ruffles that ran from her chin down the front of her dress, disappearing beneath the waistband of her best apron. It appeared the older woman's excitement exceeded even Luella's. Last night, before retiring to bed, Aunt Hattie had confided to Tressa how important it was to her that the school be a success. Her desire to see each of the girls as happily joined in marriage as she had been with her beloved Jed endeared her even more deeply to Tressa. Surely there was no more caring heart in all of Kansas than the one beating in Hattie Wyatt's chest.

Wagons turned in at the gate, and Aunt Hattie waved both hands over her head. "Park around the barn, folks, an' then come on over!"

The girls giggled, exchanging smiles or tucking wind-tossed strands of hair beneath the brims of their best bonnets. Tressa smoothed the skirt of her church dress, the only one she owned that bore a touch of lace as an embellishment. Her straw hat perched on her head, secured against the wind by two pearl-headed pins that pulled her hair. But she refused to remove them—that hat would stay put today!

Townspeople hopped from their vehicles and strode across the dusty ground toward the house. All wore their Sunday attire, women's straw hats replacing everyday poke bonnets and men's black ribbon ties contrasting sharply with crisp white shirt collars. Tressa couldn't help but remember her first glimpse of the single men the first day in Barnett. Gone were the dusty trousers, plaid shirts, and whiskered chins. With their clean-shaven faces and pressed suits, the men might have been bankers or lawyers coming to a society gathering. Only their dusty boots and well-worn hats marked them as cowboys and ranchers.

Brewster Hammond, his son Gage, and their cook arrived at the porch first, and Brewster reached past the girls to take hold of Aunt Hattie's hand. "Harriet, you've set a fine spread." His gaze swept across the neatly set tables and flapping checkered tablecloths before returning to her. A smile transformed his normally sober face. "This party'll rival my pit roast, I reckon." He gave Aunt Hattie's knuckles a quick peck with his lips and then released her hand.

Aunt Hattie flapped her bleached muslin apron at her face. "Well now, Brewster, not that we're in any competition, of course, but that's a mighty nice thing to say. Hope you an' Gage'll enjoy your time here." Her voice sounded unnaturally high, and her wrinkled cheeks held more color than Tressa had ever seen displayed.

As if suddenly realizing a good-sized crowd, including at least three dozen eager single men, stood in a half circle around her porch, Aunt Hattie clapped her hands to her cheeks and gulped twice. "Oh!

Looks like everybody's here, so let's get things started! Lunch first, folks, includin' our basket auction, an' then dancin'. That sound good?"

A rousing cheer rose.

"If you're wantin' to bid on a basket, come on over here. Ever'body else, grab yourself a plate an' dig into the food at the tables!"

Aunt Hattie waved the girls off the porch, herding them with her widespread arms the way Tressa had seen a hen shoo her chicks. The crowd scattered across the yard, their combined voices creating a happy cacophony. Aunt Hattie directed the girls to the far side of the table and then turned to the single men, who formed a crooked double line facing the baskets.

"Now, we're not tellin' you who put together these baskets, but I'll tell you the contents, an' then the biddin' will commence. Once the baskets're all bought, you'll know which lady will share your lunch. Sound good?"

The men cheered, some of them socking the air with their fists or nudging each other. Tressa stood close to Sallie, her heart pounding, as Aunt Hattie pointed to the first basket—Paralee's. Aunt Hattie called out the specialties Paralee had prepared, and bidding began. The girls held hands, shaking their heads in wonder at the amounts offered for the privilege of a home-cooked meal and the company of one of the girls.

The winner of Paralee's basket, a balding middle-aged man with bowed legs, received the congratulations of his peers, and the bidding shifted to Sallie's basket. Tressa sensed Sallie's nervousness as amounts were called. Sallie had confided she'd deliberately prepared all of the foods Cole had particularly enjoyed when they'd worked at the Lazy S in the hopes he would recognize the menu. To Tressa's delight, Cole entered the bidding, but her elation fell when he was trounced by a tall man in a perspiration-splotched three-piece suit. After the winner was proclaimed, Cole scuffed off to the corral fence, his shoulders slumped. Sallie looked longingly after him. Tressa slipped her arm around Sallie's waist in silent sympathy.

Aunt Hattie gestured toward the next basket on the table. "This here basket has a pot roast, sliced thin, a good stout cheese aged right in our own cellar, homemade bread, fresh-churned butter, sour pickles, hard-boiled eggs, an' apple dumplin's for dessert—good picnic makin's for sure! What'm I bid?"

Tressa held her breath as men clamored for her basket. At the back of crowd, Abel Samms peered over the shoulders of the other men. She'd seen his brows rise when Aunt Hattie mentioned apple dumplings. Did he remember the apple dumplings she'd baked in his kitchen? She watched, hoping his hand might rise in a bid for her basket, but instead Gage Hammond pushed to the front of the crowd and thrust his hand in the air.

"I'll give ya ten dollars for that basket!" He flashed a grin at the men behind him.

Grumbles broke across the crowd, and Luella released a gasp. Tressa glanced at Luella's furious face. The resentment in the girl's eyes made Tressa spin away, and as she turned she spotted Abel clumping across the ground toward Cole.

Aunt Hattie harrumphed. "Gage Hammond, this's s'posed to be a friendly bid. We left off at a dollar, four bits. Why don'tcha go to a dollar, six bits?"

" 'Cause I haven't had good apple dumplin's in a coon's age, an' I'm willin' to pay ten dollars for 'em, that's why. I figure biddin' high'll speed things along." He dug in his pocket and withdrew a paper bill, which he held between his first two fingers. "Ten dollars . . . anybody wanna top that?" He looked over his shoulders both left and right. The other men dug their toes in the dirt, heads low, and muttered.

Gage threw a triumphant grin at Aunt Hattie and strode forward. "Guess that means I'm the winner." He pressed the bill into Aunt

Hattie's hand and then ambled to the edge of the crowd, where he stood with crossed arms and a smirk on his face.

Aunt Hattie cleared her throat and moved on to the next basket.

Tressa's mouth felt dry. Lunch with Gage Hammond? The man made her skin crawl! And if she ate with Gage, Luella would certainly seek revenge.

Bidding on the final two baskets went far too quickly, and Aunt Hattie gestured for the girls to come stand behind their baskets. She called, "Those o' you who didn't win a basket, don't worry—there's food a-plenty on those tables. Help yourself, an' when lunch is done, we'll get that fiddle playin' so's you all can dance an' get to know each other a mite. Enjoy your lunch now!"

Gage held back until the other men led their lunch partners away from the table. Then he strode forward and offered Tressa a wink. "Well now, Miss Tressa, it'll be pure delight to sample your fine cookin'." He hooked the basket handle with one elbow and held the other out to her. "C'mon, let's find us a shady spot."

Tressa felt Luella's glare boring into her back as Gage guided her across the ground toward the barn. A nervous titter escaped her dry lips. "We aren't going to eat in the barn, are we?"

He threw back his head and laughed. "Can you think of a better place to have some privacy?"

"But . . . it isn't *clean*, Mr. Hammond."

"Call me Gage. An' it's no dirtier than sittin' out here in the wind, gettin' dust in our food." He sped his footsteps. "Besides, it's cooler in there. Ruther be where it's cool than out in the sun."

He led her through the barn door. She blinked several times, allowing her eyes to adjust to the dim interior. "Over here," Gage prodded, nodding toward an empty stall. "We can toss one of the horse blankets on the ground an' have a nice private picnic."

Although uncertainty weighed heavily in Tressa's breast, she skittered forward and removed a thickly woven blanket from a high shelf. Her mind raced. The stall Gage had chosen was in the corner, just to the right of the barn doors. If she sat in the stall's opening, she would have a short path to the door should she need to depart quickly. She spread the blanket over the dirt floor of the stall, her chest constricting at the need to plan an escape route, yet she couldn't deny a feeling of discomfort from being in Gage's presence.

Gage plunked the basket in the middle of the blanket and caught her arm, guiding her to the far side of the colorful square of wool. With a gallant bow, he seated her, then sank down beside her. He tossed his hat aside and stretched his legs out, leaning on one elbow. "Now, isn't this cozy?"

Tressa managed a weak smile in response to his grin. "Let's eat, shall we?" The sooner they finished their lunch, the sooner they could rejoin the others.

She removed two speckled tin plates from the basket and graciously placed a sample of the different foods on his plate. Gage remained in his lounging position while he ate, saying little, but fixing her with such an attentive gaze she found it difficult to swallow.

When his plate was nearly empty he suddenly sat up. "Take off that hat, would'ja?"

"W-what?"

"Take off your hat. Seems silly to wear it in here." He lifted his hands to indicate their setting. "No sun in your eyes. Go ahead an' take it off."

"Oh, but—"

"I'll help you."

Before she could stop him, he plucked the pins from her hat and lifted it from her head. One tendril caught in the weave of the straw, and it fell alongside her cheek. She quickly tucked it behind her ear.

His smile grew. "That's better. More relaxed." He hunkered over his plate and finished the remainder of his food without another word.

Eager to have the lunch finished so she could leave his presence,

Tressa forced herself to consume the last of her cheese and meat. Her plate empty, she heaved a sigh of relief. "Would you like your dessert now?" She reached for the bowl that held the apple dumplings.

Gage caught her wrists. "I want somethin' sweet all right." He rose to his feet, pulling her with him. "But the apple dumplin's can wait."

"M-Mr. Hammond, I—"

"Now, didn't I tell you to call me Gage? Mr. Hammond's my pa. Call me Gage, Tressa."

Her heart pounded so hard it took the wind from her lungs.

His fingers tightened on her upper arms. "Call me Gage, Tressa."

She tried to form the word, but her dry lips refused to cooperate. Instead, little gasps slipped out.

He chuckled softly. "Well, that's all right. No talkin's fine, long as we're doin' somethin' else. So how 'bout a kiss, huh?" He lowered his face, but Tressa twisted her head to the side. His lips landed on her cheek.

"Aw, c'mon now, don't be shy." Gage backed her against the stall rail. He caught the loose strand of her hair and coiled it around his finger, giving it a slight pull. "Everybody knows I'm the best catch in town, seein' as how my pa's the richest rancher in Ford County. An' here I've taken a fancy to you. You oughtta be thankin' me, not playin' cat an' mouse."

Tressa's pulse pounded in her temples. Although Gage was smiling and keeping his voice low and friendly, fear created a bitter taste in her mouth. She wanted to flee, but how? He was blocking her with his widespread stance and his grip on her hair.

"So . . ." Gage's grin turned leering. "It's time to thank me for givin' such a high price for your basket. All I want is a little kiss. Luella tells me you been practicin' on Abel Samms, so you oughtta know how." He laughed again, but the sound held little gaiety. "I usually don't take another man's hand-me-overs, but I'll make an exception since you're so purty." He tipped his head toward her again.

Tressa leaned back as far as the hard plank of wood behind her shoulders allowed. Twisting her face to avoid his, she released little grunts of protest. Suddenly he gave her hair a yank that made her cry out, and then his lips closed over hers. He held her tight, one hand in her hair, the other at her waist. She pressed her fists uselessly against his chest.

The kiss increased in pressure, grinding her lips against her own teeth. The contact hurt, and she whimpered. Helpless against his strength, Tressa sagged into his arms and prayed for deliverance.

20

Abel scooped another serving of beans onto his plate. When Aunt Hattie had indicated there would be food a-plenty, she hadn't fibbed. He, Ethan, and Cole were eating like kings even without having won one of the lunch baskets. From their long faces, he guessed his ranch hands weren't enjoying the meal as much as he was, but that was their problem. A full belly was a full belly, company of a lovely lady or not.

He dropped the serving spoon back in the pot and reached for a crusty corn muffin. Just as his fingers closed around it, Aunt Hattie bustled to his side.

"Abel, I could use your help."

"What do you need?"

"I sent my men out an' about to round up all the guests so our dancin' can start, but I forgot about throwing sawdust on the dance floor." She twisted her face into a grimace. "Don't want nobody slidin' on them new boards and gettin' hurt."

Abel glanced at the white-planked wood floor waiting in the middle of the yard. At the Hammonds' yearly pit roast, they just danced on a piece of canvas spread in the grass. Aunt Hattie had gone full-out for this courting party. Abel put his plate on the edge of the table. "Where's the sawdust?"

"Burlap sack of it in the tack room at the rear o' the barn. Would'ja fetch it for me?" Without waiting for a reply, she spun and trotted toward the porch, where Brewster Hammond and his cook were standing in the shade.

Chuckling, Abel aimed his feet for the barn. That Aunt Hattie . . . she knew what she wanted and she got it done. Long strides carried him through the barn door opening, but he skidded to a halt when a soft moan reached his ears.

Squinting into the shadowy barn, he looked left and right, seeking the source of the sound. He gulped when he spotted a couple locked in an embrace against the wall of the corner stall. Embarrassment struck him like a sledgehammer. He started to hurry on past, but a pair of wide, pale blue eyes met his over the shoulder of the cowboy.

He knew those eyes, and he also knew fear when he saw it. Balling his hands into fists, he barked, "What's goin' on here?"

The cowboy angled his body sideways but curled his hands around the top rail, creating a barrier that held Tressa in place. He released a low chuckle. "Aw, Abel, you wouldn't interfere in a good time now, would'ja?"

Abel experienced a jab of fury when he recognized Gage Hammond. Behind Gage, Tressa's chest heaved. Her pale face and tear-filled eyes didn't paint a picture of a woman having a good time. "Gage, let 'er go."

"But I was just gettin' my dessert. I paid for it, wouldn't ya say?" Gage ran one finger down Tressa's arm from her shoulder to her elbow. She whimpered, recoiling from his touch.

Abel charged forward and grabbed Gage's shirt front. He yanked the man away from Tressa. Buttons popped off Gage's shirt and flew through the air. His eyes on Gage, Abel ordered, "Miss Tressa, git outta here." She lifted her skirts and ran from the barn.

Shoulders squared and fists ready, Abel faced Gage Hammond. Only knowing it would ruin Aunt Hattie's party prevented him from pummeling the young man into the ground. He spoke through clenched teeth. "Miss Tressa isn't a strumpet, an' you'd do well to apologize to her an' to Aunt Hattie."

"Apologize?" Gage rested his fingertips against his chest, his face innocent. "For puttin' ten dollars in the pot for the church roof an' showin' that little lady a good time?" He shook his head, his familiar grin in place. "I don't think so."

"Hammond, money doesn't buy you the right to force yourself on a woman."

Resting his weight on one hip, Gage slipped his hand into his trouser pocket. "Aw now, Samms, I understand if you're jealous. You tasted her first—s'pose that gives you a claim, of sorts. But I didn't see you biddin' to win her basket, so that makes her fair game." Stooping over, Gage snatched his hat from the ground and plopped it on his head. "An' you gotta admit, of all the gals Aunt Hattie brought to town, she's the purtiest. So dainty. Fits just right in a man's arms. . . ." His grin grew. "You know me—only wantin' the best."

Abel couldn't decide what to address first—Gage's wrong assumption that he'd kissed Miss Tressa or the man's improper actions toward the young lady. Before he could form a reply, Gage continued.

"Man's gotta sample the goods before he makes a selection. An' I admit, that Miss Tressa . . . she passed muster. She's just as sweet an' unblemished as a fresh-picked pear. Yessir, when a man's choosin' a wife, that's exactly what he wants—unblemished." He chuckled and gave Abel a light sock on the shoulder. "You must not've wore all the sweet off her when you took your sample."

Abel bristled, and one fist twitched in eagerness to connect with Gage's cocky grin.

Gage winked. "Now that I know what I'm gettin', I'm ready to tell Aunt Hattie that I plan to court Miss Tressa."

A startled gasp sounded from the barn's opening. The girl who had accused Abel and Tressa of dallying in Aunt Hattie's kitchen stood in the wide doorway.

Gage groaned, smacking his leg with his open palm. "Luella, what're you doin' out here? Followin' me?"

"Aunt Hattie sent me to see what was keeping Mr. Samms." She took one stumbling step forward, her teary-eyed gaze locked on Gage. "You . . . you're going to court Tressa?"

Gage pulled his lips into a grimace. "Aw, honey, don't take it so hard."

"B-but I told you the color of everyone's ribbons so you'd know where to place your bid. I thought you'd bid on mine, not hers."

A slow shrug raised Gage's shoulder. "Now, Luella, I never made no promises to bid on your basket, or for anything else."

"But—"

"We had us a good time, sure, but that's all it was. A little fun."

The girl's face changed instantly from white and pleading to a furious scarlet, her eyes flashing fire. With a growl, she rushed forward, her hands curled to claw at Gage's face. He caught her wrists, laughing as he wrestled her hands downward. "Now, stop that, Luella! You're actin' like a wildcat 'stead of a lady." Luella released animal grunts of frustration as she struggled to free herself.

Abel stepped forward and caught Luella around the waist, determined to separate the pair. If anyone was going to bring Gage down a peg or two, it would be him. Luella struggled against Abel's hold, her hands clawing at his restraining grip.

Gage shook his head, his lips twisted in derision. "This's exactly why I can't marry you. Man of my stature needs a cultured bride, not a half-crazy soiled dove."

At once, the fight left the girl. She slumped within Abel's arms and stared at Gage with a blank expression. Abel, uncomfortable at witnessing such an ugly exchange, set Luella aside and moved toward Gage. But suddenly the girl dashed between them, her eyes narrowing into slits.

"You'll regret those words, Gage Hammond. You forget . . . I've been out with you at night. I know what you *do* . . . out at night."

Abel's scalp prickled.

Gage took one lunging step forward. "Luella, you better—"

She laughed in Gage's face, then spun and raced out of the barn. Gage thudded behind her. Abel started after them, but then he remembered his purpose for coming to the barn. He hurried to retrieve the sawdust. After he'd dusted that dance floor for Aunt Hattie, he'd seek out Miss Tressa and make sure she was all right. And then as soon as the dancing started and folks were well occupied, he intended to haul Gage Hammond behind the barn and pound some sense into the reckless young man.

❧

When Tressa made it out of the barn, she ran straight for Aunt Hattie. A cluster of townsfolk were standing around the older woman, all talking and laughing, but Aunt Hattie's expression changed from jovial to concerned when she spotted Tressa. She took hold of Tressa's shoulders and peered directly into her face.

"What's wrong, Tressa-darlin'?"

Tressa managed a weak laugh. "I . . . I prayed for deliverance, and it came. Aunt Hattie, I prayed, and God answered."

The older woman's graying brows pulled into sharp V. "Girl, you ain't makin' sense. Did the sun get to ya? You're red as a beet an' limp as a boiled noodle." Tucking her arm around Tressa's waist, she turned to the others. "Fred, you reckon you can ask Cookie to get the dancin' started without me?"

"Sure thing, Aunt Hattie."

Aunt Hattie guided Tressa behind the house and pushed her onto the bench that sat below the kitchen window. Tressa welcomed the sturdy seat and the protective slash of shade. Although she was now safe, her body quivered in aftershock.

"You all right, darlin'?" Aunt Hattie wiped Tressa's face with her apron. "Sun'll do funny things to a person. . . ."

Tressa pushed Aunt Hattie's hands down. "It wasn't the sun. It was . . . was . . . " She gulped. "Oh, I'm so glad I prayed for deliverance!"

The older woman shook her head, her forehead crinkled. "You gotta tell me what you're meanin'."

Between shuddering gasps, Tressa spilled the tale of what had transpired in the barn. While she spoke, Aunt Hattie's lips formed a grim line, her face mottling with red. Tressa finished on a breathless sigh. "God answered my prayer by sending Abel Samms."

Aunt Hattie pulled Tressa to her chest, rocking her gently back and forth. "God sends us angels when we need 'em, an' I'm grateful Abel came when he did. But that Gage—" Her tone turned hard, and she set Tressa aside. "I'm gonna have me a talk with his pa." She stood and headed for the corner of the house.

Tressa leaped to her feet and caught Aunt Hattie's arm. "Oh no, please! I don't want to cause trouble!"

Aunt Hattie cupped Tressa's cheeks. "Darlin', what Gage did was *wrong*."

"B-but he didn't hurt me. Not really."

"You sayin' what he did doesn't bother you?"

The disbelief in Aunt Hattie's voice made Tressa shrink in shame. In that moment, she relived the panicked feeling of being pressed to the stall railing while his lips pursued hers. She shuddered and backed away from Aunt Hattie's touch. "Yes. Yes, it bothers me." Tears filled her eyes, distorting her vision. She grabbed Aunt Hattie's arm again. "But I don't want anyone to know that he . . . he . . ."

Aunt Hattie placed her hand over Tressa's. "Tressa, you didn't do nothin' to hang your head over. Gage is the one in the wrong."

"But can't we just pretend it didn't happen?" Oh, how she wished it hadn't happened! Her skin, where Gage had pressed his fingers, still ached from the remembrance of his forceful touch.

"Don'tcha see that by keepin' quiet about what he did, you're lettin' him get by with it? You want some other gal to be forced into a corner like he did to you?"

Tressa shook her head wildly. "No, ma'am!"

"Then we gotta tell. You stay here. I'm gonna fetch Brewster, an' the three of us'll have a talk." She whirled around the house with her jaw jutted forward and arms pumping.

Tressa sank back onto the bench and buried her face in her hands. Trembling, she fought a wave of nausea. If Abel Samms hadn't come in when he did, Gage might have— She swallowed, pushing the frightful thought aside. *Thank You, God, for sending Abel to save me.*

A hand descended on her shoulder. Without conscious thought, she released a cry of surprise and jumped from the bench.

Abel Samms stood before her, his hat in his hand and his face contrite. "I'm sorry, Miss Tressa. I didn't mean to scare you. I just wanted to make sure you were all right."

She pressed her palm to her chest, willing her racing heartbeat to calm. "Oh, Mr. Samms . . . Yes, I . . . I'm quite all right, thanks to you." Her lips quavered into a smile. "You were my answer to prayer."

To her surprise, he snorted. "Aunt Hattie sent me for sawdust or I wouldn't've been in that barn." Then his expression gentled. "But I'm glad I was there. I plan to have a *talk* with Gage. . . ."

She sensed a deeper meaning behind his simple statement. She shook her head. "No, please, Mr. Samms. Let it go."

He quirked one brow at her.

Despite the seriousness of the situation, a light trickle of laughter found its way from Tressa's throat. "Aunt Hattie intends to make sure Gage sees the error of his ways."

At that moment Aunt Hattie swept around the house, followed by Brewster Hammond. Aunt Hattie crossed directly to Tressa and put her arm around her shoulders. "All right now, Tressa-darlin', you tell Brewster what you told me."

For the second time, Tressa told her story. Heat flooded her face as shame once again gripped her. Repeating the words with Abel Samms listening in added to her humiliation, but she haltingly yet honestly recounted the events in the barn.

Brewster's lined face held skepticism. "You sure, little lady? Gage is a mischievous sort, but he's never had no complaints like this made about him before."

Abel stepped forward. "Brewster, every word Miss Tressa said is true. I pulled Gage off of her myself. Took a couple of his shirt buttons in the process. An' from what that other girl—Luella—said, I'm thinkin' Gage has been havin' his way with her, too."

Aunt Hattie sucked in a sharp breath, and Tressa experienced a rush of remorse. The older woman would no doubt assume responsibility for Luella's choice to sneak off with Gage. Tressa tipped her head against Aunt Hattie's shoulder and whispered, "Don't blame yourself. As you told me, you've done nothing wrong."

Gratitude flashed through Aunt Hattie's eyes before she turned a grim look on Brewster. "Are you gonna take a stick to that boy, or am I gonna hafta do it?"

Abel added, "Gage took off after Luella. She went runnin' in the direction of the woodshed."

"That seems fittin'."

Tressa nearly giggled at Aunt Hattie's wry statement.

Brewster heaved a sigh. Fiddle music floated around the corner, followed by the thud of feet on wood. "I'll handle it. Harriet, you best get back to your party before folks start to wonder what's goin' on."

"Abel," Aunt Hattie said, "you take Miss Tressa on out an' get her dancin'." She brushed Tressa's cheek with her rough fingertips, her smile sad. "Nothin' like a dance with a handsome man to brighten a girl's spirits." She flashed a stern look in Brewster's direction. "I'm goin' with you so I can round up Luella an' see what needs fixin' there."

Before Tressa could offer a protest, Abel replaced his hat and slipped her hand into the bend of his elbow. "All right, Aunt Hattie, I'll see she's cared for. C'mon, Miss Tressa. Let's join the party."

21

Not until Abel led Tressa to the edge of the wooden dance floor did he consider what others might think, seeing the two of them coming arm-in-arm from behind the house. His neck went hot. But it was too late now.

He gestured to the dancers. "You want to join 'em midstep or wait for the next song to start?"

A single strand of hair, pulled loose from the bun at the back of her head, framed her cheek. She guided the wavy lock behind her ear with trembling fingers before answering. "Let's wait for the next song. Aunt Hattie showed us all some dance steps, but I'm not familiar enough to join in the middle of the set."

Abel nodded, and they stood silently beneath the sun and watched the others. Several couples from town were making use of the dance floor, and the three lucky ranchers who'd claimed one of Miss Hattie's girls were beaming from ear to ear as they swung their partners in the circle. Other ranchers surrounded the platform, tapping their toes and patting their legs in time with the music. There'd be a stampede the minute the song ended as single men vied to grab the next dance with one of Hattie's girls.

Abel didn't tap his toe, but his soles vibrated with the pound of boots, making him itch to join the fun. He pondered the odd sense of anticipation. He hadn't danced in over two years—not since he'd danced with Amanda at her welcome-to-Barnett party. Oddly, the thought did nothing to dampen his eagerness to take a turn around the dance floor with Tressa.

Ethan sidled up on Tressa's other side, a shy smile on his face. "Hey, Miss Tressa. You fixin' to dance, too?"

"Yes. As soon as the next song begins."

"Well . . . could I maybe have the dance right after that?" His gaze bounced to Abel and then back to Tressa. "After you've danced with Abel, of course."

Tressa lifted her face to Abel, as if seeking his approval. He gulped, realizing he wanted to say no. But he had no claim on her, and it might quiet speculation if he handed her off to Ethan. He forced a reply past his tight throat. "Sure. Why don'tcha just go ahead an' dance the next one with Ethan? I'll go . . . have another piece of that chocolate cake."

Tressa's hand slipped free of his elbow, and Abel tromped to the dessert table. The blazing sun had melted the icing into a gooey mess, but he whacked off a piece of cake and forked a bite to his mouth anyway. He might as well have been eating sawdust for all the pleasure he took in it. Leaning his hip against the table, he stared toward the dance floor. The next song started, and Ethan whirled around the floor with Tressa. The cowboy held her at arm's length—proper and acceptable—but the sight churned something in Abel's stomach.

He jabbed another bite of cake and chewed it with a vengeance while Ethan and Tressa wove between the other couples on the floor. The same feelings that had washed over him when Tressa hurt her arm on the wire now wrapped around him. He wanted to keep her safe from harm—harm from the dangers of the world, harm from Gage Hammond, harm from any other man who might not have her best interest at heart. He *cared* about that girl.

Why he cared, he couldn't explain. He had sworn off attaching himself to another woman—especially an eastern woman—but he now found himself mysteriously drawn to a high-falutin', fine-bred woman from the East. And even though he'd made up his mind that now was the worst time to pursue a wife, his heart refused to agree.

The song slowed, nearing its end, and Abel slapped the plate onto the table. His feet broke into a trot, and he came to a halt at the edge of the dance floor just as the fiddler's final note faded away. Men strained toward the girls, raising their hands for a chance at the next dance. Abel's hand flew into the air with the others. Tressa glanced across the eager faces, and her gaze met his. A smile of relief broke across her face, and she offered a quick nod.

He bounded onto the floor, his boots skidding on the sawdust. He caught his balance and reached her in two wide strides. A trio of notes started the next tune, and Abel held out his arms. She placed one hand on his shoulder and the other against his waiting palm. After a moment's hesitation, he rested his free hand lightly on her waist.

They moved in rhythm with the music, their steps as sure as if they'd practiced beforehand. He examined the top of her head, her brown hair shining like rich molasses in the sun. If he drew her near, she'd surely fit neatly beneath his chin. He kept his arms stiff, resisting the urge to test his speculation. At first she angled her face down, as if watching to make sure he didn't step on her toes, but as the song lengthened she raised her head. Their gazes collided, and a shy smile lit her face.

Abel's heart caught in his throat. Gage's comment—"*Of all the gals Aunt Hattie brought to town, she's the purtiest*"—ran through his mind. Gage was right. She was fine-boned with a heart-shaped face and beautiful eyes. Staring across a breakfast table at her would be pure pleasure. He knew she could cook a meal that satisfied a man's taste buds and filled his belly, too. Abel's feet shifted—one step, two step, twirl—as he stared into Tressa's sweet face and considered how much richer his life might be if he were to open himself to this woman.

Vince had advised him against seeking a wife until the problem with the rustlers was settled. Why bring a woman into that conflict? As much as Abel respected the old cowboy's opinion, he wanted to cast aside the advice and go ask Aunt Hattie for permission to court Tressa.

A short guffaw blasted from somewhere nearby, followed by several snickers. Tressa ducked her head, stepping out of Abel's arms. He suddenly realized the music had stopped, but he'd kept dancing. Fire attacked his face, and he stumbled backward. His boot heel slipped off the edge of the dance floor. Arms flailing, down he went, smack on his backside in the dirt.

The snickers turned to full-blown guffaws as men pointed, slapped their knees, and hollered mocking comments. Tressa darted to the edge of the floor. She stared at him with her steepled fingers covering her lips. He ignored her sympathetic expression and pushed to his feet, dusting off the seat of his pants. Anger quickly replaced the tender feelings of moment's ago. Once again, he was a laughingstock . . . all on account of his attention to a woman.

He spun and charged toward his wagon. "Cole! Ethan! Let's go!" The two cowboys pounded to his side while laughter continued to roll. The fiddle broke into a merry tune, drowning out the sounds of mirth. Abel climbed into the wagon seat and, after glancing in the back to be sure Cole and Ethan were seated, whacked the reins down on the horses' backs. They jolted forward, and he encouraged them to set a good pace as they pulled the wagon through the gate and down the lane.

"Don't know why *we* couldn't stay," Cole groused from the back. "I was up to dance with Miss Sallie on the next song."

Abel jerked back on the reins so hard the horses neighed in protest. He whirled around in the seat. "You wanna keep dancin'? Hop on out, then. But you can plan on walkin' to the ranch when the party's over. I won't come back an' get ya."

Ethan and Cole looked at each other with their mouths hanging open. Then Cole swung an eager expression on Abel. "You mean it, boss?"

"It's a lengthy walk, but if you think another dance is worth it, I won't stop you."

"Yeehaw!" Cole leaped over the edge of the wagon. "You comin, Ethan?"

Ethan shot a nervous glance at Abel. "Yep. I reckon." He climbed out. "You sure you don't mind, Abel?"

Abel forced a reply through gritted teeth. "Go on. Be home by sundown."

❧

Hattie herded Luella toward the yard, where fiddle music and laughter filled the air. The girl's cheeks were red and blotchy from the crying she'd done. But the men would surmise the color came from the blazing sun, so Hattie didn't feel too bad about making Luella join the party.

Luella stumbled along beside Hattie, her usual brassiness absent. As much as it pained Hattie to see the girl so defeated, she couldn't help but think this comedown might prove beneficial. Luella had wasted herself on a man who'd used her and tossed her aside. Maybe Gage's rejection would make her think about consequences before acting. At least, Hattie prayed so. She hated to see a good lesson squandered.

As they neared the dance floor, several men glanced over their shoulders. Immediately they bumped one another with their elbows, grinning and pointing. Luella's steps slowed, but Hattie planted her hand in the middle of the girl's back and gave a gentle push.

"Go on now. There's *good* men waitin', an' nothin' heals a broken heart better'n a dance in the sunshine."

With a persecuted sigh, Luella lifted her chin and glided forward. Hattie stood back, arms crossed over her chest, and watched as Len Meyer and Fred Pennington scrambled for the chance to take Luella onto the dance floor. After a few moments of good-natured argument between the men, Luella's shoulders shook with merriment, and Hattie grinned. Looked like the girl was already healing. And either Len or Fred would be a good match for the headstrong girl.

Hattie sat on the porch step, her chin in her hands, and watched the dancers. What a joy to see the frivolity playing out in front of her eyes. When she'd envisioned this school, her imagination hadn't been active enough to create the picture of eager men, laughing girls, and joyful music. The seed God had planted in her heart was blossoming in better ways than she'd hoped, and her heart swelled with thankfulness. Despite the trouble between Gage and Luella, it appeared much good would result from this venture of hers.

A shadow fell across her knees, and she looked up to find Brewster Hammond standing beside the steps. She tipped sideways to peek past him. "Where's Gage?"

"Sent him back to the ranch an' told him to stay put till I get home." Brewster hitched up his pant legs and sat on the opposite end of the step. He rested his elbows on his knees and stared toward the dancers. The fiddle music nearly covered his voice as he said in a serious tone, "Harriet, I knew my son could be pranksome, but I'm speakin' the truth. I had no idea he was capable of such low-handed behavior. I apologize to you, an' I'll apologize to both Luella an' Tressa before I go home tonight."

His sagging features stirred Hattie's sympathy; however, Brewster needed to assume his part in Gage's misconduct. "Never had young'uns of my own, but I do remember my mama keepin' a firm hand on me— said foolishness was bound up in a child's heart an' it was her beholden duty to drive it from me." She chuckled. "She had a way of drivin' it that kept it from comin' back if I took a notion to sample it."

Brewster cleared his throat, smoothing down his steel-gray mustache. "I s'pose I didn't do my duty by Gage in that regard. But after Amy died, I . . ." He heaved a sigh. "I spoiled him, Harriet. An' look what he's become. A selfish man seekin' only to please himself."

She gave his knee a brisk pat. "Not too late to change it, Brewster. Gage still has some growin' in him. I'll be prayin' you find a way to turn him around."

Brewster angled his head and looked directly into her eyes. "Thank you, Harriet."

She gave a nod, and they sat in silence for several minutes while the fiddler played and the dancers whirled on the wooden dance floor. Hattie relaxed, nodding in beat with the music and bouncing her toes against the ground.

Suddenly Brewster sat bolt upright. "Harriet, would you like to dance?"

"Me?" She pressed her hand to her chest. Her heart pounded beneath her palm.

Brewster searched the area, a teasing glint in his eye. "Don't see nobody else named Harriet hidin' in the bushes, do you?"

The unexpected humor took Hattie by surprise, and she laughed. But then she quickly sobered. Not since she was seventeen years old had she stepped onto a dance floor with anyone but Jed. After all these years, could she allow another man to lead her in a dance?

Brewster sat waiting, his face expectant and his hand extended. Oh, what was a dance? Might be fun. With a self-conscious chortle, Hattie placed her hand in his. She tossed her apron aside as they stepped onto the dance floor and joined the others mid-dance. To her surprise, her feet managed to follow Brewster's—not as smoothly as she'd followed Jed's lead, but she and Jed'd had years of practice. When the song ended, she discovered a sense of disappointment. She'd enjoyed being swung around the circle on Brewster's arm.

He bowed, his smile wide. When the next song started, he raised his eyebrows in silent query, and Hattie reached for him again. After three more dances, she was huffing and puffing, and she noticed the girls looked wilted, too. Although suppertime was still a good hour away, she decided it was time to bring the party to a close. Those poor girls looked purely tuckered.

The Hammonds' cook raised the fiddle to start another tune, but Hattie shook her head at him. "Thanks, Cookie, but we're gonna give you a rest."

"Aw, Aunt Hattie!" The protests rose, but she waved her hands at the blustering men.

"Now, fellas, I'm glad y'all had a good time, but these poor girls have just about danced the soles off their shoes. They've danced ever' dance, an' y'all have had breaks in between. It's time to call it quits."

The men muttered but then nodded in reluctant agreement.

Hattie shooed the girls to the porch, and then she addressed the crowd again. "Thanks for comin' an' spendin' some time with us, everyone. I'm thinkin' there might be a fella or two who's set his sights on one o' my pupils. If that's the case, you look me up after church service tomorrow an' we'll see about grantin' permission to court. Remember the courtin's gotta be agreed on by the fella, the gal, an' by me." She plunked her fists on her hips and glared down the row of men. "An' I'll be the toughest to convince, so you best be mindin' your manners, ya hear?"

A good-natured chorus of "yes, ma'am" rang, and Hattie laughed. She wiped the sweat from her brow, then waved the folks toward their wagons. "Have a good night's rest. We'll see you in service tomorrow."

The townspeople headed across the yard, still laughing and talking.

Hattie blew out a breath and started for the porch to give the girls directions for cleanup, but Brewster caught her by the elbow and pulled her aside.

"Harriet, I—" He swallowed, his Adam's apple bobbing mightily. "I had a good time."

She smiled, remembering the pleasure of dancing with him. "I did, too, Brewster. Thank you."

"An' I was thinkin' . . ." He smoothed his mustache with his leathery finger, his eyes darting toward the girls and then back to Hattie. "I been without a woman at my place for a good many years. . . . Gage'd surely benefit from a female's influence. So I was wonderin' . . ."

Hattie narrowed her gaze. "Brewster, are you thinkin' o' courtin' one o' my girls?"

His wiry brows flew high.

She crossed her arms over her chest. "Them girls're young enough to be your daughters."

"Harriet, I wasn't thinkin' of your girls. I was thinkin' of . . . well . . . of you."

Hattie's mouth lost its ability to stay closed.

Brewster patted her shoulder. "Don't answer me now. I know it's come as a surprise."

He was sure right about that. She clacked her jaw shut.

"We'll talk tomorrow after service. Right now I gotta get home to Gage. Him an' me've got some serious talkin' to do."

22

Tressa curled her fingers over the edge of the wagon bed and rested her chin on her knuckles. The other girls were also clinging to the wooden side as if they needed support as they peered across the sunny churchyard. Tressa imagined they must resemble crows perched on a fence rail, but no laughter accompanied the thought.

In the shade cast by the simple wood-sided chapel, Aunt Hattie was jotting notes on a pad of paper with the stub of a pencil as a man spoke and gestured flamboyantly. Behind that man, a line of ranchers waited for their chance to approach Aunt Hattie. The sight made Tressa's mouth dry and her chest tight. She had danced at least once with each of those men yesterday. Would one of them ask permission to court her?

Her gaze traveled from man to man, and her heart skipped a beat when her eyes encountered Abel Samms at the end of the line. Ethan and Cole flanked him, and all three men held their hats in their hands. The picture of them holding their hats even though they stood in the sun rather than in the shade sent a quiver of pleasure down her spine. She'd learned that the cowboys removed their hats as a sign of respect. Apparently Abel, Cole, and Ethan viewed this courting business seriously.

Sallie tapped Tressa's arm. "I danced twice with that man talkin' to Aunt Hattie, an' he asked me if I was good at cookin' an' cleanin'."

Tressa examined the tall man. She couldn't recall his name, but she remembered the suit. It had been dusty and sweat-splotched yesterday, and it was in no better condition today. Apparently he didn't know how to give a suit a good brushing. Or he had simply chosen not to. She wrinkled her nose in distaste. "What did you tell him?"

"The truth. I *am* good at both cookin' an' cleanin'. Do ye suppose he's askin' Aunt Hattie permission to court me?" Sallie sounded worried.

Tressa gave her a bright smile. "Don't fret, Sallie. Remember Aunt Hattie said the courting would have to be approved by her, the man, and the girl. You won't be forced to court anyone against your will."

Sallie sagged with relief. She tipped her head toward Cole and released a soft giggle. "See Cole in line there? He promised he would be. An' he promised to ask Abel to speak up for 'im, to let Aunt Hattie know he'd be a responsible husband even though he has no ranch of his own . . . yet."

"Yet?"

Sallie nodded eagerly. "He says he's been puttin' money aside an' has a way of gettin' more. He intends to buy his own place. He's thinkin' that with such fine plans, Aunt Hattie'll surely tell him yes."

"Oh, I hope so, Sallie."

The tall man in the rumpled suit strode away, his shoulders stiff and his mouth set in an angry line. The next man—Glendon Shultz, Tressa recalled—stepped forward. He and Aunt Hattie put their heads close together, and Aunt Hattie scribbled furiously on her pad.

Tressa nibbled her lip. A tiny bubble of hope grew in her middle, seeing Abel in the line. Of all the men who had attended yesterday's dance, Abel was the only one she'd wish to have court her. Remembering the way he'd defended her against Gage and then held her so tenderly in his arms on the dance floor told her he was strong yet gentle. Her heart quivered in her chest with desire to step into his arms again. Then uncertainty smote her. What if he were only in line to support Cole?

She closed her eyes briefly, offering a prayer for God to calm her fears. In her nightly reading, she'd found the words Aunt Hattie had once quoted in the Bible—God's claim of offering His children peace and not evil, thoughts that would lead to an expected end. If God devised that expected end, then it would never be second best.

She sighed, remembering the secure feeling of Abel's hand on her waist as he led her in a dance. Country dancing was much less dignified than the affairs she had attended in New York, but swinging in a circle with Abel Samms on a sawdusted dance floor had been much more fun than sweeping through a ballroom with Tremaine Woodward. How she hoped Abel cherished those shared moments as deeply as she did. If Aunt Hattie called her over when Abel stepped up to speak to her, then she would know. Her heart pattered with anticipation, and a prayer formed effortlessly: *Please let Aunt Hattie call my name!*

Aunt Hattie suddenly cupped her hand beside her mouth and called, "Mabelle! Come on over here, please!"

Mabelle sent a frantic look down the row of girls before scurrying from behind the wagon and across the yard to Aunt Hattie's side.

Sallie nudged Tressa. "Are ye thinkin' she'll say yes to bein' courted by that man? He's not so much to look at, is he?"

Tressa agreed that Glendon Shultz might be considered homely with his round, ruddy face, but he smiled often and seemed even-tempered. "Looks aren't everything," Tressa whispered in reply. "Looks fade, but character remains."

" 'Tis true." Sallie flashed an impish grin. "But I'd still rather be courted by a handsome man . . . like Cole!"

Mabelle came running back to the wagon, her face flushed and eyes bright. "I've got a beau!" she gasped out, fanning herself with her hands.

The girls murmured their congratulations, and Mabelle received their hugs before climbing into the wagon and collapsing in a heap of skirts and petticoats. The interviews continued, and a subdued Luella accepted Fred Pennington's request to court her. Paralee refused Bob Clemence but agreed to allow Jerome Garner's visits. Luella and Paralee joined Mabelle in the wagon, and finally Abel, Ethan, and Cole stepped up to Aunt Hattie. Sallie grabbed Tressa's hand.

After a few minutes of chatting, Aunt Hattie gestured to both Sallie and Tressa. "Come on over here, girls."

Girls! Then Cole wasn't the only one who wished to come courting. Tressa's legs trembled as she followed Sallie across the hard ground. Over the past half hour, while waiting to be called by Aunt Hattie, perspiration had dampened Tressa's hair. Her dress—fresh and crisply pressed that morning—clung to her clammy skin, hindering her movement as she walked across the churchyard. Although earlier she had longed to be beckoned to Abel Samms' side, now she wished to find a place to hide. How unappealing she must look in her sweat-stained dress, her hair clinging to her neck in moist tendrils.

Aunt Hattie folded her arms over her chest and tapped her elbow with the pencil. "Girls, I got a request here from Cole wantin' to court Sallie an' Ethan wantin' to court Tressa."

Tressa sent a startled look at Abel. He swished his hat against his pant leg and kept his head low.

"Thing is, neither o' these fellas own a ranch. They don't have a home, either, except a bunkhouse. I'd like nothin' more than to give permission, but . . . I just can't." Sincere remorse colored Aunt Hattie's tone.

Tressa experienced three strong emotions at once—relief that she needn't be the one to turn down Ethan, deep sorrow for Sallie, and dismay that Abel Samms hadn't requested permission to court her. She looked at Sallie, and the tears glittering in her friend's eyes chased away any thoughts of herself. Slipping her arm around Sallie's waist, she tipped her forehead against Sallie's and whispered, "I'm so sorry."

"Aunt Hattie, we're gonna head on home now." Abel took two backward steps, slipping his hat into place as he moved. "Cole, Ethan, let's go. Vince's waitin' in the wagon." The three departed, Cole looking longingly over his shoulder at Sallie, and Ethan scuffing up dust with the toe of his boots. Abel marched on, his shoulders squared and arms swinging. Tressa swallowed the lump that filled her throat. *Lord, what do You have planned for Sallie and me?*

Aunt Hattie slipped her pad and pencil into her skirt pocket. "Let's head home, too." She looped elbows with Tressa and Sallie and held their pace to a lazy saunter. "Sallie, you need to know that Orval Day—tall feller, soft-spoken—also asked to court you. I told him to rethink his reasons—got the feelin' he's more interested in a housekeeper than a wife—but if you're of a mind to allow his visits, I won't stand in the way, 'cause I know he's got a thrivin' ranch an' would take good care o' you."

Her arm tightened, pressing Tressa's elbow against her ribs. "An', Tressa—"

"Harriet?"

A deep voice intruded. The women stopped and turned. Brewster and Gage Hammond stepped off the church porch and strode across the ground toward them. Tressa subconsciously slipped halfway behind Aunt Hattie.

"Could Gage an' me have a word with you an' Miss Tressa?"

Sallie skittered sideways, gesturing toward the wagon. "I'll just be joinin' the others. . . ." She scurried away.

Mr. Hammond nodded solemnly at Tressa. "Gage here has somethin' he'd like to say to you, Miss Tressa."

Gage held his hat two-handed against his stomach. For the first time, no smirk creased his face. He looked directly into her eyes. "Miss Tressa, I want to apologize for behavin' like I did yesterday. I shouldn't've been so forward, an' that's a fact. It won't happen again."

"It sure won't," Aunt Hattie muttered, her chin tucked low.

"Truth is," Gage continued, shooting an apprehensive glance at Aunt Hattie, "I do like you. I meant it when I said you were purty, an' . . . if you'd have a mind to let me . . . I'd like to court you."

Tressa reeled. Courted by Gage Hammond? A flutter of whispers floated from the wagon, and Tressa knew the girls had overheard Gage's request. Surely the others would think her foolish for refusing, yet how could she agree to be courted by a man for whom she held only revulsion?

Mr. Hammond cleared his throat. "Gage isn't the only one who'd like to come courtin', Harriet. As I mentioned yesterday, it'd be a pleasure for me to spend time with you." He cupped his hand over Gage's shoulder. "I reckon this isn't a quick-made decision for either of you, so Gage an' me'll head on home now. Give you ladies a chance to think things over. Harriet, I'll come by . . . Saturday evenin'? That gives you a full week to decide whether or not you'd agree to me courtin'."

Aunt Hattie nodded slowly, her eyes wide. "S-Saturday evenin' oughtta be fine, Brewster. I'll be certain the coffeepot's on."

"An' I'll come, too, Miss Tressa." Gage inched forward, and Tressa battled the urge to retreat the same distance. "We can talk more then."

Aunt Hattie bid them farewell and bustled Tressa to the wagon. Tressa sat in the corner of the wagon bed, her face angled away from the others. She ignored the girls' excited chatter and turned her thoughts inward. Could she possibly set aside her aversion for Gage and allow him to court her? Had his apology been sincere?

She stared at the passing landscape, the tall grasses and blue sky a blur as her mind continued to race. If she married Gage, and Aunt Hattie married Mr. Hammond, then she and Aunt Hattie would be family. The thought held appeal. She had grown to love the older woman deeply. Certainly she would never want for anything, being Gage's wife. As Gage was so proud to claim, the Hammonds were the wealthiest family in the county. They also had a cook on staff, so her duties would be much less stringent than if she married someone else.

Closing her eyes, she deliberately tried to conjure the image of Gage as he'd stood in the churchyard, his hat pressed to the belly of his Sunday suit, his face contrite. But another image intruded—his leering grin as he'd forced his lips to hers. She shivered. Then a memory of Abel chased away the ugly picture. She smiled as she recalled his relaxed, smiling face as they'd danced on the planked floor in Aunt Hattie's yard. A pressure built in the center of her chest, quickly becoming an ache of longing. Why couldn't Abel have asked permission to court her?

"A second-best chance is better than no chance at all." Her aunt's words rang once more through her head. Abel didn't want her, but Gage did. A life as Mrs. Gage Hammond would carry prestige in this little Kansas ranching community. She could do far worse. . . .

Looking skyward, she formed a silent plea. *God, is Gage a part of Your plan for me? If so, please help me view a life with him as something other than second best.*

23

Abel carried a spoonful of gritty white mush to his mouth. If it hadn't been for tiny bits of brown peel left behind by the paring knife, he wouldn't have known what he was eating. Ethan had boiled the potatoes until they were hardly recognizable. He'd also boiled the taste right out of them. Abel swallowed the flavorless mush and pushed his spoon into the mound on his plate to scoop another bite.

Vince made a sour face and pointed with his fork at the charred beef steak curled against his serving of potatoes. "I reckon boot leather would be easier to gnaw to pieces than this."

"Aw, Pa . . ." Ethan snorted. "I never claimed to be a cook."

"Good thing, too, 'cause you'd've been lyin'."

Ethan bumped his father with his elbow. Then he sent an apologetic grin around the table. "Sorry it's so bad. I kinda forgot I was cookin' an' left things on the stove too long."

"How can you forget you were cookin'?" Cole poked at his steak with the point of his knife. It didn't even leave a dent behind.

"I walked out to get milk from the cellar an' . . ." Ethan's face flooded with pink. He hunkered over his plate, scooting a shriveled pea from one side to the other with the tines of his fork. "Well, I saw some yellow flowers growin' outside the fence, an' I started thinkin' how ladies like flowers an' how I wished I could pick some of them an' take 'em over to Miss Tressa, an' I plumb forgot that the food was cookin' on the stove." He blew out a noisy breath. "Sure do wish I could be courtin' her. . . ."

Vince flumped back in his chair, rolling his eyes. "Not again."

Abel held his tongue, but he wanted to agree with Vince. Every night for the past week, the talk had turned to courting. Cole was determined to gain approval to court Sallie. Each evening after supper, he'd saddled a horse and rode the range—"thinkin' time," he called it. With Cole bent on courting Sallie, Ethan focused on figuring out a way to court Tressa. At least Cole kept his thinking to himself; Ethan's thoughts always tumbled out of his mouth.

"I'd treat her right, Pa," Ethan said, turning defensive. "You know I would."

Vince gave his son's shoulder a clap. "I don't question that for a minute. But the plain truth is that you're a cowboy. A common ranch hand." A bitter edge crept into Vince's voice. "If Aunt Hattie says only ranchers can court her girls 'cause ranch hands don't have the means to support a wife, you're just gonna hafta accept it."

"But a man can hope, can't he?"

Abel grunted. "I hope one of you winds up with a wife, 'cause if we hafta keep eatin' meals like this, we'll all need suspenders to keep our britches in place."

Vince blasted out a laugh. "I guess I'll be needin' some of those suspenders soon, 'cause I can't eat this." He pushed his plate away. "Might as well empty it in the slop bucket, Ethan."

Cole swiped his napkin across his mouth and rose. He lifted his hat from the back of the chair and headed for the door. "Goin' ridin'."

"Check on the herd while you're out there, an' make yourself seen.

Been almost two weeks now since any cattle've turned up missin'—wanta keep those rustlers from helpin' themselves to any more of my herd." Abel tossed the words at Cole's retreating back.

Ethan gathered up the plates and carried them to the kitchen. When he was out of earshot, Vince leaned forward. "Abel, what do you think about this courtin'? Cole's all a-dither. He nearly drove me crazy this week talkin' about how he's gonna find a way to marry Miss Sallie no matter what Aunt Hattie says. He's got Ethan purely champin' at the bit to do the same with Miss Tressa. An' neither one of 'em's got so much as a pot or pan to offer a bride." Vince shook his head. "Can't see how any of this is gonna come to good."

Abel downed the last of his coffee. "Aunt Hattie's a woman of her word. If she says only ranchers can court her pupils, then that's the way it's gonna be. Besides, it won't take long an' a rancher around here'll lay claim to the girls. Then Cole and Ethan will have to stop their nonsense." A pang twisted Abel's gut, and he knew it wasn't hunger. Thinking of Tressa with someone else didn't set well.

"Now, ya know I got a heap of respect for Hattie Wyatt, but her only lettin' ranchers court them gals seems a might unfair. Bothers me to see my boy so tangled up inside. A feller's pay shouldn't matter so much. I managed to support a son on a ranch hand's pay for many a year." Vince swished his hand through the air, as if discounting his own words. " 'Course, it just bein' the boy an' me, weren't no trouble for us to live in a bunkhouse together. Man has a wife, he oughtta have a little house to offer her."

He hooked his elbow over the back of the chair and glanced around the room. Pursing his lips, he pinched his whiskery chin. "You know, Abel, I just had a thought. If you was to sell this place to me, then Ethan an' Tressa could live here. I'd just go on stayin' in the bunkhouse."

Abel jerked upright, connecting his spine with the chair's ladder back. "Sell out? But where would I go?"

"Dunno. Town. Open up a little store or somethin'." The man

chuckled. "Oh, I know you're tryin' to follow in your pa's footsteps. But just 'cause your pa ranched don't mean you have to. You're young yet—you could do most anything."

"But I *want* to be a rancher."

"Now, Abel, don't get your feathers all ruffled. It was just a thought, considerin' all the trouble of late. Wondered if you might want to try your hand at somethin' else." Vince gave a one-shouldered shrug. "I know Brewster Hammond's made several offers on the place. If you do entertain sellin', would ya sell instead to the man who helped build this ranch from the ground up?"

Abel drew a deep breath. "If I planned to sell, Vince, of course I'd offer the place to you before I'd sell to Hammond. Pa'd much rather you had it, seein' as how you an' him worked so hard together."

"Side by side, equal in sweat an' blood," Vince agreed in a congenial tone.

"But I'm not sellin'. Not if I can help it." Abel gritted his teeth. Last night he'd done a careful calculation of the current stock prices and the head he would have available to sell come fall. He'd just about break even if no other catastrophes—manmade or nature-made—befell the herd. He might need to start growing a money crop in addition to his feed to bring in some extra funds until he could rebuild the herd again, but he'd make it through.

"That's fine, Abel." Vince pressed his palms to the tabletop and unfolded from his chair. "But if you change your mind . . . I've managed to set aside a nice little nest egg. Make a good down payment on the ranch. An' you know I'd take good care of the place. Practically feels like mine already considerin' how many years I been here."

Then Vince shook his head, chuckling. "Aw, listen to me goin' on. Sound like an old man." He flashed a grin. "Don't pay me no mind, Abel. You hang on to it, if that's what you're a-wantin'." His bony shoulders lifted in a shrug. "A man's gotta do what a man's gotta do."

❧

Tressa sat in a tufted chair in the corner of the parlor with her hands in her lap and her ankles crossed, just as her aunt Gretchen had taught her. Gage Hammond perched straight-spined and solemn in the matching chair across a tiny piecrust table. How absurd to sit with such formality in this simple parlor on the untamed plains of Kansas; how ridiculous to try to impress a man whose presence she abhorred. Hysterical laughter fought for release, but by clearing her throat she managed to hold it at bay. If she laughed, her visitor might think she was enjoying herself, and that would be presenting a falsehood.

Aunt Hattie poured aromatic liquid from a tall rose-painted china pot into matching cups, added heaping spoons of sugar, then splashed cream into each serving. After swishing the spoon through each cup's contents, she offered the tray of coffee and fresh-baked oatmeal cookies to Mr. Hammond. He took two cookies and a cup, smacking his lips. "Mmm, looks good, Harriet."

Aunt Hattie held the tray toward Gage. He took a cup and a cookie, but he set the items on the table between the chairs rather than carrying either to his mouth. His gaze remained pinned to Tressa's face, unnerving in its probing focus.

Tressa ignored the cookies—she had no appetite—but she accepted a cup with a weak smile of thanks. She sipped the strong, sweet brew and willed the evening to pass quickly. On the other side of the small room, Aunt Hattie and Brewster Hammond sat side-by-side on the settee and visited quietly. She wished they would include her. Apparently Gage didn't realize that propriety dictated he must start their conversation.

Minutes ticked by until Tressa had nearly emptied her cup. If Gage hadn't spoken by the time she took her last sip, what would she do? Follow his lead and sit and stare in silence? How silly they must appear!

She reached to place her empty cup next to Gage's full one on the little table, and his hand snaked out and captured her wrist. A little squeak of surprise left her lips before she had time to snatch it back. Gage's fingers slid to her hand, and he took a firm grip.

"C'mon, Tressa. It's a pleasant evenin'—smells like rain in the air. Let's go sit on the front porch. We can talk there."

Tressa sent an imploring look to Aunt Hattie, but the older woman was tipped forward, deep in conversation with Mr. Hammond. Tressa would receive no assistance there. With a sigh, she nodded and allowed Gage to lead her out the front door. The moment they stepped outside, the scent of rain captured Tressa's attention. She inhaled deeply, drawing the essence into her lungs. Without effort, a smile grew on her face.

Gage grinned. "Smells good, don't it? I like a summer rainstorm, an' this's fixin' to be a good one. Lookee out there." He pointed to the east, where clouds formed thick, gray puffs. Flashes of lightning turned the clouds into Chinese lanterns. His hand curved over Tressa's shoulder and his breath stirred her hair as he added, "Won't be long an' we'll be hearin' the thunder."

His touch sent tiny spiders of apprehension up her spine. She stepped away and gestured to the chairs in the corner of the porch. "Shall we sit and listen for it?"

Gage released a soft snort, but he nodded and followed her to the chairs. They sat and gazed across the landscape for several minutes before Gage suddenly leaned toward her. Involuntarily, she leaned the opposite direction, banging her ribs on the armrest of the chair.

"So've you decided? You gonna let me court you?"

Tressa sucked in a sharp breath. Although she'd prayed fervently for God's will concerning her relationship with Gage, no answer had floated down from heaven. Aunt Hattie had indicated her heart would tell her when the right man began courting her. Her heart had not pattered in anticipation of Gage's visit; all week she had dreaded the moment when he would ask to court her.

"You'll have an easy life, ya know. My pa intends to keep Cookie even after he marries Aunt Hattie. Figures she's been runnin' this place all on her own an' would welcome the chance to sit back an' let somebody else do the work for a change. We'll live in the big house with Pa an' Aunt Hattie, so you won't need to do no housecleanin' or cookin', either; everything'll be done for you. Pa's got plenty of money, so I can buy you some new clothes—purty clothes like the gals in the East wear instead of those homespun dresses you been wearin'."

His disparaging glance swept from her head to her toes and back to her face. A disarming smile quickly replaced the critical look. "Purty girl like you oughtta have purty clothes. We'll ride into Dodge City on Monday. There's a dressmaker there who can sew you up some fancy duds."

Gage seemed quite familiar with the city and its businesses. Tressa briefly wondered if he'd taken other girls to the Dodge City dressmaker.

He continued. "While we're there, we'll stop by the mercantile and look at their gold rings. They don't have a big selection, but some are real nice. Bet you'd like one with a stone in it, wouldn't ya? Maybe a blue stone. What're they called?" He scratched his head, his brow furrowed. Then his face lit. "Sapphires. My ma had a sapphire neck-lace. Pa keeps it in a velvet box in his humidor since he don't smoke no more. Or maybe you'd rather have a locket you can hang around your neck. You could put my picture in it."

Tressa remembered the picture Sallie had discovered in Abel Samms' highboy. Again curiosity attacked her. Who was that pretty lady?

"So . . ." Gage tipped his chair back on two legs and rocked. "What time can you be ready to go? We oughtta leave plenty early— no later'n six o'clock—'cause Dodge is a goodly distance. You can be ready by then, right? Good."

Tressa gave a start. Had she uttered a word of approval? His assumption that she would readily agree to his plan—to drive such a far distance with him without the benefit of a chaperone—left her speechless with shock.

Apparently Gage took her silence for agreement, because he thumped his chair down on all four legs and bolted to his feet. "I'll go let Pa know I'll be needin' the calash on Monday. We don't use it except for special occasions, but it's got a fold-up top so if it's still rainin' we won't get wet. While I'm in there, you want me to tell Aunt Hattie you got yourself a beau?"

Gage's assumptions had carried him too far. She must bring things to a halt! Tressa leaped to her feet. "Gage, I—"

The front door opened, and Aunt Hattie and Mr. Hammond stepped onto the porch. Aunt Hattie held Mr. Hammond's elbow with both hands, and from the smile on her face, Tressa surmised the older woman had found more pleasure in Mr. Hammond's company than she'd found in Gage's.

Mr. Hammond approached his son; Aunt Hattie glided along beside him as easily as if she floated on air. "Harriet an' me've decided to spend some time together, get to know each other better. She's asked us to Sunday dinner."

Gage shot Tressa a grin. "That'll be fine, Pa. Give me a chance to see Tressa, too." He clomped to Tressa's side and slung his arm around her waist. She sucked in a lungful of air and held it while he announced, "Come Monday, me an' Tressa are ridin' into Dodge an' pickin' out some jewelry."

Aunt Hattie searched Tressa's face. "Tressa-darlin', are you an' Gage . . . ?"

Finally Tressa's tongue unloosed. Pushing away from Gage, words poured from her lips in a torrent. "I appreciate your kind offer, Gage, but I am not yet ready to make such a significant and life-changing commitment. I have prayed diligently this week, and I shall continue to seek God's guidance concerning whom I should allow to court me. It would be unfair of me to accept your attentions when I am still so ambivalent, so I must humbly decline your offer of a . . . a ring or other piece of jewelry that would signify our courtship."

The first roll of thunder reached their ears, ominous in its delivery, but Tressa believed nature's storm would be much milder than the one brewing in Gage Hammond's eyes.

24

Abel jogged toward the bunkhouse, dodging raindrops. He gave the door three sharp raps before opening it. A crash of thunder chased him over the threshold.

Ethan stood near one of the small windows, looking out. "Listen to that thunder, boss. Gonna be a real gully washer."

Abel ran his hand over his head, removing the water droplets from his hair. "So far it's more noise than wet, although I suspect that'll change here shortly. Clouds are dark as night. But the wet doesn't worry me nearly as much as the noise. Cattle might get spooked by the lightnin' an' thunder. I'm thinkin' we should throw on our ponchos an' go out—keep the critters company."

Vince rose from his bunk and sauntered to the door. He swung it wide and looked from east to west. His face crunched into a look of concentration. Snapping the door closed again, he raised one shoulder in a shrug. "Wind's movin' fast. Storm could blow through in less'n an hour. A couple of men oughtta be able to keep the cattle calm for that amount of time."

Another loud crash shook the bunkhouse, and the clouds seemed to open up. Heavy drops of rain pelted the earth and bounced off the bunkhouse roof. Abel shot a nervous glance toward the door. "You really think two men'll be enough, Vince?" Abel owned the ranch, but Vince had more experience. He respected the man's opinion.

"Oh, sure. One on each side of the herd. Keep 'em from stampedin' an' tearin' down the fence. That barbed wire could do a heap of damage to 'em if they tried to run through it." Vince's unruffled reply smoothed the edges of Abel's fear.

Cole plucked a slicker from a peg on the wall and tossed it over his head. "I'll go. A little rain don't bother me."

"I'll go, too." Vince donned a slicker and plopped his hat on his head. "I'll take my harmonica an' sing the dogies a little tune. That oughtta keep 'em calm."

Cole swung on Vince. "I can handle 'em myself."

Abel shook his head. "Vince advises two men out there, Cole, an' he makes good sense. If the herd stampedes, it'll take two of you to get 'em turned from the fence. 'Sides that, always good to have a buddy close by in case somethin' should happen—like a lightnin' strike or a horse buckin' you off."

Cole snorted. "I never been bucked off in my life."

"Well, you've had a short life," Abel retorted, "an' we want it to be longer. Better to be safe."

"Want me out there, too, Abel?" Ethan headed for the remaining slicker.

"Naw, you stay here," Vince answered before Abel could. "Cole an' me'll get it covered. No sense in you gettin' drenched if you don't hafta."

Ethan paused with his hand on the slicker, looking over his shoulder at his father. "I can go 'stead of you, Pa."

Vince chuckled. "How you gonna keep the herd quiet? You can't hardly get air through a harmonica, let alone play a decent tune."

"I could maybe sing."

"That's even scarier'n thunder."

Ethan laughed. "You got me there."

Abel said, "Then it's settled—Cole and Vince, head on out. Soon as the storm passes, come back in, but stay with the herd until the lightnin' settles down. An' stay low. No sense in makin' yourself look like a lightnin' rod by sittin' high in your saddle."

"Sure thing, Abel. C'mon, Cole." Vince clumped out the door with Cole on his heels.

Lightning flashed outside the windows, followed by an enormous clap of thunder. Ethan's expression turn fretful. "You s'pose Pa an' Cole'll be okay out there? Haven't had a storm like this in ages."

Unease twisted Abel's insides, too. Should he have gone instead of sending his men? If something happened to either of them, it would be on his shoulders. But he tried to reassure his young ranch hand. "You heard what your pa said—wind'll carry that storm right on through. Won't be long an' they'll be back, wetter'n a duck in a puddle, but otherwise fine."

"S'pose you're right."

"While we're waitin', wanna play a game of dominoes?" Abel had planned to spend the evening going over his books, but he figured Ethan could use the distraction. Besides, no matter how he tried to juggle the numbers, they always came out . . . depressing.

"Sure!" Ethan retrieved the box of dominoes from beneath his bunk, and the two spent an hour lost in the game, ignoring the raging storm outside the bunkhouse walls as best they could. Ethan was setting up for the fourth round when the bunkhouse door flew open and Vince stumbled through. Water dripped from his hat and slicker, leaving a puddle on the floor. He dropped the rain-dark items next to the door and shook his head, causing water droplets to fly in every direction. Ethan jumped up and scuttled for a length of toweling.

Vince ran the towel over his hair and face. "Land o' mercy, that was some rain! Creek's up a good six inches, Abel . . . but it'll probably settle back in its banks by mornin'."

"Herd handle it all right?"

Vince walked straddle-legged to his bunk and began stripping off his wet clothes. "Oh, they fidgeted some—sure didn't like them lightnin' flashes. But the music seemed to keep 'em calm. No troubles at my end. An' since Cole never fired his shot, he must've done all right, too."

Abel heaved a sigh of relief. "Well, glad you're back. Thanks for checkin' on the herd."

"No problem, Abel. That's what I get paid to do, now, ain't it?"

Vince's tone had a grumpy edge, but Abel chose to ignore it. Anybody who'd gotten as soaked as Vince had deserved to complain a bit. "Reckon I might stick around here until Cole gets back—make sure he didn't have any problems." He gestured to the table, which was scattered with dominoes. "Wanna join the game?"

"No, thanks. Think I'll shimmy under these covers an' warm up."

Vince was soon snoring from his bunk, and Ethan and Abel played another three rounds before Ethan began yawning. He stretched his fists over his head. "What time is it?"

Abel retrieved his pa's pocket watch and peeked at the round face. He jolted in surprise. "Almost midnight."

"No wonder I'm tired." Ethan's face stretched into another yawn, then he gave a start. "Midnight? Where'n thunder is Cole?"

❧

Tressa stirred, pulled from a deep, dreamless sleep. Slumber had not claimed her until late into the night. The unpleasant end to the evening, with Gage stubbornly refusing to accept no as an answer to his request to court her, had prevented her from sleeping. So she'd read her Bible, seeking words of comfort while a storm raged outside the window.

Now she lay still, staring into the dark room with her brow furrowed, trying to determine what had roused her. Silence reigned. No thunder grumbled or raindrops beat upon the roof. The storm had passed. But the fresh scent of moist earth filled the room, carried in on a cool breeze through the open window.

With a little shiver, she tossed aside the covers and dashed to the window, where the damp curtain flapped lightly. Her feet encountered a puddle. She released a little grunt of frustration. Why had Sallie opened the window in the middle of a rainstorm? The wet wood squeaked as she pushed the window frame down until it met the sill. Hugging herself, she peered out at the black night.

Sheets of gray clouds hid the stars from view, but the moon's light created an eerie glow behind the clouds. Another shiver shook her frame, and she felt her way back to her bed. She crawled in, moving slowly to avoid disturbing Sallie. And then she suddenly realized why the room was so quiet. No snoring came from Sallie's side of the bed. The girl was gone!

Tressa jolted upright. Hands outstretched, she groped her way through the dark room to the door and stumbled into the hallway. Her pounding pulse roared in her ears, hindering rational thought.

Standing in the middle of the silent hallway, she forced herself to calm. Might Sallie have gone to the outhouse? No. Ever since Luella began sneaking out, Aunt Hattie had locked the outside doors and kept the key in her room at night. The girls used chamber pots in their rooms. Perhaps she'd gone downstairs for a drink of milk.

Tressa lit a lantern, then crept downstairs and peeked in every room. No Sallie anywhere. Her heart pounding, she checked the front and back doors, but both remained locked. Tressa stood at the base of the stairs, confusion holding her captive. If Sallie was no longer in the house, she had to be outside. But with the doors locked, she couldn't have gotten outside.

Except through the window. "Oh, Sallie!" Tressa forced her feet to move. "I must alert Aunt Hattie."

Tressa stumbled up the stairs. She stubbed her toe in her hurry, but she ignored the pain and darted into her room to quickly don a dress before pounding on Aunt Hattie's bedroom door. Seconds later the door swung wide.

Aunt Hattie shielded her eyes from the harsh light of the lantern. "W-what's goin' on, girl?"

Tears flooded Tressa's eyes. "Aunt Hattie, Sallie is gone!"

Aunt Hattie shook her head, as if trying to clear it. "You must be dreamin', Tressa. I been lockin' this house tight as a drum. She can't have got out."

Nearly dancing in nervous excitement, Tressa said, "I think she went out the window."

The older woman gasped. Bedroom doors opened at the far end of the hallway, and the other girls peered out with bleary eyes. Paralee asked, "What's all the noise about?"

"Nothin' that need concern you." Aunt Hattie waved her hands at the girls. "All o' you, go back to bed. I'll take care o' this." After a moment's pause, they closed themselves back in their rooms.

Tressa clattered down the stairs and into the kitchen on Aunt Hattie's heels. "What are you going to do? Oh, Aunt Hattie, she's been crying in her pillow every night, but I never dreamed she would—" She clamped her hand over her mouth, holding back a sob.

Aunt Hattie cupped Tressa's face between her palms. "Don't you start blamin' yourself. The blame rests on my shoulders, an' that's a fact. I knew she was moonin' over Cole Jacobs, but I sure never thought she'd . . ." She heaved a sigh. "Young'uns do foolish things when their hearts are achin'. . . ."

Abruptly, she snatched the lantern from Tressa's hand and charged to the back door. After retrieving a key from her robe pocket, she unlocked the door and stepped outside. The dinner bell's *clang-clang-clang!* pierced the night. She stomped back into the house and slapped the key onto its hook.

"Men'll be in soon as they can pull on their britches. I'm goin' up to get dressed—reckon my sleepin' is done for tonight. Get a pot o' coffee brewin'. The men'll want somethin' to fortify 'em before I send 'em out."

Tressa scurried to obey, her movements clumsy as fear clawed at her heart. How had Sallie managed to climb down from the window? How frightened she must have been, running through the rain with the thunder booming and lightning flashing! Where had she gone? Would the men be able to track her across the muddy ground?

After setting the coffee to brew, she tossed several strips of bacon into a frying pan and then began mixing biscuit dough. The men would certainly appreciate some food in their bellies, and her hands needed something to do. A plaintive meow interrupted as she rolled the dough on a floured board. She dashed across the floor and freed Isabella from the pantry.

With sticky fingers, she swept the cat into her arms. "Oh, Izzy-B, Sallie is gone! She sneaked away in the night!" Tears stung her nose, but she sniffed hard. Crying wouldn't bring Sallie back. "I'm so frightened. . . ."

A snippet from last night's Bible reading in Psalms crept into Tressa's mind, and she whispered the words to the cat. " 'What time I am afraid, I will trust in Thee. . . .' " Closing her eyes, she buried her face in the cat's warm fur. A prayer for Sallie's safety and the men's success in locating her winged from her heart. Peace flooded her frame as she released Sallie into God's hands. Revived, she set Isabella on a kitchen chair, washed her hands in the wash bucket, and quickly cut biscuits.

Just as she placed the pan of fat biscuits in the oven, a rustle of activity at the back door indicated the arrival of the ranch hands. They clustered in the kitchen, rubbing their eyes and yawning, but they eagerly accepted the cups of hot coffee. Aunt Hattie bustled in shortly after they arrived, fully dressed, her gray hair combed into a neat bun.

"We got a problem, fellas." She quickly informed them of Sallie's disappearance.

"So that explains the ladder leanin' against the side of the house," one of them said.

Tressa paused in removing the crisp bacon from the pan. "Ladder?"

"Under the window. We seen it when we came in," the man confirmed.

Slapping her hand to her cheek, Aunt Hattie groaned. "Sallie couldn't've put that there herself. That means somebody helped her." She shot a grim look in Tressa's direction. "An' I think I know who."

Tressa nodded as she realized Sallie and Cole must have planned this escape.

"I reckon I oughtta—" Aunt Hattie's words were interrupted by a fierce pounding on the front door.

Tressa jumped. "Could that be Sallie?" Her heart lifting with hope, she raced for the door with Aunt Hattie and the ranch hands thumping behind her. The other girls clustered on the stairs, holding to the rail and peering down with wide, curious eyes.

Aunt Hattie stepped past Tressa, key in hand, and pulled the lace curtain aside. "It's Abel Samms." She raised one brow and quirked her lips into a wry grin. "Guess that confirms our suspicions about who ran off with Sallie." Aunt Hattie twisted the key in the lock.

Abel stepped over the threshold, swept his hat from his head, and offered a quick nod. "Aunt Hattie, sorry to bother you at this hour, but I'm missin' me a ranch hand. Cole Jacobs." Abel's puzzled gaze flicked across the gathered people before returning to Aunt Hattie. "Was plenty worried, too, seein' as how he didn't come back after checkin' on the herd in the middle of that storm. But now I'm just all-fired mad."

Aunt Hattie touched Abel's arm. "You want some coffee, Abel? An' a biscuit with bacon?" She turned and spotted the girls on the stairs. "Well, since you're all up, make yourselves useful. Mabelle, get the biscuits out o' the oven; Paralee, turn them biscuits and bacon into sandwiches for the men. An' Luella, perk us a fresh pot o' coffee."

The girls scrambled to obey.

"I don't want nothin'." Abel crossed his arms tightly over his chest, his brows low. "I was hopin' I could maybe talk one or two of your men into helpin' me search for Jacobs. I've got Vince and Ethan out fixin' my fence." The muscles in his jaws bulged as he clenched his teeth. "Near as we can tell, Cole must've cut through it an' took a good three dozen of my cattle when he headed out."

Aunt Hattie reared back in surprise. "But then how could he've—?" She shook her head and drew in a deep breath. "Abel, the reason my men're in here rarin' to go is 'cause Sallie sneaked down a ladder in the middle o' the night. She's gone. I figured Cole put that ladder up an' she took off with him, but I don't see how he could've done that if he was herdin' a bunch o' cattle. You sure them beefs didn't knock the fence down an' take off outta fear durin' the storm?"

"The fence was *cut*." Abel's formidable expression made the fine hairs on the back of Tressa's neck prickle. "I don't see how my cattle an' my ranch hand could turn up missin' at the same time unless Cole cut that fence an' stole from me." His tone changed to a growl as he added, "We don't find those cattle by mornin', I'll go see the sheriff an' have a warrant put out for Cole's arrest."

Tressa's heart pounded as a conversation she'd had with Sallie flooded back. She touched Aunt Hattie's arm. "Aunt Hattie, Sallie told me Cole had a plan to get money so he could buy a small ranch and win the right to court her. Do you think . . ." She flicked a glance at Abel's stony face. "Do you think his plan was to steal Abel's cattle?"

Aunt Hattie stared at Tressa for several silent seconds, her brow crinkled into lines of worry. Then her expression cleared, and she whirled on her men. "Bob, go check if we're missin' a horse. If Sallie went with Cole, chances are she's ridin'. Frank, you take a lantern an' see if you can read how many feet were wanderin' around out there." Turning to Abel, she gave his shoulder a pat. "Don't you worry now, Abel. We'll get to the bottom o' this. I guarantee you that."

25

Sheriff Tate hitched his waistband higher. The pants drooped back below his round belly as soon as he let go. "We been searchin' for three days, Abel. That's more'n enough. Way that ground was stirred up, those cows could've been sent in any direction. No way of knowin' where Cole took'em, an' that's that." The portly man pooched his lips. "He planned good, takin' off in the middle of a rainstorm."

Abel gritted his teeth. "You could send wires to cattle buyers— let 'em know what my brand looks like an' have 'em be watchin' for a man matchin' Jacobs' description." It irked Abel to no end to have to do the sheriff's investigation for him. But the man was too lazy to lift a hand. If Abel hadn't threatened to wire the state's marshal, Tate wouldn't have even saddled a horse and gone tracking.

"Now, Abel, you know Jacobs'll be wantin' to unload them critters to somebody who won't be askin' questions. So he ain't gonna go somewhere he'll need to prove ownership. He'll likely take 'em to Indian Territory an' sell 'em to the army for Injun food. They'll buy most anything to feed the Injuns livin' on the reservations." The sheriff worked his whiskered jaw back and forth, his watery eyes narrowed to slits. "Them cows're gone, Abel. Accept it an' move on."

Abel slammed his hat onto his head and stormed out of the sheriff's office. *Accept it an' move on.* The words taunted him. How could he just accept it? Those cattle represented a loss Abel couldn't afford. His boots stuck in the mud, slowing his progress toward his wagon. He scraped off as much of the muck as possible on the wagon wheel spokes before climbing onto the seat. As he released the brake and plucked up the reins, Brewster Hammond clopped down the boardwalk toward him.

"Hold up there, Samms."

Abel held to the reins and waited for Brewster to reach the wagon.

The man curled his hands over the wagon's side rails. "Any luck in locatin' those cattle?"

A bitter taste filled Abel's mouth. "No. An' that lazy coot of a sheriff isn't doin' nothin' to try."

Brewster gave a derisive snort. "Wouldn't expect anything less. That man'll be voted out next election." He twisted his face into a grimace. "I reckon it'll be harder to keep your place goin' without proceeds from the sale of those head."

Abel didn't bother to reply. Brewster, as well as everyone else in town, was aware of Abel's precarious situation.

"Keep in mind, I'm still interested in buyin' your spread. 'Specially now with Gage fixin' to take a wife."

"Gage is courtin'?" Abel was surprised the town's grapevine hadn't reached him with that piece of news. Usually anything about the Hammond family spread quicker than honey on a hot biscuit. Abel knew Aunt Hattie had agreed to Brewster courting her, and even though he wouldn't have put the two of them together, he figured she was old enough to make up her own mind.

"Yep. Gage has set his sights on Miss Tressa Neill, an' I'm inclined to support him. She's a sweet little gal with a pretty face, an' seems to be right smart to boot—a good match for Gage."

Abel's stomach clenched. Tressa and Gage? After being forced into a compromising position by the man, she'd agreed to his courting? It didn't make sense. Then his thoughts turned cynical. Maybe Gage's wealth had turned her head. Living on the Hammond ranch would put her in a prominent position in Barnett.

Brewster grinned. "Who knows? Maybe in another year I'll be bouncin' a grandson on my knee. All the more reason to add to my land holdin's. Gimme somethin' to hand 'im when he's full grown."

The thought of Tressa bearing Gage's children made Abel squirm. He set his jaw. "Sorry, Brewster, but as I told you before, my place isn't for sale. You'll have to look elsewhere to find land for your future grandson."

"All right, Abel." Brewster slapped the wagon side and stepped back. "But remember the offer's still open. You let me know if you change your mind."

Abel smacked the reins down, urging the horses out of town. He felt sick to his stomach. He'd promised his pa he'd hang on to the ranch, but this latest loss crushed all hope of keeping that vow. It took money to run a ranch—to buy feed, to pay ranch hands, and to keep Uncle Sam satisfied. He might be forced to sell. But not to Brewster Hammond.

≈

"You must be the stupidest girl ever born." Luella ran a squeaky wooden rolling pin over a lump of dough on Saturday afternoon, working it thinner and thinner. The contemptuous remark stung, but Tressa continued plucking wet feathers from the dead chicken and refused to rise to Luella's bait.

"When are you going to give up your snooty ways and allow Gage

243

Hammond to court you? It's not likely you'll find a better match."
Luella's caustic tone carried a hint of melancholy.

Tressa glanced toward the work table, and despite Luella's mistreatment, compassion stirred in her breast when she glimpsed the girl's sad face. Mabelle and Paralee had gone to town with their beaus for dinner at the café. Although Fred Pennington had committed to courting Luella, the man's efforts to woo a woman were sorely feeble. He arrived at the Flying W each evening and spent a few minutes with Luella, but he never brought her gifts like Mabelle's and Paralee's beaus, and he had yet to take her to town for dinner or out for an evening drive.

"You ought to be thankful Gage Hammond shows even a trace of interest in you." Luella clacked the rolling pin to the side, picked up a sharp knife, and ran it across the sheet of dough, creating long, skinny noodles.

Tressa carried the freshly plucked chicken to the dry sink and began cutting it into pieces with a butcher knife. "I'm not ungrateful, Luella. I know Gage is paying me a compliment by wanting to court me." Her nightly prayers hadn't awakened fond feelings for the young man. Instead, images of Abel Samms always interfered with her focus. Her heart ached each time she thought of how Cole Jacobs had stolen from him. The anger Abel displayed no doubt masked his deeper feelings of betrayal.

Luella lifted a string of dough and placed it over the wooden drying rack. "A man like Gage Hammond won't wait forever."

Tressa bit down on the end of her tongue to still any further argument. Luella would continue haranguing her no matter how she responded. Silence was often her best defense. She layered the chicken pieces in a pot and ladled in water—"enough to drown the bird," as Aunt Hattie had taught her. Grunting a bit with the pot's weight, she carried it to the stove. Remembering Aunt Hattie's recipe, she added salt, pepper, and a bay leaf, and then placed the lid on the pot.

She crossed to the table and helped Luella lay the remaining noodles over the wooden rack, thankful that the girl had ceased her diatribe. She hummed as she worked. In a few hours, the noodles would be dry enough to break into pieces and add to the soup. Her mouth watered. They would have a fine supper.

The moment Luella draped the last noodle over the rack, she put her hands on her hips and scowled at Tressa. "So are you going to finally let Gage Hammond start courting you or not?"

Tressa sighed. She couldn't imagine why Luella was so eager to have her matched with Gage Hammond after going to such lengths to secure him for herself, but she found the girl's endless badgering tiresome. "Luella, it wouldn't it be fair to accept Gage's attention when I don't love him."

"Love," Luella snorted. "We have to be practical, Tressa, and take whatever chance we're offered."

"You mean like Evelyn, who returned to New York to marry a man older than her own father?" Tressa caught Luella's dress sleeve, her desire for answers overpowering her determination to avoid further animosity. "Do you really believe Evelyn is happy in a loveless marriage even though she has lots of money? And think of Sallie—she risked everything to be with Cole, not because he's wealthy, but because she loves him. Who do you think is happier right now, Luella—Evelyn or Sallie?"

For a moment, Luella gazed out the window, her expression wistful. Then, with a huff of breath, she wrenched her arm free and pasted on a scornful look. "We weren't talking about Evelyn and Sallie. We were talking about you. You're going to lose your chance for a husband and a family if you don't set aside your romantic ideas and accept Gage Hammond's offer. And if you refuse him, Tressa, you really are a fool." She turned and flounced out of the kitchen.

Tressa sank onto a kitchen chair and rested her chin in her hand. Was is it a foolish, romantic idea to wait for love? Although she'd been young when her mother died, she remembered the tender looks her parents shared across the dinner table. She also remembered the sense of security that surrounded her when she glimpsed their devotion to each other. How could she forget her father's impenetrable sadness after Mama's death? Sadness so deep could come only from the loss of something infinitely precious. Perhaps her parents hadn't shared many years together, but they had shared love. And their lives—including Tressa's—were richer because of it.

Each time Aunt Hattie spoke of her Jed, a special look came into her eyes. What was that, if not love? Tressa was certain Aunt Hattie would not marry Brewster Hammond—no matter how wealthy and powerful the man—unless she loved him.

Her thoughts skipped backward to the evening when Aunt Hattie told her God had used her aunt and uncle to bring her to this place for a God-planned purpose. Tressa wanted desperately to believe that God had someone special waiting for her—someone who would love and cherish her as deeply as her father had cherished her mother. Could that person possibly be Gage? And how could she know for sure?

Jumping up from the table, Tressa hurried to the garden, where Aunt Hattie was snipping green beans from their vines. She smiled when she spotted Tressa stepping over the low fence.

"Ah, you got that chicken simmerin' already? Then you can help me pick beans. Can't hardly keep up with 'em. Fool plants grow new beans every night."

The word "fool" propelled Tressa forward. She knelt and buried her hands in the sticky leaves of a plant, searching for beans. "Aunt Hattie, how can one know if love is growing in her heart for a man?"

The older woman shot Tressa a speculative look. "Well, Tressa-darlin', I reckon it's different for every woman, but I can tell you how I knew I was fallin' in love with Jed."

Tressa sat on her haunches and listened intently, the green beans forgotten.

"Got to be where my ears hungered for the sound of his voice. Day just wasn't complete if we didn't have a few minutes o' time together. I wanted to *give* to him—not just things, mind you, but pieces o' myself. My thoughts, my dreams, my feelin's . . . and I trusted him to keep those things safe." Aunt Hattie stared across the garden patch, her lips curved into a sweet smile. Tressa wondered what the older woman was envisioning in those moments of silent reflection. "The day he said 'I love you' to me, why, my heart nearly took wing an' flew right out o' my chest, it made me so joyful inside. An' I knew. I just knew I loved him."

"How long did it take?"

Aunt Hattie's head jerked, her surprised expression meeting Tressa's. "How long? Well now, missy, I'm not sure a person can know how long it takes love to grow. Kind o' like these bean plants. You put a whole passel of seeds in the ground, but they pop up one by one—on their own time, y'see. But with sunlight an' water, eventually they all sprout." She chuckled. "That's probably not a good example, but you see what I mean. Love needs nurturin' an' attention to grow."

Nurturing and attention . . . Tressa flung her arms around Aunt Hattie's neck and squeezed. "Thank you, Aunt Hattie!"

"Gracious, girl, you're welcome." Aunt Hattie patted Tressa's back. "But let loose o' me now before we tumble into these plants an' squash 'em flat!"

With a laugh, Tressa released her hold. "Aunt Hattie, is Mr. Hammond coming for supper tonight?"

"He sure is. I told him we was havin' chicken an' noodles, an' he said wild horses wouldn't keep him away."

"Do you suppose I could ride to the Double H and . . ." She lowered her head.

Aunt Hattie lifted Tressa's chin. "An' what, Tressa?"

Tressa drew in a fortifying breath. "Gage wants to court me, but

I've resisted him because I don't love him. You said God has plans for me here. How can I know for sure those plans don't include Gage if I never spend time with him?"

Aunt Hattie grimaced. "Oh now, Tressa—"

"But you just said love takes nurturing and attention. I haven't even given Gage a chance. Shouldn't I at least allow time to see if a seed of love will sprout between us?"

For several seconds, Aunt Hattie peered uncertainly into Tressa's face. Finally she sighed. "I reckon it wouldn't hurt. You wantin' to see if he'll come with his pa to supper tonight?"

Tressa nodded eagerly.

"All right, then." She waved a dirty hand toward the barn. "Saddle up Spotty an' ride on over there."

Tressa jumped up and started across the garden.

"But mind how you ask him. You're just wantin' some time to get to know him a bit better. Careful you don't give him the idea you're ready to start courtin', or you might get stuck with somethin' bigger'n you can handle."

Tressa called over her shoulder, "I'll be careful!" Fifteen minutes later, she was heading down the lane astride Spotty's broad back. The Double H sat behind Abel Samms' ranch, and to reach it she would need to travel past the Lazy S and then turn north. She could shorten the distance if she cut along the property line between the Lazy S and the Flying W. Abel Samms' barbed wire fence would lead her directly to Hammond land. Then she could cross the Hammonds' pasture. For a moment she nibbled her lip, wondering about the wisdom of such a choice. Traveling by road would take longer, but it would be safer.

Glancing skyward at the sun's position, she realized the afternoon was slipping by quickly. A shorter route would ensure she could reach the Hammonds' ranch and return to the Flying W in time to set the table. The decision made, she gave the reins a tug. Spotty snorted in protest, but he obediently trotted out into open pasture.

26

After a half hour of riding beneath the sun, Tressa regretted her impulsive decision to cut across the Lazy S and invite Gage Hammond to supper. Perspiration dribbled down her forehead, stinging her eyes. Her dress stuck to her skin. Strands of hair, worked loose during her bouncing journey on Spotty's back, clung to her cheeks and neck. Why hadn't she waited and invited Gage to Sunday dinner after church, rather than making this unpleasant trip by herself? He'd certainly be less than impressed by her disheveled appearance when she finally arrived at the Double H.

A burbling creek's melody reached her ears, and her mouth seemed to turn to cotton in response to the cheerful song of the water. The horse nodded his great head, releasing little snorts, and she laughed. Apparently Spotty wanted a drink, too.

"All right, big boy. Let's stop for a minute or two." She pulled back on the reins and slid down from the saddle. The horse trotted eagerly toward the water with Tressa holding tight to his reins. He lowered his head and slurped noisily.

Tressa tossed the reins over Spotty's neck, then sat on her haunches and scooped up the sparkling water with her hands. The cold liquid trickled down her wrists and chin when she drank, but she didn't mind. Her dress would dry, and the moisture refreshed her. She drank until her thirst was quenched.

Spotty submerged his nose in the water and then snorted, spewing little drops on the side of Tressa's head. With a giggle, she leaped to her feet and stepped backward. "Now you stop that!" She gave his reins a gentle pull. He dug in his front hooves and refused to move, so she turned stern and gave a mighty yank. With a snort of protest, he allowed himself to be led away from the creek.

Suddenly Tressa realized she'd made a mistake by getting down from the horse's back. The stirrups hung high to accommodate her shorter leg length when sitting in the saddle—too high for her foot to reach when standing on the ground. She had always climbed a fence and slid directly into the seat, but no sturdy wooden fence was available to her now. How would she remount Spotty?

Catching hold of the saddle horn with one hand and the cantle with the other, she tried lifting her foot high enough to place her toe into the stirrup. Spotty shifted, and she hopped twice on one foot before losing her grip.

"Spotty, stand still!" She tried again, but her skirts prevented her from seeing her foot, and she continually missed the stirrup. However, she bumped Spotty's ribs with her knee, and he whinnied, rolling his nose toward her as if to tell her to stop bothering him.

She stomped her foot in frustration. "Oh! I suppose I'll have to the walk the rest of the way. Unless . . ." She tapped her lips thoughtfully. The barbed wire fence appeared flimsy, but if the wire was strong enough to hold back cattle, perhaps it would support her weight. If so, she could climb on the wires and get into the saddle.

"Come here, Spotty." She tied his reins to the top wire to keep him from scooting away from her, then she slipped between the horse and the fence. Holding on to the saddle horn, she placed her foot on the lowest wire and lifted herself. Her sole slipped on the thin wire, and her dress caught in the barbs. *Rip!* Tressa gasped when she saw the large tear in her skirt. For a moment her resolve wavered, but she had no other choice. Either climb the fence or walk the remaining distance to the Hammonds' ranch.

Taking in a deep breath, she made a second attempt to climb the barbed strings. Her legs quivered with the effort of balancing on the narrow wire, but she made it to the second line. She poised to heave herself into the saddle, but once again her foot slipped. Arms flailing, she landed flat on her bottom. The fall forced the air from her lungs with a *whoosh.*

Spotty whickered and shifted his hindquarters away from her. She lay on her back, her chest heaving as her lungs tried to regain the lost air. Eventually her breathing calmed, and she sat up. Her back throbbed, but she managed to get to her feet. Hobbling forward, she untied Spotty.

She held the reins for a moment, looking north and then west. Should she continue on to the Double H or simply return to Aunt Hattie's? The desire to go home, to wash the sweat and dust from her face, and to change into a fresh dress overrode inviting Gage Hammond to eat chicken and noodles.

"I will invite Gage Hammond to dinner tomorrow after church," she told the horse. "But for now, we are going home."

At the word "home," Spotty perked up his ears and nickered. Tressa held Spotty's reins as she limped back toward the road. Pain stabbed her back with every step, and she was hot and sweaty, but somehow the beauty of the landscape crept into her soul, chasing away her frustration. A stout breeze encouraged the tips of the tall grass to dance and sway, as if the blades were whispering secrets. Scrubby trees, their branches bowed from the force of a persistent north wind, waved their leaf-dotted boughs in welcome. The clear blue sky stretched from the horizon, dazzling in its immeasurable expanse.

Her face aimed toward the sky, Tressa said, "You truly have created a beautiful world, God. When one moves quickly, she misses the glorious details. Thank You for the opportunity to slow down and see the prairie in all of its splendor." The simple prayer revived her even more than the drink of cool water had.

Tressa's gaze roved over every inch of the open country as she made her plodding progress. Speckles of blue amidst the grass caught her eye, and she hurried her feet to a patch of tiny, pale blue flowers. One hand pressed to her lower back, she stooped over to pick a few of the delicate blooms, and something else captured her attention— evidence of a recent campfire.

"Stay here, Spotty." She tossed his reins over the top line of barbed wire and moved forward to explore. The cleared patch rested just on the opposite side of the fence. In its center, rocks circled a jumble of charred wood, and a branding iron rested inside the circle of rocks.

Tressa crinkled her brow. Aunt Hattie brought her calves into a pen to brand them. Did Abel have his men brand their cattle out on the range? She pressed her memory and recalled an enclosure between Abel's barn and the bunkhouse with a similar fire pit for branding. Did they brand in two locations?

Careful to avoid the barbs in the wire, she leaned in as far as she could. Tipping her head, she looked again at the branding iron, and then she jolted backward, releasing the wire so quickly it twanged. Instead of an S lying on its side—the Lazy S brand—this iron possessed two H's, the second one slightly higher than the other and sharing a center stem—the Hammonds' brand for the Double H.

Why was a Double H brand lying at the edge of Abel's pasture? Heart pounding, she glanced up and down the fence line. She limped back and forth as quickly as her aching back would allow, examining each post, and she found several places where the wire had been restrung. The fence had been cut and repaired—possibly more than once. An ugly picture began to form in her mind.

"Spotty, we need to hurry home. I need to tell Aunt Hattie what I found." As she reached for the horse's reins, a pop similar to a firecracker sounded in the distance, then a high-pitched *zing* whizzed by her ears. She froze, her skin tingling with awareness. Spotty neighed, dancing with his front feet and tossing his head. His reins slipped from the wire.

Tressa looked around, seeking the source of the sound, and a second *pop-ziiiiing* came. Spotty screamed. A ribbon of red formed on the horse's neck. Realization struck Tressa, followed by terror. Someone had fired a gun at them!

Spotty whirled and took off across the pasture, his reins bouncing at his knees. Tressa took two stumbling steps after him, and a third shot rang. With a screech of fear, she dove facedown in the grass. Curling her arms over her head, she begged God to protect her.

❧

Hattie dipped water from the reservoir to cover the snapped green beans. The aroma of chicken rose from the pot on the stove, and she licked her lips in anticipation of supper. Chicken and noodles was hardly the fare of kings, but Jed had always loved it—said it stuck to a man's ribs. Hattie chuckled as she stirred pieces of bacon and chopped onion into the green beans. Her Jed had never been one to complain, no matter what she put on the table. Pleasured a woman to cook for a man like that.

Her hand stilled. Brewster had said his cook would stay on and see to the kitchen chores should Hattie choose to marry him. What would she do all day if she didn't cook and clean and garden? All her life, her hands had been busy. "Idle hands are the devil's workshop," her ma had preached, and Hattie had kept the devil at bay by working, working, working. . . .

She set the spoon aside and crossed to the kitchen window. Paralee and Mabelle, back from their excursion into Barnett, were hanging towels on the line and chatting, their laughter carrying through the open window. Upstairs, Luella was remaking all the beds with fresh sheets. A smile of satisfaction tugged at Hattie's lips. The girls had become true ranching women. They'd all be fine wives for Barnett's ranchers.

A pang of regret nicked her heart when she thought of Sallie. She wished she'd paid better attention to the girl's melancholy—maybe she could've kept her from running off like she did. But she couldn't do anything about it now. Sallie was gone, and soon Mabelle, Paralee, and Luella would marry and move to their own ranches.

The lid rattled on the chicken pot, and Hattie scurried over to turn the damper and reduce the heat. She didn't want broth boiling over across the stove. Tressa wouldn't appreciate having to clean up such a mess. Another pang struck as she considered Tressa's future. No peace filled her heart when she thought of Tressa marrying up with Gage Hammond. Brewster was finally taking a firm hand with his son, and that was certain to bring some change, but Hattie suspected Gage would always be more interested in what pleased him than in pleasing somebody else. Tressa deserved better than that.

Despite all her prayers for the girls to find their God-chosen matches, the only one who'd stepped up to court Tressa was Gage Hammond. Hattie snorted. "God, I've spent my life believin' You know best, but I sure have to wonder about Gage an' Tressa. Don't seem right to me." She picked up the wooden spoon to give the beans another stir.

A *bang-bang-bang* on the back door nearly scared her into throwing the spoon across the kitchen. She yanked the door open and glared at

Clyde, who stood on the little stoop. "What'n thunder are you tryin' to do—knock the door down?"

He pointed to the yard, where Spotty stood near the corral fence, his neck lathery and sides heaving. She scowled. Tressa knew better than to ride a horse hard enough to make him lather. And why hadn't the girl unsaddled him and put him in the barn instead of leaving him out in the sun?

"Miz Wyatt, Spotty just come gallopin' into the yard, an' from the looks of 'im, somebody winged him with a bullet."

Hattie's heart skipped a beat. "What?" She barreled across the ground to the horse. Pink lather showed where the animal's neck had been bleeding. "Tressa wasn't ridin' 'im?"

"No, ma'am. He came just like this."

Hattie spun and headed for the barn, calling orders over her shoulder. "Tell the girls to see to supper. Tend to the horse. I'm ridin' to the Hammonds'." Looking skyward, she added, "Dear Lord, wrap Your arms o' protection around that girl. Please don't let nothin' bad happen to my Tressa!"

❦

Tressa had no idea how long she lay in the grass. Her heart pounded so hard her chest hurt. Her muscles ached from holding herself stiff and still. She longed to rise and run home to Aunt Hattie. To feel safe within the confines of the Flying W. No shots had followed the third one, but what if the person were still out there, waiting for her lift up her head? He might not miss the next time.

So she remained flat on her belly, her face pressed to the ground, listening for any clues that her attacker could be drawing near. The whisper of the grass, soothing earlier, made her quake in fear that it covered the sound of footsteps. The wide open sky, so beautiful, now mocked her with its inability to hide her. She repeated a verse from

Psalms again and again—" 'What time I am afraid, I will trust in Thee' "—but still fear paralyzed her.

Suddenly a flapping noise, accompanied by the squawk of a bird, came from somewhere beyond Tressa's head. What had startled the bird into flight? She bit down on her lip to hold back the screech of fear, and she tasted blood. " 'I will trust in Thee. . . . I will trust in Thee. . . .' " The whisper rasped from her dry throat. Might her words bounce from the hard ground to God's ears?

❧

Hattie set her horse at a reckless pace. Questions crowded her mind. Why would someone shoot at Tressa? Had she been hit like Spotty? Did she lie somewhere hurt and bleeding? The lack of answers made her pulse race, and she dug her moccasin-covered heels into the horse's ribs and demanded, "Yah! Yah!"

The gate to the Lazy S lay just ahead. Hattie had planned to head right on to the Hammonds', but when she spotted Abel pitching hay from the barn loft's opening into his wagon bed on the ground, she pulled the horse's reins and turned in at the gate. She clattered directly to the wagon and brought the animal to a halt.

"Abel, you been workin' out here all day?"

"Pret' much." He stood the pitchfork on its tines and frowned down at her. "Somethin' happen?"

Quickly, Hattie explained Spotty showing up with a gunshot wound and no rider. "Didja hear any shots?"

"No, but if it happened while I was inside the barn, I wouldn't've. Those rock walls block out nearly everything."

Hattie gestured anxiously. "Well, she was headin' for the Hammond place to ask Gage to supper. Didja see her ride by here?"

"Haven't seen nobody come down that road all day, 'cept for you just now, but I might've been inside the barn when she went by." Abel caught the pulley rope that hung from the peak of the barn and came down hand-over-hand. "Or she might've cut across the pasture between our places."

Hattie groaned. "She could be anywhere. I was hopin' to spot her along the road. . . ."

"Can't spare Vince an' Ethan—they're out with the herd—but I'll saddle a horse an' help you look."

"I'd be obliged. Don't mind tellin' ya, I'm plenty scared."

"You head on to Brewster's place—get some more men to go lookin'. I'll double back an' ride the fence line, just in case she left the road." He squinted up at her. "You got a pistol with you?"

Hattie patted her hip where her sidearm always rode.

"Good. Fire a shot in the air when she's found." He headed for his barn.

Hattie gave the reins a yank, and the horse wheeled around. A hard nudge in his ribs, and he took off at a gallop. The sooner she reached the Double H, the sooner they'd find Tressa. "Yah, Rudy, let's go!"

27

Worry nibbled at the back of Abel's mind as he searched for signs of hoofprints heading off the road and across the grazing land. In all his years of living in Barnett, he'd never heard of anyone taking a shot at a lady. To think someone had done so now rattled his sense of well-being.

Don't let her be hurt. The words formed in his heart, but they weren't a prayer. More of a demand to anybody who might be listening. When he'd learned Miss Sallie had sneaked off, he hadn't experienced an urgency to locate her and make sure she was safe. But the moment he'd been told Miss Tressa was missing and could be hurt, fear had clawed its way to the very center of his soul.

He also wanted to find the shooter. Any man worth his salt took care with his weapon—knew what he was aiming at, and usually hit the target. His stomach churned at that thought. If she'd been shot, it was best he found her instead of Aunt Hattie. The old woman didn't need such an ugly picture in her mind.

Hurry . . . Gotta find her . . . He scanned the area, seeking any sign of Tressa. He forced his brain to release the worry and just focus. He searched back and forth across the prairie, up and down the road, and then at the ground, alert to anything out of the ordinary. And finally, a little more than a mile from the Flying W, he spotted a set of shod horse tracks veering from the road into the pasture.

They had to belong to Tressa's horse. Hope pounding through his chest, he angled his horse in the direction of the tracks and rode slowly, his head high, eyes seeking. He considered calling out for her, but if the person who had shot at her was still somewhere near, he could put himself in peril. So he used his ears and his eyes and searched diligently.

He followed his own fence line, noting places where the grass had been mashed down, offering evidence of Tressa's progress. With his head angled to the side, looking down, he almost missed something rustling in the breeze just ahead. Instinctively, he pulled back on the reins and swiveled his eyes forward. Rumpled calico fabric . . . a woman's dress!

He leaped from the horse's back and stumbled the few yards forward to where she lay on the ground, unmoving. No blood stained her clothes, but maybe the bullet had entered from the front. Fearful of what he would find, he advanced slowly. He bent down on one knee and gingerly placed his hands on her shoulders to turn her over.

Releasing a scream that pierced his eardrums, she sprang to life. She rolled to her back and kicked out with both legs. Her arms thrashed, connecting with his chest and shoulders. The terror in her eyes melted him, and he captured her wrists. "Tressa! Tressa, I'm not goin' to hurt you. I'm here to help!"

For several more seconds she continued to rail against him, little animal grunts of fear leaving her lips, while he continued to reassure her with calm promises. Then just as suddenly as it had begun, the fight went out of her. She wilted into a defenseless heap. He released his hold on her wrists but caught her shoulders to help her sit up. Her muscles quivered beneath his palms.

She stared at him with wide, unblinking eyes. "A-Abel?"

The sound of his given name on her lips caused his heart to skip a beat. She must be very unsettled to forget her manners. "That's right." He glanced down her front, seeking signs of injury. To his great relief, she seemed unhurt. Only very badly frightened.

"How . . . did you know . . . I needed help?" Her words came out in little gasps.

Abel maintained a soothing tone, giving her shoulders a gentle squeeze. "Aunt Hattie sent me out lookin' for you. She was worried sick when your horse come back without you. 'Specially since he had a gunshot wound." Abel licked his lips and darted a glance around the area. "Were . . . were you hit?"

She shook her head. Fine strands of tangled hair were clinging to her cheeks and neck. "No, I wasn't hurt. But I didn't know what to do. I thought if I got up, he might—he might try again to shoot me." Her chin crumpled. "Why would someone want to shoot me?"

"I don't know. . . ." The fearful confusion dimming her blue eyes made Abel long to soothe her worries away. Only the knowledge that she was being courted by another man kept him from gathering her into his arms. But he had to offer comfort somehow. "Maybe it was just a hunter shootin' at some quail or a deer, an' his shot went awry."

She sat in silence, her gaze boring into his, as if considering his explanation. Suddenly she let out a little huff. "Well, he nearly frightened me to death. Hunters should exercise greater consideration when there are people nearby."

A grin twitched at Abel's cheek. Her high-falutin' speech attested that she was returning to normal. He strode to his horse and tied the reins securely to a fence post. He then removed his pistol from its holster. "Cover your ears, Tressa. I'm gonna fire off a shot to let Aunt Hattie know I found you."

She pulled up her knees and hunkered forward, squeezing herself into a ball with her hands over her ears and her eyes closed tightly. Abel fired the shot and then quickly holstered the gun. He took hold of her hands, pulling them from her ears. She sent him a wary look.

Gage Hammond was a lucky man, Abel thought as he gently helped Tressa to her feet. "Let's get you back to the Flying W. Aunt Hattie'll be eager to see that you're all right." Holding her hand, he headed toward his horse.

"No, wait! I forgot . . ." She pulled loose and hobbled to the fence. On tiptoe, she pointed to the other side. "Over there—see that fire pit?"

Abel frowned. "I see it."

"There's a branding iron, but it— Oh!" She clapped her hand over her mouth and stared at him, her eyes once more filled with fright.

Concern sent him forward several feet. "Tressa, what is it?"

"It . . . it's gone." She looked rapidly back and forth. Whirling to face him, she caught his shirt sleeve and shook it. "There was a branding iron lying right there in that fire pit."

Abel shook his head. "Tressa, you must be mistaken. That's not a brandin' pit—a brandin' fire would need to be bigger. I reckon one of my men started a fire out here to keep warm at some time, or maybe to heat up a pot of coffee. We don't do any brandin' out on the range."

"But I saw a branding iron, Mr. Samms. It was there, and now it's gone." Her shoulders rose and fell with the speed of her breathing. "Do you . . . do you think the person who shot at me might have come and taken it away?" Tears pooled in her eyes. "I was lying right over there. He . . . he could have easily killed me." Her voice rose with hysteria.

"Now, Miss Tressa, don't go gettin' yourself worked up."

"But . . . but . . . it was there, and now—"

Abel grasped her shoulders, giving her a slight shake. "Miss Tressa, stop it. You been out here for quite a while. The sun'll do funny things to a person. Even make 'em see things that aren't there."

She knocked his hands loose. "I *know* what I saw! There was a branding iron lying right next to those pieces of charred wood!"

"All right, all right . . ." He held up both hands. "I believe you."

Her eyes narrowed.

He sighed. "Well, maybe I'm havin' a hard time believin' you. Can't figure why somebody would be brandin' out here." At her irritated huff, he added, "But maybe they did."

"And then someone walked off with the branding iron while I was lying in the grass not twenty feet away?"

He had no answer to that. He held out his hand. "C'mon, Tressa. I fired off that shot. Aunt Hattie an' the others'll be headin' to the Flyin' W to check on you. I need to get you back."

He swung into his saddle, then pulled her up behind him. "Hold tight." Her arms curved around his waist. The touch sent a jolt of reaction through his insides. *The sun'll do funny things to a person.* Had the sun caused the strange response? Somehow, he didn't believe so.

"Let's go." He clicked his tongue on his teeth, and his horse headed for the road.

✍

Hattie tucked the fresh-smelling sheet beneath Tressa's chin and gave the girl's cheek a gentle pat. "There now. You just get yourself a good sleep, an' by mornin' you'll be right as rain."

Tressa sighed, burrowing against the pillows. "Aunt Hattie, I'm so sorry I ruined your supper plans."

Hattie waved her hand. "Pshaw! Don't be silly. Why, Brewster'n me'll have plenty o' chances to sit an' eat chicken an' noodles together. You're more important than any dinner. You oughtta know that by now."

The girl's eyes flooded with tears. Hattie sat on the edge of the bed and patted Tressa's leg through the sheets. "Here now. What're them tears all about?"

Tressa shook her head, tangling the long strands of hair that lay across her shoulders. "You make me feel like somebody special."

"An' that makes you want to cry?"

"Yes, ma'am."

Hattie chuckled. "Well, Tressa-darlin', I'm not tryin' to make you cry, but you are special. I've come to love all you girls. Even Luella. But you . . . there's just somethin' that makes my heart reach out to you. Never had no young'uns o' my own, but I figure God's given me a glimpse of what a mother might feel toward a child by plantin' a seed o' love in my heart for you."

One tear spilled down Tressa's cheek. She pulled her hand from beneath the sheets and placed it over Hattie's hand. "I love you, too, Aunt Hattie."

Tears pricked behind Hattie's nose. She sniffled. "I best skedaddle out o' here an' let you rest. You had a rough day."

Tressa's hand tightened on Hattie's. "Please stay."

Sympathy held Hattie in place. "You still feelin' scared about that rifle goin' off?"

"Yes. Something . . . isn't right, Aunt Hattie."

The girl spoke the truth. If someone could take shots at a girl as sweet and harmless as Tressa, then there was certainly something wrong in the world. But Hattie pushed her lips into a smile. "What's that, darlin'?"

"I tried to tell Mr. Samms, but he wouldn't listen to me. He said the sun was making me see things that weren't there. But I know I saw a Double H branding iron lying near a fire pit on Lazy S land."

The hairs on Hattie's arms prickled. "Double H? You sure?"

"I'm very sure. And I walked along the fence and saw places where somebody had cut the fence and then fixed it again."

"Did you show these things to Abel?"

"That's what's so odd. I tried to. But after he came, the iron was gone. So he didn't believe that I'd really seen it. That made me mad, so I didn't try to show him the fence."

An uncomfortable prickle snaked across Hattie's scalp. Tressa might have stumbled upon the rustler's camp. And if she'd been seen out there, the rustler was probably the one who shot at her. If he suspected she knew too much, he might try again.

She bolted to her feet. "You don't worry now, you hear? I'll talk to Abel, an' between the two of us, we'll get things figured out. You just sleep."

"Will you pray with me before you go?"

Hattie would never deny a request like that. She took Tressa's hand and closed her eyes. "Dear Lord, thank You for bringin' Tressa safely home today. Thank You for Your love an' protection. Give her peace now an' let her rest knowin' that You're here with her an' You won't ever leave her side. Amen." She patted Tressa's cheek and smiled. "Can you sleep now?"

"Yes, ma'am. Thank you." The girl rolled to her side and curled into a ball.

Hattie blew out the lamp, pulled the window shade down, and tiptoed out of the room. Once in the hallway, she stopped and replayed Tressa's statement about the branding iron. At one time Abel had suspected Gage Hammond of stealing his cattle. It would be an easy thing for the man to do, with their spreads side by side. And Brewster wanted to buy Abel's land. Could the two of them have been filching Abel's cattle and using a running iron to change the brand in the hopes that Abel would give up and sell his ranch?

When she'd arrived at the Double H today, Brewster was in the house and responded to her plea for help without one second of hesitation. But Gage was off somewhere. Hattie clenched her teeth. If Gage had been off somewhere firing shots at Tressa and then hiding that branding iron, she'd have a piece of his hide. And Brewster's, too!

❧

"Mm-mm, that was good grub."

Abel nodded to acknowledge Vince's satisfied statement.

The old cowboy leaned back in his chair and patted his belly. "Reckon we could talk Aunt Hattie into sendin' food over ever' day? That was the best chicken an' noodles I've had in years."

Considering the reason Aunt Hattie had sent Abel home with a crock of chicken and noodles, Abel hoped she wouldn't ever find need to repay him with dinner again. Every time he thought about Tressa lying facedown and unmoving in the grass, he experienced another jolt of panic. "Don't get to countin' on it. This was a thank-you."

"What'd you do for her?" Ethan asked around a mouthful of noodles.

Although Abel hadn't intended to discuss the afternoon's search for Tressa with his hired hands, he decided if someone was out there firing a rifle, the men should know. He told them about Tressa being frightened by three rifle shots, one of which injured her horse.

Ethan sat bolt upright, his eyes wide. "She all right? She didn't get hurt, did she?"

"She's fine. But she was plenty shook up. Can't blame her." Abel scowled. "Bothers me that she was so close to my land when it happened. Makes me wonder where those shots came from. . . ."

Vince cleared his throat. "Uh, Abel? Was she out by the northwest pasture?"

Abel sent Vince a puzzled look. "Yes. Why?"

The man scratched his chin. "Might've been me, then, that shot at her."

"Pa!" Ethan nearly came out of his chair.

"Now, not on purpose, mind you. I was out checkin' the fence, an' I spotted a badger. Sent off three shots to scare him away." Vince's face twisted with remorse. "If'n I'd known Miss Tressa was ridin' out there, I wouldn't've fired my gun, but I was down along the creek—

that rocky place where the water made a gulley. Hard to see from down there."

Abel blew out a breath of relief. Even though Tressa had a close call, at least he knew no rustlers were roaming his property. "I'm sure it was an accident, Vince. Tell Aunt Hattie about it at church tomorrow. It'll ease Tressa's mind to know nobody meant to hurt her."

"I'll do that, Abel. I surely will." Vince unfolded his lanky frame and reached for his hat. "Since Ethan's on clean-up duty, I'm gonna head on out an' check what's left of the herd one more time—bring 'em in a little closer. I sleep better knowin' they're closer to the house."

"Fine, Vince. Thanks." Not until Vince had closed the door did Abel consider what he'd said. *"What's left of the herd . . ."* The words were a reminder of how much Abel had lost. He was relieved Tressa was safe, but what would it take to keep his ranch safely in his hands?

28

"Gage, I'm telling you, I saw a Double H branding iron on Mr. Samms'
land!" Tressa folded her arms across her chest and glared into Gage's
smirking face. "Do not presume to tell me what I have or haven't
witnessed with my own eyes!"

Gage laughed. "You're cute when you get all fired up."

Tressa blew out a breath of aggravation. She had hoped the man
who claimed a desire to court her, wed her, and share his life with her
would do more than ridicule her story of the missing branding iron.
"I am certain that branding iron was carried away by the person who
shot at me—no one else was out there. And he's probably the same
man who has been stealing Mr. Samms' cattle. I will discover the truth,
Gage—whether anyone wants to believe me or not!" She whirled away
from him and headed across the churchyard.

Gage clumped up behind her and caught her arm. The mischievous
expression of moments ago had disappeared. His lips formed a surly
line, and his eyes sparked with something that sent a chill through

Tressa's body. He pulled her behind the flowering bushes that grew at the corner of the church building and gave her arm a shake. "Spunky's one thing, but you're takin' this too far."

Tressa puckered her brow in confusion. "But the truth needs to be uncovered, Gage."

"Tryin' to uncover the truth could cause you a heap of trouble, Tressa."

The threatening tone stole Tressa's breath. "Gage . . . you?"

His hand tightened painfully on her arm. "Don't go jumpin' to more conclusions. You think you got it all figured out, but you don't, so it'd be smart to just keep your mouth quiet." Suddenly his grip relaxed. "I ain't out to hurt you, Tressa. I like you—like you lots. I want to marry up with you. But it grieves me deep down to have you thinkin' ill of me. You need to let those ideas go. A man and wife . . . they gotta trust each other, now, don't they?"

Although the words were warm, they were delivered with a menacing undertone that chilled Tressa from the inside out.

"No sense in gettin' everybody all worked up over some brandin' iron that prob'ly wasn't even there to start with. What rustler'd be foolish enough to leave his runnin' iron layin' out in the open?" Gage laughed, shaking his head. "Silly little city gal, don't know how things're done in the West." He gave her arm a squeeze and then released it. Hooking his thumbs in his pants pockets, he winked. "We ain't gonna talk about this no more, Tressa. You just tell yourself that fall you took from the fence made your head fuzzy, an' let it go. Everybody'll be better off."

Tressa gaped at him. "Did you see me fall when I tried to remount Spotty?" If he saw her fall, he had been out in the pasture, and that meant—

Curling his arm around her waist, he pulled her tight against his side. "Didn't I just say to let it go? You think too much, Tressa. Purty girl like you has no need for thinkin'."

His possessive arm around her waist bound her as tightly as a new rope to his side. He escorted her to the wagon, where Aunt Hattie and Mr. Hammond stood visiting with Glendon Shultz, Fred Pennington, and Jerome Garner. Aunt Hattie frowned briefly when she saw Gage and Tressa approaching, but she quickly flipped it into a smile.

"Here you two are. We was just fixin' to head to the Flying W for dinner. All the fellas are comin' so they can spend the afternoon with their gals. Gage, you comin', too?"

"Wouldn't miss it." Gage aimed his lips at Tressa's temple, but she shifted her head slightly, avoiding the contact. His eyes sparked, but he released her and offered an easy grin. "Pa, I'll get our rig." He turned a loving look on Tressa. "You wanna ride with Pa an' me, darlin'?"

"The girls're comin' with me so's we can get lunch put on the table before you fellas get there," Aunt Hattie interjected.

"All right, then." Gage sauntered to the Hammonds' buggy.

Tressa scrambled into the back of the wagon with the other girls, all the while wondering what she should do about Gage. Was he a rustler? A liar? If so, who should she tell? Aunt Hattie was set on marrying Brewster—she couldn't burden the older woman. Abel didn't believe her. Oh, if only Sallie were here! She could share these troublesome thoughts with Sallie.

Oh, Lord, what should I do?

~

Aunt Hattie's succulent beef roast stuck in Tressa's throat. She picked at the stewed carrots and potatoes, moving the chunks of vegetables back and forth on her plate rather than carrying them to her mouth. The others around the table chatted while they devoured the meal, seemingly unaware of Tressa's discomfort. Gage sat on her right, leaning close to whisper in her ear, smiling and attentive as a good beau should be, but she couldn't set aside the look in his eyes when she'd told him about the Double H branding iron lying out in

Abel's pasture. He knew more than he was willing to concede, and mistrust had formed a gigantic stone in her stomach that blocked the desire for food.

Unable to bear his presence one second longer, she pushed her chair back and tossed her napkin onto her plate. "Aunt Hattie, I believe I'll go to the kitchen and whip some cream to put on our dessert." She forced a smile as she informed the men, "Spice cake, baked fresh this morning before we left for church."

Luella jumped up. "I'll help you."

Tressa sent Luella a startled look. The girl had never volunteered to assist Tressa with any task. But perhaps Luella needed a brief escape from Fred Pennington. Although the man wasn't unkind, his inattentiveness to Luella stood out in stark contrast to the other young men who gazed with adoration at their chosen brides-to-be.

"That's fine, Luella."

Luella trailed Tressa all the way to the cellar. As Tressa skimmed cream into a small pitcher, Luella said, "I'm glad to see you're allowing Gage to court you."

Tressa placed the wooden lid on the milk crock and sighed. "I can imagine what it looked like in there, with Gage constantly touching my arm and whispering in my ear, but we are *not* courting." She wouldn't accept wooing from someone she distrusted. "I'll make sure he understands that before he leaves today."

Luella's eyes widened. "But you have to let him court you! If you don't, he'll—" She clacked her jaw shut and headed for the cellar stairs.

Tressa hurried after her, mindful of the full pitcher. "Luella, please wait!"

The other girl came to a stop at the base of the earthen stairs. Sunlight poured in from the cellar's opening, highlighting the fear in Luella's face.

"Has Gage threatened you in some way?" Tressa placed her hand over Luella's forearm. "Please tell me."

Luella turned and grabbed Tressa's shoulders, giving her a little shake. Cream splashed out the top of the pitcher and dotted Tressa's dress. "Gage wants you, Tressa, and Gage always gets what he wants. Do you really believe you'll be able to live happily with someone else in this community if you deny him? Gage will make your life miserable, just as he's—" Again, she broke off.

Tressa wriggled free of Luella's grasp. "You've been after me for days to accept Gage's attention. I know you aren't pushing me at him because of any affection you feel for me. So why are you so interested in seeing me married to Gage? What hold does he have on you?"

Luella's eyes filled with tears. "I can't tell you."

"Then he *is* threatening you!" Tressa held the cream pitcher against her stomach with one hand and captured Luella's hand with the other. "We need to tell Aunt Hattie, Luella. Gage needs to be stopped before—"

"No!" Luella jerked loose. She dried her eyes with her skirt. "You don't understand. If Gage doesn't get what he wants, everyone—you, me, Aunt Hattie—we'll *all* pay the price. So stop asking questions and let him have what he wants." Her voice turned wheedling. "It'll be a life of ease and comfort, living on the Hammond ranch. And Aunt Hattie will be there, too—I know you like being with her. So accept him, Tressa. Take what he's offering and be grateful."

Luella spun and charged up the stairs. Tressa followed more slowly. *What time I am afraid, I will trust in Thee.* . . . The words whispered through her heart. She set the pitcher of cream on the ground and closed the cellar door, then slipped to her knees in the grass. "I can't trust Gage, God, but I can trust You." She spent several minutes in communion with her heavenly Father, discovering a sense of peace despite the uncertainties that still plagued her mind. After whispering amen, she rose and carried the cream to the kitchen.

As she stepped through the back door, she heard a commotion at the front of the house. She set the pitcher aside and hurried down the hallway. The girls and their guests were all crowded around the front door. Sheriff Tate stood in the center of the group, holding out his palms as if staving off a fight.

"That's all I know, folks. Telegram from Dodge didn't give me no more details than that." He puffed his chest with self-importance. "I gotta head over to the Lazy S now an' let Abel know Jacobs has been apprehended."

Tressa's heart skipped a beat. She grabbed the closest arm. "Paralee, what is happening?"

Paralee crowed, "Cole and Sallie were arrested in Dodge City! Sheriff says they're sitting in a jail cell. Soon as the sheriff there can arrange it, they'll be brought to Barnett for prosecution!"

Aunt Hattie followed the sheriff out the door, and the gentlemen hurried after them. Tressa clung to Paralee's arm, her knees quivering. "Prosecution? For what?"

Paralee stared at Tressa as if she'd taken leave of her senses. "For cattle rustling! The night Cole Jacobs and Sallie sneaked off, Abel Samms lost over thirty head of cattle. Everyone knows Cole and Sallie stole those cattle. When the judge finds them guilty, Cole might be hanged!" She broke loose of Tressa's grip and charged out the front door after the others.

Tressa stood in stunned disbelief. *"Everyone knows Cole and Sallie stole those cattle. . . ."* Tressa started to run after the sheriff to tell him about the branding iron she'd seen, but Gage's threats and Luella's advice stopped her. She didn't dare talk to the sheriff—and especially not in front of Gage.

Luella had intimated Gage might harm Aunt Hattie if Tressa refused his attention, so she wouldn't involve Aunt Hattie. The only other person who knew about the branding iron was Abel Samms.

He hadn't seemed to believe her tale, but if she told him how Gage had threatened her, he might be more willing to listen.

Tressa turned and ran out the back door. She made her way to the barn and saddled Spotty as quickly as her trembling hands would allow. With luck, she could sneak off without being seen. Cole Jacobs was certainly guilty of stealing the heart of one of Aunt Hattie's girl, but if her suspicions were correct, he was innocent of cattle rustling. Regardless of the harm Gage might inflict, she couldn't stay silent and allow an innocent man to be hanged.

29

Abel propped his hand against the rough doorframe and watched Sheriff Tate heave himself into the saddle and ride away. He remained in the doorway of his house for several minutes after the sheriff's horse left the gate, staring unseeingly across the yard. Why didn't the news that Cole had been arrested give him more pleasure? Shouldn't he feel . . . something?

He closed the door and turned to face the dinner table, still scattered with the remains of the simple lunch he, Vince, and Ethan had consumed. He supposed he should clean up the mess, but instead he headed for his bedroom and crossed directly to the highboy. The top drawer—seldom used—squeaked as he eased it open. He plunged his hand beneath the pile of folded linen handkerchiefs that hadn't seen daylight since Pa's death, groping until his fingers encountered what he sought.

He plucked it out and then sat on the edge of his bed and gazed at the tiny frame holding Amanda's image. She'd told him an artist in Central Park had painted the minuscule portrait. He knew little about art, but whoever painted the picture was surely talented. The artist had captured Amanda's beauty perfectly.

The little gold-filigreed frame—no bigger than a silver dollar—looked ridiculous in his rough, callused palm. Just as Amanda's velvet dress and lace parasol had looked ridiculous against the simple storefronts in Barnett when she'd stepped off the stage. She'd wrinkled her nose when she'd glimpsed the town, and no matter how her letters had promised undying devotion, he'd known from the look on her face when she entered his house she wouldn't be staying. Amanda hadn't *fit*.

But Miss Tressa had cooked at the stove, milked the cow, swept the wide-planked floors, and dug in the garden, all the while humming a cheery tune. When he'd held her in his arms and danced at Aunt Hattie's, their feet had known how to move together. Even though she'd been raised in the city, she hadn't looked out of place either in his house or swirling around that wooden dance floor under the Kansas sun. Instead, she'd been at ease. At ease in his house, at ease in his arms . . .

Abel shook his head to clear Tressa from his thoughts and returned his attention to the picture within the gold frame. He stared for long moments at Amanda's beautiful smiling face as if waiting for her to come to life and speak to him. Then he closed his fingers over the image and sighed. He hadn't taken out the portrait in months. Why did he need to look at it today? He suspected it had something to do with Fred, Glendon, Jerome, and Gage all fluttering around their chosen gals in the churchyard earlier. Regret had nearly strangled him. He should've laid claim to Miss Tressa when he'd had the chance. Aunt Hattie'd tried to tell him he'd let his feelings about Amanda's betrayal hold him at a distance from Tressa, but he wouldn't listen. And he'd been wrong.

He strode to the highboy and opened the top drawer, intending to bury the portrait under Pa's linen handkerchiefs again. But his hand froze in midair. He needed to bury it, but not in a drawer where he'd encounter it again and again. He needed to bury it for good. He needed to bury the hurt of Amanda's rejection for good.

A lump of longing rose from his gut and lodged in his throat, bringing with it the unexpected sting of tears. He hadn't cried in years—not since he'd laid Pa in the ground next to Ma. Men didn't cry over nothing. Even Ma hadn't wasted tears over spilled milk. So there must be something big eating at his insides to bring tears to the surface.

He slammed the drawer shut and spun toward the bedroom door. Maybe if he put Amanda's portrait in the ground next to Ma and Pa's graves, he could finally let loose of the pain she'd inflicted. And then he'd be free to move on.

Eagerness propelled him forward. He grabbed his hat from the rack by the front door and headed for the barn. Plans unfolded in his mind as his feet clumped against the ground. He'd saddle a horse, ride out to the gravesites, and bury Amanda and his memories of her once and for all, and then he'd ride over to Aunt Hattie's and let her know he wanted to—

He careened to a halt as abruptly as if he'd collided with the barn's rock wall. He completed the final thought: *let her know he wanted to court Miss Tressa.* He couldn't court Miss Tressa. She'd already been claimed by Gage Hammond. He'd seen the way they'd sauntered across the churchyard together, hip to hip. Tressa belonged to Gage now.

He hung his head, glaring at his closed fist. The sharp edge of the gold frame dug into his palm. What was the use? Even if Tressa hadn't already accepted Gage's offer for courtship, Abel didn't have anything to offer her anymore. His pa's ranch would transfer to someone else's hands soon—he wouldn't have the money to keep it running. He was seven times the fool for mooning over Amanda, for losing his pa's hard-won ranch, for not following his heart in pursuing Miss

Tressa . . . *Fool!* He absorbed the word, accepting its sting like a well-deserved strapping.

Heaving a sigh, he turned and shuffled back toward the house, but then he stopped and squared his shoulders. Even if he couldn't have Tressa, he still needed to let loose of the bitterness that had been his constant companion since Amanda's return to the East. The judge would mete out vengeance for Cole's betrayal, but it was up to Abel to excise the hurt caused by Amanda. He'd bury the portrait and state a vow over its tiny grave to never let the woman represented by the picture torment him again.

The decision made, he headed for the barn. Just before he arrived at the wide opening, the sound of hoofbeats reached his ears. Someone was coming at a desperate pace. He whirled around and spotted Aunt Hattie's Appaloosa, ridden by a slim female rider, turn in at his gate. He took one stumbling step forward, his jaw dropping in surprise.

The horse clattered to a halt next to him, and Tressa slid down from the saddle. She panted as if she'd run the distance rather than riding. "Abel—I mean, Mr. Samms, I . . . I need to talk to you."

Vince appeared in the barn's doorway. "Abel? Somethin' wrong?"

Abel barely flicked a glance at the man. "Everything's fine, Vince. Finish up in the tack room an' then rest. Shouldn't be workin' on Sunday anyway."

"Sure thing." The man strode back into the barn.

Abel slipped Amanda's portrait into his shirt pocket and gave Tressa his full attention. "What is it?"

"The sheriff . . . has he been here?"

Abel nodded. "Yep." Resignation weighted his shoulders. "He told me Cole's been apprehended an' there'll be a trial. He'll pay a price, but I prob'ly won't get my cattle back. No sign of them anywhere." He didn't add how that final loss guaranteed the loss of his ranch. Why should she care? She'd be living high and fine at the Double H.

"He came by Aunt Hattie's, too, and interrupted our dinner to tell us the news of Cole and Sallie's capture. Paralee says Cole might be hanged." She shuddered. "But, Mr. Samms, I truly don't believe Cole is guilty of rustling."

Abel glanced down the lane. "Aunt Hattie send you over?"

"No one knows I'm here. I . . . I sneaked off. I couldn't let Gage know what I was doing." Tressa told of a puzzling conversation between herself and Gage and then repeated a warning given by Luella. With her brow puckered and fingers twined together, she finished, "I know Mr. Rylin apologized this morning for accidentally shooting at me, but that still doesn't explain the branding iron or its strange disappearance. And I am very certain Gage means to discourage me from seeking it."

Abel frowned, carefully processing everything Tressa had shared. Although Gage hadn't said anything that could be considered a direct threat or a confession, if what Tressa said was true, then the man sure was hiding *something*. Abel ran his hand down his face. "Miss Tressa, that iron you saw—"

"Kindly do not try to tell me I imagined it!" She squatted, her skirts mushrooming around her. With her finger, she traced several lines in the dirt. "It looked just like this—two H's, the second one a little higher than the first, with the first H's second stem acting as the second H's first stem. I've seen the brand many times on Gage's horse."

Abel ignored the jealousy that pinched at her words.

She glared up at him, her eyes squinted against the sun. "It was a Double H branding iron, and it was on *your* property."

He stared at the scratchings in the dirt to avoid looking into her eyes, and suddenly realization struck so hard his knees buckled. "Tressa! Look . . ." He squatted and planted the tip of his finger at the top of the lower H's first stem. Slowly, he drew a sideways S that followed the first stem to the crossbar, slid on the crossbar to the second stem, worked its way up to the crossbar of the higher H, and finished by gliding across the crossbar and then downward where it met the base of the final stem. "A person could hide my brand pretty easy by puttin' a Double H right on top of it."

Tressa stared at him in amazement. "I never realized . . ."

"Neither did I till you drew it out there." He grabbed her hand and pulled her to her feet. "C'mon. We need to go scout around that fire pit. See what else we can find."

"Shouldn't we just go see the sheriff?" She nibbled her lower lip.

The worry in her pale blue eyes gave Abel pause. She'd had a good scare by being fired at, and he might be putting her in danger by dragging her along. "Here." Taking her arm, he hurried her to her horse. He grasped her narrow waist, lifted her onto the saddle, and then placed the trailing reins in her hands. "You head on back to Aunt Hattie's—reckon she's wonderin' where you are by now. I'll go out an' nose around."

"Absolutely not! If you're going, I'm going, too. I'm the one who spotted the branding iron in the first place." Her eyes sparked, daring him to deny her.

Despite the seriousness of the situation, a chuckle rose from Abel's chest. Who would've thought this fancy city girl could turn so fearless? She was dead set on going, and he'd just waste time arguing with her. "All right. Let me saddle a horse, an' we'll ride out there together. But then—" he pointed his finger at her—"I'm takin' you to Aunt Hattie's an' that'll be the end of your involvement."

She turned her nose in the air, but she didn't argue.

Abel trotted into the barn and nearly collided with Vince. "You still in here?"

"Just headin' out," the man replied, sliding his hand into his pocket. "You goin' somewhere with Miss Tressa?"

Abel hesitated. He didn't want to lie, but he couldn't tell the truth, either—not without pulling Vince into the mystery. He offered a half-truth. "I'm ridin' her back to the Flyin' W."

Vince gave a nod. "Good thing. Reckon Gage Hammond wouldn't be too pleased to have you spendin' time with his intended."

Abel brushed past Vince without responding, and Vince ambled out of the barn. Vince's gentle warning ran through Abel's mind as he rode next to Tressa across his pasture. If Gage was brazen enough to steal cattle and threaten women with silence, what else might he do? Another worrisome thought struck—what if Vince wasn't the only one who'd fired a rifle yesterday? Could it be coincidence that he fired three shots at a badger around the same time someone else was taking shots at Tressa?

He glanced at Tressa. Her bonnet hid much of her face from view, but the sweet turn of her jawline was enough to hold his attention. The determined jut of her jaw, despite her small frame, gave him a glimpse of her inner strength. Why should she care so much about finding the truth?

"Miss Tressa, you know this really ain't your concern." He swallowed when she aimed a disgusted look in his direction. "Not that I don't appreciate you wantin' to help find out who's been runnin' off with my cattle, but . . ." Fear tied his vocal cords in a knot. "You could get yourself hurt."

"What time I am afraid, I will trust in God." She raised her chin and fixed him with a challenging look. "Every time I pray for His protection, He answers." She smiled, her lips and cheeks rosy. "Most of the time He sends you. Do you find that odd?"

Abel cleared his throat. "That's prob'ly just happenstance."

"Hmmph. I choose to believe God hears my prayers and uses you as His hands to rescue me." Her smile turned impish. "Did you know there's a Chinese proverb that claims if you save another's life, you are forever responsible for that person?"

He gulped twice. "Well now, I'm not sure you could go as far as sayin' I saved your *life*. Might've saved you from some serious regrets by pullin' Gage off you in the barn, but—" He reined his horse to a stop and waited until she did the same. "I gotta know, Miss Tressa. How can you forgive Gage for tryin' to force himself on you?"

The teasing look in her eyes faded. "In all honesty, Mr. Samms, it isn't easy. But I've recently developed a relationship with God, and I've been spending quite a bit of time reading the Bible to get to know Him better. God is very clear on His expectation concerning holding a grudge. He advises not to let the sun go down on our anger, and in another place Jesus instructs the disciples to forgive seventy times seven." She released a soft laugh. "I'm not a disciple, but I believe those words apply to me, too. If I refuse to forgive Gage, then I disobey God." Her eyes glittered with unshed tears. "I truly don't want to disobey my heavenly Father."

Her words wormed their way to Abel's soul and tickled his insides. He shifted in his saddle. "I admire your stand, Miss Tressa, but it takes a heap of forgiveness to let a man who wronged you be your beau."

She shook her head. "Gage is not my beau."

He blinked twice. "But I thought—"

"*Everyone* seems to think so." She tilted her head to the side and plunked a small fist on her hip. "Have you noticed how quickly rumor becomes fact in this community? *Everyone* has already convicted Cole of cattle rustling. *Everyone* has me married to Gage Hammond." Her frown grew fierce—a ridiculous expression for someone so pretty. "But let me state quite unequivocally, I have not accepted Gage's request to court me, and I have no intention of accepting it. If it means finding work in town and supporting myself rather than getting married, then so be it. But I will not marry a man I cannot trust or for whom I have absolutely no affection."

Struck dumb by her lengthy, emphatic speech, Abel could only stare at her in amazement. A bead of sweat rolled down his temple, awakening him from his stupor. He nodded once and said only, "All right."

They continued in silence and reached the area where he'd

discovered Tressa cowering in the grass. He hopped down from his horse and reached to help her dismount, but she slid down without his assistance. Leading the horses, they walked along the fenceline, searching for the fire pit.

The wind flipped Tressa's bonnet brim inside-out, and she snapped it back in place. Holding her palm above the brim, she scanned the area. "I don't understand . . . that fire pit was here . . . wasn't it?" Her puzzled expression matched Abel's confusion.

He dropped the horses' reins over the top line of barbed wire and walked slowly forward, his eyes down and seeking. He came to a halt when the grass beneath his feet shifted, exposing a patch of dirt. "Well, I'll be . . ."

Tressa darted forward. "What is it?"

"Look at this." He crouched down and swept the grass aside with his hand. Three long sweeps revealed the fire pit. "The rocks're gone, and somebody laid grass over the area to hide it." He shook his head, rising. "Somebody sure has gone to a lot of trouble."

"Do you think it was Gage?" Tressa's voice trembled.

Abel blew out a breath. "Seein' as how he tried to scare you off, that seems a sound guess." Anger swelled as he added, "I'm takin' you to Aunt Hattie, an' then I intend to—"

A rifle blast cut off his final words. Fire attacked the back of his shoulder as he spun and dove at Tressa. Ignoring the searing pain, he flattened himself over her body and pressed his face into the curve of her neck. Her pulse beat against his cheek.

From yards away, a man's voice called, "You were warned, but you wouldn't listen. This's what happens when snoopy little ladies stick their noses where they don't belong. Somebody gets hurt. Maybe you'll listen next time."

30

Hattie tapped her foot and fingered the pipe in her apron pocket. If Brewster Hammond wasn't sitting in the other porch chair, she'd take out the pipe and enjoy a smoke just to calm her jangled nerves. Where *were* those young'uns?

Brewster reached out and patted the back of her hand. "No sense in worryin'."

Hattie managed a weak chuckle. "Oh, I know worryin' is a plumb fool waste o' time. But it's not like Tressa to just take off without sayin' somethin' to somebody. Why, if Luella hadn't seen her headin' out, who knows how long it would've took us to figure out which way she went."

"But Luella did see her, an' Gage is out lookin'. He'll make sure she don't come to harm."

Brewster's words did little to calm Hattie's fears. The worry that Tressa might've ridden off to avoid Gage's attention niggled at the back of her mind, but she didn't voice the concern. Brewster didn't take well to criticism of his son. Hattie suppressed a sigh. Gage's self-ish behavior—and her need to hold her tongue about it—would be a constant thorn of irritation if she were to marry Brewster.

The thought saddened her. She'd grown fond of Brewster over the past days. Although not as gentle and talkative as her Jed, he treated her respectfully and had even given her permission to bring more girls to her school after they were wed. The word "permission" had rankled—she hadn't answered to anyone for a good long while—but she appreciated his recognition of the importance of the Wyatt Herdsman School. It meant a lot that he wouldn't stand in her way.

But that Gage . . . She released a little snort. If she and Brewster were to enjoy a permanent relationship, they'd have to come to some agreements about his boy's behavior.

Unable to sit still any longer, Hattie pushed off the chair and paced the porch, her eyes scanning the land for a puff of rising dust or the sight of a horse. *Lord, seems these days I'm always prayin' for You to keep that girl from harm, but . . . please keep her from harm. Bring her safely home again.*

Brewster caught her from behind, curling his arms around her waist and holding her in place. He pressed his cheek to her temple. "Harriet?"

Her pulse raced faster than a gopher escaping a coyote. She hoped her heart didn't give out. "Yes, Brewster?"

"You could pace until you wear the paint off the porch boards, an' it won't make no difference. How can I help you stop worryin'?"

She turned in his arms and looked up into his face. Genuine concern was etched into the grooves of his forehead. Warmth spread through Hattie's middle. Her arms itched to sneak up and coil around his sunburned neck. Did old ladies really have feelings like this? "Maybe . . . we could do the same as all those young couples an' go for a drive?"

He chuckled. "A drive sounds fine."

"An' while we're out, can we look for Tressa?"

His lips tipped into an understanding smile. "If it'll ease your mind. Let's go."

❧

"Do you think he's gone?" Tressa pushed the words past her tight throat. With Abel's bulky frame holding her down, she found it difficult to draw a deep breath.

"I . . . I think so."

"Then could we get up?" His weight seemed to increase by the minute.

"I'll try."

She felt him lift, then he groaned and collapsed on her again. "Mr. Samms, please! You're impeding my breathing."

"I'm sorry. I'll try again."

At last he rolled from her body. She scrambled onto all fours, drawing in deep drafts of air. How wonderful to fill her lungs! Then she looked at his inert body. Concern sent her scuttling forward. "Mr. Samms, are you all right?" Red seeped through his shirt, just below his right shoulder. She gasped. "Were you hit?"

He squinted at her. "Burns like fury. I . . . I'm thinkin' I shouldn't move around too much."

"Yes, lie still. We need to stop the bleeding." Tressa lifted her skirt and ripped a ruffle free from her well-worn petticoat. She wadded the cloth and pressed it against his wound.

His face contorted. "Am I bleedin' there? It hit me in the back. Must've gone straight through."

"Oh, Abel . . ." Tears distorted her vision, but she blinked them away and tore another strip of fabric loose. "Can you roll to your side long enough for me to apply this to your back?"

He gritted his teeth and complied. A greater amount of blood had soaked through the back of his shirt. Tressa wanted to cry, but she set her jaw and jammed the wad of cloth against the seeping wound. "Lie back down."

He flopped flat on his back, letting out a low moan. "Horses took off, didn't they?"

For the first time, Tressa remembered the horses. She looked to where Abel had tossed the reins over the fence, but the spot was empty. "They're gone." She touched his crimson cheek. Although the sun was beating down, his skin felt cool and clammy. A shiver of fear shook her.

"Shoulda tied 'em good. I know better. . . ." His face pulled into a horrible grimace. "You gotta go for help. It'll take you a while to reach the road on foot. You'd best get goin'."

"I can't leave you!" She stared at him, aghast.

"Unless you think you can cart me out of here on your back, you're gonna have to." He grabbed her wrist and gave it a feeble squeeze. "Please, Tressa. I . . . I'm hurtin' bad an' feelin' mighty weak. Go. . . ."

With a strangled cry, Tressa got to her feet, but they refused to budge. "What'll you do if a . . . a coyote or wildcat comes near?"

"I got my sidearm. Can you take it out of the holster an' put it in my hand?"

His fingers brushed hers when she placed the wooden grip in his palm. She fought the desire to weave her fingers through his and hold tight.

He curled his hand around the grip and gave her a weak smile. "Thanks, Tressa. Now, go."

Tressa swallowed hard and blinked back more tears. Compassion and fear tumbled through her stomach, creating a rush of emotion so overwhelming she thought she might collapse. "Abel, I—"

"No talkin'. Just go."

She choked back a sob and jolted to her feet, then dashed off across the pasture in the direction of Abel's ranch house. "Don't let him die.

Please, God, don't let him die," she prayed over and over as she ran. Never had she run so far, so fast, in the heat of the day. Her muscles ached in protest, but she willed her legs to carry her forward.

Tears rained down her face, blurring her vision. The uneven ground tried to turn her ankles, and her skirts tangled around her knees. With a frustrated cry, she stopped and swished the tears away. Then she lifted her skirts to an indecent height and took off again. Her feet stumbled, her chest burned, but somehow she managed to continue. She had no choice—Abel's life depended on her reaching help.

"Tressa! Tressa!"

She whirled around, her hands pressed to her heaving chest. A horse galloped toward her. Gage sat in the saddle. Her gaze fixed on the slim case bouncing against his leg. The wooden stock of a rifle poked out from the leather sheath.

With a shriek of terror, she caught her skirts and staggered forward. "Please, God—please, God . . ." But was she pleading for Abel or for herself?

Gage rode directly into her pathway and reined in. The horse whinnied, lifting up on his hind legs as Gage leaped from its back and ran to her. She tried to escape him, but her tired legs refused to carry her away. He clutched her shoulders and bent down to peer directly into her face. "What're you doin' runnin' around out here? You could get sunstroke!"

"Let me go!" She fought against his restraining hands, her breath coming in gasps that left her weak and trembling. "How could you do it, Gage?" She began to weep, her chest heaving with the sobs. "You didn't have to kill him!"

Gage scowled. "What're you talkin' about?"

"Abel!" She pounded her fists on his chest. "You shot him! He's lying out there bleeding—maybe dying! Are cattle worth more than a man's life?"

Gage's face drained of color. His hands fell from her shoulders. "This has gone far enough. I never thought . . ." He jolted, reaching for her again. She tried to retreat, but he grabbed her wrist and pulled her toward his horse. "Come on, Tressa."

"No! No, let me go!"

"Tressa!" He whirled on her, giving her arm a jerk. "We're gonna go get Abel's wagon. Then you can show me where he is. We'll get him to the doctor."

She stopped squirming, staring at him in amazement. "Y-you'll help me?"

"I never meant for anyone to be killed." Gage's voice rasped out. He mounted the horse, then leaned down and grabbed her arm. He swung her onto the horse's rump.

She grabbed the saddle's arched cantle. "Go! Go!"

The horse pounded across the ground, closing the distance to Abel's ranch. When they careened into the yard, Tressa slid down before Gage dismounted. Her legs crumbled beneath her and she fell, but she quickly bounced to her feet and took off for the bunkhouse, yelling for Vince and Ethan.

"Tressa, quiet!" Gage ran up beside her and covered her mouth with his sweaty palm. "Don't . . . call . . . Vince."

❧

Abel licked his dry lips. *I should have brought a canteen. Sure could use a drink.* He lay with his eyes closed but senses alert. The fire in his shoulder had faded to a dull, persistent throb. Sleep tried to claim him, but he deliberately jiggled his right arm. The tiniest movement created a wave of pain that chased sleep away. He couldn't risk losing consciousness.

He gripped his pistol in his left hand so hard his fingers felt numb. If something threatened him, he'd fire a shot. Only a miracle would let him hit the target, his aim was so bad with that hand, but maybe he could scare critters away.

His thoughts drifted to Tressa. Had she reached the ranch by now? Was she on her way back with the wagon? *Please let her be comin' back soon. Don't know how much longer I can hold on.*

Had he prayed? Been so long, he hardly knew how anymore, but he sure hoped God would take that plea as a prayer. He was more scared than he'd ever been.

Hoofbeats vibrated the ground beneath him, and his heart lifted with hope. "Tressa?" The word came out in a strangled gasp—too soft to be heard—but it felt good to say her name. So he repeated it. "Tressa . . ."

The hoofbeats stopped, and after a few silent seconds he heard a squeak. Leather. From a saddle. He frowned. Why hadn't she brought a wagon? He'd never be able to mount a horse with his useless right arm. He tried to sit up, but nausea attacked him and he broke out in a cold sweat. He flopped back with a groan.

A shadow fell across him, and he squinted into Vince's face. He nearly cried with relief. "Thank God you found me. Vince . . . get me on your horse. I need a doctor. I've been shot."

Vince squatted on his haunches and grazed Abel's shoulder with his fingers. A shudder rolled through Abel's body with the slight touch. Vince pulled his hand away and examined his stained fingertips. Clicking his tongue against his teeth, he shook his head. "Yep, you sure have. Bleedin' a lot, too." He wiped his fingers on his pant leg and then looked down at Abel. "Bet you're a-hurtin', huh?"

Abel groaned. "Yes, I'm hurtin'. Hurtin' bad. Vince, get me some help. I need help. . . ."

"Ain't much fun to need somethin' you can't have, is it?" Vince planted his boot on the barrel of Abel's gun, pinning it to the ground. He plucked a blade of grass and then rested his forearms on his knees, toying with the strand of green. "For years, I've had a need—to own my own place. Be my own boss. But . . . haven't seen it come to pass."

"Vince . . ." Black dots swam in front of Abel's eyes, making it hard to focus, but he thought the man smiled at him.

"Your pa an' me was best friends. I came all the way from South Carolina to the Kansas Territory to help him start this ranch. Fought off Injun attacks, an' lived through dust storms that turned the prairie black. Never once complained or shirked from anything he asked of me. Worked as hard as two men gettin' that ranch goin', an' your pa told me again an' again how he couldn't've done it without my help. But then what does he do but up an' die an' leave it all to you."

Vince tossed the grass blade aside. "I didn't do all that work just to take orders from his wet-behind-the-ears son. He could've bequeathed me some land. But he didn't. And you—" He bumped Abel's arm with his fist. "You wouldn't sell." He shook his head, his expression sorrowful. "That was a mistake, Abel. See, if you'd just sold me the ranch, I wouldn't've had to shoot ya."

"Y-you?" Abel wanted to jump up, to pummel Vince, to punish him for the hurt he'd inflicted. But all he could do was lie on the ground while Vince went on in a conversational tone.

"I did everythin' I could to convince you to sell, but you wouldn't budge. Would've been so much better if you'd just let me buy the place. But it'll be mine now. With you dead, an' you havin' no heir, it makes sense for the land to go to your pa's best friend, the man who stayed around an' helped you keep the ranch a-runnin'."

Vince stood, his knees cracking. "Don't you worry now. I'll be sure to bury you right next to your folks an' your baby brothers. An' I'll take real good care of the ranch, just like it was my own." He paused. "Sorry it had to end this way, Abel, but I got too much of my life invested in that ground to let it go." He turned and strode away. Moments later, hoofbeats retreated.

Tears slid from Abel's eyes. *It's over, God. No way Tressa could make*

it all the way to the ranch on foot. My life's ebbin' out—I can feel it—an'
I'm scared, God. Tressa said when she's afraid, she trusts in You. I want
to trust in You again. Please forgive me for bein' so contrary and blamin'
you for Pa's dyin' and Amanda's leavin'. I was foolish an' stubborn. I'm
sorry, God. Please let me know You're here with me.

A feeling of comfort flowed from Abel's head to his toes, causing
fresh tears to fill his eyes. *Thank You, God. Thank You.* . . . Despite
his pain, despite his weakness, despite Vince's treachery, his soul felt
at peace. He could let go, and go home.

31

Hattie held Tressa tight against her chest. The girl had cried herself to sleep, exhausted from running so hard in that blistering heat and being scared half out of her wits. Even in sleep her body continued to convulse with sobs. Hattie pressed her cheek to Tressa's sweaty hair. As soon as the doc finished with Abel, she'd have him take a peek at Tressa.

Lord, I'm beggin' You, save Abel's life. He's got so much more livin' to do.

The last thing she'd expected when she and Brewster rode down the road was to encounter Gage in Abel Samms' wagon, driving that team like there was no tomorrow. And when she'd looked in the bed to find Tressa cradling Abel's head in her lap, him lying white and still . . . She shook her head to dispel the image. Who'd've thought such things could happen in Barnett?

Now, Brewster and Gage sat side-by-side on the bench against the far wall of the doctor's small sitting room. Gage hunched forward, his face buried in his hands. She'd never seen the boy so broken. Finding Abel near death must have affected him deeply.

"Gage?" She whispered his name, unwilling to disturb Tressa. At first, she thought he hadn't heard, because he didn't so much as flinch. But after a few seconds he lifted his head and met her gaze. "Thanks for actin' so quick in gettin' Abel to the doc. You might've saved his life."

Gage stared at her blankly for several seconds, and then his face contorted into a horrible scowl. A single harsh sob burst from his lips. He drew up his arm, hid his face in his elbow, and began to sob wildly.

Brewster slung his arm across the boy's shoulders. "Son?"

Gage's body shook with the force of his weeping, and Brewster shot Hattie a helpless look. Hattie gently transferred Tressa to the bench seat and scurried across the floor to kneel in front of Gage.

"Gage? What's wrong?" She used her gentlest voice, a tone she never thought she'd use with Brewster's wayward son.

His muffled voice came from behind his arm. "I . . . I'm scared."

His admission raised a rush of maternal compassion. Taking hold of his wrist, she pulled his arm away from his face. "I know it's scary to find a man laid out like that, but—"

"No!" Gage swiped his forearm across his eyes, darting a frantic look across his father and Hattie. "You don't understand. I . . . I . . ." He clamped his jaw shut, his Adam's apple jerking with several large gulps.

Brewster curled his big hand over Gage's knee. "Gage, you gotta talk to me, son, or I can't help you."

Gage spun on the seat. "You'll help me, Pa? You won't let 'em hang me?"

Brewster drew back, his mouth falling open. "H-hang you?" Suddenly he lunged forward, grabbing Gage's shirt front. He growled, "What've you done?"

Hattie caught Brewster's wrist and wrestled his fingers away from Gage's shirt. Gage stormed to the corner of the room. He crossed his arms over his chest and hunched into himself, his head low.

Brewster strained toward his son. "Gage, I asked you—"

Hattie placed her hand over Brewster's mouth. She tipped her head toward Tressa, who was sleeping fitfully a few feet away, and mouthed, "Not now."

Brewster removed her hand from his mouth with an impatient sweep of his own hand, but he gave a brusque nod and remained silent. He glared at his son, fury and fear alternately flashing in his eyes. Hattie sat beside him and held his hand.

A door squeaked open, then clicked closed, and footsteps echoed from the hall. Tressa stirred, sitting up and staring, red-eyed, toward the hallway opening. Hattie jumped to her feet and greeted Doc Kasper as he entered the sitting area. She searched his face for signs of Abel's condition, but the man was well practiced at keeping his expression unreadable. She blurted out, "Tell us, Doc. Is he still breathin'?"

The doctor plucked his spectacles from his face and slipped them into his shirt pocket. "He's a lucky man. Bullet went straight through so I didn't have to go digging for it, and far as I can tell it missed anything that would make it a mortal wound. I cleaned him up good and bandaged him tight to prevent more bleeding." Doc Kasper rubbed his eyes with his finger and thumb and then finished, "He's lost a lot of blood and he won't be using that arm for a good long while, but he's young and strong. I expect him to make a full recovery."

Hattie turned her face toward the ceiling and clapped her hands once. "Thank You, Lord!" Tressa scuttled to her side. She slipped her arm around the girl's waist and looked at the doctor again. "Couldja give Tressa a look-see now? She—"

"I'm fine," Tressa put in. She turned an imploring gaze on the doctor. "Can I go see him?"

"Not today. He needs rest more than visits. You all look like you could use a great deal of rest. There's nothing more you can do for Abel."

Before Tressa could argue, Hattie turned the girl toward the door. She intended to see that Tressa followed the doctor's instruction and went straight to bed. Brewster and Gage followed them out the door.

Out on the boardwalk, Hattie turned to talk to Brewster, but Brewster was looking sternly at his son. "Gage, you want to tell me why you're worried about bein' hanged?"

Gage flicked a quick glance at the women, and his lips formed a stubborn line.

Brewster grabbed Gage's arm and shook it hard. "If you're in trouble, boy, now's the time to speak up. You wait till the sheriff finds it out on his own an' it'll only be worse for you. Talk!"

Tressa scooted close to Hattie. Hattie understood the girl's nervousness. She'd never seen Brewster so forceful. She held her breath, waiting for Gage to respond.

"All right!" Gage jerked his arm free. "I . . . I been puttin' our brand over the top of Abel Samms' an' mixin' his cattle into our herd."

"You been *what*?" The veins on Brewster's neck stood out.

Although Hattie had long awaited the day Brewster would take his son to task, apprehension now gripped her. Brewster looked angry enough to hang Gage himself.

"I been pilferin' his cattle, Pa, a few head at a time—whatever Vince cut loose."

Hattie shot Brewster a startled look. Vince'd been stealing from Abel?

Brewster clenched his fists. "What'n thunder would make you do such a stupid thing?"

Gage held out his arms in supplication. "It wasn't my idea, Pa! Vince come to me—said the only way you'd ever get Abel off that land was to force him off. If Abel couldn't keep up, money wise, he'd have to sell. So Vince cooked up a scheme to blend the Lazy S cattle in with ours. A herd big as ours? Nobody'd notice a dozen or so extra head. Vince said Abel'd be sure to sell out when he couldn't make money off the ranch no more."

He whirled on Tressa. "It was his idea for me to court you, too. Said Abel was settin' his sights on you, an' he might just take you for a wife. That'd make him less willin' to leave his home. So he had to get you out of the way."

Tressa gasped and clung to Hattie's arm. Hattie gave the girl's hand a comforting pat. Shaking her head, she said, "Gage, this is all a little hard to swallow. Why, Vince Rylin's been workin' the Lazy S for as long as I can remember. He practically raised Abel! Why would he help you take Abel's ranch from him?"

Gage blinked, his face blank. "I . . . I don't know. I just knew Pa wanted the land, so I helped Vince." He turned to his father, and tears pooled in his eyes. "But I never meant for nobody to get hurt. When Vince told me he'd taken some shots at Tressa—scarin' shots, he called 'em—I said I'd had enough an' I wouldn't help him no more. But he said if I quit or told anybody, he'd tell the sheriff he saw me puttin' the runnin' iron to Abel's calves an' get me arrested. I didn't know what to do."

Brewster stood with his arms at his side, his stony expression aimed beyond Hattie's shoulder.

"Pa!" Gage stared into his father's stern face. "You said you'd help me. What're you gonna do?"

Hattie held her breath, waiting for Brewster to speak. In the past, he'd excused Gage's misdeeds—making amends with a smile or a discreet passing of paper money. If he excused Gage this time, she'd be done with Brewster. She couldn't pledge her life to a man who would knowingly overlook unlawful behavior.

Brewster's hand snaked out to grip his son's upper arm. Tears shone in his eyes, but his voice was firm. "You an' me are goin' to the sheriff an' you're gonna tell him what you just told me."

Gage gaped at his father, fear dancing in his eyes. "Pa! You'd turn me in? But . . . but they *hang* cattle rustlers!"

Brewster spoke through clenched teeth. "You're going to do the right thing for the first time in your life. I can't get you out of this one, son, an' even if I could . . . I wouldn't. You gotta face up to this wrongdoin' an' make your own amends. Now come on." Dragging Gage by the arm, he pounded down the boardwalk toward Sheriff Tate's office.

Tressa squeezed Hattie's arm, her eyes wide. "Aunt Hattie, do you think Gage will be sentenced to hang?"

Hattie hugged Tressa to her side. She ached for Gage and for Brewster, yet her heart sang at the choice Brewster had made. "I don't know, darlin'. Maybe since he didn't act on his own an' is 'fessin' up to his actions, the court'll go easy on him."

"Oh, I pray so." She appeared to wilt, her shoulders slumping and head dropping.

She steered the girl toward Abel's wagon. They'd take it to his ranch and care for his livestock as best they could. If Gage's story was true and Vince Rylin had been behind the evil-doin' of late, he wouldn't be doing Abel any favors.

She helped Tressa onto the seat, then scuttled around to the other side and climbed aboard. As Hattie took up the reins, Tressa placed her hand over Hattie's wrist. A smile trembled on her lips. "I'm so glad it's over."

Hattie bobbed her head in a nod, but she kept her lips tightly closed. No, it wasn't over. It wouldn't be over until the sheriff talked to Vince Rylin and Abel's shooter was brought to justice.

32

"Sallie!" Tressa exclaimed when she stepped into the dining room Tuesday morning and spotted her friend sitting at the table with Paralee and Mabelle. Sallie jumped up and met her in the middle of the floor. The two girls hugged, laughter ringing.

Tressa pulled back. "When did you get here?"

"The sheriff brought me out yesterday evenin' while ye was sleepin'. I stayed with Luella so I wouldn't be disturbin' ye." Sallie's face pinched in sympathy. "Aunt Hattie said ye had reason to be tired."

Tressa chose not to dwell on the frightful experiences of Sunday afternoon. Her day of rest yesterday, alternately sleeping and praying, had restored her energy and her spirits. Now she would focus on getting Abel well. Tressa took Sallie by the shoulders. "Are you going to have to go back to jail?"

Sallie shook her head, her red curls bouncing. "The judge threw out the charges against Cole an' me, thanks to Gage speakin' up an' sayin' he an' Mr. Rylin stole away with those cattle the night we sneaked away to find a justice of the peace."

"Oh, I'm so relieved you're all right and you're back." Then Tressa's jaw dropped. "A justice of the peace . . . Sallie, are you and Cole married?"

Sallie hunched her shoulders, giggling. "We are. I love him so much, Tressa, an' he loves me, too. I do regret worryin' everyone, but we didn't know how else to be together."

Tressa hugged Sallie again. "I *knew* you and Cole hadn't stolen those cattle."

"Jail was a fearsome place, Tressa. I prayed an' prayed to God to have the judge let me go." Sallie flicked a glance over her shoulder toward the doorway that led to the kitchen before whispering, "Although to be truthful, I'd almost rather have faced a jail cell than Aunt Hattie. She gave me a most terrible scoldin'!"

Tressa laughed. Looping her hand through Sallie's elbow, she led her to the table, and they sat as Luella entered carrying a platter of fried eggs and pancakes. Aunt Hattie followed with a pot of coffee. She sat and sent a smile around the table. "Sure is good to have all o' my girls here this mornin'." Her gaze lingered for a moment on Sallie and then drifted to Tressa. "Tressa, would you like to say grace?"

Tressa bowed her head and offered a heartfelt prayer of thanks for Sallie's safe return and a plea for Abel's full recovery. She asked God to bless the food, and everyone echoed her amen.

While they ate, Sallie regaled them with the tale of climbing down the ladder in the thunderstorm to meet Cole and of their ride across the rain-soaked prairie. "When we planned our sneakin' away, we didn't know the sky would open an' pour down rain, but Cole said it was God's way of coverin' our tracks an' any sound we might've made. 'Tis hard, stayin' on the back of a rainslick horse, but Cole held me tight. He got me to Dodge safe an' sound." Sallie grinned. "But you'll likely never see a more bedraggled bride an' groom than what we was that night!"

Tressa marveled at Sallie's determination to be with the man she loved. How perilous the journey must have been. Yet Sallie spoke as if she'd done nothing of great magnitude. She simply *had* to be with Cole, and nothing—not even a vicious thunderstorm—would have keep her from him.

"After we waked the justice of the peace an' Cole gave him two dollars as payment for his service, we found a hotel that'd let us take a room." Sadness pinched her face. "Burdened me that Cole had to sell his granddaddy's gold pocket watch to get us money, but he said I was worth more'n the watch could ever be."

With a sigh, Sallie continued. "I started waitin' tables in a café an' Cole did the sweepin' an' such in a dry goods store, but it weren't his kind of work. He missed bein' in the open, minglin' with cattle. It was almost a relief when the sheriff found us and said he'd be sendin' us back to Barnett. Cole hoped Mr. Samms might let him be workin' at the ranch again."

"But you were being sent to Barnett to face prosecution!" Paralee sat wide-eyed, staring at Sallie. "Weren't you afraid?"

Sallie shrugged. "We knew we'd done no wrong. I was fearful, for sure, but Cole told me he'd been prayin' for the truth to be found. An' it was, thanks to Gage confessin' his part in the stealin'." Sallie's face clouded. "Surely do feel bad about Mr. Samms bein' hurt like he was. Cole says he'll stay at the Lazy S an' help until Mr. Samms is all better." Sallie turned to Aunt Hattie. "What do ye think will be happenin' to Gage?"

Aunt Hattie put her fork on the edge of her plate and sighed. "It'll be up to the judge, o' course, but Brewster an' me've been prayin' for leniency. Gage did admit to his crime. That's gotta count for somethin'."

"An' Mr. Rylin?" Tears winked in Sallie's eyes. "When Tressa an' me worked that week, I took a likin' to the man. Can't hardly believe he's involved in such awful dealin's."

Aunt Hattie sighed. "Whole community's shocked, Sallie. Why, Vince Rylin's one o' us! Brewster says the sheriff plans to send out a posse to locate Vince—no one's seen hide nor hair o' him since Sunday service. His poor son is worried sick. . . ."

Luella glared in Aunt Hattie's direction. "I don't care a fig about what happens to Vince Rylin, but Gage Hammond deserves to be drawn and quartered for what he did!"

A gasp left Tressa's lips at the bitterness that spewed from Luella.

Aunt Hattie tipped her head. "You got some strong feelin's there."

"Yes, I do." Luella spat the words, her narrowed eyes glinting with malice. "He stole more than Abel Samms' cattle. He also took—" Tears flooded her eyes, and her chin quivered.

Aunt Hattie put down her fork. "Luella, what're you sayin'?"

Luella flashed a rebellious look around the table. "I know what you're thinking. You all know I sneaked off at night to . . . to be with Gage. But no matter what you might believe, I didn't let him have his way with me. I told him he'd have to wait until after we were married, and that's when he said he'd court me. But he lied."

She sent a scathing look at Tressa. "Instead he courted Tressa. And when I confronted him about his lies, he told me I'd have to convince Tressa to marry him or he'd tell all the men in Barnett that I'd been a . . . a prostitute in New York and had given myself to him for free." The venomous tone took on a hint of anguish. "He stole my dignity. How can I ever get that back?" She jumped up and ran from the room. The clatter of her feet on the stairs didn't cover the sound of her weeping.

Aunt Hattie tossed her napkin onto the table. "Mabelle an' Paralee, you two clean up the breakfast mess. Tressa, I was plannin' to drive to town an' check on Abel, but I think I better stay here." She shot a meaningful glance toward the stairway. "Would you go in an' see how he's doin'? Sallie, you go with her—an' take a rifle. Don't want none o' you girls roamin' alone until Vince Rylin is caught." She charged around the corner and thudded up the stairs.

Sallie pushed her plate aside. "Let's go, Tressa." As they hitched the horses to the wagon, Sallie said, "When we've left the doctor's office, do ye think we might be able to go to the Lazy S an' let me have a smidgen of time with Cole? I'm missin' him terrible."

Tressa lifted the traces over the horses' backs and wrapped them around the brake handle. "I don't see why not. Maybe we could go to the Lazy S first. We can return Abel's horses to his barn since Cole and Ethan are there to care for them. Then we'll go to town."

In short order, the girls had tied Abel's pair of geldings to the rear of the wagon and were heading down the road. Tressa flicked the reins and let out a giggle.

Sallie grinned. "What're ye laughin' at?"

"Me." Tressa laughed again at Sallie's puzzled expression. "Consider how very green I was when I arrived. Would you have thought I would learn to drive a wagon, ride a horse, or milk a cow?"

"Ye've surprised me, for sure. An' yourself, too, I'd wager."

"Oh yes." Tressa sucked in her lips, organizing her thoughts. "Shortly after I came, Aunt Hattie told me that God had orchestrated the events that brought me to Kansas—that He had something special planned for me here. She was right. I found God and accepted Him as my Father." She gave Sallie a tear-damp smile. "I've never been happier, Sallie, even though so many frightening things have occurred. I'm uncertain of what will come next, yet I trust that God will take care of me."

Sallie sucked in a breath and grabbed Tressa's hand. "Oh, Tressa! It gives my heart such a lift hearing ye speak this way! The night Cole an' me run off, we had a talk about God. It were important to him that I be believin' the same way as him. I tried to say I'd accept God just to make Cole happy, but the words wouldn't be comin' out of my mouth. Then I thought about Aunt Hattie—how kind she was, an' the way she prayed to God like she *knew* He was there listenin', an' suddenly I was cryin'. I asked God to come to me. I asked for myself an' not to please Cole. An' He came to me, Tressa."

"I'm so happy, Sallie." Tressa gave Sallie's hand a squeeze and then turned her attention forward. She let out a gasp. "Sallie, look!" She pointed to what remained of Abel's barbed wire fence. The posts lay on the ground, the clipped wires coiling across the grass like snakes lazing in the sun.

Sallie clapped her hands to her cheeks. "Who would've done such a thing to a man lyin' wounded in bed?"

Tressa's heart thumped. "Vince Rylin must have come back. . . ." She pulled the reins, guiding the horses off the road and into Abel's pasture. "Do you see any cattle?"

Sallie rose up on the seat and scanned the area. "He must've run 'em all off."

Numb, Tressa let the reins lay slack in her lap. The horses clopped onward without direction, and Tressa jolted when the wagon rolled by the bare patch of ground that had housed the branding fire pit. She gave the reins a jerk and pointed to the dirt patch with the blackened center. Her eyes found another dark spot, and her heart lurched. Slowly, she climbed down from the wagon and walked to the place where Abel's blood had seeped into the soil.

Sallie squatted beside her. "What is it?"

Tressa couldn't answer. Abel's blood had literally been poured into this ranch. How would he recover from the loss of his herd? How many burdens must one man bear? She lifted her head and spotted Abel's gun lying in the grass. She picked it up, holding it away from her body.

Sallie's round eyes stared at the gun, asking a silent question.

"It's Abel's," Tressa said grimly. She carried the pistol to the wagon and laid it carefully on a crumpled gunny sack. Abel would surely want it back. She stared down at the gun, remembering placing it in Abel's weak hand. "Sallie, I know men need weapons for hunting and for protection. But what possesses a man to aim something so dangerous at another human being and pull the trigger?"

Sallie dashed over and gave Tressa's shoulders an understanding pat. Suddenly she stooped over and plucked something from the grass. "Tressa?" On her palm, she held the delicate gold-filigreed frame she'd taken from Abel's highboy the week they had worked in his kitchen.

Tressa took the frame and gazed once more into the face of the lovely stranger. The image was now dust-marred, the frame bent, but the woman's beauty was undeniable.

"Why do ye suppose it was out here?" Sallie asked.

Tressa swallowed the tears that gathered in her throat. "Abel . . . Mr. Samms . . . must have been carrying it with him, and he lost it when he was shot." The implication made her chest ache. A man wouldn't carry the image of a woman who meant nothing to him. Abel must care deeply for this woman, whoever she was. She slipped the little frame into her pocket. "We'll give it to him when we visit him today. I . . . I'm sure he'll be elated to know it wasn't lost."

A sob tried to escape, but she pushed it down. Hadn't she just told Sallie God had something special planned for her? She must stop thinking of what she wanted and simply trust God to give her what she needed. "Let's get these horses to the barn now, and—"

"Tressa!" Sallie pointed across the pasture. A wispy black cloud rose from the prairie a few miles ahead.

Smoke! Tressa broke out in a cold sweat. Aunt Hattie had sternly cautioned the girls about the danger of fires sweeping across the plains. She claimed a fire could destroy acres of land in a few minutes, aided by the strong Kansas wind and dry ground. "Get in the wagon, Sallie— quickly! We must stop that fire!"

33

Abel's breakfast plate teetered on his belly. He'd never eaten in bed before, but Doc Kasper refused to let him sit up to a table. He'd also never wrangled a fork with his left hand, but he couldn't lift his right hand. So he lounged against a stack of pillows, clutched a fork in his left fist, and tried to feed himself scrambled eggs.

Couldn't the doc's wife have brought him something easier to eat, like bread and butter or a biscuit? Half the bite of eggs bounced down his chin and landed on his chest, but he shoved the remainder into his mouth and chewed. Impatience tried to capture him, but he shoved the feeling away. Eating might take twice as long as it ought to using his clumsy left hand, but at least he wouldn't starve.

He'd been playing the "at least" game ever since he'd awakened in the tall bed in the back room at Doc Kasper's office. He'd been shot, but at least he wasn't dead. His arm hurt like blue blazes, but at least no permanent damage had been done. He'd lost a good friend with Vince's deception, but at least he'd found his way to God again. After two years of running from God, it felt good to be standing in His presence once more. The first opportunity he had, he'd thank Aunt Hattie for her prayers.

Doc Kasper's wife bustled in and looked pointedly at his plate. "You still eating?" She tsk-tsked at him. "If you'd let me help you, you could have an empty plate and a full belly by now."

"But if I let you feed me, I'll never figure out how to take care of myself. None of my ranch hands is gonna be willin' to shovel food into my mouth." Immediately, he wished he could snatch the comment back. He still hadn't told anyone that Vince had shot him. He needed to come to grips with it himself before he could say the words out loud. "Besides, my belly's already full. You can take the plate away."

She quirked a brow at him. "You won't regain your strength if you don't eat."

Abel sighed. He jabbed another forkful, but he didn't try to bring it to his mouth. "When does the doc think I might get to go home?"

Mrs. Kasper poked at the bandage on his shoulder. The prodding hurt, but he held still and let her finish her perusal. "No fresh bleeding this morning. That's good." She backed up a step and propped her hands on her hips. "I figure when you're able to stand on your own and the doc's sure your wound won't open up again, he'll release you." She stabbed her index finger at him. "Now you eat every bit of those eggs." Her nose in the air, she strode out of the room.

As soon as she closed the door, Abel set the plate aside. He wasn't one to disregard an order, but his arm ached from the effort of controlling the fork, and all he really wanted to do was sleep. He recalled the doc telling him sleep was good medicine. "Well then," he muttered to himself, "I'll just swallow another dose of rest."

He nestled into the pillows, but as he was drifting off, a flurry of men's voices and the clatter of horses' hooves brought him fully awake. By pushing his left arm against the mattress he managed to roll to a sitting position. The room swam, and he braced himself against the mattress for a few minutes until the dizziness passed. Then he wrestled himself into his trousers, which he found draped across a chair in the corner of the room. He looked around for his shirt, intending to fling it around his shoulders, but he couldn't find it. At least the bandages hid a good portion of his torso. Bare-chested, he stumbled to the hallway.

Holding the wall with his good hand, he made his way down the hallway and into the small waiting area at the front of the doctor's office. Mrs. Kasper stood in the doorway that led to the street, looking out. Abel glimpsed men milling excitedly, some on foot, some on horseback. Fear stabbed him. Could it be a lynching party? Sheriff Tate would be powerless against a mob of angry men, and according to the doc, folks in town were plenty irked with Gage Hammond. They'd be even angrier if they knew Vince had put a bullet in his shoulder.

He shuffled up behind the doc's wife. "What's the commotion?"

Mrs. Kasper spun around, and her mouth dropped open. "Abel Samms, you get right back in that bed!" She grabbed his left elbow and tugged him toward the bedroom. He had no choice but to do as she said—she had a firm grip for a woman—but he looked over his shoulder. Although the men were gone, dust still billowed in little clouds above the road.

He flopped onto the pillows and let Mrs. Kasper lift his legs onto the mattress. His shoulder throbbed and his head spun, but at least he'd proved he could walk a few feet if he took a mind to. "What was all the excitement about?"

"Apparently there's a fire." Mrs. Kasper tossed the sheet over his legs. "But the men will handle it. You are *not* to get up again without help." She sucked in air, her face pinching into a scowl. "Oh, look! You got yourself bleeding again, Mr. Samms!"

Abel submitted to the woman applying pressure to his wound until the bleeding stopped. She changed the bandage and then tucked the sheet under the mattress snugly, trapping him in place. "Now, you sleep."

Feeling like a chastised child, he said, "Yes, ma'am." But he didn't sleep. Fire was the prairie's biggest enemy. Whose land was burning?

Were cattle in danger? Would it consume someone's house or barn? Worry ate at him, compounded by his inability to join his neighbors in battling the blaze. He groaned, "I wish I could *do* somethin'!"

You can pray.

The thought seemed to drop from heaven and bop him on the head. *I can't beat down the blaze with a gunnysack, but at least I can pray.* Snapping his eyes closed, he prayed for the safety of the men who were battling the blaze, for the livestock that might be in the fire's path, for success in stopping the fire before it ravaged too much of the land. He finished, "And God, be with the owner of the property. Give 'im strength an' peace to face this loss."

Before he could utter an amen, he fell asleep.

❦

"Whoa!" Tressa secured the traces and leaped from the wagon. The sight of yellow flames licking at Abel's house sent spasms of fear through her belly, but she couldn't let fear make her helpless. "We need buckets!" she hollered as she ran to the barn to retrieve the milk bucket.

Sallie lingered beside the wagon, seemingly mesmerized by the dancing flames. Tressa shoved the milk bucket into her arms. "Fill it and throw the water on the house! I'm going to find more buckets!" But Sallie didn't move. Tressa gave her a push toward the well. "Sallie, go!"

Sallie's wild eyes met Tressa's. "Where's Cole? He's supposed to be here, at the ranch. Where is he, Tressa?"

Tressa froze. If Cole were there, surely he'd be battling that blaze. Unless . . . She refused to give the unpleasant thought root. "He's probably out trying to round up cattle. He'll be in when he sees the smoke. Now hurry, Sallie—we've got to get water on that house before it's completely lost!"

Sallie finally stumbled toward the well, and Tressa ran back into the barn in search of buckets. The horses nickered nervously in their stalls, their nostrils flaring and eyes rolling. She longed to comfort them, but there wasn't time. She found one bucket in the tack room and she ran it to the well. The crackle and roar of the fire filled her ears, covering her pounding heartbeat. When would Cole arrive and help? She and Sallie couldn't fight this fire alone. *God, send help, please!*

She cranked the handle, drawing up water. Sallie dashed over and held out her bucket to be refilled. As Tressa splashed water into Sallie's bucket, she yelled, "We need more buckets. Do you suppose there are any in the bunkhouse?"

Sallie handed the full bucket to Tressa. "I'll go see!" She took off running, and Tressa carried the bucket to the house and tossed its contents as high as she could. She recognized the futility of her efforts, but she couldn't stand aside and do nothing in the face of such a calamity. She dashed back to the well and grabbed the handle.

"Tressa! Tressa!" Sallie's terrified screeching pulled Tressa from the well. She scrambled to the bunkhouse and tripped through the door. Sallie was kneeling on the floor next to Cole, who lay battered and unmoving. Tears streamed down Sallie's face. "Oh, Tressa—my Cole, my Cole . . . someone's killed him, for sure."

Tressa dropped to her knees and cupped Cole's cheek with her hand. His breath brushed her skin. "He's not dead, Sallie. I think he's just unconscious." Several purple splotches decorated his face, and her heart wrenched. "Someone beat him badly."

"But why would anyone hurt Cole? He's as gentle as a lamb. He'd not even go out of his way to be steppin' on a bug." Sallie leaned over Cole, hugging his head and crying into his hair. Suddenly Cole groaned, lifting his hand to push at Sallie.

Sallie sat up, her hands fluttering to touch his cheek, his hair, his shoulder. "Cole . . . Cole . . ."

He opened his eyes and looked around, as if confused by his surroundings. Then, without warning, he leaped to his feet and staggered for the door.

Sallie rose clumsily and chased after him. "Cole, you're hurt! Please lie down an' let me tend your wounds!"

"Gotta stop him." Cole swayed, and Sallie caught his arm. "Can't let him burn the place."

Tressa took his other arm and helped Sallie guide him to the table in the middle of the small room. "Who, Cole? Who was here?"

Cole flopped into the nearest chair, his eyes wide. "Vince. He was crazy—drunk as a skunk. I never seen him like that. Stumblin' around, claimin' Abel should've died. Said he'd shoot every cow an' burn every buildin' on the place if it couldn't be his. Ethan tried to stop him, an' he knocked him down. So Ethan yelled he wouldn't stay an' be a witness to it—an' then he rode off. I tried to stop Vince, an' . . ." Cole touched his forehead where a huge purple lump had formed. He looked at Sallie helplessly. "I . . . I tried, honest I did, but he . . . he was like a madman. I couldn't stop him."

Suddenly he sniffed the air. He groaned. "Oh no, he's gone an' done it. I shoulda stopped him . . . I shoulda stopped him, Sallie."

Sallie hugged Cole's head to her chest and murmured to him. Tressa dashed back to the yard, intending to throw more water on the house, but the sight that greeted her eyes brought her frantic race to a heartbreaking halt. The roof of the house was engulfed. Flames glowed behind every window and danced beneath the eaves. The fire roared and cackled like malevolent laughter, and a chill wiggled down Tressa's spine. Even if a dozen people battled the blaze, they wouldn't be able to save the house.

She sank down on the little stoop outside the bunkhouse's doorway and watched the flames eagerly devour the wooden structure. The loss made her chest ache. Such damage Vince had wrought. *God, why? Why did evil have its way here today? I want to believe that You have good plans for Your children, but, dear God, I don't understand. . . .*

She remained so focused on the fire, she hardly noticed the caravan of wagons and riders pouring onto the property. Men swarmed the grounds, creating a bucket brigade and soaking every building, including the outhouse, to prevent the fire from spreading.

No one made an attempt to save the house—as Tressa had feared, it was beyond saving. Sallie and Cole joined her, and she battled tears as she stood to the side and watched the others work. Aunt Hattie and the other pupils arrived with sandwiches and jugs of lemonade, which the smoke-stained, sweaty men eagerly consumed.

Fred Pennington sidled up between Aunt Hattie and Luella. "We've pret' much done all we can. Me an' Jerome'll stick around an' watch that the wind don't carry any sparks to the pasture." He looked at Luella, who was fiddling with the cork on a lemonade jug, her gaze averted. "Why don't you ladies go on back to the Flyin' W."

Luella didn't lift her head, but she said, "I can stay, too . . . keep you company . . ."

Paralee skittered forward. "And me."

Fred gave one slow nod. "We'll take you ladies home later then, if it's all right with Aunt Hattie."

A lopsided smile creased Aunt Hattie's face. "I think that's fine." She turned to Cole and Sallie. "You comin' with me, Sallie?"

Sallie tucked herself beneath Cole's arm. "I'll be stayin' here in the bunkhouse with Cole. I won't be leavin' him."

"I expected as much."

One by one, the townspeople and neighboring ranchers drifted away. Cole and Sallie, their arms twined around each other's waists, ambled off to the bunkhouse. Fred and Jerome positioned themselves on opposite sides of the smoldering house, and Luella and Paralee stayed close to their respective beaus.

Aunt Hattie put her arm around Tressa's shoulders and walked her to the wagon. As they drove away from Abel's ranch, Tressa stared over her shoulder at the blackened, broken timbers that had once formed a house. Glowing embers became yellow eyes peering back at her, and she shivered.

A heavy sigh came from the other side of the wagon seat, and Tressa looked at Aunt Hattie. The older woman's face sagged, her features drawn and tired, but she offered a sad smile. "Well, missy, it's just you an' me." She chuckled. "Reckon that's how it'll be soon, too. Sallie's already hitched with Cole; another few weeks an' Mabelle an' Paralee'll be havin' their joint weddin'." She cocked her head to the side, one eyebrow high. "I wondered for a while whether Luella'd accept Fred—he's such a quiet one an' she's so flighty—but from the looks o' things today, I figure she's plannin' to say yes."

Tressa remembered Luella's mad dash from the dining room. Had it only been this morning? It seemed as though she'd lived two lifetimes in the last ten hours. "Were you able to assure Luella that Gage's lies hadn't reached the community?"

Aunt Hattie nodded. "But we need to be prayin' for that girl. She carries a heap o' anger. Her life before she come here . . . well, it wasn't so good." She shot Tressa a meaningful look. "When you grow up without bein' shown love, it makes you uncertain how to reach out for it when you're big."

Once again, Tressa experienced a rush of gratitude for the affection she'd received from her parents before moving into her aunt and uncle's home. She'd been given an example of loving that she longed to emulate in her own life. "I'll pray for her."

"You're a good girl, Tressa."

"Aunt Hattie?" Her voice sounded raspy, her throat raw from breathing smoke. "Do you think someone from town will let Mr. Samms know about his house?"

Aunt Hattie harrumphed. "Oh, he'll know before sundown. Barnett's not exactly known for keepin' secrets."

"I didn't get to check on him today, so I'd like to go tomorrow."

The older woman's lips twitched. "Why sure, darlin'. First thing in the mornin' you hitch a horse to the wagon an' ride on in to town. I'd think lookin' at your purty face would be good medicine for Abel."

Tressa cupped her hand over the little gold picture frame that still rested in her pocket. She hoped the pretty face in the picture would be good medicine for Abel. Everything else in his house was gone. This one remaining belonging would surely bring him a small measure of joy.

34

For a man in need of rest, Abel sure had to deal with a passel of disruptions. He folded his good arm behind his head and stared at the ceiling as he replayed snippets of conversations he'd had with the string of visitors who'd come and gone.

When Glendon Shultz and Bob Clemence had shown up yesterday right after supper, all grubby and smelling of smoke, to tell Abel his house was gone, one thought had struck: *I prayed for myself.* And the strength and peace he'd requested for the person whose land was threatened by the fire washed over him even as one fat tear rolled down Glendon's cheek, leaving a clean trail in the soot that stained his face. He'd ended up comforting his neighbors, assuring them he'd be all right. They'd crept away, murmuring that the news must have tetched Abel's head to make him so calm. But Abel knew it was God giving him strength.

An hour after Glendon and Bob departed, Brewster Hammond had come in, his face sad but determined. Sitting on the edge of the bed, he'd withdrawn a leather packet from a pocket inside his jacket and laid it on Abel's pillow. "This here is every penny you'd've earned over the past few years if those cattle hadn't been stolen from you. Gage kept a count, an' when he took my cattle to market, he handed over the proceeds from your purloined beef to Vince."

Abel had argued, "You don't owe me nothin'. Vince's the only one oughtta be makin' restitution."

But Hammond shook his head. "Nope. My boy was involved, an' I'll settle his debt. I can't go backward an' keep Gage from followin' such a hurtsome path, but at least I can make things right with you. You keep that money, Abel—use it to build a new house on your property."

Abel had nearly swallowed his tongue. "You mean you don't want to buy my land no more? This'd be a good time for me to sell, what with my house gone, my cattle run off, an' me not even able to carry a fork of eggs to my mouth."

"You keep that land, Abel. I wanted to expand my holdings so Gage . . ." Brewster's chin had quivered. Giving Abel's good shoulder a solid pat, he'd repeated, "You keep that land. It's what your pa would've wanted, an' God'll give you the strength to rebuild."

Before leaving, Brewster had shaken Abel's hand and promised to pray for him. Abel couldn't help but marvel at the change in the older rancher's demeanor. He'd seemed broken, yet somehow stronger than ever before.

The most difficult visit came shortly after breakfast this morning. Sheriff Tate had told Abel that a burned body, along with an empty jug of whiskey, had been found in the rubble of his house. No doubt Vince Rylin. Fury had swelled Abel's chest when he realized Vince probably had deliberately set the fire. But before he could give vent to the feelings, he'd suddenly thought of Amanda. He'd carried a grudge against her for two years, and holding on to it had turned him away from God. Did he want another grudge separating him from his heavenly Father?

Flesh battled with spirit, a silent tug-of-war under his skin. And suddenly Tressa's voice echoed through his memory: *"God is very clear on His expectation concerning holding a grudge. He advises not to let the sun go down on our anger. . . ."* Abel released his breath in a whoosh, choosing to let the anger go. He looked the sheriff square in the face and said, "Vince was like an uncle to me all durin' my growin'-up years. He was my pa's best friend. Don't know what made him turn on me, but . . . I pray God'll have mercy on his soul."

The sheriff had stared at him like he'd taken leave of his senses. Abel then asked, "What about Ethan?"

"No idea where the boy went, but accordin' to Cole he tried to buck his pa. I'm pret' sure he ain't involved in none of these dirty dealin's."

Thinking about it now, Abel couldn't help but mourn the loss of the man who'd been so important to his family. He offered up a prayer that Ethan would return. Ethan was the closest thing to a brother Abel had, and he didn't want to lose him along with everything else.

The doctor's wife bustled in, chasing away his melancholy thoughts. Clean sheets filled her arms. "Mr. Samms, since you're awake, can I move you to a chair long enough for me to change your bedding?" She wrinkled her nose. "You've been lying on those sheets for two days now. They're stale."

Abel swallowed a chuckle. There'd been times he'd gone a full two *weeks* without washing the sheets on his bed at home, but he didn't figure Mrs. Kasper would be pleased to know it. "That'd be fine, ma'am." Pain attacked his shoulder when he strained to sit up, but the sharp throbs dulled after he settled into the chair in the corner of the room. He sat very still and watched Mrs. Kasper whip the soiled sheets from the bed. The sight brought another image to mind—Tressa, in his bedroom, stripping his bedding.

Deep regret smacked him at the thought of Tressa. What a scare Vince had given her. Vague memories—of her hands stroking his hair, her lips brushing his cheek—lingered on the fringes of his mind, but he couldn't be sure if the memories were real or imagined. Really, it didn't matter much. God had used Tressa to reopen his heart to the idea of loving, of building a family. At last he'd healed from the pain of Amanda's rejection.

"All right, Mr. Samms." Mrs. Kasper's shrill voice broke through his thoughts. "Let's get you back in that bed."

Abel grimaced. "Can't I stay in the chair a little longer? Been layin' down so much my backside's nearly forgot its purpose."

The woman clapped her hand over her mouth, and Abel feared he'd scandalized her. But her shoulders shook in silent laughter. After several seconds, she lowered her hand and gave him a crooked half scowl, half smile. "Very well, Mr. Samms. But only for a few more minutes." Snatching up the rumpled sheets, she headed out the door.

Abel leaned his head against the chair's high back, cupping the elbow of his injured arm with his good hand to keep from jiggling his shoulder. As soon as that wound healed, he could go home. Eagerness to return to his ranch made his feet itch to carry him out of the room, down the hallway, and all the way to the Lazy S.

Then he remembered the fire. He didn't have a home waiting anymore. And if the house was gone, everything inside it was gone, too. The furniture Ma had carted all the way from South Carolina to Kansas—enough to fill two wagons—had been burned to cinders. He glanced at his trousers and then at the new, neatly folded shirt resting on top of the bureau across the room. They were the only clothes he owned. The money in the packet Brewster had brought in wouldn't cover everything he'd need to reestablish himself.

"What'll I do now, God?" He whispered the words aloud. But it wasn't a whiny complaint—just a heartfelt desire for guidance. The strength and peace he'd prayed for earlier once again flooded him. He smiled. "At least I still got the barn an' bunkhouse. There'll be a roof over my head until I can rebuild."

He yawned. That bed was looking better minute by minute. He drew in a deep breath and called, "Mrs. Kasper?"

Within seconds, the woman scurried into the room.

"I'd like to rest again now, if you'd help me, please."

Her firm arm around his waist offered support as she guided him to the bed. He leaned into the pillows, releasing a sigh of contentment. "Thank you, ma'am."

"You're welcome. Have a good rest." She flipped the sheets to his chin and headed to the door. But she came to a stop in the doorway and plunked her fists on her hips. Abel looked at her straight spine and aggravated pose. What had he done to rile her now? But she sent the scolding comment to someone in the hallway. "You can't visit right now. Mr. Samms needs to sleep."

"Oh . . . I apologize. I'd hoped . . ."

Abel's heart fired into his throat when he heard the timid response. He jammed his left elbow against the mattress and pushed himself up. "Tressa?"

Tressa peeked into the room. Her pale blue eyes—wide and hopeful—met his. A smile curved her lips, doubling the beat of his pulse. He gulped and gave Mrs. Kasper his best pleading look. "Just one more visitor this mornin'? It'll be the last one."

Mrs. Kasper's scowl deepened. "Mr. Samms . . ."

"I'll sleep all afternoon. I promise."

The woman let out a mighty huff, shaking her head. "Taking care of you is worse than caring for a dozen cantankerous children." She threw her hands in the air. "All right! Wear yourself out. But don't complain to me later on when you're too tired to eat your dinner!" She stomped past Tressa, still muttering.

Tressa hovered in the doorway, her hands clasped at her waist. Abel flopped back on the pillows and waggled his fingers at her. "Her bite's worse'n her bark. Come on in."

She sent a furtive glance down the hallway. "Are you sure it's all right? If you need to rest . . ."

"I'll rest this afternoon. Please." He beckoned again, offering a smile. "Come in. I'd like to talk with you."

Slowly, she advanced a few feet forward, stopping midway between the door and the bed. Her eyes traveled from his face to his bandaged shoulder. Her forehead crinkled briefly, and then she met his gaze again. "Does it still hurt?"

Truthfully, the dull throb never left, but he shook his head. "Not much." So many words cluttered his brain, he didn't know what to say first. "Miss Tressa . . ."

"Yes?" She tipped her head, her face sweetly attentive.

He wanted to leap out of the bed and crush her in his arms. He swallowed. "Thank you for goin' after help like you did. Probably wouldn't still be alive if you hadn't taken off that way."

Her chin quivered. "You wouldn't have been out in that pasture, wouldn't have gotten shot at all, if I hadn't taken you there."

"That what you think? My gettin' shot's your fault?"

She bobbed her head once, so slight he almost missed it.

"Aw, Miss Tressa, don't blame yourself. It would've happened no matter what." Remembering Vince's emotionless recital, Abel cringed. Yes, Vince had been gunning for him, and it had nothing to do with Tressa. He said, " 'Sides, I'm kinda glad it come about."

Her eyes flew wide. "W-what? You're glad you were *shot*?"

Abel chuckled. "I know it sounds odd, but . . . layin' out there, hurtin' an' scared, I got to thinkin' what you said about trustin' God when you're feelin' afraid. So I called out to Him. An' He answered. He took me back, an' I told Him I won't be doin' no more strayin'."

"Oh, Abel . . ." Tressa's eyes filled with tears, and she took one step forward. "Aunt Hattie was right. Sometimes a bad thing *can* be a good thing."

"Aunt Hattie's usually right." Abel shook his head. "Save ourselves a lot of time an' bother if we'd just listen to her an'—" He clamped his mouth shut. There were other things he wanted to tell Tressa—feelings he could barely contain—but what could he offer her now? His house was gone, his hired hands were gone, and his cattle were scattered.

He shouldn't be making declarations of love and devotion when there were no assurances he'd have the means to take care of her.

The silence between them lengthened, and suddenly Tressa gave a little start like someone had poked her in the back. She stuck her hand in her pocket and pulled something out. Taking one more step forward, she held out her hand and bobbed it.

Something glinted in the light. Abel squinched his eyes at the object. "Whatcha got there?"

Leaning forward, she deposited Amanda's portrait in the little gold frame on the edge of the mattress and then scuttled backward. "Sallie found it lying out where . . . where you'd fallen. Your house, and everything in it, was destroyed by the fire." Her voice sounded tight, like the words got stuck and she had to push them out. "But this wasn't ruined. I thought you'd like to have it . . . as a reminder of . . ."

He stared at the gold frame, and the irony of the situation hit as solid as a boulder dropping on his head. A laugh built in his chest. He cleared his throat, trying to hold it back, but it exploded out.

❧

Tressa took a stumbling backward step. Abel's laughter filled her with confusion. What could he possibly find funny? He'd suffered such loss—his long-time hired hand, his home and belongings, his cattle, and very nearly his life! Was this laughter a maniacal response to overwhelming sorrow? Perhaps she should retrieve the doctor. She spun toward the door.

"Miss Tressa, please—wait!"

She turned back at his breathless request. He held his palm to his shoulder as he continued to shake with laughter, but the raucous sounds of mirth ceased. Finally he drew a deep breath and released it, lowering his hand to his lap.

He sent her a crinkly smile. "C'mon over here, Miss Tressa. Lemme tell you about this little picture."

Hesitantly, she approached the bed, maintaining a decent distance between the two of them. She listened as he told her the woman's name and his relationship to her. Jealousy reared its ugly head when he shared he'd intended to marry the girl, but empathy at Amanda's desertion chased the envy away.

After the story ended, Tressa stared at him in amazement. "Abel—Mr. Samms—how do you bear it all? You've truly lost more than any man ought to. It seems so very unfair!" As soon as the words escaped, she bit down on her tongue, silently berating herself. She'd come to offer encouragement, but instead she'd reminded him of his troubles.

"Unfair?" Abel scratched his head, his forehead puckered. "Yep, probably is unfair by most folks' reasonin'. But to tell you the truth, it's best that Amanda's gone. She'd've never been happy here, an' I'd've missed out on—"

Something in his eyes made Tressa's pulse race. She wanted to explore the strange reaction, but when she opened her mouth a question spilled out. "But don't you still love her? You . . . you carried her portrait with you. . . ."

He plucked up the frame and bounced it on his palm. "Reason I had this with me the other day is I was plannin' on buryin' it—givin' my old feelin's for Amanda a . . . well, a funeral of sorts. Puttin' her to rest. I knew it was time for me to move on. 'Cause, Miss Tressa . . ." His whisker-dotted cheeks, pale from his ordeal, streaked pink. "I'm findin' myself drawn to . . . someone else."

She held her breath, her heart caroming against her ribs. Her mouth formed the word *who*, but no sound came out.

He sighed and closed his eyes, collapsing against the pillows. "But it wouldn't be fair to say it, 'cause I can't meet Aunt Hattie's rules about providin' for a wife."

35

Two opposite emotions attacked Tressa: elation—*He loves me!*—and despair—*His pride will imprison his feelings.* She tried to speak, to tell him how she felt. "Mr. Samms, I—"

"I'm tired, Miss Tressa." The words rasped out, proving his exhaustion. "I appreciate you comin' to see me an' bringin' me . . . bringin' me . . ." He swallowed. "But I need to rest now." Grunting a bit, he rolled onto his good shoulder, hiding his face from her.

Without another word, Tressa gathered the shards of her shattered heart, turned, and left the room. Her chest ached so badly, breathing became torture. But somehow she made her way to the wagon, climbed aboard, and aimed the horse toward Aunt Hattie's. By clenching her jaw, she held her tears at bay.

At the ranch, she guided the horse directly into the barn, leaped down, and released the animal from the rigging. She gave the horse a few scoops of oats, then walked stiffly across the yard to the house.

She wanted to escape to her room, bury her face in the pillows, and cry this intense hurt away.

But when she clicked the front door shut behind her, Aunt Hattie's voice called from the kitchen, "Tressa, that you?"

She sucked air through her nose, forcing down the tears. "Yes, ma'am."

"How's Abel this mornin'?"

Tressa's lips quivered. Her chest grew tight. On a strangled sob, she barked out, "Positively mulish!" Then she clattered up the stairs and slammed the door to her room. Throwing herself across the bed, she pressed her face into her elbow and let loose a torrent of tears.

Pounding footsteps reached her ears, and hands curled around her shoulders, forcing her to roll over. Tressa took one look at Aunt Hattie's concerned face, and her wails increased in volume.

The older woman swept Tressa against her chest and patted her back. "Lands, darlin', what'd that man say to you? 'Cause injured shoulder or no, I'll give him a piece o' my mind if he—"

"He loves me, Aunt Hattie," Tressa blubbered into Aunt Hattie's shoulder. "He won't say it, but I know he does. Oh, Aunt Hattie . . ." She rubbed her eyes with her fists. "You said when a woman loves a man, her heart feels as though it would soar out of her chest. But my heart has turned to a lump of clay. It's heavy and dull, and it will never soar." She dissolved into more wild weeping. Aunt Hattie held her and patted her and let her cry herself out. Eventually the loud sobs faded to shuddering sniffles, and Tressa pulled back.

"Aunt Hattie, why must love hurt so much? I love Abel. But he can't truly love me or he'd do as Cole did with Sallie and steal me away. Home or no home, money or none, if he genuinely cared for me he would find a way for us to be together."

Aunt Hattie clicked her tongue against her teeth. She lifted her apron and wiped Tressa's cheeks dry and then cupped Tressa's face in her hands. "Darlin', you can't be judgin' Abel for not doin' what

Cole would do. They're two different men, an' each has his own way o' bein'.'"

"But—"

"No. You thinkin' ill o' Abel for not bein' like Cole is no better than Abel thinkin' ill o' you for comin' from the same world as Amanda."

Tressa jerked free of Aunt Hattie's gentle hold. "I am *nothing* like Amanda! She made promises she refused to keep!"

"But you're both from the East, so Abel figured you'd never fit in here."

"That's the most ludicrous thing I've ever heard. Why, just because two people hail from the same area doesn't mean they are similar in every way."

Aunt Hattie raised one eyebrow. "You listenin' to yourself? You just proved your own point. You can't be condemnin' Abel for not sweepin' you away to some unknown future." She smoothed the hair from Tressa's face. "I'm not tryin' to criticize Cole—he's young an' brash an' acted in the only way he knew how to keep from losin' the girl he loved. But Abel's a man o' deep convictions. Responsible. Those're good traits, Tressa—things any woman'd want in a husband."

"But his convictions might keep us apart!" New tears threatened, but Tressa sniffed hard and brought herself under control.

"Have you prayed about this?"

Tressa jolted, suddenly feeling guilty. "P-prayed?"

"Sure, prayed." Aunt Hattie emphasized her words with a nod of her head. "Missy, God has a special plan for you, but it appears to me you're runnin' willy-nilly, tryin' to fix everything yourself instead o' trustin' Him to lead you."

Tressa toyed with a loose thread in the bed's quilt. "But . . . but what if God . . ." She couldn't finish the question, too fearful of the answer.

"Has somethin' different in store than what we want?"

Tressa gave a quick nod, her head low.

"Well, this I can guarantee you: God doesn't always do things the way we think they oughtta be done."

Tressa's head shot up, her gaze colliding with Aunt Hattie's.

A soft smile warmed the older woman's face. "He always does 'em *better*. An' when we follow His lead, we discover what's best for us. God doesn't want you to hope only for second best—He wants you to find His very best." She caressed Tressa's cheek. "You gotta trust that, darlin' girl."

Tressa bit down on her lower lip, absorbing Aunt Hattie's words. Even Abel had said Aunt Hattie was usually right. At that moment a high-pitched meow interrupted. Isabella leaped onto the bed and curled herself in Tressa's lap. With a small laugh, she gathered Isabella beneath her chin and sighed into the cat's fur. "I wish I were as wise and brave as you, Aunt Hattie."

The older woman swept her hand down Isabella's back. "An' I wish I were young an' beautiful an' owned a flyin' horse." She chuckled, and Tressa smiled. "Truth is, darlin', I'm not wise an' brave. I just have faith. An' I believe that you're gonna see God's very best worked out in your life." She rose. "You stay up here for a while, cuddle ol' Izzy-B—somethin' soothin' about runnin' your hands over a purrin' cat. An' do some talkin' with God. When you feel better, come down an' give me a hand with supper. Brewster's comin', an' Cole an' Sallie'll be joinin' us, too, seein' as how she doesn't have a way to cook in that bunkhouse over at Abel's. You'll want to be free o' those tears before they get here."

Tressa waited until Aunt Hattie left the room. Then she transferred Isabella to the mattress and slipped to her knees beside the bed. "God, I'm sorry for not placing my hope in You. I want to be like Aunt Hattie—full of faith. Every time I've asked for Your rescue, You've come. So rescue me now, God. Take away my hurt and fear and help me find Your plan. Lead me to what You deem is best."

Hattie listened to the cheerful conversations happening around her dining table. Every chair was filled; every face bore a smile—even Tressa's, although her eyes were still red-rimmed from her crying bout. A feeling of satisfaction filled every ounce of Hattie's frame.

She'd prepared a feast fit for a Sunday—roast beef with potatoes, carrots, and onions. The food and the crowded table turned the meal into a party, and it was fitting. She had reason to celebrate: Sallie'd returned, safe and sound; Abel was healing; each of her girls—save Tressa—was preparing to marry a good, godly man; and even she, old as she was, had been offered a second chance at love. God's blessings were plumb overflowing, and Hattie couldn't keep a smile from her face.

"You folks ready for dessert?" she asked. "Got a tall cake with a thick chocolate icin', if anybody's interested." A rousing cheer rose, which Hattie took to be a yes. She bounced up. "I'll go fetch it." As she headed for the kitchen, someone knocked on the front door. She changed direction, calling over her shoulder, "Paralee, go get that cake an' a servin' knife, wouldja?"

With a happy bounce in her step, she reached the door and threw it open, then stepped back in surprise. Ethan Rylin stood on her doorstep. For long seconds they stared at each other, Hattie's jaw slack with shock and Ethan as sheepish as she'd ever seen a man. Then she found her senses and snapped her mouth shut. "Ethan. Come on in here, son."

Sweeping his hat from his head, Ethan stepped into the house. He fixed a sad gaze on Hattie. "Ma'am." A burst of laughter carried from the dining room, and his face flooded with color. "Oh . . . I'm interruptin'. I'll—"

Hattie captured his elbow. "You'll join us."

He pulled loose of her grasp. "No . . . no, I can't. I just need to talk to you. Outside." He dashed out the door before she could argue.

Hattie scuttled to Brewster and whispered in his ear, "Ethan's on the front porch. Me an' him are gonna have us a little chat."

"Want me to come, too?"

Although she was capable of handling the situation alone, she discovered she wanted his support. She nodded, and he followed her outside. Ethan was waiting on a chair at the end of the porch, his hat hooked on his left knee. Hattie sat beside him, and Brewster leaned on the railing. She squeezed Ethan's shoulder. "I'm glad you come back. We were worried about you, son."

Ethan nodded, his face stoic. "I had to come back. I . . . I went by the Lazy S." He shook his head. "Can't believe all what Pa done. . . ."

Hattie took a deep breath. "Ethan, about your pa . . ."

He blinked rapidly. "He's dead, ain't he?"

"Yes. I'm sorry."

"How?"

"They found 'im in the house. The fire . . ."

For long seconds Ethan sat in silence, his jaw muscles twitching. Then he sighed. "At least I won't see him hanged for rustlin' an' tryin' to kill Abel." He looked back and forth from Hattie to Brewster, his eyes wide. "I didn't know any of what he was doin'. He kept givin' me money—claimed he'd been roundin' up strays an' sellin' 'em. Said to tuck the money away so's we could buy our own little place. I believed him. I didn't know he was rustlin' from Abel's herd. If I'd known, I'd've . . ." He dropped his head.

Hattie grabbed his hand. "Ethan, Abel's worried about you."

His head shot up. "He is?" Then he looked down again. "I can't face 'im. Not after what Pa done."

Brewster cleared his throat. "Abel's gonna need some good hands to rebuild his ranch, an' he knows you're a good hand."

Ethan kept his head low. "No. No, I couldn't stay around here. Be too hard, with folks knowin' about Pa an' all. They'd always be whisperin', watchin' me . . . I gotta find someplace else to go. Start over. But . . ." He pulled a rolled wad of bills from inside his shirt. "All the money Pa gave me is here. I haven't spent a penny of it." He plopped it in Hattie's lap. "Would you give it to Abel for me?"

His pleading gaze made Hattie's heart ache. "Ethan, won't you at least go see Abel? Let him know you're all right?"

He shook his head and stood. "No, ma'am. Better for all of us if I just . . . go away." His boot heels dragged as he scuffed his way off the porch, his head hanging. Moments later he swung into his saddle and pounded away without a backward glance.

Hattie turned to Brewster. He opened his arms, and she stepped into his embrace. Her cheek against his shirt front, she said, "This ain't exactly a happy endin' to my day, Brew."

He rubbed his hand up and down her spine. "An' I'm afraid the next days won't be much better, considerin' Gage's trial is comin' up next week an' Abel'll be comin' home to a pile of black soot. At least my men've found nearly fifty head of his cattle. That's somethin' good."

Hattie sighed, enjoying the security of Brewster's arms. Been so long since she'd leaned into someone else's strength she'd almost forgotten how pleasant it could be. She nestled closer. "Need to take this money in to Abel. He'll need every penny he can find to get his ranch up an' runnin' again. He's got a heap o' work waitin'."

Brewster took hold of her shoulders and peered into her face. "Seems to me that boy could use some prayers. Should we pray for him now?"

Tears stung behind Hattie's nose. With his only son in dire trouble, he still had the heart to pray for a neighbor. "Brewster Hammond, I love you."

He smiled. "Harriet Wyatt, I love you, too."

36

Tressa glanced around the small, crowded courtroom. Every seat was filled, and people stood three deep along the walls. It appeared most of the town of Barnett had turned out to see Gage sentenced. She, Aunt Hattie, and Mr. Hammond had arrived early, so they sat behind the railing that separated the defendant from the spectators. Gage was close enough to touch, but Mr. Hammond held to Aunt Hattie's hands instead. Seeing the anguish in the older rancher's eyes pierced Tressa's heart.

God, I know Gage must be punished, but please don't let them hang him. Please spare Mr. Hammond that pain.

The judge set aside the small pile of yellowed papers over which he had been poring for nearly half an hour. As his head rose, the entire congregation of people seemed to hold its breath. Silence fell, an unearthly silence that made the fine hairs on Tressa's neck tingle.

"The defendant will rise."

Gage flashed a frightened look over his shoulder before jolting to his feet. The chair legs screeched on the wooden floor, and Tressa cringed. The sound reminded her of opening a door with rusty hinges. Might the trapdoor of a hanging platform make a similar sound?

The judge cleared his throat and pinned a solemn look on Gage. "Gage Hammond, finding you guilty of aiding and abetting a known rustler, for deliberately selling stolen goods, and for giving those proceeds to a man other than the owner, I hereby sentence you to two years in the Ford County jail."

Murmurs and disbelieving gasps broke out across the room. Someone yelled, "Only two years? For what he done? Should be *thirty* years!"

The judge banged his gavel and aimed a stern look at the crowd. He laid the gavel down and folded his arms on the high wooden bench. "You folks need to remember that *I'm* the judge, not you. Besides that, the man he wronged asked me to go easy on Mr. Hammond. If Abel Samms can forgive, then you people ought to be able to do the same."

Another murmur came from the onlookers, but it held amazement rather than anger.

Tressa's heart sang at the judge's words. How difficult it must have been for Abel to choose to forgive Gage. Yet he'd done it. It seemed Abel had adopted a policy of releasing hurts rather than carrying grudges. And then a question winged through her mind: *And what about you? Will you forgive?*

She sat up straight, startled, as she contemplated the question. What *about* her? Although she hadn't viewed her feelings as a grudge, in those moments she realized she needed to release the resentment she carried toward her aunt and uncle. If Abel could forgive Gage and Vince for the harm they'd inflicted, then surely she should be able to forgive Aunt Gretchen and Uncle Leo for their cold treatment. Bowing her head right there in the crowded courtroom, she asked God to help her forgive her aunt and uncle.

The judge's stern voice pulled her from her inner reflections. "Young man, you need to be aware that it is within my power to sentence you to hang. I could lock you away for the next fifty years. But I chose two years of incarceration—one year for each of those you engaged in unlawful activities against your neighbor."

Gage hung his head, his meek pose so different from his former brash bearing.

The judge continued. "Along with Mr. Samms' plea on your behalf, the fact that the money has been returned to its rightful owner and that you willingly admitted to wrongdoing influenced my decision. I believe there's hope for you." He removed his spectacles and rubbed the bridge of his nose. "You're young, and you've got a lot of life ahead of you. Use the next two years to turn yourself around. When you return to Barnett, I'll expect to see a reformed, law-abiding citizen."

Gage nodded respectfully. "Yes, your honor. Thank you, sir."

Tressa averted her gaze as Brewster leaned across the short railing and hugged his son. The pair clung, their fingers clutching handfuls of fabric. The agony expressed in the gesture nearly broke her heart. The sheriff strode forward and took Gage's arm, pulling him from Brewster's embrace. Brewster stood, silent and unmoving, until Gage disappeared behind a solid wood door. Then he reached for Aunt Hattie. "Let's get out of here."

They worked their way through the murmuring crowd and emerged onto the sunny boardwalk. Tressa nearly gaped in amazement. How could the day be so normal? Sun hanging in the sky, birds singing from bushes, people bustling in and out of shops . . . Shouldn't the drama that had unfolded inside the courthouse be reflected on the outside, as well?

Mr. Hammond let his head drop back, and he released a heavy sigh. "Two years . . ."

Aunt Hattie slipped her arm around his waist and rested her head against his shoulder. "It could've been worse, Brew. Our prayers were answered."

Mr. Hammond gave Aunt Hattie a one-armed squeeze and then turned his attention to Tressa. "An' some other prayers've been answered, too." A weak smile quavered on his lips. "Doc Kasper caught me this mornin' an' said Abel's well enough to go home."

Tressa's heart skipped a beat. "H-he is?"

"Yep. An' we're gonna give 'im a ride. C'mon, ladies." He looped one hand through Tressa's elbow, curled his other arm around Aunt Hattie's waist, and led them to the doctor's office.

Tressa held back. "I'll wait out here."

"Nope, you're comin' in." Mr. Hammond gave her a nudge that sent her through the doorway. "Got some things to tell Abel, an' it'd be good for you to hear 'em, too."

Tressa sent a puzzled look at Aunt Hattie, but the older woman just winked in return. Tressa followed Mr. Hammond and Aunt Hattie down the hallway to Abel's room. When Mr. Hammond knocked, Abel's familiar voice called, "Come in."

Just hearing his voice caused her heart to flutter. Part of her wished to turn and run from the doctor's office—to avoid adding more pain to her already battered spirit—but her desire to see Abel hale and healthy prevailed. She trailed Aunt Hattie into the room.

Abel stood beside the bed, buttoning his shirt with one hand. His right arm hung in a sling, a reminder of his injury, but his face was freshly shaved and his cheeks held a healthy rosiness. Aunt Hattie bustled forward and planted a kiss on Abel's cheek. Tressa wished she could do the same. Only she wanted to kiss his lips. Shocked by that brazen thought, she scuttled to the corner of the room and perched on a ladder-backed chair.

"Abel, good to see you on your feet." Mr. Hammond slipped his hands into his trouser pockets and studied Abel.

"Good to be on my feet." Abel's gaze flitted to Tressa. A brief spark lit his eyes, and then he turned to face Aunt Hattie. "I'm grateful for the ride to the ranch. Doc says I shouldn't try ridin' a horse or drivin' a team for a couple of weeks yet." He released a rueful chuckle. "That'll make it pretty hard to get any work done. . . ."

"Won't be a problem," Mr. Hammond declared. He pointed to the bed. "Sit down for a minute, Abel. We got some talkin' to do."

Abel's expression turned wary, but he sat and gave Mr. Hammond his attention. "What is it?"

Mr. Hammond crossed to Aunt Hattie and slung his arm around her shoulders. "Harriet an' me've been doin' a lot of prayin' an' thinkin' durin' the two weeks you been holed up here. Now, we know you're a growed man, but sometimes even growed men can use a little help."

Abel started to rise.

Mr. Hammond held up his hand. "Hear me out. Then you can decide if you want to heed what we say or not. Fair enough?"

Abel offered a solemn nod. He sank back onto the edge of the bed.

"Your spread an' mine are back-to-back, makin' it easy for my men to take an extra swing across your property an' keep an eye on your herd. They've rounded up a goodly number of your wanderin' cattle, an'—with Cole's help—they been rebuildin' your fence to keep 'em in place till you got back."

The man shifted, his boots scuffing the wood floor. "An' seein' as how our spreads are so close an' I got a big house with lots of room, I'd like you to come stay with me until the men of town can come together an' build you a house of your own."

Tressa watched Abel's face for signs of rebellion, but although he appeared uncertain, he listened without argument.

"Cole wants to stay on." Aunt Hattie continued where Mr. Hammond had left off. "He an' Sallie've been sleepin' in the bunkhouse but eatin' their meals at my place. Not very convenient. Seems like a person could build an addition on the back o' the bunkhouse and add a . . . what do they call 'em?"

"Apartment," Tressa contributed.

All three sent startled glances in her direction, as if they'd forgotten she was there. Then Aunt Hattie nodded, turning back to Abel. "That's right. An apartment. Their own little place."

"That'd still leave most of the bunkhouse open for you to bring on extra hands to replace Vince an' Ethan," Mr. Hammond added.

"You're gonna need furnishings, too." Aunt Hattie settled next to Abel on the bed and placed her hand over his knee. "Folks in town've been talkin', an' they'd like to give you a house-raisin' an' then throw a housewarmin'. Bring you things to at least get you started. Would . . . would you be acceptin' of it, Abel?"

Minutes ticked by while Aunt Hattie, Mr. Hammond, and Tressa waited for Abel's response. Tressa discovered she was clasping her hands so tightly her knuckles ached. She relaxed her grip, flattening her palms on her thighs. How she hoped Abel would swallow his pride and accept their help! She'd never heard more sincere offers of assistance. *Let him say yes, Lord, please!*

Eventually, Abel cleared his throat and rubbed his finger under his nose. He shook his head twice, staring at the floor. Then he lifted his gaze to look directly into Aunt Hattie's face. "You're really somethin', you know that? All you got to do, all your own worries . . ." He included Mr. Hammond by swinging a grin in his direction. "An' you've been frettin' over me." He chuckled softly, shaking his head again. "Really somethin' . . ."

Aunt Hattie patted Abel's knee. "But what do you say?"

Abel puffed his cheeks and then blew out the breath. "Aunt Hattie, I been layin' in this bed for two weeks with nothin' much to do except stew an' pray. Gave up the stewin' midweek an' told God He'd have to see to things 'cause I just couldn't. Asked Him to . . ." He gave a self-conscious chuckle. "To rescue me. An' what does He do but send you." A grin stretched across his face. "What I say is yes, an' thank you. Thank you, Aunt Hattie . . . Brewster."

Then his gaze fixed on Tressa. "An' Miss Tressa?"

His softly worded query seemed to float across the room and coil itself around her with a blanketing warmth. The way he'd uttered her name—softly, with tenderness—made her breath catch. She heard love in the gentle timbre of his voice.

He stood, wavering for a moment before planting his feet wide. Bouncing a glance from Mr. Hammond to Aunt Hattie, he said, "There're a few things I need to discuss with Tressa. Could you give us a moment of privacy?"

Aunt Hattie's grin turned knowing. "Why sure, Abel. Take all the time you need." She took Mr. Hammond's hand and tugged him out the door. Tressa watched the pair disappear around the corner, her heart hammering so hard she feared it might explode. She shifted to look at Abel and discovered he stood a mere two feet in front of her chair, his brown eyes boring into hers with a look of adoration that nearly melted her into a puddle on the floor.

"M-Mr. Samms?"

Very slowly, he went down on one knee before her, reaching out to capture her hand. "Miss Tressa, I owe you an apology. I wasn't fair to you when you was here last. I was thinkin' of myself 'stead of you—thinkin' of what I couldn't give you 'stead of what I could. But I've had plenty of time to think while I been layin' here healin', an' I know now I had it all upside-down."

His thumb traced a lazy circle on the back of her hand, sending shivers of awareness all the way to her shoulder. She almost forgot to breathe.

"You see, Tressa, I was just a boy—seven, eight years old—when my folks packed us up an' moved us to Kansas. I'd plumb forgot how there was nothin' when we arrived. Nothin' but empty prairie, far as the eye could see. No house waitin', no big ol' mooin' herd of cows.

No means, really, of carin' for a family. But my pa an' ma worked together an' they built a house. Then a barn. Then they purchased a few cattle. They built a *life* together, Tressa. It was a good life, an' they were happy."

She nodded. "They loved each other very much, didn't they?"

The corners of his eyes crinkled. "Yep. They did."

"So all the hard work was joy, simply because they did it together."

Tears winked in his dark eyes, and sadness tipped his lips into a brief frown. Then he jolted to his feet, pacing the short length of the room. "That's right. An' that's what I almost denied myself. The joy of buildin'—the joy of workin' together." He spun to face her, his shoulders heaving with a mighty sigh. "But God an' me've been sortin' things out in my head . . . an' in my heart." His expression gentled, turning boyish. "Right now, Tressa, all I got to offer you is me. But if you'll have me, I'll do my best to make you happy."

A joyous giggle spilled from Tressa's throat. She leaped from the chair, ready to throw herself into his arms, but she remembered his injury in time. Instead, she took his sun-toughened hand in hers and pressed her lips to its knobby knuckles. "And I shall do my utmost to bring you happiness, as well."

He slid his fingers along the line of her jaw and gazed at her as tenderly as Papa had looked into Mama's face. "You've already brought me plenty of happiness just by openin' up my heart to lovin' again. Thank you, Tressa."

"Oh, Abel . . ." Tressa placed her fingers lightly against his chest. "You've given me so much, too."

He tipped his head. "I have?"

She nodded. "Yes. One thing you gave me is the freedom to forgive."

Puzzlement creased his brow. "How'd I do that?"

Laughing softly, she guided him to the chair. When he sat, she took his free hand between hers and peered directly into his face. "In court today, the judge told everyone how you asked for leniency for Gage. You have every right to be angry and spiteful and to demand a severe punishment. But . . . you forgave him instead. And your actions gave me the courage I needed to forgive my aunt and uncle."

Abel's face hardened, and his fingers clamped down on her hands. "What'd they do to you?"

She rushed to assure him. "They didn't hurt me, but they . . . they didn't love me. They made me feel unwanted." She discovered a sense of freedom in stating the words aloud. Licking her lips, she added, "It wasn't my idea to come to Barnett—they sent me against my will, and I've resented them for it."

A sudden thankfulness rushed over her. Had her aunt and uncle not sent her, she wouldn't have met Aunt Hattie or Isabella or Sallie or any of the others, and she wouldn't have fallen head-over-heels in love with Abel Samms. She'd thought of Kansas as merely her second-best chance, but God had given her so much more than she'd ever hoped.

To Abel, she said, "But I decided no more resentment. I'm going to follow your example and forgive those who've hurt me."

Abel shook his head, his eyes sparkling. "I forgave Gage an' Vince 'cause you reminded me that's what God wants us to do. So you set the example first."

Recalling the day she and Abel had ridden across the pasture together, another memory surfaced. "I think I also told you that since you'd saved me, you were responsible for me." Heat flooded her cheeks at her bold statement, but she continued peering directly into Abel's face.

His face split with a grin. "Darlin', it would give me great pleasure to be responsible for you for the rest of my life. Should we go tell Aunt Hattie?"

Tressa hunched her shoulders, another giggle trickling out. "I think it might be best to *ask* Aunt Hattie."

He laughed and stood, drawing her to his side. He brushed a kiss across her temple. Her heart fluttered like the wings of a dove, threatening to carry her feet from the floor. If a kiss on her temple produced such a reaction, what might a kiss on her lips do? She tipped her head, unconsciously lifting her face toward his.

"C'mon, Miss Tressa. Let's go see if Aunt Hattie'll talk Paralee an' Mabelle into makin' their double weddin' a triple one!"

37

Tears pricked behind Tressa's eyes as Brother Connor opened a little black book and cast a bright smile across the congregation.

"Ladies and gentlemen, we have gathered today to witness the union between this man and this woman. And this man and this woman." His focus bounced from Paralee and Jerome to Mabelle and Glendon. "And this man and this woman." His smile broadened as his focus shifted again to include Aunt Hattie and Mr. Hammond.

Abel's hand over hers tightened, and his breath stirred her hair as he whispered, "Disappointed we ain't up there, too?"

The minister's voice faded into the background as Tressa pressed her shoulder against Abel's and scooted closer to him. "A little. But I agree with Aunt Hattie." She turned her hand palm up, linking fingers with him. "We'll have our own special day after a time of courtship, which—" a soft giggle escaped her lips—"I'm enjoying immensely."

Over the past few weeks, she and Abel had taken several long walks, hand-in-hand, through pastures filled with peacefully grazing cattle. On buggy rides, with Tressa holding the reins and Abel curving his good arm around her waist, they'd talked and laughed and planned their future. The days had been a time of growing heart-to-heart.

Twice he'd kissed her beneath a star-speckled sky while the light breeze swished her skirts and lifted strands of her hair to tickle his cheek. Those moments carried her to heights of joy she hadn't known existed. She would have been willing to live in his barn's loft, only to be with Abel, but Aunt Hattie had insisted Abel must at least have a house built before they could exchange vows.

Tressa smiled, remembering how the older woman had spluttered, "You can't be takin' Tressa to no barn even if it does have a sturdy roof. 'Sides that, a girl deserves to be wooed. You get some wooin' in, let the townsfolk get a house built, an' *then* we'll talk nuptials."

Although at the time impatience to be joined in every way with Abel had nearly made her want to crawl out of her own skin, she was now happy they had waited. They would have their own wedding in the late fall, when Abel's arm was no longer in the sling and the little three-room house the men were building on his land was completely finished. She'd requested a railed porch where she and Abel could sit in the evening and watch the stars creep out to decorate the vast, velvet prairie sky, and a solid door they could close to seal themselves away, just the two of them. Abel had heartily agreed.

"I now pronounce you, and you, and you"—Brother Connor's happy announcement broke through Tressa's musings. She sat up, holding her breath—"man and wife. Gentlemen, you may kiss your brides."

The congregation rose to its feet, applauding wildly. Abel's arm slipped around Tressa's waist, holding her close. She rested her temple against his jaw, clapping with the others while tears ran freely down her cheeks. Yes, this was best—to stand within Abel's strong embrace and see Aunt Hattie happily married to Brewster, to trust that God's good plans for her would be fulfilled.

She tipped her face toward Abel's. His lips brushed her forehead, and then he smiled down at her, his warm brown eyes gazing into hers with an adoration that flooded her with delight. *Oh, dear God, thank You for gifting me with this man.*

Her aunt and uncle might have sent her to Kansas to find a second-best life, but guided by her heavenly Father's gracious hand, she'd discovered fulfillment beyond her wildest hopes through the God-bestowed gift of Abel's love.

Acknowledgments

In August of 2008, my parents, husband, and I went on an Alaskan cruise to celebrate my folks' fiftieth anniversary. On the ship, we met a woman who, upon learning we were from Kansas, mentioned she'd attended a herdsman school in Kansas. She went on to explain she'd married a rancher, but he didn't have time to teach her the skills she needed to help him on the ranch, so he sent her to a herdsman school for an education in ranching. A little bell rang in the back of my mind.

A couple of weeks after returning from the cruise, I had the opportunity to visit with a few other authors, including *Tracie Peterson*. I shared this woman's experience and mentioned how I'd like to find a way to turn it into a story. Tracie said, "You know what could be fun? Do a mail-order bride type story with inept women from the East coming to a herdsman school to learn the skills they need to be good wives for western men."

The bell clanged wildly, and Wyatt Herdsman School was born.

I didn't catch the name of the woman on the ship, but I'd like to express my gratitude to her for planting the seed and to Tracie for splashing it with enough water to make it grow. Thank you muchly!

As always, I need to say thank-you to my family. It isn't easy to live with an author, but they do it with grace. *Mom and Daddy, Don,*

Kristian, Kaitlyn, and Kamryn . . . thanks for putting up with me and my characters.

Speaking of characters, to my grandsons, *Connor, Ethan, Rylin, Jacob, and Cole* . . . thanks for letting Gramma borrow your names for this story. (*Adrianna*, patience little princess—your turn's comin'.)

Spending so much time in my office alone would be unbearable were it not for my critique group members who are only an email away. *Eileen, Connie, Margie, Ramona, Judy, Donna* . . . bless you for all you do to keep me sane.

People who commit to praying for someone else's ministry must be earning extra crowns in Heaven. *Miralee, Cynthia, Kathy, Rose, Ernie, and others at First Southern* . . . there aren't words to tell you how much you mean to me.

Writing a book is not a one-person occupation, and I am so grateful to my editor, *Charlene*, and the *entire staff at Bethany House* for partnering with me. What an incredible privilege to be a member of the Bethany House family.

Finally, and most important, endless appreciation and admiration to *God*, who opened this pathway to me, who lovingly guides me in directions I would never imagine for myself, and gifts me with more than my heart can conceive. May any praise or glory be reflected directly back to Him.

KIM VOGEL SAWYER is the author of fifteen novels, including several bestsellers. Her books have won the ACFW Book of the Year Award, the Gayle Wilson Award of Excellence, and the Inspirational Readers Choice Award. Kim is active in her church, where she leads women's fellowship and participates in both voice and bell choirs. In her spare time, she enjoys drama, quilting, and calligraphy. Kim and her husband, Don, reside in Kansas and have three daughters and six grandchildren. She invites you to visit her Web site at *www.kimvogelsawyer.com* for more information.

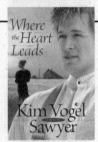